IN MEMORIAM

Lyndsie Clark

Cover Art by Nova Kodex
ISBN: 978-1-961578-00-5
Library of Congress Number: 2025910554

To James, my "ideas man." Without your unwavering support, this dream would never have come true.

And to my grandmother, Leslie Skinner Jagiello (1928-2025), the matron of our family. You always believed in me, no matter how far from the path I strayed.

Foreword

At its heart, this book is about resilience—both on the battlefield and in the soul. It explores what it means to rise above oppression and fight against systems designed to break us, whether those systems are political, social, or deeply ingrained in our own minds. Too often, power is wielded through division, through the dehumanization of others, and through the suppression of emotions that make us whole. But true strength is not found in the absence of feeling or in blind obedience to authority. It is found in the courage to resist, to reclaim humanity, and to stand up for those who cannot stand up for themselves.

This struggle is not new. The oppression of marginalized groups, the silencing of dissent, and the erosion of empathy have been recurring forces throughout history. In the United States, these forces have taken many forms—from the forced displacement of Indigenous peoples to the enslavement of Africans, and from the internment of Japanese Americans to the persecution of LGBTQ+ communities. The damage caused by "othering" those who are deemed different has persisted since the founding of this country, spreading like a virus and weakening the very foundation of the nation we claim to cherish.

Initially, I wrote this book as a social commentary on these cycles of oppression, particularly in light of the political climate that emerged from the 2016 presidential election and still persist today. As a descendant of immigrants who fled war, poverty, and tyranny, I have always believed that this country should be a place of refuge and opportunity, not exclusion and hate. Yet, history has shown us time and again how easily people can be divided—how fear can be used to justify atrocities. However, if oppression is a cycle, then so too is resistance.

This is also a story about men—the way they are shaped by war, by expectation, and by a culture that demands strength but denies vulnerability. In addition to the external battles, this book is also about the unseen battles fought in silence, for instance, the suffering of men in our hyper-masculine, male-dominated society. In our culture, men are often expected to embody strength through stoicism and to suppress fear, pain, and grief in favor of a hardened exterior. Nowhere is this more apparent than in the military where vulnerability is often mistaken for weakness, and the weight of trauma is expected to be carried alone. Many veterans suffer in silence, turning to substance abuse or, in too many cases, suicide, because seeking help has not been normalized. But strength is not the absence of struggle—it is the willingness to confront it head-on. Through this story, I seek to challenge the rigid expectations placed on men, especially soldiers, and to show that courage is not just found in battle, but in allowing oneself to feel, to grieve, and to heal.

A Legacy of Soldiers

While I have never served in the military, or grew up in a military household, my extended family has deep ties to the armed forces. I was raised to internalize the pride of serving this country, but I also deeply felt the tragedy of war. Hearing stories from my grandfather and other relatives, I learned that war isn't just about victory. It's also about the aftermath—the cleanup, the rebuilding, and the people left behind.[1]

My great-great-grandfather, Colonel George Skinner was a US Army medical officer during WWI. He helped set up hospitals in France for war victims and was also the surgeon who successfully performed the first animal bone transplant into a human forearm.

His son, Colonel Leslie Skinner, also served in the US Army between WWI and WWII. He melded an armor piercing shell and with a solid fuel rocket (using the expertise he learned from Robert A. Goddard, the father of US rocketry). To test it, he and his colleague Lieutenant Uhl, took a pipe from a pile of scrap for the housing. Together, they successfully fired it at (and destroyed) a captured German tank. Hence the recoilless rocket launcher, or the Bazooka, was born.

Additionally, my grandfather, Major Walter A. Jagiello (married to Col. Skinner Jr's daughter—My grandmother Leslie) was a graduate of West Point and then began his military career at Dachau in the aftermath of WWII. Later, he earned a Silver Star and two Purple Hearts for his acts of bravery in Korea. His brother, Joseph A. Jagiello, who served in the US Marine Corps in Korea, was killed in action at Chosin Reservoir. He was only twenty-six years old. It took the family years to recover his body.

These are only fragments of my family's military history, but I include them here because I want to illustrate that soldiers are more than just their

[1] The scene in Ch. 28 with the man in the closet and the detonator is inspired by a story my grandfather Jagiello shared near the end of his life. He carried guilt over what many would call an act of self-defense. War forces people into impossible choices I can barely comprehend, but I've done my best to portray those moments with the sensitivity and gravity they deserve.

service records. My relatives were fathers, sons, inventors, poets, sculptors, travelers, wine-drinkers, jokesters, lovers of Tabasco sauce, bus drivers, and tour guides. They carried on despite what war took from them, despite what they endured to ensure that others could live in peace. Their sacrifices should not be forgotten, nor should the ideals they fought for be eroded by those who seek to strip away the freedoms they died to protect. In order to keep these memories fresh, I have included a list of my military relatives in Appendix 2.

On Men, Emotion, and War

While I hope this story will reach a wide audience, I especially hope it will speak to men. In today's society, they are as much on the receiving end of toxic masculinity as women, though their struggles frequently go unnoticed. Even as progressive as this country has become, many boys are still raised with rigid expectations: be strong, be brave, be angry. But never be fragile. Never be scared or sad. Never be sensitive.

The military culture amplifies this ideology. Soldiers are trained to suppress their emotions, to function as efficient, detached warriors. And yet, when the war ends, when the battlefield is replaced by a quiet home, those same soldiers are expected to reintegrate, to feel again, to become whole. But how can they do that, if no one ever taught them how?

Many don't. Every day, an estimated seventeen US veterans take their own lives. Men, in general, account for nearly 80% of all suicides. Not because they don't feel pain—but because they've been taught they're not allowed to. Instead of seeking help, they drown in silence, addiction, and self-destruction.

In this story, I attempt to explore the duality of man—both as an agent of war and as a flawed, vulnerable human being. Strength is not the absence of emotion. It is the ability to carry both pain and hope. It is knowing when to keep fighting, and when to ask for help.

A Call to Action

If you are struggling—whether you are a veteran, an active-duty soldier, or simply a man who has been told to endure in silence—know this: seeking help is not weakness. It is one of the bravest things you can do.
And for those who have not walked this path, I ask only that you listen.
War doesn't end when the guns go quiet. The battle continues in the minds of those who fought. If we truly wish to honor our soldiers, we must give

them more than just medals and folded flags. We must give them the space to heal. We must fight for them as fiercely as they have fought for us.

Part One

Xi'an, China

- 1 -
C.E. 2252 June 16

in memoriam: /ˌin məˈmôrēəm/ a Latin phrase equivalent to "in memory (of)", referring to remembering or honoring a deceased person.

* * * * *

We were on our way to Xi'an when the rods fell, leveling the metropolis. Hot wind breathed the sickly sweet tang of death over my face. Xi'an's distant skyline loomed, the carrion-encrusted teeth of a massive monster that had just devoured the lives of its twenty million citizens. It belched acrid fumes as it digested their dreams, their futures, and their fears. Oily fingers of smoke clung to the dark, mangled frames of 'scrapers, their vacant windows staring forlornly across the plain.

Xi'an, whose name meant "Western Peace," was once considered the root of Chinese civilization. Now, it was just a smoking ruin, twisted under a sky clogged thick with haze.

We jogged down a wide commuter maglev track, the late-spring heat already oppressive. Debris from the shock wave and the hollow shells of magcars blocked our path, blanketed in a thick layer of soot from the fires still burning around us. My heavy pack pinched into my shoulders. Sweat dripped down my back to pool just above the waistline of my pants. The temp meter on my Radlon suit read forty degrees Celsius.

"Street Dogs, form up!" my platoon leader shouted, waving his arm in a circular motion.

We came to an untidy stop, tripping over our own gear and elbowing each other in our haste to 'form up.' Standing in a mess, I surveyed my fellow soldiers. As new recruits, we hadn't seen real fighting yet. Some of us never thought we would. But, now faced with the blackened corpse of Xi'an, I knew it didn't matter whether we joined up for money, duty, or to get a piece of the action. The fight would come for us soon enough.

Our officers knew it too. Many were already veterans of the resistance, either here or in America. They had tried to prepare us, but we neither understood nor cared. How could we? We were too young to be driven by the fire of revolution. Too young to care about any picture bigger than ourselves.

The officers knew that, too.

"Pathetic," scolded Staff Sergeant Mitchell, our senior NCO. His accent twanged like an out-of-tune guitar. "My ancestors, heroes of World War Three, would be rolling in their graves at the sight of you lot!" He continued.

He referred to a war over a hundred years ago between us genetically modified savants and the machine-enhanced people we called mechs.

It was a war that tore the world asunder. It was a war our ancestors had lost.

A fire crew rushed past, jostling us with shoulders and equipment, and drowning out Mitchell's insults. They chased a spreading line of flames that was headed toward a silo of hovervehicle fuel. They were too slow.

The flames hit the silo, and the block erupted with a *whoosh* of heat and fumes. The heat hit me in the face and my eyes burned. I choked, snapping my visor down. The air filtration system of my Radlon suit kicked in just as fast, pulling the smoke away.

"Move back!" Mitchell shouted as we stumbled away from the inferno in a mass of legs and arms.

"Stupid private," I cursed to myself when I finally caught my breath. I had thought we were safe, this far from the epicenter. It was the first mistake I'd make here in China, but not the last.

Shouts rang out over the roar of flames. "Wǒmen xūyào bāngzhù!"

Most of us stared in the direction like lost sheep until one of my squad mates snapped through the comm. "They need help!"

I looked over at the private who'd spoken. His name tag read *Rostbane.* I remembered him from basic, a soft boy barely of military age with styled hair and manicured hands. Now he tossed his head in annoyance, attempting to dislodge the curly golden lock the mask trapped against his forehead. His eyes pierced through mine.

"Are we going to help or not?" He urged, tilting his head toward the commotion.

"No…why—?" I began, fear gripping at my chest.

This wasn't my platoon. I was no leader.

But something pushed at me…determination and…action? I couldn't fight the feeling. Soon it became mine. I *had* to help these people.

"Of course!" I shouted, the words tearing from my lips as if pulled by an invisible string.

A second man echoed my statement, then we were running toward the burning building and leaping over red-hot coals before I could even see his name tag.

As minimally outfitted as we were in our second-hand suits, the fire crew wore even less: grimy coats and jeans, decades-old respirators. Pushing past the gathered men and women, I skidded to a stop. A wall of flame roared from the ground, chewing at the remnants of an old holoboard broken from the roof of a nearby movie hall.

A woman, her eyes red from fumes, rattled a string of Chinese at me so fast I couldn't comprehend it.

"She says the fire surrounded them. Two of her crew are still trapped," Rostbane said from behind me.

Damn. I shook my head. The guy knew a helluva lot of Mandarin for an American from New Colorado. Based on my own upbringing, I was lucky I even learned a first language as well as I did.

"I've got this," I said, still feeling that odd sense of urgency. I turned to the man next to me. "You in?"

The craggy faced private, Ferryman, gave a curt nod. "Hold on," he replied, lifting his hands like a conductor.

The billboard broke apart, charred chunks of what looked like wood flew away. I don't know what impressed me more: the existence of ancient wood in Chinese cities, or the machinations of a Kinetic—a savant who could move objects with his mind.

"Okay," the 'Net replied, breathing hard. "Let's go!"

Slipping through the remnants of the fire, we found two people huddled in the only clear spot on the floor of the burning theater. I reached a hand down to grasp the small gloved one of a teenager, thirteen maybe. She stared back with eyes both afraid and resolute, pleading with me over her ill-fitting respirator. I gasped in surprise.

"Yéyé," she said without hesitation, pointing to the man, "Tā shòushāngle."

Her companion, a man in his sixties, wore no protection from either flames or smoke. Burns covered his bare arms.

Sweat rolled down my brow, but I couldn't brush it away. My eye twitched. Heat seeped through my boots.

"Her grandfather is injured."

"Thanks, Rostbane," I grumbled. I could see that.

I lifted the girl to him, and he shepherded her through the flames. "It's JR, by the way," he called back, disappearing past the curtain of orange.

Ferryman helped the man up with another wave of his hand, an invisible force pulling him to his feet. The two of us guided him from the wreckage, allowing him to collapse only when we reached the crowded, and only marginally cooler, boulevard.

The old man looked up at me, his red-rimmed eyes wet with tears. "Xièxiè," he said through dry lips.

A shout came over the babble from the man's grateful companions. "Lilly, Rostbane, Ferryman! What the *hell* do you think yer doin' going off like that?"

Shit. Mitchell again. He sure did like yelling at us.

"You could have gotten yerselves killed! What have the officers told you?"

"Sarge…Isn't this…our job?" I asked.

"Unless we're *not* supposed to help people?" Rostbane added, flames reflecting in his golden eyes.

Mitchell glowered and grabbed Rostbane by the shoulder, dragging him back in line. "Yer not supposed to get yourselves killed before your first assignment. Stupid private," Mitchell snapped.

He shoved me next, and I stumbled into Rostbane. The man muttered something not too kind about the sergeant, but I held my tongue. We hadn't even arrived at the barracks yet and I'd already gotten myself into trouble.

Second mistake. Stupid private. I thought, cursing myself again.

Then, I saw the relief on the faces of the Chinese fire crew and the teenager's happy smile. The old man's hoarse words echoed in my mind:

Xièxiè—*Thank you.*

The first Mandarin I learned.

* * * * *

We approached the blocky warehouse serving as our barracks.

Ferryman whistled through his teeth. "Shee-it," he said, eyes glued to the city in the distance, "who could do something like this?"

"Monsters," I replied, already exhausted. The adrenaline high from our earlier rescue had long since faded, leaving me reeling beneath the magnitude of the disaster we now faced.

"The government," Rostbane added. "Lightbar Industries works its people to death in their stupid tech factories and then gets pissed when they ask for more vacation time or mental health policies."

I gestured toward the city. "I think this problem went deeper than just overworked employees with a lack of health care."

Rostbane snorted. "But that's always where it starts, isn't it? The fight comes later."

"That's why we're here," Ferryman added, voice dry. "To fight the meching CORPs."

"Maybe that's why you're here," I sighed under my breath. "But not me."

(I was a dumb, twenty-something who'd knocked up his fiancé and dropped out of school.)

"I'm here for the money."

"'Course you are, dustboy," Rostbane laughed. "You probably grew up thinking that the CORPs are the ultimate evil, giving mechs every convenience, while you savants scrape by in the slums."

"Well, that's not wrong!" I snarled, the sudden urge to defend my position rising in my gullet. "They raid our neighborhoods and take those with the best Skills to Greysoft-knows-where."

Ferryman grunted in agreement. We'd grown up in the same place. He understood.

"Yes, Lilly. They do," Rostbane said with a roll of his eyes. "But your common, everyday mech is not immune to wickedness of the CORPs. Here in China, Lightbar doesn't care what you are, as long as you work. And they'll abuse you all the same."

"You're shitting me."

Rostbane shook his head and pointed to the city. "The citizens of Xi'an put their tech differences aside decades ago so they could stand up to a greater enemy. One who weaponizes capitalism and greed."

"Well, it looks like they're not standing now," Ferryman grumbled.

He had a point. None of us had known we'd be entering an active war zone. Or a massacre, as the case may be. Kinetic weapons of this magnitude weren't supposed to exist, beyond speculation. As technology goes, historians and weapons experts would have written it off as an antique Weapon of Mass Destruction.

But there was no denying the carnage wrought by the vengeful rain. Gravity, normally the ally keeping us on this spinning rock, had worked against the citizens of Xi'an, destroying the city with kinetic energy and the resulting heat and shock wave. No recorded nuke blast during The Third had been as large.

"But we'll get 'em back," someone else said behind me. "Give them what monsters deserve, right?"

I shrugged. What else could I do but believe him? We were a squad of idealistic young toughs. We had no idea what we were doing.

As we filed into the warehouse, I pulled my visor off, allowing my eyes to adjust to the low light. It felt great being free of the humming electronics so close to my sensitive ears.

"Nǐ de míngzi?" the man at the intake desk asked me, wiping sweat from his broad face. I gave him a blank stare. Rostbane, jostled somewhere toward the back of the line, couldn't translate this time.

"Pardon?" I said. "I'm American."

The man looked as if he'd eaten something sour but repeated with a heavy accent, "Your name?"

"Oh, uh, Robert Lilly."

"Robert Lilly from America?" The man entered the information on an ancient computer whose keys still clicked.

"New Colorado," I clarified. A look of confusion crossed his face. "Yeah…Just America."

A commotion drew my attention toward the center of the open atrium.

Two soldiers in gray fatigues held a black clad figure by each arm. She struggled, yelling at the top of her lungs, "Let me go, you Neanderthals!"

A third soldier lay gasping on the floor. Blood pooled from his open mouth, spraying red droplets across the concrete, glistening in the flickering LEDs.

The man at the desk cleared his throat angrily. He held out his hand. I fumbled through my suit's pockets with shaking fingers, one eye following the struggle. I pulled out the slim tablet containing my orders paperwork and passed it to the clerk.

"Nǐ de fángjiān shì sānshíwǔ hào," the man said to me, alternating his gaze between my tablet and a computer screen.

"Huh?" I asked.

He frowned again. "Your room. Number thirty-five."

He thrust a matte-textured chip toward me along with my tablet. I snatched it, muttering a "thank you" and hurried away. I focused back on the woman. She had thrown both the soldiers from her arms, though they appeared to be twice her size. Someone raced past me: Rostbane, no longer wearing his helmet. He raised a hand toward her though didn't go so far as to touch.

She whirled; fist poised for a punch. I braced for impact. This wasn't going to go well.

"You don't want to do that," he said calmly.

She froze in mid-swing, her fist inches from my squad mate's calming stare. Slowly, she lowered her arm while simultaneously twisting her mouth into a frown. Her chest heaved.

"You're a…" she muttered to Rostbane and ripped her eyes away. "Dammit."

Then she looked at me. I flinched at her gaze.

You know that moment in life when you realize you're about to make some pretty bad decisions? Well, the two before were nothing compared to what came next.

My eyes connected with her deep brown ones. The gentle rise of her cheekbones flowed down to a sharply pointed chin; her tawny skin tinged with the pink flush of rage. Her clenched fists turned the muscles of her forearms into tight cords, protruding sharply. Her gaze glowed with a fire I couldn't ignore. This woman would not hesitate to break me, or Rostbane, just like the bleeding soldier. She terrified me, yet I couldn't look away.

"Rostbane!" Mitchell shouted. Everyone jumped as if awoken from a sluggish dream. "Get yourself back here and check in."

The man strode purposefully past me, and I remembered his neatly groomed beard and perfectly tousled hair from orientation. I'd written Judas Rostbane off as a partyboi—too arrogant for his superiors, and too pretty to be of much use in a fight. He cracked me a confident smile.

"Nailed it," he whispered in my ear. He took his place back in line. The haughty tilt of his chin made it seem as if he held the eyes of the whole room.

Again, a feeling washed over me in a warm, golden glow. I relaxed. *Maybe I should join Rostbane for a drink?* Not as subtle this time. I slapped myself mentally. *No, Robert.* Rostbane was a Sway—a savant who knew how to use his Skill of persuasion for maximum effect. Shaking my head, I turned away, hearing his chuckle echo across the hall or directly into my mind. I couldn't quite tell which.

I looked back at the woman. She glared at the soldiers, who kept their distance. Her jaw clenched. The fallen soldier's breath rasped. Several others loaded him onto a stretcher. *Hopefully he won't die,* I thought. The prognosis didn't look good.

I approached the woman, still tense like a trapped animal. "Hey," I said raising my hands in submission, "Everything okay?"

She nodded, looking around at the growing circle around us.

"What happened?" I asked, wondering why I felt the need to insert myself in this situation… and wondering if I would regret it.

She took a deep breath, but her words still came out through gritted teeth: "No one touches me without permission."

Despite the harshness in her voice, I could sense hesitation—a slight tremble. Her hands shook, though she held them in tight fists.

"I'm Robert," I said, sticking out my hand, not really sure what I was doing. Then again, no one else was doing anything so what did I have to lose?

Your intact bones, my inner voice told me, noting the woman's taught muscles. *Don't screw this up.*

She looked at my hand, then at me, confused.

"You're supposed to shake it," I clarified. "It's an old gesture from before the Pandemic Era."

A smile, quickly suppressed, fluttered across her lips. Taking my hand in a crushing grip, she shook it back and forth. *Not exactly,* I thought but didn't feel the need to correct her. "Mara," she replied finally.

Her hand was like a vise! I pulled away, attempting to stifle a tiny exclamation of pain.

"You're one of those...strong people, aren't you?"

"Tank," she corrected, allowing herself a slight chuckle.

"Yeah. I've never met a female Tank before," I replied lamely. How could someone make me feel both nervous and fascinated?

"Not many of us," she shrugged.

"Make way," came a gruff voice behind me.

Everyone around snapped to attention with a salute and parted for an officer with a stern frown to pass through.

Glancing between the bloodstain, Mara's grimace, and the tablet still clutched in my hand, the officer frowned deeper. Her name tag said *Healey* and the four-pointed gold star on her crisp jacket indicated she was a major.

"Soldiers, stand down!" Major Healey shouted, her rounder vowels and a liquid *r* indicating her Candalaskan upbringing. "What the hell is going on?" Her shouts made me flinch, but Mara stood calmly, staring up at her.

I opened my mouth to stammer but soon remembered my training. "Sir!" I saluted, holding my orders in front of my face like a shield.

Mara didn't say anything.

Major Healey peered at the tablet.

"Private Robert Lilly. You're from the new platoon of Americans?"

"Yes, Sir!"

"Getting into trouble already?"

"I…" I had no idea what to say. *No. Yes. Maybe.*

"No," Mara said in a low voice, "He had nothing to do with it."

Healey nodded, "Then get to your bunk, Private Lilly and try to stay out of trouble. Briefing is at zero-six-hundred tomorrow!"

"But, sir," I said, then regretted it when the major turned her focused gaze on me. "Mara didn't do anything wrong," I continued uncertainly.

"Lilly, this is none of your concern," Healey snapped. She glanced at the bloodstain on the floor. "Dismissed."

I shrunk into the crowd but hesitated after only a few steps. *What would happen to Mara?* I watched the exchange, peering between two higher ranking soldiers.

Healey studied her. "Private—?" she stopped when she didn't see a name tag on Mara's open jacket.

"Dark, Sir," Mara said, her low tone just short of respectful.

"Private Dark, you will be escorted to the detention wing until we figure out what to do with you." The major touched Mara's elbow gently. "We can't have uncontrolled Tanks in this unit."

I could feel the hair rise on the back of my neck while Healey's electromagnetic Aura charged. How a Spark had been able to keep it together long enough to make Major, I didn't understand. None of the Sparks I'd known could suppress their volatile personalities or the quick use of their EMP when tensions ran high. However, Healey's stoic mask returned a moment later and the characteristic Spark anxiety faded. I finally turned to leave.

Mara glanced over her shoulder at me, pushing a piece of choppy black hair from her eyes. She smiled slightly as if to ask, *Will we meet again?*

I gave a slight nod.

She chuffed.

"Dark!" Healey said again, tugging her elbow.

Mara's anger drained, and she nodded in compliance. "Understood, Sir," she said contritely. Healey led her off. Two lesser officers trailed behind the women, keeping a prudent distance. Everyone had just witnessed what happens when you made a Tank angry.

* * * * *

"Yo, Rob!" Rostbane shouted, storming through the door of my bunk, "Did you see that shit, you blond bastard?"

Startled, I sat up. My forehead slammed against the low ceiling of my upper-bunk bed. I grunted, glaring at the intruder.

"Rostbane," I said blandly, "I think you have the wrong room."

"JR, please," he said, waving his datapad. "And says right here, room number thirty-five."

Great…

"So anyway, what'd ya think?" he asked, putting a hand on his hip.

"About your stunt in the intake room?"

"Yeah. Did you like it?"

"No. What the hell were you thinking?"

"Nah," Rostbane waved it off. "I knew what I was doing. But what were *you* thinking?"

I didn't answer.

"Yeah, I saw it," he winked at me. "Mara is somethin'. Stubborn. Dangerous. *Hot.* There's just something about a woman who could break you in half…" He shivered. "I could go for that."

"You will not, you insufferable playboy," I growled.

Rostbane chuckled, climbing onto my bed. Unlike me, he didn't have to hunch as he sat next to me. "You want her?"

I scooted away from him with a scowl. "No one *gets* her. She's a person, Rostbane."

He snorted. "You working-class boys are no fun. Get married. Pop out babies when you're practically babies yourselves. How many you have? Two? Three?"

"I'm not married."

Rostbane's eyes widened. "That's a surprise. Engaged, then?"

I grunted, casting sheepish eyes to my lap.

He laughed. "Nailed it! I'm good, aren't I, Rob?"

"Leave me alone."

He scoffed. "But engaged ain't married. You could totally go for Mara."

"I have a son on the way," I said, my voice tight.

"Guess you're not so different," Rostbane laughed. "So, do you love this woman? Or were just…not prepared?" He pointed to his crotch suggestively.

"I wasn't—I mean, I'm not—" I stammered. I really wanted to punch the annoying smirk off Rostbane face. "It's what I had to do, okay?" Heat rushed to my cheeks.

Rostbane rolled his eyes. "I get it. You working-class savants have short lives, but it doesn't mean you have to lower your standards. Enjoy your life a little, ya know?"

"This conversation means little coming from a guy who apparently enjoyed life—and his dead father's inheritance—so much that he had to join the army to keep himself out of jail."

Rostbane contorted his face in a look of mock hurt, "Rob, you wound me," he pouted. "Fine. We won't talk about the mistakes of our pasts. But we're stuck here so why not make the best of it?"

"This isn't a vacation, Rostbane."

He sighed, "For fuck's sake, Rob, it's JR. Rostbane was my father, piece of shit that he was."

I grunted. I didn't much care about his father. Or him for that matter.

"Anyway, you gotta lighten up or this place will kill you—quicker. Do whatever you want, but try to find someone, okay?"

"I'm not finding anyone. I'm engaged, remember?"

"Okay then, try not to think about Mara. But don't come crying to me when you're blue-balled and lonely." He launched himself off my bed, landing on the ground with a thump.

I felt that thump in my chest, as if my heart had momentarily stopped. His words struck a bitter note. A wave of lust washed over me, quickly replaced with deep, heavy guilt.

"If you keep flappin' your mouth," I said calmly. "I'm going to punch you."

Rostbane sighed. He settled into the lower bunk. "Whatever you wish. I'll ignore your repressed sexual energy for now. And don't worry, I'll leave your girl alone."

"Not my girl," I said, flopping on my back and placing the pillow over my head. "And no one calls me Rob."

"And no one calls me Rostbane," the younger man taunted. "Guess we've reached an impasse." He gave a dramatic sigh, but didn't say more.

I ground my teeth. I wanted to punch JR even more, now that I recognized the truth in his words. My finance, Constance, was a continent away and Mara was here, in this very building. My heart beat faster and my 'repressed sexual energy' bubbled to the surface. My sweatpants grew tight.

A tickle wrapped around my spine, my hips, my thighs. My skin prickled with unrequited longing. It felt familiar, yet unfamiliar at the same time. Wiping a drop of perspiration from my forehead, I gave an involuntary grunt.

A faint chuckle came from the bottom bunk.

That asshole!

"Will you stop it?!" I finally snapped, thankful the man below couldn't see my very real flush…or the hard-on in my sweats.

The sensations fled all at once, leaving the sweat to dry cold on my brow.

Rostbane laughed again. "Sorry…couldn't help it."

My racing heart slowed. I ground my teeth together until I could speak without shouting. "If you *ever* use your Aurawave on me like that again, I'll rewire your Radlon suit inside out and cook that laugh right out of your lungs."

I could almost hear the roll of Rostbane's eyes when he gave a half-hearted "yes boss" in reply.

Pressing my sweaty palms against the cool concrete wall, I reluctantly admitted that Rostbane was right. It *had* been a while. Before boot camp, certainly, but I couldn't remember how long before that.

This deployment was going to be long indeed.

* * * * *

Rostbane's words turned over in my head as I tried, in vain, to fall asleep.

"Do you love her?"

I didn't even know. Yes? I supposed I did.

A savant like me, living under the radar in a cartel-controlled city didn't have many options career-wise. I attempted college to make something of my inherent Skill—I could always find mechanical work fixing maglev tracks or working on rich people's planes. But college money ran out. I met Constance. Mistakes were made.

Is that love? How the hell was I supposed to know.

What I did know, however, was that I had a son on the way. A new, fragile life, dependent on me. I faced a tough choice: get a job or abandon my family.

Why not both?

I ran away to the army for money and time away from my bad decisions. From my desire and my half-hearted promise of marriage. The money helped salve the shame I felt about my decision. Besides, I needed time to think and maybe see the world a little. I was still way too young.

And Constance was…older than me in many ways, though not in years. I didn't like the way she looked at me with that frozen, dreamlike gaze or the way she winced every time I fixed our dryer with a coat hanger and some spit. It was almost as if I pained her with my very existence.

But she didn't understand. She didn't have a Skill. Not one I could identify, anyway, like I could with Rostbane's Aurawave. And while she never outright claimed to be techist, I knew the signs when I saw them. My fiancée didn't like the mechs, which wasn't a problem since we tended to keep apart from them, but she didn't seem to like savants much either.

Techism has a long and storied history in the United Corporate Cities of America, (or UCCA as most of us call it), starting many decades before The Third. Savants and mechs, fighting over who'd be the dominant race, and True Humans resisting the pull of both sides. You had to be born a savant, but you could *make* yourself a mech. One of those was unnatural.

A person's belief on which *one* that was, depended on the group they claimed to be a member of. True Humans were not born with any Skills and also refused the addition of mechanical modifications. Maybe they had it the easiest—able to go between groups with little notice—or the hardest, never having a place in society.

Giving up on sleep, I powered up my handheld. The machine came to life with a blink of light, an electrical current flowing through my fingertips. Everything wanted to have a place, a purpose. Even machines. I'd always felt lucky as a savant. I knew what I was. Where I belonged. I didn't have to subject myself to painful, disfiguring modifications which required constant upgrades. More importantly, I didn't have to buy into the capitalist rhetoric of the CORPs.

Staring at the screen, I studied my reflection as it powered up.

Did I *really* know who I was?

I had to give it to Rostbane. However aggravating I found him, he was always unapologetically himself, Skill and all. There was something honest about that. Same with Mara. Like me, she fell into the category of savants who couldn't activate their Skills. They were ever-present. She would always be exactly as she was. And that attracted me something fierce.

Conducting a quick security scan on my handheld, I siphoned bandwidth from the compound's server room. An illegal thing for a private like me to do, but I wasn't taking much, and I knew how not to get caught. I searched for Mara's file.

My fingers whizzed across the touchscreen, but my mind drifted back to Constance. No Skill. No mods. Yet, mysterious, nonetheless. Surrounded by sadness and…a peculiar kind of darkness. I should have fled the moment I saw the darkness in her eyes, but like most young men, I followed my dick.

And now it pointed in a different direction…

Stop it, Robert. You're on a dangerous path, I told myself.

I shouldn't even be thinking of Mara like this, but my irrational heart (and other things) didn't care. She was beautiful and strong, and she had one thing Constance did not: a Skill.

Did I want her? Hell yeah, I did.

But I wasn't that kind of person, was I?

As Rostbane had so annoyingly pointed out, I already proposed to the first woman I'd fucked. I failed romance spectacularly.

Already, the regrets piled up.

Mara was a trap. This whole place was a trap.

In response to my thoughts, the woman's file popped up on the screen. I scrolled through the info, skipping over personal information I didn't have any right to until her current status popped up on the screen.

DETAINED. BRIG 3.

Only a short walk from my bunk.

Yes. Mara was *definitely* a trap.

One I would happily fall into, it seemed.

- 2 -
C.E. 2252 June 17

Morning assembly. Our bleary-eyed group of recruits stood at attention, me more so than some. I slapped my cheeks to try and startle myself awake. It only somewhat worked. Buzzing from jet lag, I had lain awake all night thinking about Mara and Constance and trying *not* to think of why I was there.

Now, even staring into the middle distance, my eyes unfocused, I couldn't close myself to the images flashing across the holovision boards in front of me. The city—or *former city*—of Xi'an, taken by drone footage at first light.

Dense smog still hung low over the city, pierced only by the jagged tops of ruined scrapers. Flames danced across dark slicks of oil, their glassy surfaces reflecting the ragged facades of shops and restaurants. Charred shells of vehicles slumped into greasy puddles. Bodies were everywhere. At first, the sooty flesh and blackened bone camouflaged well with the ruined city, but the longer I looked, the more often I saw a separated limb in the middle of a blasted boulevard or a set of eyes staring vacantly between two cracked struts.

I would find many dead in this city, and a few still alive.

I wiped sweaty palms on my cargos and swallowed through a tight throat. Was I ready for this? Were any of us?

Major Healey strode up to the podium, the sharp clacks of her hard-soled boots echoing across the temporary stage. Lesser officers fanned out around her, mostly captains and lieutenants, like our platoon leader, Lieutenant Ames. He stared out over the assembled crowd with an impassive frown and sharp gray eyes that aged his youthful face.

"Fellow soldiers," Healey addressed the crowd. "Five months ago, the Mayor Zhelan Liu of Xi'an requested aid from the Candalaskan Militia. The workers had attempted industrial reform via peaceful protests and legal declarations before that, but Lightbar ignored their voices. Mayor Zhelan's request was for weapons and manpower, but our Prime Minister didn't want to start a war."

"Looks like the war started anyway!" someone shouted from the crowd.

"Indeed, Sergeant Mezei," Healey replied sharply, casting a glare at the stout, red-haired man sporting a cat's head stitched onto the back of his jacket. "For those of you who are new to this conflict, let me be clear: this is no ordinary war. After a year of fighting for liberation, the destruction of Xi'an is not just a setback—it's a tragedy. We've lost too many of our own to those rods."

"Candalaskans?" Ferryman mumbled beside me. "I didn't realize so many were already here."

Healey's voice grew stronger, cutting through the room like a blade. "Yet we will not be deterred. Our cause is just. For too long, the citizens of China have suffered under the oppressive hand of Lightbar Industries. In cities across the country, they sicken and die from working conditions that would make the slums of the UCCA look like a paradise. Their children inherit their suffering, unable to raise a hand against the CORPs. And this fight isn't just for China's savants—it's for the mechs and Trues here, as well."

A wave of murmurs swept through the crowd, quickly silenced as Healey continued.

"China is different from North America or Europe. Unity is their defining feature."

"Unity between the classes?" Ferryman whispered skeptically. "How does that even work?"

"They say you can conquer China, but in two generations, China will conquer you," Rostbane muttered on my other side. "Guess Lightbar didn't get the memo."

I shrugged, remembering what the officers had drilled into us during Basic: China's size made it impossible to conquer. Yet arrogant people kept trying.

Healey's voice dropped, heavy with conviction. "I know this isn't what many of you expected to hear. Some may feel confused—or even betrayed. But now is the time to cast aside those doubts. Put your prejudices to rest. We face a greater enemy: Lightbar Industries. And through Lightbar, we'll strike at the heart of every CORP that stands in our way!"

Even though Lightbar hadn't publicly claimed responsibility for the rods, the truth hit me like a hammer. The CORPs persecuted savants everywhere, but we'd always directed our anger at mechs—they were the CORPs' people, after all. Now, realizing a company could abuse its own as well stirred a different kind of fury in me. For the first time, I questioned everything I'd been taught.

Beside me, Rostbane's fists clenched, his face twitching as he forced a cocky smirk. I could feel his agitation radiating off him, prickling my bare arms. He already knew. Maybe he wasn't the air-headed glitterpony I'd pegged him for after all.

"I know you have many questions," Healey continued with finality. "But for now, we must help those in need. The citizens of Xi'an."

With that, the lesser officers took over and we dispersed into our smaller regiments for the briefing. When Ames approached us, a cold sweat broke out under my collar. It was time.

He addressed our platoon in his cool, even voice. "Street Dogs, form up!"

From the first time I met him, Ames had made me nervous. He smiled easily, and never raised his voice, but his eyes flashed from time to time as if he noticed something unsettling that he couldn't forget. He wore his calm, unwavering demeanor like a hard shell.

He stared over our heads as he spoke. "We don't yet know the extent of the damage to the city, or why exactly it occurred. We've heard no word from Mayor Zhelan, or the others from the Council of Five. Timeseers tell us they are alive," he said, referring to those savants whose Skill allowed them to see into the future. "It is our job to search the city in hopes of finding them."

"We have to find five people in a scrap pile of a city filled with corpses?" Rostbane whispered, eliciting an annoyed frown from Ames.
I shook my head. The council was likely dead, and if they weren't…well, from the looks of the city, they probably wished they were.

* * * * *

"Hey buddy," someone said, following me onto the hovervan.

Charger's Beard! I cursed to myself. Rostbane seemed to have taken to me like a stray cat to a hot dog vendor. He slid into the seat next to me.

"Rostbane," I said blandly.

"JR, please," the man repeated. "How many times do I have to tell you?"

I had no desire to banter with him this early in the morning. When we'd started basic together, he'd refused to get his perfectly manicured hands dirty, leaving work for "unrefined" city boys like me. At the time, I didn't care. I'd grown used to dirt. High society was what scared me.

I stared out the side window, hoping he would get the hint and leave. He didn't.

"So, city cleanup," he continued with a sarcastic guffaw. "Looks like we get the fun job."

"Looks like."

His Aurawave pressed on me. As much as I wanted to deepen my frown, I felt the corners of my mouth lift into something resembling a smile. Damn Sways.

An officer placed a gun in my hands—a massive megasonic rail gun. I caressed the cold, heavy barrel meant to propel tiny metal slugs at twenty-five times the speed of sound. We'd made this gun for maximum destruction. And it wanted to fire.

"Quite the weapon for an S-n-R mission," Rostbane chuckled without humor. "Do they really think the half-dead inhabitants of this city are this much of a threat?"

I shrugged but agreed with his sentiment. "This is a hell of a gun."

Even if it was excessive, it felt good to hold a weapon again. Guns spoke more clearly, and less often, than humans. They never argued or criticized.

"Hopefully we don't have to use this," Rostbane snorted. "I'm a terrible shot."

"I'm not," I replied, a fond memory finding me in this burnt-out city. "My uncle first took me shooting when I was seven, in the back alleys by his apartment. We used to peg bottles and trash cans with his homemade shotgun. Sometimes, I'd even get a rat."

"For supper, no doubt," Rostbane snorted in disgust.

"It was wonderful," I finished with a sideways smirk. "My uncle was a lot like me. We rarely needed to talk. The guns did that for us."

"Why, Rob, I think that's the most I've ever heard you say without complaining. Are we…friends…now?"

I grunted, biting the inside of my cheek. So much for opening up.

But Rostbane was undeterred. "I'm sure your uncle is proud of you," he said.

"He's dead," I responded flatly. "Fell during one of the raids."

Rostbane offered his condolences, but I tuned him out.

Of all the people to be stuck in a platoon with, it had to be an overly talkative, terrible shot, smarter-than-he-looked dandy.

Fuck my luck.

The van drove until debris clogged the road.

"A'ight! Everyone out!" Mitchell snapped through our comms. "We're walkin' from here."

The heat hit me first. Unlike the annoying heat from the previous day, the air outside wrapped me in a cloying, suffocating swelter. My brow prickled with sweat, droplets sliding down my temples to soak the collar of my tight-fitting radlon suit. Even through the thick material, I could practically feel the fires burning miles away.

The odor hit next, twisting its acrid fingers through my filtration mask.

"Smells like barbecue," Rostbane's voice crackled through my helmet comm followed by the ear-splitting frequency of comm-static.

"Yeah, but worse," Ferryman chimed in once the noise faded.

Realizing what made up the cooked meat and burnt wood smell, my stomach churned. Some visceral instinct screamed in the back of my mind.

Danger.

"I never liked barbecue, anyway," Rostbane continued. He sounded ill.

My light-sensitive visor brightened and dimmed in response to a bulbous cloud drifting across the sun.

Someone else in my unit said something in Chinese and others laughed. It was the joyless, nervous laugh of those not ready for what they were about to see.

"Cut the shit," Mitchell snapped. "Pay attention. We don't know what may be lurkin' here."

"Or not," Rostbane mumbled. "No way anyone could be alive in here."

Mitchell's visor swung toward us, and I froze, unsure of who was the target of his darkened gaze. He made a gesture with his hand, two fingers pointed at his visor and then directed at us. I swallowed hard.

Rostbane's lips opened again, but this time I jabbed the butt of my gun into his ribs. Last thing I wanted was to be the recipient of any more officers' ire.

Doctor Tien, the platoon's medic, held a heartbeat wand in her right hand, stuck out like a staff. She stared at the tiny screen of her handheld, across which were scattered tiny red dots.

The heartbeat wand beeped once, twice, three times. She pointed to the side of the road, waving her hand sharply three times. Four fingers. Four fingers. Two Fingers.

Ten paces off the ruined road we trod, across broken ground littered with detritus. Power lines wound through the rubble like snakes waiting to strike. Most lay cold and dead, just like the city around us, but several still thrummed with power. I felt it like a low bass note, pulsing just below my sternum.

"Stop," I muttered, thrusting my rifle in front of Rostbane. "That one's live." I pointed to the line with the tip of my gun.

Rostbane whistled through is teeth and gave me a grateful nod. After that, I noticed him always hanging behind me a pace. He might be obnoxious, but he definitely wasn't dumb. Begrudging respect blossomed in my chest.

When I saw the first bodies, or pieces of bodies, it didn't register at first. Blackened by char and crusted with the red-brown stain of blood, they should have horrified me, but they didn't. Some looked like tech, while others were clearly flesh, though I remembered what Healey had said. It didn't matter. Human was human.

Still, I felt neither rage nor disgust from these sightings. We'd been warned about compartmentalizing, but I didn't realize it would happen so fast. That is, until we came upon the first "survivor."

We heard the wheezing breath before we saw her, the raspy sound resonating from behind a large chunk of stone. She leaned against the blackened metal supports, which stuck out like ribs from the concrete, her passage to the ground marked with a shiny red streak on the wall.

She wore only tatters, held on by a thick, caked layer of soot and blood. Her face…I staggered, reaching out to steady myself on a still-hot girder. Blackness tickled the edges of my vision, and my head emptied of thoughts. Behind me, Rostbane flipped up his mask and retched. Others knelt in silent respect. Doctor Tien approached with caution, wary of startling the woman. However, she didn't seem to register the approach, just continued to stare at me with one wild eye.

She seemed middle-aged—at least, that was my guess, though the destruction to her face made it hard to tell. The right side was frozen in an expression of shocked confusion, while the left was a charred mass of blackened blisters. Her hair and parts of her scalp had been singed away, exposing patches of shockingly white bone where bloodied flesh peeled back. The skin around her eye socket sagged, dragging downward to reveal a bulging, bloodshot orb, its iris swallowed by a dilated pupil clouded with white. Her mouth twisted in a grimacing frown, as though she had been caught mid-scream.

I couldn't look away and eventually the woman's lips twitched. "Jiùmìng…" she said to me, "Wǒ de háizimen… Wǒ de jiātíng … Wǒ de háizimen."

I would come to know these words well over the next few days: "Help…my children…my family."

Tien responded to the woman in a soft voice and finally she registered the doctor's presence. She mumbled back, weakly pointing behind her with raw fingers.

"Jiùmìng…Wǒ de háizimen…"

"This woman speaks of a square," Tien said in English for our benefit, "where more survivors are waiting for aid. About one and a half kilometers west."

"Copy," Ames said from somewhere at the front of the column. "Squad Four, get this woman to the compound and then return with medical reinforcements."

"No more reinforcements are available," someone else answered, "but we'll try."

"Do your best," Ames commanded. "The rest of us will go west. Do what we can."

A handful of Chinese soldiers began coaxing the woman onto a stretcher under the watchful eyes of Doctor Tien. The rest of us stood frozen like idiots.

"Y'all heard the Lieutenant," barked Mitchell, startling us into action. "Move out!"

As one we lurched forward, our stomachs sick and our eyes clouded with smoke, trying not to imagine what we were about to come upon.

"Well, they say if you haven't been to Xi'an, then you haven't been to China!" Rostbane piped up through the comm, but even he couldn't keep the quaver out of his voice.

Even Mitchell didn't even bother answering this time.

* * * * *

"State your business, private," commanded the bored guard at the door.

"Robert Lilly, Sir!" I responded, unsure of the guard's rank. "Mara is… assigned to my platoon. The lieutenant wants her briefed," I lied.

The guard looked at me, slightly confused, then shrugged. Clearly detailed questioning had not been part of his briefing. Turning on his heel he said, "Cell three. Follow me." He stopped in front of the third door, though there was no number on its frame.

It had a digital lock. I looked away to reassure the guard I wouldn't see the code. I didn't need it anyway. As I entered, I trailed my fingers on the locking mechanism. Electricity tickled my fingertips, telling me everything I needed to know. Yes. I could crack this one. The Xi'an outskirts bunker clearly hadn't been built for high security.

Mara sat on a low aluminum bed, back against the wall and knees tucked to her chest. She still wore her boots as if ready to move at a moment's notice and tilted her head over a reading tablet. She twitched at the sound of the latch, telling me she'd only been pretending to read.

When the guard closed the door behind us, she met my gaze immediately.

"Oh. It's you." Her lips broke into a smile.

I nodded. "Robert Lilly. From America. We met yesterday."

Mara nodded, but the smile didn't fade, "I remember. How'd you find me?"

"I…" Suddenly I realized I probably should brag about hacking the personnel database or lying to the guard. However, saying "I wanted to see you again" sounded far too corny. I doubted Mara was the type to appreciate it, anyway. Finally, I settled on, "How are you doing?"

Charger's Beard, that was lame.

Mara chuckled at my awkwardness, "Bored. What's going on out there?"

Thank Greysoft for Mara's directness! I exhaled my nervous breath. "Lots," I tried to chuckle back.

She gestured next to her on the bed. "Tell me," she said. "I didn't come all the way to China to languish in a cell. "You find the council yet?"

I shook my head.

"We didn't even make it past the first camp of survivors." I swallowed hard and felt the bile creeping up my throat. I had skipped dinner, too nauseous to eat, and now my stomach was grumbling in sick protest.

Don't faint or throw up Robert, I told myself. I wanted to make an impression on Mara, but not *that* way.

"Have you ever been in a fight before?"

Mara snorted. "Plenty."

I remembered the previous day. I gave an awkward cough, "I mean like…War?"

She shook her head. "I just enlisted this year. Took me a while to convince them I was old enough."

"How…?" I began but Mara interrupted me.

"Nineteen. But my birth records don't officially exist, so it took extra time."

Nineteen. Younger than me. Younger even than Rostbane. I studied the hard angles of her face and had a difficult time believing that.

"So…the survivors?" she asked, prodding me with a rock-hard elbow.

I grunted. Stammered. She was so green, yet her frown spoke of a hard life.

"Are you sure you want to hear about it?"

She looked at me with earnest eyes, "I can handle it."

Nodding and mentally steeling myself, I began.

"Imagine a square surrounded by rubble. The moment you step from the hovervan, the smell hits you like a maglev truck, even through your MOPP suit. The air is thick with the sickeningly sweet tang of death and eye-burning, bitter smoke. Scores of people—savants, True Humans, and mechs—cluster in the meager shade of ruined walls. Their collective gasps hum through the otherwise quiet courtyard."

"Most are too wounded to go on. Some are too alive to succumb to death, but others already lost that battle, their lifeless bodies lying where they fell. No one has the energy to move them."

I coughed once, trying to rid the tremble in my voice.

"Your unit doesn't have enough doctors. Your squad mates can't do much either—combat lifesaving or rudimentary care—that's it. The medic goes from person-to-person for triage. She must choose who to treat. We bypass the most gravely injured because we don't have the resources. Many times, we cannot even ease their suffering before death, though some beg us to do so. We can transport some to the makeshift medical tent, but mostly we just give them water and maybe food."

I paused. Steeling myself for the last line of my speech—the speech I practiced all the way back to the barracks so I wouldn't choke up in front of Mara.

"Then, we leave."

Mara didn't respond. She considered me, sitting next to her on the bed, her gaze inquisitive, sympathetic.

"It's not how I expected this deployment to start." I laugh mirthlessly. "Fuck, I don't know how I expected this deployment to start, to be honest."

Placing a hand on my shoulder, Mara gave it a squeeze. She must have noticed my pallor.

"Uh, sorry," I mutter, suddenly becoming aware of how dirty I was—T-shirt encrusted with soot and sweat, scuzzy boots, hair matted.

Greysoft help me! I think. What an idiot I'd been to forget all about personal hygiene. I tried to scoot away, to put some distance between us in my embarrassment, but Mara just gripped my shoulder harder.

"It's fine," she snorted, then chewed on her lip for another moment of thought. "What a fucking mess," she finally said, "Those CORP bastards!"

She slammed her hand into the concrete wall with a loud thud. A spiderweb of cracks ran across the surface. Powder dusted my hair. Suddenly, I realized that it wasn't the walls keeping Mara in the brig, but her own sense of duty.

"That's why I need to be out there. Not rotting in this sell for some stupid NJP bullshit." After a moment's silence she admitted, "Though, it was probably a bad idea to break the sergeant's jaw."

"Yeah, remind me not to get on your bad side," I said, attempting a grin.

Mara smirked. "He deserved it though. Anyway, are *you* okay?"

"Am I okay?" No one had asked me that yet. Not even nosy Rostbane. I shrugged. "Yeah, I'm fine."

"Bullshit," she snorted, brushing a sweaty lock of hair from my temple.

"Lilly, time's up!" the guard snapped, unceremoniously flinging open the door.

I glared.

Mara patted my hand, "It's okay. Just come back tomorrow."

"Oh…I…" I stammered. "Okay."

"But make sure to take a shower next time!" she called, and I caught her sticking out her tongue in good-natured mockery.

Blushing up to my ears, I stumbled out behind the guard.

"She's right about the shower," he muttered to me through a gentle chuckle. "Part of your platoon, my ass."

* * * * *

"So, how's Mara?" Rostbane asked as I returned to my bunk.

"How'd you know?"

"What else would be more important than a shower after the shit show that was today?" He ran a hand through his still damp hair.

"It's none of your business."

"You are *so* not fun."

I grunted. I had to admit, *shit show* was pretty accurate. Even though his cavalier attitude had returned, the lines on his forehead told me it was only superficial.

"Well, shower quick. The mess is only open for another hour and I'm starving."

"You waited for me?"

"Obvs," Rostbane responded.

"But we're not friends," I protested.

He laughed. "We're somethin' though. And that's close enough for me."

I hadn't come here to make friends. Joining the resistance was supposed to be about getting paid, staying focused, and keeping my distance. But after a day like today? Maybe having someone to talk with about stupid shit wouldn't be the worst thing.

"Fine," I muttered, pretending reluctance. "Give me ten minutes." Grabbing my towel, I headed for the showers. And as I walked away, I realized I didn't so much mind that he'd waited for me.

- 3 -
C.E. 2252 June 22

A child's shoe lay half-buried in the rubble, the pink cartoon rabbit on its side barely visible. I crouched, brushing ash from the torn canvas, and tried not to think about the rest of her. The air reeked of burnt plastic and decay, and even through my MOPP gear, the stench clawed at my throat.

The rods had flattened everything here. Entire blocks reduced to skeletal remains of buildings and piles of blackened debris. A month ago, this had been a neighborhood. I imagined homes, schools, and little shops with candy jars in the windows. Now it was a graveyard.

Someone behind me shouted, and I turned to see Rostbane pulling a woman out of the wreckage. Half her face was smeared with soot, her eyes wide and hollow. She clutched a bundle to her chest—a blanket, frayed at the edges and empty. The soldier in me wanted to help her, to do something, but there was nothing left to give. Not for her. Not for anyone.

We'd been at this for a week now, and it wasn't getting any easier. Every day, more of the same: mothers screaming for their children, fathers digging with bare hands, the elderly staring at the horizon as if the dead might return. I thought I'd learned to bury the grief by now, but it followed me like a shadow, just waiting until I let my guard down.

That night, during my regular visit with Mara, I finally did.

"No word on the trial," she grumbled, staring at the ceiling of her cell. "They're dragging this out on purpose. I swear, I'm going to die of boredom before they decide anything. What about you? What'd you see out there today?"

I hesitated, leaning against the wall and keeping my eyes on the floor. "You don't want to know."

She gave me a sideways look, then reached out and squeezed my hand. "I don't mind."

I swallowed hard. "A boarding school," I said finally. "It was half-buried under debris. Still full of…bodies. Kids. And the parents were there. They'd walked two days to find hope—" My voice cracked, and I couldn't finish.

Mara sat up. "Shit," she said quietly.

"I can't—" The words caught in my throat. My chest tightened, like it was caving in. "I can't do this."

The grief I'd been pushing down all week hit me like a blow to the face. I slumped against the wall, gasping for air as sobs forced their way out of me. My helmet clattered to the ground, and tears spilled down my cheeks, hot like the scorched ground of Xi'an. My body shook with the force of it. I wanted to curl up and disappear.

"You can," Mara whispered.

She wrapped her arms around me, pulling me close. Her chin rested on my shoulder, sharp and unyielding, but her embrace was steady, grounding. She didn't try to shush me or offer hollow reassurances. Just held me until the worst of it passed.

When the tears slowed, I realized how warm she was. Her hands stayed firm on my back, her breath even against my neck. It had been six months since anyone touched me like this. Longer since I'd let anyone close enough to try. A quiet longing stirred in my chest—something I wasn't sure I knew how to handle.

I shifted, pulling back slightly, and her hands dropped to her lap.

"Thanks," I muttered, trying to sound casual, though my voice was still hoarse.

She tilted her head, studying me with an amused smirk. "For what?"

For not letting me drown. For holding me together when I couldn't do it myself. For making me want something other than survival, even if I didn't know what to do with it.

But I just shook my head. "Nothing."

As I grabbed my helmet and stood, guilt flickered at the edge of my mind. Two problems. First, I felt myself yearning for the woman in front of me. And second… I'd already given someone else a ring.

* * * * *

The sounds coming from my bunk didn't exactly scream *military professionalism*: springs squeaking in rapid rhythm, a woman's breathy giggles, and—of course—Rostbane's voice cutting through it all.

"You like that, kitten?"

I froze mid-step, my hand hovering over the door handle. For a second, I thought I must've misheard him. *Kitten? Really?* My brain stumbled between cringing and laughing.

Wow, what a creep. But still, the guy had managed to score a hookup in the middle of a war zone. I had to give him credit for that—objectively impressive, even if it grossed me out.

Part of me considered turning around and letting him finish. Leave the man to get his rocks off in peace. But then I thought about what he'd do if the roles were reversed—bursting in, laughing his ass off, probably filming the whole thing for future blackmail.

I smirked to myself. *Yeah, no way I'm letting this slide.*

Gripping the door handle, I threw it open with as much dramatic flair as I could muster. "Hey, asshole! Let's get di—" I stopped dead in my tracks, putting on my best shocked-and-appalled face.

Rostbane, gloriously naked, stood at the foot of his bunk, deeply engaged with a petite brunette bent over the edge of the mattress. She gasped, her wide eyes snapping to mine, though her lips were still curved in a telltale expression of pleasure.

"Whoa," I said, holding up my hands as if to shield myself from the scene. "Wow. Did not need to see that."

The woman scrambled awkwardly to cover herself, one arm crossed over her chest while the other reached back to tug the blanket around her hips. Rostbane, of course, made no such effort. He turned to me with a bead of sweat rolling down his forehead and a smug grin plastered across his face.

"Dammit, Rob," he said, brushing a damp lock of hair from his face. "You ever heard of knocking?"

I ignored him and gave the woman a quick once-over, unable to stop my lips from twitching into a grin. "Nice work, JR. She's cute. Hi, by the way," I said to her, giving a small wave. "I'm Robert."

She blinked, her mouth opening like she wanted to respond but wasn't sure what to say.

Rostbane frowned. "Well, thanks, but could you not?"

"What? Interrupt?" I asked innocently, leaning against the door frame. "I'm sorry, am I ruining the vibe? You've been in here for, what, half an hour? Some of us are hungry."

Rostbane groaned, his frustration finally breaking through. "Charger's Balls, Rob, I'm busy!"

"Busy with what? A cardio workout?" I asked, arching an eyebrow. "Wrap it up, lover boy. Mess closes in thirty."

The woman let out a soft, nervous laugh, looking between the two of us like she thought this was all some kind of bizarre joke.

Rostbane sighed dramatically, rolling his eyes so hard I thought they might stick. "Fine. Give me five minutes."

"Five minutes? That's generous," I said, leaning closer to the woman with a mischievous grin. "Better get ready for the best thirty seconds of your life," I whispered to her.

Her cheeks flushed pink, and she let out a startled giggle as Rostbane glared daggers at me. "Rob. Out."

"Don't keep me waiting! That reconstituted protein won't eat itself." I called as I ducked out the door, leaving it slightly ajar just to be an ass.

I leaned against the wall outside, shaking my head and laughing quietly to myself. Somehow, Rostbane had turned seduction into an art form—albeit a crass, obnoxious one. Still, watching him charm women with that absurd confidence made me wonder how he pulled it off so easily.

Maybe I should ask him for tips. Charger knows I could use the help.

* * * * *

"You called me JR."

"Huh?"

A quiet bustling hung over the mess hall this evening. Most of the soldiers had already eaten and were either on patrols or catching whatever sleep they could get in their limited downtime. The smell of reheated rations hung in the air—over-salted mystery meat and stale bread rolls, but at least the food was hot. I grabbed my tray, slumping into a seat across from Rostbane.

"That was the first time you've called me JR."

I blinked, caught off guard. "Huh. Didn't even realize I did."

"Yeah, well, don't think I didn't notice," he said, leaning back in his chair. His usual smirk was there, but softer this time, more genuine. "What happened to calling me 'Rostbane' like some drill sergeant trying to keep me in line?"

I shrugged. "After the shit I've seen this week, maybe I'm just tired of pretending I live in a bubble. Or maybe," I added with a sly grin, "I feel bad for your latest conquest."

"You know," he began, jabbing his fork at a particularly unappetizing slab of protein. "Guess what I *didn't* get to finish thanks to your little stunt?"

I smirked, popping a dry cracker into my mouth. "What can I say? I'm a fan of the classics. Nothing like a good, old-fashioned cock-block to spice up a boring week."

Rostbane snorted, shaking his head. "You're a real piece of work, Lilly, you know that?"

I shrugged again. "Well, someone's gotta look out for you."

Rostbane barked out a laugh, loud enough to draw a few side-eyes from nearby tables. "Shit, Rob, just admit it. You like me."

"Like you?" I said, feigning horror. "Don't flatter yourself, JR. You're barely tolerable."

"See! You did it again!" he said, grinning as he reached across the table to swipe the bread off my tray. "Clearly, you like me enough to call me JR. Baby steps, Rob."

I sighed but didn't stop him from stealing the roll. "You're impossible."

"More or less impossible than you, hmm?"

I shook my head. I supposed, once again, Rostbane wasn't wrong.

We ate in comfortable silence for a moment, the sounds of clinking utensils and distant chatter filling the room. My thoughts drifted to the days we'd spent slogging through the wreckage of Xi'an, the despairing faces of the survivors, and then to Mara, locked away from it all, waiting for a verdict that felt like it would never come. It was awful to feel so useless on two fronts.

"You ever think of breaking the rules for someone you care about?" I asked suddenly, my voice low.

Rostbane's scoffed. "I grew up in a cartel, Rob," he said. "Breaking the rules was our M-O. What are you thinking?"

"Breaking her out of the brig."

His chewing slowed, expression cautious as he swallowed. "Who? Mara?"

"Yeah," I said, glancing around to make sure no one was listening. "I mean, we both know the trial's just a formality. They're going to punish her no matter what, and for what? Protecting herself?"

He leaned forward, his voice barely above a whisper. "You're serious? You'd risk that for pussy?"

I made a sound of disgust and glared at Rostbane.

"Sorry! Sorry!" he said, holding up his hands in surrender, "I know you said it's not like that. It's just…that's a big step to take for someone you don't really know."

"I know." I hesitated, picking at a crumb on the table. "But she doesn't deserve to sit in there. That's all I'm saying. It's bullshit."

"You're not wrong," he said, his tone unusually somber. "But, do you realized what would happen if we tried something like that? It wouldn't just be her ass on the line—it'd be ours too. They'd make an example of all three of us."

"Yeah," I muttered, my shoulders sagging. "I realize that."

He studied me for a moment, then leaned back with a sigh. "Look, I get it. She's a good person, and she doesn't deserve to be trapped like that. But if you're seriously thinking about pulling something, you better make damn sure you've got a plan. And I mean a real plan, not just some half-baked idea fueled by guilt."

"I'm not planning anything," I said quickly, though the thought had crossed my mind more than once. "It's just…hard to sit around and do nothing."

"Yeah, well, welcome to the military," Rostbane said, his smirk returning, though it didn't quite reach his eyes. "Sometimes doing nothing is the hardest part."

"Right…"

We lapsed into silence again, the weight of the conversation settling over us. It wasn't until Rostbane started stealing food off my tray again that the tension broke, his grin returning full force.

"So," he said, tossing a piece of meat into his mouth. "About earlier—you really think I only last thirty seconds?"

I laughed despite myself, shaking my head. "What, you want me to run a stopwatch next time?"

"Please, like you could handle it," JR shot back, his grin widening. As annoying as he was, I couldn't help but feel a little lighter. Since we'd arrived here, JR always had a way of relieving tension—of making the unbearable seem almost manageable. And maybe, just maybe, calling him "JR" wouldn't be so hard after all.

- 4 -
C.E. 2252 June 24
0600 hours

"Rob! You gotta come to the Commons…like, now!" JR announced, rushing into our bunk.

It was day eight of the search-and-rescue expedition and I was thoroughly done. I had come here to fight evil corporations and blood-thirsty mechs, not clean up their messes. Today, I dallied slightly in putting on my radlon suit, hoping maybe I would be left behind if I were late. At this point, it was almost worth getting the brig. Maybe they'd lodge me near Mara…

"What's going on?" I asked.

"It's crazy!" he said, "Just c'mon!"

I sighed heavily, wrenching up the zipper on my tall boots crusted in whatever foul amalgamation of ash and chemicals we picked up in the city. My feet hurt just looking at them.

I followed JR into the hallway. Soldiers rushed past, barely noticing us.

"What's going on?" I asked again, "Are we being attacked or something?"

JR shook his head, golden curls quivering. "At least—I don't think so. But they're really not sure."

"They?"

"The officers." When I gave the other man a blank look, he rolled his eyes dramatically. "They heard some chatter over the radio. Something about knowing where the mayor is."

"I see?"

"Then, these drones, man. They're everywhere."

"Drones?"

I whipped my head toward a window. A black mechanical shape whizzed by, stopped, then doubled back. I could hear the whir of its propeller and feel the direction of its flight path as it zipped back and forth.

"See?" JR was still talking, "They want us to turn on our holo-Vs or something like that."

"How do *you* know all this?"

"Like I said, I heard them chatting."

"Behind closed doors?" I asked, raising an eyebrow at him.

He coughed, "In Major Healey's office."

"Dammit, Rostbane!" I cursed.

At least the man had the decency to blush.

"You were spying on them?"

He shrugged. "If you want to call it that."

I shook my head, unsure what else I would call it. Letting that go, I watched the drone pass nearby.

"Screw the Commons," I said to him, "I wanna see what these drones are doing." Mechanical things were much more my speed than fancy vidscreens.

I peeled away from JR.

"Wait! Where are you going?"

"Outside." I stopped. "You comin' or not?"

"Fine," he replied, though his faint smirk belied his reluctance.

My vision sparkled when I stepped outside. The low morning sun cast bright yellow-gold streaks over the nearly empty parking lot, reflecting off the windscreen of a lone maglev truck. I wiped tears from my eyes. Maybe I should have grabbed my helmet?

Too late now.

I counted twelve drones circling the compound.

"Holy hell…" JR muttered. "What are they?"

"Standard-issue media drones," I explained. "You know, for like news casting and such."

"But there are so many. Are they dangerous?"

I shrugged. "Not really. Pretty dull AI actually. Not like peacekeeping or even messenger drones, which have something much closer to free will. If only I could…aha!"

I snatched one out of the air. It struggled against my grip, its tiny propellers slapping against my thick fingers.

JR gaped.

I studied it briefly. A soft breath of air tickled my palm—a fan cooling the tiny microdrive.

"No info stored here, but it is transmitting something…"

I concentrated on the radio waves pulsing through my fingertips.

"Waiting for feed," I murmured with a shrug. "Probably a broadcast."

I let it go. The drone levitated from my hand and resumed its lazy pacing.

JR snorted. "Looks like we weren't the only ones who had this idea." He pointed around.

A group of soldiers—American, Chinese, Candalaskan— streamed through the doors.

"What the hell is going on?" someone asked us, but JR just shook his head in confusion.

A low tone reverberated through the air, making my ears itch. The drones stopped their pacing, hovering in a circle around us.

"Are you *sure* we're not about to get pasted?" JR whispered in my ear.

"Yeah," I muttered back. "Just chill."

Holorays drifted from the drones' projector lenses. Streaks of red, blue, and yellow melded and solidified into shapes—one shape—the head and shoulders of an orange-skinned man with badly bleached hair. He held his mouth in such a way, that I would not have been surprised if his whole face had been a pre-fabbed floor model from some cheap mech department store.

Unfortunately, I recognized him. We all did. Somebody booed in a bellowing voice, and others followed suit. JR and I remained quiet, whether out of anticipation for the man's speech or some ill-founded suspicion that Sir Normal Rose, CEO of Lightbar Industries, would actually hear us.

And Rose was not someone you wanted to piss off. He smiled down at us in that frozen image. As the CEO of the newest CORP in the Triumvirate, I supposed he had a lot to smile about. None of it good for us, however.

"Ugh," JR groaned, disgusted. "Since Lightbar joined the Triumvirate, they've been nothing but trouble. CEO Mirabel is probably rolling in his grave."

"Mirabel Industries was no saint either," I reminded JR. "You know, they just started The Third World War. That's all."

"Oh, trust me, I know," JR added. "It's how my family got their money…"

I raised an eyebrow at him, but he waved it off. "They didn't support the mechs or anything. Just gathered up what they left behind. Totes legit."

"About as legit as anything," I conceded. "At least you didn't grant them sanctuary like Greater Ireland."

JR made another sound of disgust. "Right? But if we had, maybe they wouldn't've collapsed and let in an even worse boss."

"Worse?"

JR grimaced as he regarded me. "You don't follow CORPs news?"

I shrugged. "I've never paid much attention to the Triumvirate goons in their tall towers, playing politics."

"Even if those politics affect you?"

I didn't reply. Up until this point, though, they hadn't—at least not enough for me to notice.

But JR gestured to the ruined city behind us. "Guess it's time to start paying attention."

I grunted in agreement.

"Citizens of Xi'an," the head of Rose said, "Lightbar Industries understands you have been looking for your mayor and her council in the ruins of your city. You need fear no longer, because I am here to assure you of their wellbeing. We were able to get them out of the city before the rods fell, thus sparing their lives."

"You mean, you kidnapped them," JR said under his breath, spitting on the concrete.

The black background behind Rose's head began to fade and his image shrank until it revealed a corner of a room and a black-clad mech guardsman slouched there. The hood of the mech's sleeveless vest obscured his face but left his arms visible. Both were meched up to the elbow, the jointed steel glinted in the spotlights. He played with something in his right hand, a look of boredom on his features. Upon closer inspection, I realized that the object wasn't in his hand. It *was* his hand.

And it was a gun I'd only read about in collector mags. Resembling a vintage armor-piercing FN 5.7 handgun, the thing was attached directly to the man's wrist. He flicked it in and out of its forearm housing with an ominous click-clack, click-clack.

The room brightened further, and a spotlight shone on four bound prisoners all on their knees.

"Citizens of Xi'an," Rose said, repeating his earlier address, "I present to you…your council."

I winced. No wonder we couldn't find them.

The camera (a drone, I assumed) panned across each person, lingering on their faces. The first member was a completely unremarkable man in a business suit, neither ugly nor attractive, with a receding hairline and hooded eyes. He hunched almost in two, his eyes downcast, utterly defeated.

The second, a woman, also wore a business suit and neat ponytail. A thick metal bit was wedged between her teeth. She stared at the camera with sad eyes with only a hint of fear.

"That one's a Sway," JR whispered in my ear, nudging me sharply with his elbow.

"How do you know?"

"The gag."

Made sense. A Sway's power came from their Aurawave, but their words could magnify that power ten-fold, making them one of the more dangerous savants. I wondered if JR had ever been similarly gagged.

A feral roar ripped from the holo as the third member, a man, strained against his bonds, which were more numerous than the others'. The mech guard slammed his pistol into the side of the man's head which slowed, but didn't completely stop, his struggling.

A head taller and probably a hundred pounds larger than the other members, the man was bound with thick metal straps over shoulders, chest, waist, and thighs, pinning his arms to his sides. Three chains connected him to the floor via a collar around his neck. His jaw clenched tightly beneath a dark steel muzzle and his eyebrows pressed together, almost touching. After spending a week with Mara, I recognized the visceral rage of a Tank.

The last member, a woman, surprised me the most. With silver lips and an asymmetrical hairstyle dyed bright pink, she looked like she belonged in a nightclub, not an administrative council. Even more surprising were the delicate wires that snaked over the bare part of her scalp, across her cheek, and down her neck. They disappeared beneath the collar of her metallic scoop-neck crop-top.

She stared directly at the mech guard with a blank expression, one eye a natural misty gray and the other a sparkling bright lilac. She barely moved —I couldn't even see her breathing—and I wondered if I was looking at a doll rather than a mech. But then her mouth twisted in a snarling grimace at Rose and the illusion shattered.

"Citizens of Xi'an," Rose repeated for a third time, once we'd all developed a suitable level of pity for the council, "your mayor wants to show you something."

I winced. For one of the three greatest leaders in the world, this man was as bright and charismatic as a pile of rocks.

The camera panned once more and focused on a fifth person. While she was not bound, the way she sat stiffly in her chair made it obvious that she was a prisoner, too. Older than the rest, with an angular face and impossibly pale skin, she wore a well-pressed pantsuit and a tidy bun. She clasped her hands in her lap and revealed neither anger nor sadness in her expression. Instead, a stoic neutrality radiated from her features, and I could not tell if she was a savant, True Human, or a mech. And maybe that was the point. Maybe it didn't matter.

"Zhelan Liu," JR breathed.

"It is an unfortunate day," Rose continued, looking at Zhelan and then at the rest of the council, "for the Council of Five had not had a chance to see the consequences of their conspiracy."

"Conspiracy my ass," JR growled.

Several of the inactive drones whirred up their motors and sped off into the city. A sick knot in the pit of my stomach told me exactly what they were about to do. But the image on our holo remained fixated on those five faces. As if in slow motion, each expression changed from fear, sadness, or rage into abject shock.

We knew they were seeing: The vaporized structures, smoldering fires, and charred corpses of their beloved city. Faint audio played through the room. The sounds of mourning. The sounds of dying.

The plain man wept. The Sway gnashed on her gag. The Tank growled, straining against the bonds, his face reddening with exertion. The mech's face flashed back to blank, but the iris of her mechanical eye dimmed, its pupil dilating to swallow all color.

Zhelan's expression didn't change much, but the chords on her neck grew tight as she ground her teeth. A flicker flashed behind her eyes that I swore hadn't been there before. Her little finger twitched.

"You five," Rose began.

He walked into view from the left side of the holo, addressing the council. Except he didn't walk. He rolled. A scooter comprised his lower half, with two bulbous wheels that trembled under the CEO's massive belly.

"You five have made a terrible mistake."

"Especially you," the guard spat under his breath, kicking at the pink-haired council member.

"Yes," Rose continued, "By aligning yourself with these savant freaks," he gestured at the Sway and the Tank, "who want 'freedom' to live their little freak lives and bear their little freak babies...."

Freak.

While Rose continued to spew his hatred, I contemplated the term.

"How are you not angrier?" JR asked me.

I took note of the daggers in the younger man's eyes. The hard scowl that mirrored the Tank's. The clenched fists.

"I—" I mumbled. "I've never heard the word from a mech before."

"Fuck, Rob. You really were sheltered."

As embarrassed as I was to admit it, JR was probably right. I mean, I knew savants were second-class citizens, but my family taught me that if I stayed out of the public eye and gave mechs a wide berth, they'd leave us alone to live our lives. But then I thought of my uncle.... Have I been lying to myself this whole time?

"He's talking about us like we're monsters."

"Kinda like how we talk about mechs, huh?" JR gave me an all-knowing look and I grew doubly embarrassed.

While I had been blithely ignoring the happenings of the world, JR had grown up embroiled in it. For all his partyboi image, right now he made me look like the vape-head.

"But mechs *are* monsters," I countered. "I mean, who could do that to themselves?"

"Are they, Rob? Have you ever met one?"

"Not personally, no," I said with a blush.

JR's eyes flashed. "Then how do you know?"

I scowled, hating that JR was right...again. I needed to step up. But hell, I'd never had someone challenge my beliefs before.

"You five," Rose repeated as if woken up from a rambling dream, practically trembling and spitting, "you have doomed your city and the people in it. You have destroyed not only yourselves, but everything."

The Council of Five lifted their heads as one.

"No, Rose," the plain man spoke, his voice strong and features etched in defiance. "You have destroyed us."

"And you're next," the mech said without emotion. "They all see."

Then her entire body stiffened, freezing in place. Only her mechanical eye relayed movement as it flickered and pulsed.

"What's she doing?" JR asked through clenched teeth.

"Broadcasting," I replied. I had no doubt that all of China now watched what we did.

The guard punched the woman in the cheek, causing several of the tubes to rupture. Colored fluid seeped down her cheek, but she didn't cry out or even flinch. Her body remained rigid.

Rose's voice wavered as he continued. "Only destruction can come from an alliance between the superior race and this race of genetic mistakes."

"Race is a construct. It means nothing," JR scoffed.

"Citizens of Xi'an, survivors of Xi'an, and visiting soldiers, hear me now."

"If he says, 'citizens of Xi'an' one more time, I swear…." JR muttered but I couldn't reply.

Wherever the drones had parked in the city, they projected this spectacle. And people were watching from squares and parking lots, streets and rooftops, doorways and alleys. The citizens of Xi'an, already bruised and beaten, were about to get one more kick in the teeth.

"We have sent the warning, and you have not listened. We will give you one more chance. Surrender the city within forty-eight hours and you can stop the violence. Maybe this will help you understand the seriousness..." He waved a bloated, stubby-fingered hand in a small circle.

The guard straightened and lightning-fast fired the pistol with an echoing snap. A red blossom appeared on the purple-eyed mech's forehead. Her human eye closed as she fell forward to the floor, but I noticed her lilac eye remained open and bright.

My gut wrenched.

A silent command drifted between Rose and the guard.

Two more shots followed.

My heart skipped a beat.

The Sway and the plain man also fell, face forward, into the floor

A hot tear bubbled in the corner of my eye and my whole body went as rigid as that of the mech.

The Tank struggled with renewed vigor, his face molten red, tears coursing down his cheeks. But no fourth bullet came. It would have been wasted, anyway. Tanks were pretty much bulletproof.

The guard flicked his pistol into its housing, *click-clack,* and picked up what looked like an oxygen mask connected to a tube in the floor. He jammed it over the Tank's face, a vacuum sealing it around his mouth and nose. With a hiss, orange smoke filled the mask.

Fighting harder, the Tank jerked his body within the restraints. Tight chords in his neck stood out like steel cabling, and his muscles bulged as if they were about to burst. The color of his face went from red to white, yet still he fought.

The band around his chest popped free, then one of the chains. Two more chains snapped and the fearful surprise on Rose's face was almost heartening. The Tank ripped off his mask, but it was too late. Just as he managed to shove himself to his feet, his eyes rolled back into his head. He collapsed, hitting the floor like an anvil, and convulsed. White foam frothed from his mouth. His death spasms cracked the remainder of his restraints, and probably a few of his bones. Eventually, he too lay still.

My stomach twisted further. I curled over the hard knot, feeling as if I were about to vomit. I choked back the bile, but only barely. That single tear singed my cheek like a licking flame.

The crowd around me had dropped into a deep, heavy silence as if they could contain their breath and thus, help the Tank survive the poison. But when the man fell, they dissolved into wails and shouted curses. The camera focused back on Zhelan, who no longer tried to hide the bitterness from her features.

She stood and advanced toward Rose with a step so swift I barely saw her move. She grabbed his collar, pressing her face close to the microphone clipped to his lapel. She spoke in Chinese. The automatic subtitles struggled to keep up.

"You can destroy homes. Torture. Kill. But ——can't destroy the dream. The seeds of freedom——sown——will grow in the blood-soaked soil you've created. We—they—will nurture them because the dream is greater than anyone——any person. We will fight. We will die a hundred ——thousand—— deaths for our freedom. With every death, a thousand more will rise. Your power will crumble. Crumble—— beneath the weight of our resolve. The world——they—— will remember. *We do not kneel.*"

Then, she let go of Rose and threw both hands wide. One rested on the guard's exposed gun and the other pointed at Rose. Her glower filled the frame. Sparks shot from the mech's arm. He screamed. A blinding white light consumed the view. I ripped my eyes from the holo, but even in the dark of my closed eyelids, I saw the imprint of Zhelan's face.

Static screeched in my ears and I only opened my eyes once the sound faded. The holo-V had dissolved. Drones littered the concrete, now just mere hunks of twisted metal. Everyone stood, frozen in one moment.

I gasped. Breath coming back as if I'd been drowning. My knees buckled. I sank to the concrete, feeling outside of my body but also painfully within it. JR staggered beside me, placing a hand on my shoulder for balance. I felt the ghost of his Aurawave, hovering thin and far away.

Then, like a boomerang, a tidal wave of emotion smacked me in the face. A sharp stab of anger in my chest mimicked a heart attack. A flood of despair threatened to drown me. And a cold twist of terror slid through my side like a blade. JR growled. The growl turned into a roar. He screamed his rage at the sky, feral and possessed.

It ended as quickly as it had come.

It took my racing heart longer to slow.

"What the hell was that?" I asked when I had enough breath to talk.

"Nothing like the threat of death to make you feel alive," he replied in deep, husky tones, dropping to a crouch beside me. He traced his tongue over the thin trail of blood from his bitten-through lip and uncurled his fingers from my shirt.

"Sorry about that," he said, contemplating the pinkish tinge that indicated the return of blood. "I tried to keep it in."

I sighed, finally able to wipe the tear from my cheek. "You really feel things, don't you?"

JR nodded. "Inconvenient at times for sure. How are you feeling?"

"I feel angry," I said lamely.

"That's an understatement," he replied with a humorless laugh. "I feel like I want to paint the whole of China orange with that man's blood."
I snorted, because even *that* felt like an understatement.

* * * * *

"Rob, this is insane!" JR panted behind me, his voice laced with a rare edge of panic. "This is even crazier than anything I could think of!"

The shock of the murder scene still burned in the back of my mind, but it was no longer paralyzing. Now, it fueled me. My boots pounded against the metal floor as I tore down the corridor, my mind fixed on one goal: get Mara out of lockdown.

"Well, if you think that," I said gruffly, glancing back at him, "then go start writing your will, because when Lightbar's forces descend on us, you're gonna wish we had a Tank on our side."

JR hesitated, his lips twitching like he wanted to argue, but no words came out.

I slowed my pace just enough to make sure he could hear me clearly. "Or," I added, "you can go back to doing exactly what the higher-ups tell you. Die on command. No questions, but no adventure either. Just a meaningless death in a war someone else is calling the shots on."

The silence stretched between us, heavy and electric. For a second, I thought he'd give up, but then he sighed. His boots fell into rhythm with mine. A grin tugged at my lips.

"Fine. I'll overlook your insubordination. Just this once."

But the spark in his eyes told me this wouldn't be the only time. JR, I would come to find out, was always up for an adventure.

"Good. I'll need your help, anyway."

He snorted. "I see. And what would you have done if I'd walked away?"

I shrugged. "Figure out another half-baked plan, I guess." I ripped off my rank insignia and shoved it into my pocket.

"Wow, you really are a reckless bastard," JR muttered, but he ripped his badge off too.

"And you're still here."

"Yeah, well," he grumbled, "someone's gotta make sure you don't get us both killed."

"Do you have a better plan?"

When JR didn't reply, I quickly explained my plan.

He groaned. "You owe me for this, Rob," he mumbled. "And, if we *do* get in trouble, I'm totally throwing you under the bus."

I chuckled. "I doubt that. Who else would put up with you?"

As we rounded the corner, a soldier blocked our path with his arms crossed over his chest. I snapped my face into some semblance of authority and JR did the same, though, I'm sure it looked even better than mine, knowing JR.

The guard, marked with the rank of PFC, looked as if he'd just stopped his session of nervous pacing. He huffed, pressing the comm against his ear as if desperately waiting for some word from the officers.

"Morning, Private," I said, puffing up my chest.

JR slid behind me, obscured by my bulky frame. The private, at least five inches shorter than me, looked up, mouth twisted in confusion.

"State your business, um…" He searched my uniform for a rank. Finding none, he repeated, "Just state your business."

"Orders from Major Healey," I replied in a tone several octaves lower than my usual. "All Tanks are to report to the front lines."

The guard cocked his head at me, stepping from foot to foot, anxious. He looked as if he wanted to believe me, but he took his training too seriously. "And you are?"

Steeling myself, I said the first name that came to my mind. "Biggs. Captain…Marshal Biggs."

For a moment, I thought the soldier wouldn't take the bait. He stared at the empty space where my insignia should be with a healthy dose of skepticism. Then I felt it. JR's Aurawave caressed me like a soft tide. The man's frown faded.

"Sir! Yes, Sir!" He gave a sharp salute. "I'll take you to her."

"No need," I said, unsure of how long JR's Skill lasted. "I've got it. You are relieved, Private."

The guard relaxed and saluted again. "Thank you, Sir."

"That was close," JR said once the guard had walked off. "Let's kick it up a notch. We may not have much time before our friend realizes he's been duped."

"Right," I said, swallowing a lump of anticipation. "Halfway there."

When we reached Mara's cell, I studied the lock. It was an old fashioned one, with bright numbers lined up on a touch screen. I crouched, placing a finger on either side of the housing, gaze softening. My other sense took over.

The lock whispered to me, a subtle hum of data and intent. Reaching out with my mind, I visualized the intricate pathways within the metal exterior. Currents of energy flowed like rivers, ones and zeros weaving together in a delicate, pulsing web.

All things want to open, my uncle's voice echoed in my thoughts, deep and resonant. *Or close. Or run. Or compute. Or destroy. What you need to do is convince the machine of its true purpose.* Then, it will comply.

I didn't manipulate the lock, but rather, *thought* it open. I imagined the currents bending to my will, each line of code unraveling, realigning, obeying. The machine's consciousness—cold, mechanical, and simple— lingered at the edge of my mind. I coaxed it gently, soundlessly instructing it. *Your purpose is to yield. To grant entry. To release.*

A faint pulse of acknowledgment rippled back to me, and then, with a quiet click, the door unlocked. It drifted inward, the movement as smooth and compliant as the machine itself.

JR grunted in approval behind me, his voice low but impressed. "That's a neat trick."

I suppressed a grin as I rose.

"Hey," I said, loud enough to make myself known, but not so loud as to startle Mara. No one wanted to confront a startled Tank.

She stood on the back of a chair, precariously tilted against the wall, its metal headboard already bent and gripped the ledge of the high, narrow window. It creaked as she turned, her eyes alight with hope, glinting in a ray of morning sun.

For the love of Greysoft…those eyes. I blinked those thoughts away.

"Robert?" she jumped off the chair and it clattered to the floor. "What the hell is happening out there? Those drones—That video…"

"C'mon," I jerked my head toward the door. "We'll talk on the way out of here."

She cocked her head. "And the guard?"

"We sent him on his way." I indicated JR.

A mischievous smile played on her lips. "I see…"

She picked up a worn black leather bomber jacket and shrugged it on. A size too big, it hung past her hips but fit her muscular arms perfectly. I shuddered when she took hold of my elbow, her grip both soft and strong.

"Then let's go," she said.

Little did I know at the time just how far we *would* go in the coming months.

0900 hours

"Wait. The CEO murdered five people on public holovision and then threatened the survivors?" Mara asked. "Wonderful."

"Yeah, it wasn't good," JR said.

"'Not good' may be the understatement of the millennium," I snorted. "The Council was obviously loved by the citizens."

"This is gonna get messy," Mara sighed.

"Mess*ier*," JR emphasized.

Turmoil surged around us. Soldiers and officers running every which way; most of them unsure what they were doing. Elbowing our way through the throng, we strode toward Mara's bunk for a quiet place to talk, trying to look purposeful so no one would give us an assignment.

Once we were crammed into the small one-person room, which had probably started life as a utility closet, JR and I stood awkwardly while Mara overturned a battered crate filled with clothing. She sat on her cot and gestured to us. JR was quicker, sinking down onto the crate, which left me the cot—right next to Mara. In the inches of space between us, I could practically feel her. I struggled to focus on the conversation at hand.

"Damn, girl," JR mumbled. "How'd you get your own room?"

Mara chuckled, "When they want you to join the brute squad, they try to be extra generous."

JR looked confused.

"Meaning they put us in danger first," Mara gave a dry laugh.

JR nodded, eyes wide, and turned to me. "Alright, Rob. What's the plan?"

I hesitated, pressing my lips together to avoid admitting the truth: I didn't have one.

"They're going to regroup any minute now," JR continued, filling the silence. "And once they do, we'll get our orders. Then…" He raised his arms in a dramatic shrug.

"Then we march into whatever half-baked operation they throw us in," Mara cut in sourly. "And keep marching until it gets us killed."

"You really think it'll be that bad?" I asked, though deep down, I suspected she wasn't wrong.

She shrugged, her gaze drifting to some unseen horizon. "What I've seen so far doesn't inspire much confidence. Too many soldiers from too many places. Different training. Different priorities. No cohesion. No listening." Her voice dropped. "We're not a unit. We're just pieces on a board."

"Thinking about that guy whose jaw you broke, huh?" JR said, a sly grin tugging at his lips.

Mara startled, her head snapping toward him. "I thought you *weren't* one of those creepy mind-reader savants."

"I'm not," JR replied easily, leaning back with a satisfied smirk. "I just read faces. And yours? Very expressive."

Mara snorted, rolling her eyes. "Great. Now I know who to avoid when I'm trying to have a private thought."

As if it heard us, my handheld buzzed. A glow on the screen read, ORDERS DELIVERED. I tapped on the paper-shaped icon and began to read.

JR's brow furrowed with concern.

"What?"

"Looks like Mara was right. The Street Dogs' platoon will be part of the front-line troops." He groaned. "Fuck…that…shit…"

"So, why did we join the army again?" I sighed.

"Cuz you wanted money, and I was about to be arrested," JR said helpfully.

Mara chuckled.

"What's so funny?" JR asked, sounding as hopeless as I felt.

"Well, I don't know about you," she pointed at the golden-haired man, "but I know enough about Robert to know he's too fragile to last a minute on the front line."

"Uh, not sure that makes me feel better," JR quipped. "If Rob's too fragile, then I'm a delicate fucking flower."

I snorted.

Mara smiled a bit defiantly, looking at her balled fists. "It's not a bad thing. Not all of us were meant to punch the crap out of mechs with our bare hands. I'm guessing my squad'll be up there with you."

"Your squad?"

JR and I exchanged a glance, and I realized I'd never asked Mara what platoon she was part of.

"The Black Cats."

My jaw dropped. "That's the brute squad you were talking about earlier?"

She nodded, her lips curving in a small, knowing smirk that made my stomach do something weird.

"Who're they?" JR asked.

I allowed myself another moment of obvious gaping, enjoying—for once—that I knew more about something than JR.

"The Black Cats are not just any ol' unit," I explained, forcing my voice to sound casual. "They're the best of the best. Have you never heard Mitchell talk about them?"

JR shrugged. "I try not to listen to Mitchell much, if I'm being honest. I hate that guy."

"They're an American unit. Mitchell used to be a part of it…or so he claims. Mostly Tanks, a few Kinetics or Grifters, and even some talented Mechanics."

"Ah, so no fuck-ups like me," JR snorted.

I scoffed. "Or me," I added. "I requested that assignment but didn't get picked. I don't think I was strong enough."

Mara furrowed her brow, her sharp eyes studying me like she could see straight through my self-doubt. Before I could look away, JR gave my upper arm a squeeze.

"Not strong enough my ass…" he muttered.

"Robert?" Mara said.

"Huh?" I blinked, startled out of my thoughts.

"You're staring."

Heat rushed to my face as I realized I'd been lost in admiration—not just for her obvious physical strength but for the confidence that radiated off her like a force field. I shook my head, blushing furiously, and dropped my gaze to my boots.

"Everyone loves the muscle," JR teased, poking me in the side.

I swatted his hand away, grumbling, but Mara's laugh cut through my embarrassment. It was rich and friendly, and before I could stop myself, I smiled.

Then she reached out and patted my knee, her hand lingering just long enough for my pulse to spike.

"Don't sell yourself short," she said, giving my leg a gentle squeeze before pulling away. "Just because you're not a Tank, doesn't mean you don't have strength."

A shiver ran through me, unbidden and undeniable.

"And, it seems you have other enviable traits." She tilted her chin toward her door, indicating my role in her earlier liberation.

"Should we try to run?" JR asked, the implications of our orders finally sinking in.

"You mean, become deserters?" I said with a frown.

JR shrugged, but his shoulders sagged under the weight of the question, his eyes darting to the floor as if looking for an escape route. "It's better than dying like dogs in a fight we can't win," he said, his voice lower than usual. "We could leave, disappear into the countryside. People do it all the time."

"But people are already *dying* out there," I shot back, crossing my arms. "If the CORPs don't find us first—some *very American-looking Americans*—we'll never be able to go home without being tried as deserters."

"So, what? We just line up like good little soldiers and die when they tell us to? Didn't you say we *didn't* want to do that?" JR's tone sharpened, and he glared at me.

"True, but it's at least better than running away and dying for nothing," I countered, leaning closer. "Desertion is worse than death—it's giving up. And what happens to the people we leave behind? The ones who can't run? You want to abandon them too?"

"But this is dying for nothing, Rob," JR said, his jaw tightening as he looked away. "I just don't want to be a fucking corpse in some mass grave. Is that so bad?"

"Neither do I!" I snapped. "But running won't save you. It just makes you a coward."

"Coward?" His eyes narrowed, and he leaned in so close I could smell the coffee on his breath. Hot agitation pressed against my chest. "You've got some nerve to call me that after everything I did to get her out." He jerked his chin at Mara.

I froze. "That's not—"

"Don't you dare say it's not the same." JR's voice rose now, a flush creeping up his neck. "I've *already* risked my career once today. I could've walked. Should've walked, honestly. But I didn't, because I believed in you. believed you'd do the right thing. Don't throw that in my face now."

A wave of complex emotion rocked me back in my seat—guilt and gratitude, desire and hurt. But JR wasn't wrong. He'd been there for me when it counted. And that made my resolve stronger.

"That's exactly *why* we can't run," I said, placing my hands on his shoulders, trying to keep my voice from wavering beneath the press of JR's Aurawave. "We *should* do the right thing, or everything we've done so far means nothing. We need to see this through. Together."

JR opened his mouth as if to argue, but no words came. Instead, he just shook his head, his frustration clear in the tight line of his jaw.

"Enough!" Mara's voice cut through the tension.

We both turned to her, startled. Her eyes narrowed as she regarded the two of us.

"You're both right," she said evenly, "but you're both also wrong. Running is suicide. So is blindly following orders we know are going to get us killed. We need a third option—something that doesn't involve running or becoming cannon fodder."

"How the hell do we do that?" JR asked, his voice still rough but quieter now.

Mara tilted her head, a dangerous glint in her eye. "We play their game, but on our terms. If that means bending the rules, so be it. We're not pawns —we're the players. And we need to start acting like it."

"What do you have in mind?" I asked, my voice barely above a whisper.

"We plan a trap."

JR's head snapped up, the sparkle in his eyes renewed. Somehow, Mara knew exactly how to play into JR's criminal past.

"Fine," he said. "But if this goes sideways, neither of you will ever hear the end of it."

"No problem," I countered. "We'll probably be dead anyway, so at least I won't have to listen to your bitching."

That elicited a snort of laughter from JR.

"I might survive," Mara said with a good-natured shrug.

"Well then," JR continued, "I guess Rob and I will just have to haunt you for the rest of your life."

Now, even Mara was smiling. "That sounds fun, but not nearly as fun as living in a world where you two are still alive. I guess I'll just have to make sure you guys don't die."

I felt my smile stretch wider and for a moment, the tension of war and the looming threat of becoming cannon fodder melted away, replaced by something softer. Something almost like hope.

1200 hours

The sun bore down on us with an unforgiving intensity, baking the rubble-strewn district in its fury. My radlon suit hung halfway off, the arms tied around my waist. Sweat soaked through my T-shirt which clung to me like an uncomfortable second skin, but I ignored it. There were bigger concerns —like figuring out how to keep ourselves alive against the incoming CORP troops.

We stood in a half-circle amidst the wreckage, the distant hum of drones and the clang of machinery reminding us that time wasn't on our side. JR fidgeted with a handheld scanner, while Mara cracked her knuckles, looking ready to punch a building into submission if that's what it took.

"Okay," I said, trying to focus, "what do we have to work with here?"

"My strength," Mara said matter-of-factly, like it was the most obvious thing in the world.

"My Aurawave," JR added, flashing a winning smile.

"My tactical ingenuity," Mara chimed in, her tone so casual I almost missed the smirk tugging at her lips.

Both JR and I froze mid-thought and whipped our heads toward her.

"Huh?" I asked brilliantly.

"No way," JR said, narrowing his eyes. "You're only a private like us…"

Mara tapped the insignia on her jacket, just above her chest—a location I suddenly realized I'd avoided looking at until now.

"Private First Class?" I said, blinking. "Didn't you just get here?"

She chuckled. "Tanks usually get automatic promotions after basic. Don't tell anyone. It's not as glamorous as it sounds."

"Wow, that's lucky," JR muttered.

"Not really," Mara replied, missing the sarcasm. "It just means we get sent into more dangerous combat sooner. Also, it helps us not accidentally crush you bumbling privates." She gave a sly wink in my direction.

I groaned, running a hand through my damp hair. "Right. Great. That's…comforting."

JR snorted. "Okay, but what's this about tactics? Do you actually know what you're doing, or is that just Tank big talk?"

Mara grinned wider than I'd ever seen. "Actually? It's all talk. I've just always wanted to say that." JR and I exchanged a look as she continued. "Usually, my tactic is to beat the living crap out of anything that moves."

"Fantastic," I said, pinching the bridge of my nose.

"Real funny," JR added, glaring at her.

She laughed again, the sound rich and warm, and I hated how much I loved it. It was the first time I'd seen her smile this much since we'd met, and something about it made the oppressive heat, the imminent threat of death, and my drenched shirt all seem…manageable.

"We're really screwed," JR muttered, adjusting the straps of his light armor.

"No, we're not," I said, forcing myself to focus. "We've got tools and just enough brainpower to make something work. Oh, and my mechanical ingenuity." I winked at Mara. "I actually know a thing or two about machines, though."

She snorted, stretching her back, and gestured toward the ruined district in front of us. "So, we need to figure out how to take out those mechs without getting ourselves killed."

I chewed my lip. "Correct."

"And we're really gonna ignore our orders," JR said, a note of question in his voice, "because we're gonna do something better. Right?"

Mara's eyes glinted with something between humor and determination. "Right. Let's just hope Robert's plan is as tactical as my ingenuity."

"Don't push it," I muttered, but I couldn't help the small grin tugging at my lips.

A chunk of concrete shifted under my foot, and I fell to one knee, a sharpness stabbing through my pants. I grunted.

"Wait a second," Mara pointed at my feet, she crouched down next to me, atop the pile of rubble we'd been climbing up and moved away a few loose boulders the size of my head. "I think this is a wall."

She continued to climb, showering us with debris. A fist-sized piece flew past my head.

"Hey! Watch it!" I shouted, pushing myself to my feet and climbing up after her.

"Sorry!" she called back once she reached the peak.

Joining her on the much narrower hilltop, I dropped to my knees. The pile felt steady enough, but a sudden onset of vertigo disoriented me. We peered past a large boulder and down a sheer drop-off.

"This is definitely a wall," she said, "and none too study, either."

Well, that explained the vertigo.

Shifting position, she looked at the other side, a much gentler slope of debris. "If we clear this crap, some Tanks could probably push it down."

I looked at the hill of debris. "Uh…There's a lot of crap here. We'd need more people. Maybe a 'Net or two, also."

"I can get help," Mara said, easing herself away from the ledge.

"You think we can convince others into insubordination?"

She nodded. "Well, it won't be insubordination if an officer commands it. Lieutenant Griffin owes me anyway."

"And what about Ferryman?" JR asked from behind me. "That stoic-faced bastard's one hell of a Kinetic. Makes up for his lack of social skills."

"Good point," I said. Since we were both 'dustboys' as JR called us, we shared an unspoken sense of camaraderie. Besides, he probably wanted to be away from the front lines as much as we did.

I stared across the alley to the building on the far side, which looked much more intact as I felt the gears in my mind churn. This fragile wall had absorbed the brunt of the shock wave, saving the buildings beyond from destruction.

"Mara, can you arrange the cleanup crew?" I asked, also sliding away from the wall on my ass as another wave of vertigo hit me.

"No probs," she grinned, chucking a hunk of rock off the edge.

"Now, all we need to do is figure out how to get the mechs in the alley."

"I can do that if I get access to their communications," JR said. "But again…I'd need help."

I sighed. "How many troops are we looking for? Any ideas?"

Mara made a sound of disgust. "Probably a lot. Lightbar's got creds up the ass."

"Yeah," JR added despondently, turning a piece of rubble over in his hands. "Their soldiers probably have all the best training and mods. And will *definitely* be more organized than our rag-tag crew."

I nodded slowly. Looking into the alley once more. About a hundred yards away, something caught my eye, an orangish-yellow glint in the noonday sun. I focused on that sheen in the courtyard, as bright and still as glass on this windless day. The dark shapes of half-collapsed buildings reflected off its surface.

"Water," I murmured.

Power lines towered above the courtyard; some were bowed and blackened by the blast, but others stood tall, their metal still glimmering in the light. If those unbroken lines still worked….

"All objects want to fulfill their true purpose," I said my uncle's words to JR and pointed.

"Oh no," JR muttered, "I recognize that glimmer in your eyes."

"I have an idea," I grinned.

"Of course you do."

* * * * *

"C'mon, laggard!" I called to JR as I raced through the broken streets.

"Shouldn't we be helping Mara?" he responded with a wheeze.

"She's got it! We would just be in the way."

My foot splashed in a puddle and a thin stream of water seeped across the cracked asphalt, winding its way around dead maglev cars and twisted bits of metal track.

"What are we doing?" JR yelled again. "Rob! Slow the fuck down and talk to me."

We reached a small hill. I slowed to a jog, then a fast walk, allowing JR to catch up. He coughed and heaved, clutching his side.

"What do you think about us dustboys now?" I said to him with only a few heavy breaths.

JR grumbled, placing his hand on an overturned magcar as if it would help him catch his breath. He dropped his head and said something unintelligible, but I assumed it was mostly made up of swears.

I smirked and kept walking. "Don't rest too long," I called back. "We only have somewheres around forty hours left. And there's still a lot of work to do."

JR straightened, gritting his teeth as he forced his legs to move. "Oh yeah? Are you ever gonna explain?" The younger man asked, having finally caught up. He was gasping.

The stream of water had gotten wider now by about a foot, and the hill had gotten steeper. JR continued to pant as we stumbled over a patch of rubble.

"I'm going to the courtyard I saw from the top of the wall. I think it's filled with water and some power lines are still intact. You know what water and electricity do, right?"

JR's smile became vicious. "Shock the shit out of these Lightbar scum?"

I nodded.

"Rob, Rob, Rob," the other man joked through heavy breaths, "I didn't think you'd have it in you, being a wholesome dustboy and all."

I snorted. "There's a lot you don't know about me."

By the time we reached the apex of the hill, the trickle of water had turned into a mini river, spreading across the alley. Our boots made little pip-pip-pips as we walked. My goal lay ahead: another pile of debris, likely a fallen 'scraper, with water seeping through the gaps between the stones.

"Well, this is positively *moist*," JR groaned, shaking water from his boot.

I winced at the way JR said that word, not one of my favorites, and tried to distract myself by imagining what the 'scraper had looked like before.

Compared to the squat, utilitarian buildings of the rest of the district, it was a modern marvel. Some business tycoon must have had his sights on gentrifying this lower class area. *Fat lot of good it did him*, I thought, shaking my head.

When the rods hit, the shock wave had taken it all out equally. I shivered. There were probably still bodies in there. My stomach heaved. I wasn't ready to find out.

"Rob...ROB!" JR's voice cut my doom spiral short.

I startled, running a hand through my sweaty hair.

"Sorry," I mumbled. "What's up?"

"I said…I assume this is the thing you wanted to check out?" he asked, pointing to the damp barrier.

I nodded.

"You first."

I nodded again. On the wall in the alleyway, I contemplated a metal plaque that I could not read: 天空广场.

"Tiānkōng guǎngchǎng. Sky Plaza," JR read and when I looked at him in awe, he just shrugged. "What?"

"Where'd you learn all that Chinese?"

"It's Mandarin, technically. And, rich men's sons learn languages," he chuckled, "Never thought I'd use them, though."

I clicked my tongue as I placed my hands and one foot on the rubble.

"You don't know everything about me either." JR jabbed me in the side.

I climbed, testing each hand hold before hauling up my large frame. My foot only slipped a couple of times while scaling the ten-foot barrier, but I managed to reach the top.

"Not bad for a big, clumsy oaf!" JR called out from the ground.

I snorted, swinging my leg over the lip and catching my knee on an exposed piece of rebar. The sound of ripping fabric followed, and I grunted, pausing to untangle myself. More carefully this time, I shifted my weight and swung my other leg over the far edge, lowering myself into a seat.

I strained my senses, taking in the plaza ahead of me. Slightly elevated and sprawling, it stretched out in eerie silence. The space was wide and open, though water coated its surface, reflecting the fractured sunlight filtering through gaps in the surrounding ruins. The surface rippled slightly as a faint breeze disturbed the stillness, and I could just make out the distorted reflections of the skeletal skyscrapers looming overhead.

The flooding had turned the orderly pavers into a submerged mosaic. Algae had already begun to grow, creeping between the cracked stones. At the plaza's northwest edge, the rubble of the fallen 'scraper shattered the symmetry as it sprawled across the open space in jagged piles of concrete, glass, and twisted beams. The collapse had sent waves of debris outward, breaking through the edges of the plaza and creating an uneven, chaotic border to its otherwise tranquil surface.

I sat at one of the original entrances, now entirely blocked by the wreckage. From this vantage point, the plaza felt like a fragile island of calm, perched precariously on the edge of ruin. The ankle-deep water carried the faint metallic tang of rust and something sharper, something chemical. I listened for any sign of movement, but the only sound was the faint slosh of water as it pooled and shifted in the uneven terrain. Most importantly, I couldn't sense the hum of electricity coursing through the submerged power lines.

"It good?" JR asked.

I answered by splashing into the ankle-deep water.

When I didn't get electrocuted, JR followed.

"So, we need to get Lightbar's troops in here," I began, then pointed to the power lines, "and then run current through the water."

The younger man nodded, scratching his two-day-old stubble. "And how do you propose we do that? It's a bit out of the way."

"Well," I thought about it for a second. How can we lure thousands of mechs into this huge plaza and keep them there? "We'd need a rabbit…" a light bulb flickered in my mind, and I turned to JR.

The younger man frowned for a moment before he, too, realized what I was getting at. Then he ogled at me. "Oh wait...you mean me?!"

1300 hours

Lieutenant Ames wasn't a tall man—five-foot-seven maybe—but somehow, his presence loomed larger than anyone in the room. His crisp uniform gleamed under the dim lights, every crease razor-sharp. His close-cropped hair gave him the air of a man who didn't tolerate disorder; and his frown carried more weight than any shouted reprimand. His eyes unsettled me the most—those storm-gray eyes that never quite looked at you, as if you weren't worth focusing on.

Talking to officers had always made my skin crawl. Ever since boot camp, they felt untouchable, like some higher species that moved through the world with a knowledge and power we grunts could never hope to understand. Squad leaders might beat you into submission, but an officer? They didn't need fists. Just a handful of words, delivered in a calm, measured tone, could end your career—or worse—without you even understanding how or why.

That power came with the uniform, I supposed. Officers weren't like us. They didn't scrape through basic training or choke on sand in the heat. They were plucked from fancy institutions—or so I'd heard—trained in tactics and politics, while we learned to march in formation and reload under fire. Ames embodied that divide, the line between us and them.

I shifted my weight, resisting the urge to tug at my collar. I disliked Sergeant Mitchell, but I feared Lieutenant Ames. Now, standing in his office, I felt like a bug about to be crushed under his polished boot. And yet, here I was, standing in his office. That's how much I wanted this plan to work.

JR stood beside me, spine erect and shoulders squared. He chewed on his lip, and though he clasped his hands behind his back in formality, I noticed him fidgeting with a ring on his index finger. He flicked a glance in my direction.

We'd come to the same conclusion: we couldn't do this alone. Between the three of us, we had a good team, but it wasn't enough. We needed manpower which meant going to the brass and hoping to hell they'd listen.

Ames tapped a finger on his simple desk, a deliberate, measured rhythm that made my pulse quicken. The weight of previous judgments made in this clinical office pressed down on my shoulders, the fates of soldiers like me sealed with a single gesture.

"Well?" he said, his voice calm, cutting, and expectant.

It was just a single word, but it might as well have been a gunshot.

I explained our plan, trying to keep my voice from wavering too much.

Lieutenant Ames leaned back in his chair, steepling his fingers beneath his chin. His expression didn't shift—those stormy eyes still focused just past me, unreadable as ever—but the steady tapping of his index fingers betrayed a subtle curiosity. I felt the weight of his scrutiny pressing down on me, each word of my explanation feeling like it threaded a needle.

When I faltered, he tilted his head slightly, the faintest raise of an eyebrow urging me to continue. The room felt colder with every passing second, his silence more damning than any interruption could've been. It wasn't until I finished, my mouth dry and hands clenched behind my back, that he finally moved, shifting his gaze to meet mine.

"Mitchell's gonna have a fit," Ames said, voice a low rumble.

I barely had time to react before the door slammed open with a force that rattled its frame. As if summoned, Sergeant Mitchell stormed in, his boots hitting the floor with heavy, purposeful thuds. If Ames filled the room with his attitude, Mitchell did so with his body—broad shoulders blocking the only door, thick arms crossed over his chest. His eyes, narrowed into a permanent scowl, shot daggers at me and JR.

Ames didn't flinch, didn't even blink, but I could see the slightest twitch in his jaw as Mitchell approached, an energy crackling in the room between them.

"Y'all got a problem with doing things the right way or somethin'?" Mitchell growled as he looked us over, completely ignoring Ames and protocol.

I noticed Ames stiffen at the intrusion, yet he didn't speak, just ceased his thoughtful tapping and observed the exchange.

Mitchell turned his focus on JR. "I might've expected this from you, Rostbane."

JR opened his mouth in silent protest, but Mitchell continued.

"But you Lilly?" He glared at me. "Hadn't thought you'd be the type to go behind my back."

Neither had I…until this morning, at least.

"Sergeant," Ames finally said, "with all due respect, this is a matter of urgency." He still spoke in that calm, measured tone, but now it had an edge of ice to it. "We're dealing with bigger things here than your grievances with your soldiers."

Mitchell snorted, his face twisting into a sneer. "Bigger things? You really think these two clowns can handle anything bigger 'n themselves, Sir?"

The tension thickened, but I stood my ground, holding Mitchell's stare even as the blood pounded in my ears. This wasn't just about the plan anymore—it was about proving we weren't just some soldiers he could push around.

"Sergeant Mitchell," Ames said, his tone firm, "I suggest you sit down and listen before making assumptions."

For a moment, it looked like Mitchell might argue, but instead, he scoffed and muttered something under his breath before slamming his bulky frame into a chair to stare up at me. His eyes remained focused, like a hawk ready to swoop.

"Fine," he said, his voice low and dangerous. "Let's see what you've got, Lilly. I'll try'n make sure this doesn't blow up in your faces."

"Major Healey's plan is flawed," I said, emboldened by Ames's quiet support.

Mitchell jolted. "But that don't mean we just ignore it!"

Ames blinked and studied the three of us, as if seeing us for the first time.

"Private Lilly is correct," he said in that same even tone. I had hoped to feel vindicated with Ames's agreement, but his following words left me shivering. "Under the current direction, our platoon will suffer heavy casualties. Up until now, I've had no other recourse to change the outcome."

"But, Sir!" Mitchell pressed, pushing himself up causing the chair to creak in protest. "We don't know that for sure. This—This is insubordination. Maybe treason. It could get us all court marshaled…or worse."

"Would you rather risk court marshaling or certain death for many of your men?"

"I vote not death," JR said, "respectfully, Sir."

Mitchell glowered, but I contemplated the Lieutenant. How did he speak of the outcome with such certainty? He must see something, somewhere, in between the space of this small room and the distant horizon. I had seen that look in someone before: in my fiancée's eyes when she begged me not to join the army. I didn't give weight to her imagined fears then, but the gravity in Ames' voice now made me falter.

"Lieutenant, Sir," I asked meekly, forcing myself not to flinch under Ames' gaze as it shifted back to me. "How do you know this?"

Ames paused, his eyes narrowing slightly, and for a moment, I thought he might dismiss me altogether. But instead, he gave me a smile—calm, calculating, almost... knowing. He looked back at Mitchell, his voice unwavering.

"I'll handle Healey," Ames said, a glint of something unreadable in his eyes. "Gather the men, Sergeant. We follow Private Lilly's plan."
The words hung in the air like a promise. The weight of everything that came before this moment was nothing compared to what was about to unfold. In that silence, I realized I wasn't just a faceless soldier anymore. Ames saw me—for better or for worse.

1700 hours

After a tense standoff of clenched jaws and smoldering glares, Ames and Mitchell finally reached an agreement. The Lieutenant's word was final, as it always was. Whatever Ames Saw with those foggy gray eyes wasn't just intuition—it was truth. Even Mitchell, as obstinate as a rust-locked magcar during a heatwave, couldn't argue with that, though the scowl carved into his face suggested he wanted to try.

With their approval secured, we launched into action. Soldiers from our unit began cutting down lifeless power lines and hauling them across the plaza. Others patched up the leaks in the ramshackle plaza barricade that kept the water in, while scouts scurried off to identify sniper nests hidden among the rubble. We strung the severed power lines along the precarious columns, their frayed ends concealed in the ankle-deep water—our improvised trap set with painstaking care.

Mara, somehow, got her Lieutenant's permission for the Black Cats to help our platoon clear debris from the rickety wall. I noticed Ferryman amidst the chaos—or maybe he was the cause of it. He swept his arms in fluid arcs, a maestro in the ruins; his Auranet sent boulders and shards of twisted metal flying into neighboring buildings. The thunderous crashes rattled the air, one fragment landing a hair's breadth from my head.

"Ferryman's good," Mara said in awe. "Why isn't he in the Cats?"

"Good?" I snorted. "He's…" I paused, brushing dust from my shoulder, "he's…something."

Ferryman, hearing his name, glanced over. His eyes sparkled with mischief, and with a flick of his wrist, he sent a pebble zipping through the air to strike me square on the forehead. It stung just enough to make his point.

I staggered back, rubbing my hand against the spot. "Oh, it's gonna be like that?" I shouted out, though I couldn't keep the grin from my lips.

Ferryman's answering grin was a shade too smug. "Next time, duck faster," he called back as he flicked another small rock through the air for good measure.

I dodged the rock and wagged a finger at him, my own smirk widening. "This isn't over, Ferryman!"

"Can't wait," he shot back, hands already sweeping through the air to hurl more debris into the pile Mara's team was clearing. Mara, watching the exchange, chuckled under her breath.

"Try not to get yourself mangled before the mechs show up, Robert," she said, brushing past me to direct a few others to reinforce the wall.

"Will do," I said with a roll of my eyes, even though her touch left a tingling sensation on my shoulder. Even among the chaos, the fleeting moment of camaraderie was grounding—even if it did involved a pebble to the forehead.

I turned to JR who had his nose buried deep in his handheld.

 "How's it going?" I asked him.

"Scanning…" JR mumbled. "They've got to be here somewhere."

"Who?"

"The mechs," he said as if it was the most obvious thing in the world.

"What are you…?" I began but JR exclaimed:

"Ah-ha! Found those fuckers." He took a deep breath followed by a low, muttered, "Oh, shit!"

JR had indeed found the mechs—a contingent of roughly five thousand of them, to be exact. They were camped at the base of the Qinling Mountain Range, in the long-abandoned county of Lantian, once part of the Xi'an administration.

"That means they're only fifty kilometers away," I said, thinking back to my geography course.

The man nodded, "Right on our butts."

"That orange shit bag has been amassing forces," I groaned. "How did they get here so fast?"

"What did you expect, Rob? That they wait for our invitation?"

I grumbled.

"Must've been dropped by aircraft out of Hong Kong Island," JR continued, "Rose does have all the resources of United Greater Ireland, after all."

I shook my head. I supposed it didn't matter exactly how these mechs had crossed the Qinling Mountains. They were only an hour away by speedbike and that was a problem.

"They could be here any minute," JR said in a low, awed whisper. "They could he here tonight!"

I glanced at the handheld, the blips on the screen continued to grow in number, like they were still gathering.

"They won't," I said.

JR cocked his head. "How do you know?"

"I'm just guessing. They have to know how much of a shit show it is out there. All the crap in the air is probably already messing with their scanners. They won't want to throw darkness into the mix."

"So, if they're only fifty kilometers away…" JR said, trailing off for a moment, "That's close enough for us to get there and back before tomorrow morning."

"Go into the mech camp? Charger's Beard, are you serious? And what do you mean, us?"

"I'll need your help."

I gaped. "You're joking."

"No, I'm serious Rob," he said with a half-frown uncharacteristic of his usually jovial features. "My mojo works best in person."

The thought of being that close to a camp full of mechs made my nerves twitch. "But why do you need me?"

"We'll need transpo. Charger knows I don't have the way with tech that you do."

I gave him a flat stare. "Are you proposing high-jacking something?"

"Dunno," he said with a small shrug. "However you get it, is no matter to me. Oh, and I'll need someone to make sure I get out of there or at least sing a tale of my heroics if I don't."

"Ah…There's the JR I've come to know," I said dryly.

"And love," he added with a grin.

But I just frowned. "I hope you know, I can't sing worth a damn."

"Then you'd better make sure I make it out alive."

I sighed. My friendship with JR was as new as anything, but I had to admit he'd already made my time here much more interesting. And, in addition to being the key to our plan, I realized I actually kind of liked the guy.

"Okay, I'll do it. I'll tell—"

"*Don't* tell the officers," JR cautioned, placing a hand over my wristband.

I raised a curious eyebrow.

"We've already been successful in getting their blessing once. But, I don't want to push it. Lady luck is even more unreliable than I am." He winked.

"Superstitious are we, JR?" I teased. Then, with faked reluctance I said, "Fine, we'll leave them in the dark about this part." Secretly, I agreed with him, but I'd never admit to it. Better to ask for forgiveness…if we survived.

I really hoped JR knew what he was doing.

- 5 -
C.E. 2252 June 25
0000 hours

The air outside the bunker hung still and heavy, despite the open night sky. We moved like shadows, the silent scraping of our boots across the asphalt and our careful breaths amplified the stillness. The distant hum of the compound's perimeter lights vibrated the base of my skull. I jittered with nerves. This was the most dangerous part of the plan, and we both knew it. If someone spotted us now, especially after Rose's threat, we wouldn't get a warning. A single crack of a rifle, and that'd be it.

Even if we made it from the compound, we still had to worry about Lightbar's forces. I hoped all of them were still in their camp, but there was no guarantee we wouldn't run into a scout or random patrol. If they found us, death would be a kindness. As we saw, the cold hands of Rose hands didn't just kill—they broke you. No officer, not even Ames, not even Healey, could protect us out there. Still, JR needed this. His Aurawave worked best face-to-face, and if we wanted to make sure they didn't see through our ruse, we had to take the risk.

A sleek black speedbike glinted under a nearby lamp, parked among a few boxy magtrucks and some scrappy SMRT cars the army had salvaged from the nearby junkyard. JR nudged me with his elbow, nodding toward the bike. His grin was faint but reckless.

"Guess this is where you prove you're not just a pretty face," he said.

"Healey's bike?" I looked at him in disbelief. "Yeah, right."

"I'm serious," he pressed. "The maglev tracks are dead, but that bike doesn't need any forcefields to run. Its tires make contact with the ground."

I stared at the bike in longing, still not ready to commit that level of theft.

"Besides," JR jabbed me in the side, "it'll be faster and more maneuverable than those crappy cars….not to mention more fun."

The thought of riding such a machine sent a thrill through me; goosebumps prickled my skin. It *was* the nicest vehicle in the lot and JR was right. It was also the most logical choice.

"This is crazy," I said, but touched the cool metal anyway.

JR snorted. "Right. I keep forgetting that working-class dustboys like yourself never do anything crazy."

"I hadn't until today!" I snapped back, breathing in the scent of warm rubber and fuel. But today, I'd done several crazy things in a row. What was one more?

Closing my eyes, I sensed the tetrahydrite engine and quantum drive core. Where I touched, the cool metal warmed, leeching the heat straight from my fingers. I crouched down, opening the control panel on the side of the bike, gently gripping a wire and giving it a slight tug. The internals came to life, glowing a faint blueish green with pulsing fluid. Pulling out a small metal card, I wedged it between two plates and snapped one off. The tracking chip. It clattered to the ground, a sound too loud for this silent night. I heard JR make a muffled "oof" in surprise.

"You okay?" I asked, glancing up in concern.

He nodded. "Just warn me when you're going to do something loud," he said in a tight whisper. "I'm on-edge enough as it is."

I huffed. *You and me, both,* I thought and went back to prying off the locking chip. Instead of letting this one fall, I caught it in my hand and set it down quietly. The navscreen blinked on and the word *SET DESTINATION* flashed across the screen. No passcode. Good. Caressing the internals one more time, I pushed my Aura into it—into the wires, fluid tubes, microchips, and even the metal frame.

You want to take us silently out of this city.

I formed the coordinates of the mech camp in my mind, then let that thought flow from me into the bike. Moments later, the navscreen showed our path.

It took longer than I expected to exit the city. The roadways, while quite navigable on foot, became much less so on the stolen bike. Eventually, we were able to reach the open road and sped along at a good clip.

"Getting close," JR shouted directly into my ear. I shook my head in irritation.

"I know it's loud," I shot back, "But I'm not deaf!"

I slowed my speed and JR thrust his arm in front of me where I could see the handheld strapped to his forearm. A blinking red dot indicated our location, while a mottled collection of green dots lurked at the edge of the screen.

The Lightbar Army. Several thousand vicious mech assholes who wanted us dead. And we were going right into the middle of them.

"Hope you like off-roading!" I called and veered off the roadway.

The bike bumped and jostled. JR clutched at my radlon suit, his knees digging into my upper thighs.

"Speedbike rookie?" I asked.

"Puh-lease, not in the slightest," he snorted back. "You're just a terrible driver."

I grunted, pulling the bike into a copse of twisted, stunted trees and killed the engine. "Fine, next time, you drive," I said with a pant, placing my foot on the soggy, muddy earth. With the other foot, I kicked down the stand.

"Yet another reason for me to survive this mission," JR muttered, tripping over a ratty bush and falling to his knees in a marshy puddle.

He made a sound of disgust. "I gather it rains more here than in New Colorado." He wiped slimy organic matter on his pants. "Algae is so gross."

I couldn't help but laugh at that. "So, no algae packs for you, then?"

He wrinkled his nose in response.

Algae packs had grown more popular as a food source in the UCCA due to the vast swatches of irradiated, unusable farmland left over from The Third. Cities covered the remaining habitable areas and algae was quick and easy to grow in small, hydroponic gardens. It made sense, even though many still found it unappetizing.

We continued on foot. The Qinling Mountains stretched upward against the steel gray of a vast and starry sky, their shadowy bulks a backdrop to the camp's flickering lights. Despite the danger of our mission, I took a moment to contemplate how different this landscape was compared to where I grew up. Trees covered the mountains, the dark, jagged shapes only just visible if I squinted out the lights. Trees were rare in the UCCA, mostly found in upper-crust Sky Gardens or the odd Tree Museum in the New York Metro Complex.

Even rarer were stars, only seen from the barren wastelands. Mostly, the population just stared up into endless clouds of toxic chemicals or were blinded by a psychedelic color wheel of light pollution. I probably wouldn't get many moments like this during the war…especially if we didn't live out the night.

I didn't want that to happen, so I turned my attention back to the walk. Teeth set in a grimace, I wiped a bead of sweat from my forehead, though the wet air still left my skin clammy and damp. My stomach churned and my nerves buzzed as we moved cautiously through the marshy terrain.

The camp loomed closer, its perimeter lit by a bright, bluish glow that pulsed faintly, like the breath of some slumbering beast. JR tapped my shoulder, pointing toward a patrol on the road—two mechs on scooters, their silhouettes sharp and angular against the glow. The lead scanned the darkness with eerie precision, the umber color of his digi-eyes contrasting with the lights of the camp. Even from this distance, I could feel their cold presence: the pulsing of current in their wires and the synth in their veins.

We dropped to a crouch, trying to remain still. I glanced back at JR, who was already raising his hood, shadowing his face in preparation. His grin was gone now, replaced by the taut, focused expression of someone walking on a narrow bridge. He gave me a brief nod, his hands twitching at his sides as he readied his own nerves.

I nodded back, swallowing hard, and shifted my grip on the handle of the speedbike's slim toolkit. My heartbeat thundered in my ears. The guards passed us by without even a lingering glance.

This was it—the point of no return.

As we crept closer to the camp, the faint, electrical hum of the mechs grew louder. The lights flickered strangely, casting the jagged terrain in fragmented shadows that played tricks on my eyes. I caught myself holding my breath, as if even that small sound could betray us. Then, as we crossed the last stretch of open ground, a sudden whirring sound snapped through the night like a taut wire breaking.

A mechanical hum vibrated through my core and radiated outward until it filled my limbs and made my head throb. My chest tightened and I gasped for breath, falling on my side in the damp grass.

Up until today, my encounters with mechs had been limited. It wasn't unusual to come across the occasional pair or small group in my community, but we didn't cross paths often. I had always appreciated that because I could feel them. And it didn't feel good.

When I was eleven, a troop of around two hundred mech soldiers marched through my childhood suburb, and I genuinely thought I was dying —my skull throbbed, my heart fluttered, and my lungs strained as the vibrations shook me so intensely it felt like my eyes might burst from their sockets.

Well, this was worse.

My vision sparkled as I tried to force myself to breathe normally. I curled into a ball and wanted to press my face into the mud to make it stop. JR placed a hand on my shoulder.

"Rob?" His voice drifted in as if from far away.

I just lay there, shuddering. Moaning.

He moved his hand to the back of my head, at the base of my helmet and again warmth brushed over me. The pain subsided. My stomach stopped doing flips. Soon, the pulse of their lubrication tubes no longer resonated in my veins, and my ears ceased buzzing from their electrical synapses.

"Rob?" JR asked again. "Hey. You okay?"

I looked up, his face a shadowy ghost in the pale light. Clouds drifted across the sky, behind his head of curly hair.

"You okay?" His voice rang clearer now. I focused on the movements of his lips, white teeth reflecting the moonlight.

I nodded, uncurling myself and slowly rising onto my knees. Hugging myself tightly, I kept my gaze downcast for a few more moments, focusing on the gray tendrils of grass.

"What happened?" JR asked in a low voice.

I swallowed sour saliva before taking a swig of water. "There are a lot of mechs in there," I responded.

JR snorted a chuckle, "Yeah, thousands. Remember?"

"I don't like it," I said, my voice tight.

He glanced behind him with a worried expression. We crouched at the base of a hill covered in grass and twisted bushes. The lights of the camp, now barely a glow, felt crooked and out of place in such a verdant environment.

"Me neither," he muttered. Then he let out a sharp breath. "Shit."

I followed his gaze.

A mech patrol on their way back to the camp slowed, the two members swiveling their heads in our direction.

JR stiffened beside me.

"No turning back now," he whispered, his barely audible voice laced with grim determination. "Stay hidden."

I clenched my fists and followed his command.

"Hallo, there!" he called, standing tall above the stunted brush.

The guard startled, then turned to their companion. After a moment's consultation, the slimmer of the two nodded and turned their scooter in our direction, only to abandon it moments later and continue on foot. I pressed myself against a boulder, taking advantage of the hill's large shadow.

I hoped the modifications to our radlon suits held; I had no way to test them earlier. The electromagnetic jammers would interfere with most standard infrared scanners, and the extra coat of aetherblack paint absorbed nearly all ambient light. If I'd done it right, they should render me invisible to the approaching guard.

As she drew closer, I could make out the apparatus on her face—all lenses, wires, and severe angles. The metallic surface gleamed faintly, etched with intricate circuitry that pulsed a soft, ominous red. Twin optical sensors glowed where human eyes might have been, scanning with an unfeeling precision. The rest of her face, the scarred flesh of her human cheeks and chin, contrasted sharply with the mask. A faint hum emanated from the device, its own mechanical heartbeat.

She raised her magrifle and pointed it directly at JR.

"State your name and authorization," she said, her voice firm but more human than I expected.

Her gaze must have unnerved JR, because he stumbled over his words.

"We were just…uh…surveying the perimeter and…"

The guard tilted her head and flicked the power-up switch on her rifle.

With a deep breath that puffed up his skinny frame, he tried again. "We were surveying the perimeter, and we have some troubling news."

This time, the warm caress of JR's Aurawave washed over me. Initially, I began to feel his unease, which just heightened my own dread, but soon reassurance replaced it. Keeping my eyes fixed on the mech, I watched her response.

At first, it seemed as if nothing was happening. That concerned me. I didn't fully understand mechs, though with all their technological parts, they should be right up my alley. I had just never taken the time to learn much about them. I knew they were born human, but upon reaching adulthood, they altered their physique with technology. Some kept their mods superficial, but others were more artificial than flesh. Maybe JR's Skill didn't work as well on them.

However, as he talked, I noticed the woman's tight grimace soften. Her gun wavered. She shifted the weight onto one foot, listening to him. Her finger left the power-up switch, and the gun moaned, it's lights dimming.

"….rebel land mines on the road," JR was saying, "so it's not safe for patrols. Send your partner home. Tell him you'll catch up."

Finally, she nodded, tapping her ear-piece. She mumbled something I didn't catch. The man on the roadway gave an answer I didn't hear, though I felt the vibrations of his voice in my chest.

"I'm sure," the female guard said sternly. "Gar out."

It felt like it took the man an eternity to power up his scooter, but eventually he continued down the road, disappearing behind a hill a few agonizing moments later.

The woman who identified herself as Gar stared at JR, a faint smile on her lips, the only indication that his Aurawave still encompassed her. The red lights on her ocular shuddered then brightened. The woman shook her head.

"Who are you?" she demanded, fumbling for her gun.

Fortunately, JR had slipped it from her hands and passed it to me.

"State your name and authorization," she snapped, still unsure where the rifle had gone.

Without thinking I heaved to my feet and swung the gun in a half circle connecting with the side of her head. Blood blossomed against her pale hair, and she crumpled. The light in her ocular faded, and the pulsating rhythm of electricity through her wires ceased. My skin no longer itched from the tingling of current, though a moment later I felt her backup systems engage to a more rhythmic pulsing.

"She dead?" JR asked, his face pale in the silvery moonlight.

I shook my head. "Just unconscious."

"Really?"

"Check her pulse."

He knelt in the mire and felt around the woman's neck. He grunted an affirmative after a few seconds.

"Then we better hurry."

0300 hours

Someone was shaking me.

"Rob…we gotta go."

"No. I'm fine, thanks," I muttered.

"Rob!"

I snapped awake, blinking blearily up at JR. "What…?"

"I told you not to wait more than an hour."

"Okay…?" I forced my sluggish sleep-addled brain into action.

"And it's been two."

Oh…right. After I'd knocked out that guard, we bundled her up onto her scooter and JR, wearing her jacket, took her only Charger knew where. Then, apparently, I'd fallen asleep on the dry ground beside that boulder.

"Sorry," I mumbled.

"Well, I'm glad you did," he continued with a slight smile. "But we have to go. Now. STAT. Vamanos."

"Okay, ready." I stumbled to my feet, then took a step back. "Hey, that jacket looks good on you."

He narrowed his eyes. "Fashion feedback later. Leaving *now*!" He tugged at my sleeve.

"Did you succeed?" I asked him.

"More or less," the younger man huffed.

"Who'd you piss off?"

JR grumbled under his breath. "Doesn't matter. I didn't die. That's the important part."

I glanced at my partner. His brow was furrowed and his skin pale. He practically clung to my sleeve as we hiked back to the bike.

The important part indeed…

0400 hours

A bleary-eyed Lieutenant Ames opened the door of his bunk and saw two muddy, frantic grunts standing on the other side. Those grunts were us, recently returned from the mech encampment in old Lantian County. But, even as he wiped the sleep from his eyes, a smile danced on the Lieutenant's lips as if he'd been expecting us.

"Lieutenant Ames, Sir," JR said with a hasty salute, "I have some troubling news."

Ames furrowed his brow and, without a word, opened the door to usher us inside.

Being in a Lieutenant's quarters was both more and less nerve-wracking than being in his office. It forced me to see Ames as a person—wearing a T-shirt and sweats, bed rumpled in the corner, with a very mundane bottle of water on the small night table. Unsure if I was ready for this level of informality, I kept my eyes trained on Ames, slightly downcast out of respect.

Again, Ames said nothing but gave JR permission to speak with a slight nod of his head.

"The Lightbar army will be advancing at zero-six-hundred *today*."

I tried not to flinch at that information.

Ames's eyes widened slightly. He glanced at his wrist-unit. "As in…two hours from now?"

JR nodded. "At sunrise, more or less."

"Are you sure?"

"Completely."

"Who did you hear this from?" Ames still sounded convinced. "Intelligence hasn't heard…" He trailed off as if unwilling to divulge too much information.

But his face said it all.

JR mumbled something, chin tucked to his chest.

"Pardon?" Ames asked.

"From a captain in the Lightbar Army," JR repeated louder, though not by much.

Now the man narrowed his eyes, skeptical. "And you can confirm this,

Lilly?" he asked me.

When JR mentioned we needed to go the Lieutenant right away, I didn't question him. The version of JR that left the mech camp, was not the one I knew. This version was serious, hard, and haunted—more akin to how I thought a cartel son would be. I didn't ask why we were waking up Ames, but the look on new JR's face told me I wouldn't get an answer anyway. So, I trusted my friend. Now, it was his turn to trust me.

"Yes, Sir," I started, then back-peddled. "I mean, I didn't hear the information first-hand, but I trust JR. He knows what he's doing."

Ames sighed and wiped a hand over his face. Normally so confident, now I heard his voice waver with uncertainty. "Before I act, I need to ask how you acquired this information, Private Rostbane."

With a stuttering breath that belied JR's confidence, he said, "I went into the mech encampment."

At this, Ames took a step back in surprise. "You went *into* the mech encampment? And did Lilly?"

JR shook his head. "Just me, Sir. Rob—er—Lilly waited outside."

Pink flushed the Lieutenant's cheeks. "Do you realize how stupid that was?" he said, raising his voice at us for the first time.

But JR set his jaw firm. "With all due respect, Sir, it was not stupid.... Well, okay, it was a little stupid, but it was the only way. I'm a Sway, remember? Talking to people is kind of my jam."

"And what was the point of this…side mission?" Ames asked.

"We needed to get the army to go where we wanted them. For the plan to work," I said as JR's agitation wormed its way under my skin. He was doing a fair job of not being insubordinate, but I worried his patience was wearing thin.

"Also, Rostbane is correct," I continued, "we didn't have any better options."

Turning to his nightstand, Ames opened a drawer and pulled out a flask. Taking a long swig, he shook his head. "And you chose not to run this part of the plan by me....why?"

I took a breath, my mind racing for an appropriate lie.

"To be honest, Sir," JR said before I could speak, "we were hoping you wouldn't need to find out."

Ames chewed on that for a moment but found nothing to argue about. Instead, he said, "You also realize that leaving the compound after hours is a direct violation of the rules? That could get you brig time."

"Respectfully, Sir," I said, having found my words at last, "if this plan fails, there may be no brig to return to."

"Or soldiers to put in it," JR mumbled. I winced again, but Ames wasn't stupid.

He nodded in reply, regarding us like a father disciplining his two boys. With a resigned sigh, he passed the flask to me.

"Oh, Sir, I couldn't…" I muttered, but his gesture was insistent.

"As the leader of this mission, you probably need it as much as me." He fixed me with his steely gaze.

"But I'm not…" I stammered and took the flask anyway. I had nothing better to do with my hands. *Who the hell made me the leader?* I railed to myself as the burn of liquor slid across my tongue.

"This whole thing was your idea, was it not?"

"It was an idea," I said, looking at JR for backup.

But the younger man just gave the Lieutenant a shrug.

Thanks for having my back, I thought to JR, though I understood his reticence. He didn't want to be the leader any more than I did. And, I suppose, I did kick off these events when I broke Mara out of detention.

"Anyway," Ames said with a resigned sigh, "you two have solid intel of the Lightbar Army's early arrival."

I tried to give the flask back as I nodded, but Ames waved his hand, so I handed it to JR instead.

An awkward silence followed. Ames frowned and cracked his knuckles. His gaze lost focus as he thought. JR and I fidgeted, passing the flask back and forth.

Finally, Ames said, "I'm sorry I did not see this coming. However, the intel doesn't surprise me."

"That's good," JR mumbled, tongue loosened by the liquor, "because it sure as hell surprised me…" He coughed, "um, Sir."

"But we can work with this," I said quickly, before Ames could register JR's words.

The Lieutenant raised an eyebrow.

"Our trap is almost ready," I continued. "We just need a rabbit…to lead the mechs to the plaza. We already have a speedbike."

Ames scratched his chin, then frowned. "You're talking about Healey's aren't you?"

I gave a hesitant nod, clearing my throat. "I—" I stammered the next line, unsure what I was even volunteering for, "I'm happy to do the task and take respon—."

"No!" JR interrupted me. "You have to do all that stuff with the power lines…" he took a deep breath as if disbelieving the words about to come out of his mouth, "I'll do it."

A slow smile spread on Ames's lips and his gray eyes practically sparkled.

"And that, Private Lilly, is why you're the leader of this mission."

I just wish I knew what *that* was.

0700 hours

"Where *are* they?" JR shot to his feet.

The wall we were sitting on wobbled, sending a shower of pebbles cascading down its face.

"Whoa," Mara cooed, placing her hand on the stone beside her as if to still the shock wave with just a touch.

"It's just…" JR began to pace, "They should he here by now! I *hate* waiting!"

"Well I don't love it either!" Mara snapped back. "But that doesn't mean you get to ruin our hard work by springing the trap early. Especially while we're all sitting here!."

We were all getting testy.

None of us had slept well, or in our case, at all. The three of us had reconvened in the bunker just long enough to shovel a scalding, half-cooked MRE into our faces. Then, it was back to work to oversee the completion of our projects. We couldn't afford an error.

However, once everything had been checked and rechecked, it was time to wait. And, as JR had stated, that was the hardest part. I tried to keep myself busy jogging between Mara's crumbling wall and the preparations at Sky Plaza, but everything was as it should be. All we needed now was an army of mechs.

"Maybe you need to eat something," I said around a mouthful of protein bar, tossing one to JR. It tasted like stale chocolate, with the texture of Styrofoam mixed with poorly set concrete. Swallowing it with difficulty, I had to admit it was doing a poor job of keeping the exhaustion at bay.

I checked my handheld and noticed my step count read near seven miles. That would do it.

JR took several sulky bites from the bar. "This is not gonna work, you know," he said. "I need the thrill of adrenaline, the threat of dan—"

"Hey guys," Mara said, jabbing her elbow into my ribs. She pointed ahead of her.

A streak of black caught my eye. The glint of sunlight off something metallic.

I scrambled to my feet, showering the broken street below with more dust.

"That enough threat of danger for you, Rostbane?" Mara asked, rising more carefully.

A flock of birds rose screaming into the air.

"Shit," JR jumped, struggling into the top half of his radlon suit.

I staggered back a step. Despite how ready I thought I was, now that the mechs had arrived, I was all nerves and impulses.

Mara raised her rifle, using the scope to peer between the buildings.

"That's not good," she muttered, and I wondered, yet again, how she could be so calm while my mind was racing in fifteen directions at once.

"What?" JR asked, zipping up his suit.

"They're closer than they should be," she muttered, ticking her fingers up one-by-one, silently counting. "I think they're walking down the next street over."

"No," JR breathed, "That's not good. No good at all. Isn't this Yulan Road?"

Mara lowered the scope and made a face. She passed the rifle to me. "No," she said dryly. "*This* is Jinlong Avenue. *That's* Yulan Road."

JR uttered a string of very colorful curses.

Squinting into the scope, I picked up the vanguard of the mech forces—a company of several hundred elite, shining soldiers. The morning sun shot rainbows off their black chassis and rounded pot helms covering once-human heads. They moved as one, a sentient oil slick oozing through narrow alleyways and between dilapidated warehouses.

"How did I screw that up?" JR mumbled. "I was so sure…"

"It's not your fault," I said clapping him on the shoulder. Then continued before he could protest, "Where are the warning sirens? We were supposed to have guys monitoring the streets."

"They must be dead," Mara said without emotion. "Don't worry. I have a backup plan."

"You didn't trust me?" JR almost whined.

Mara snorted, rummaging around in her pocket. "No. I mean yes. I mean…I did trust you but you're a—what—twenty-two-year-old private…?"

"Twenty.…"

"Okay, a twenty-year-old private who's never seen combat before. You can't account for everything."

She rolled three silver balls, each about the size of a marble, between her palms.

"What are you gonna—" JR asked, Mara's affront forgotten.

"You boys may wanna get down."

She looked at us with a devilish smirk, the balls hovering centimeters above her palm, and whistled sharply. Cocking her arm back, she whipped the balls toward the shining, surging, liquid darkness. They spread out in a triangle-shaped arc, catching sparkles of sunlight and reflecting the white puffs of clouds hanging far above.

"Oh crap!" I said and grabbed the sleeve of JR's radlon suit.

Despite his protests, I dragged him down the ramp to the wall's lip and shoved him behind a berm made of concrete and metal.

"What the fuck, Rob?" JR snapped, rubbing an elbow he had knocked against the berm.

A skull-splitting *bang* thundered through the air, the shock wave of the explosion rocking the ground beneath our feet. Debris rained down on us like tiny razors. I ducked my head under my arms, pulling up the helmet of my suit. Once the din subsided, I risked a glance past our berm.

Mara stood uninjured on the wall as it shuddered beneath her, laughing her ass off.

"Did you see that shit?" she called down to us. "Beautiful!"

I grumbled, standing up to dust myself off. A gaping hole yawned where buildings once stood, and a newly minted pile of rubble closed off Yulan Road. The mech unit would be forced to come down our street now.

"Beautiful? More like crazy," JR mumbled, though there was admiration in his voice. "I hope you've got more of those shiny bombs," he called back to Mara.

She just grinned and whistled again, the sound eerily familiar to the squawk of the carrion crows.

"I guess that's our cue," I muttered with an exasperated sigh. "C'mon people. We've got mechs to dust."

Mara gave me a straight-backed salute—one I didn't think I deserved —and leapt down the backside of the wall, her boots crunching on gravel and broken glass. The soldiers waiting at street level scurried toward their positions. JR and Ferryman looked at me expectantly and with as much authority as I could muster...

...I began to run.

* * * * *

"See anything?" JR's voice called up to me. He was sitting on a speedbike we'd stashed earlier, at the mouth of Sky Plaza.

"It's quiet so far," I said staring through my pocket laser range finder, and gripping my knees tighter on the ladder of the power pole.

Sky Plaza was now a shallow lake, the water lapping at our knees as we'd trudged through it earlier. We'd managed to patch the major leaks, though we never found the source of the water. At this point, it didn't matter. It had done what we needed.

Ferryman had already joined the other Street Dogs in the ruins. I could just barely see glimpses of their gray-black uniforms tucked into the jagged remnants of shattered buildings and the faint gleam of sniper barrels peeking through gaping window frames. Additional shadows shifted behind the rubble, 'Nets and Sparks.

I dropped my PLRF to the cord around my neck, tucking it into my vest. Squinting my eyes against the sun until my visor dimmed, I climbed higher. This particular pole canted at a precarious angle over the plaza but seemed sturdy enough to hold all two-hundred pounds of me. Fortunately, the ladder was on the top side of the slant, so I didn't need to hang like a spider monkey.

Keeping my focus on the piece of power line that line hung into the water, I repeated the order of operations in my mind. I needed to turn on the power at exactly the right moment.

"I fuckin' hope I can do this," I muttered to myself.

Holding up the range finder again, I tried to focus it on the streets outside of the plaza, sweeping it back and forth.

"Anything?" JR called again when he saw me pause.

I shook my head.

"Where are those damn birds when you need them?" he grumbled. Then, "Hey, Rob?"

"Uh…yeah?"

"What about your mech-sense thingy? Can you do that on command?"

Now, there was an idea…

Releasing the scope, I closed my eyes. Gripping tighter with my thighs, I pushed up the sleeves of my suit and raised my hands. I'm not sure I needed to do that part, but something about the grand gesture made this silly action make more sense. I've always been able to sense machines—specifically, the electrical current passing through them—and while I couldn't turn this sense on or off, I had learned how to ignore it when I needed to.

I also learned how to lean into it, to feel the coming and going of current. The pulse of power. Power lines and hovervehicles felt different, as did mechs. Electrical current, synthetic fluid, and human blood coursed through their bodies together, creating impulses unique only to them.

Focusing on my Aura, I pushed it out in all directions.

Soon, a throbbing ache blossomed at the front of my skull, a feeling I'd been getting uncomfortably familiar with. A large surge followed, hitting me like a cold splash of water to the face. I gasped, opening my eyes up. The world spun. I threw myself forward on the ladder, gripping a rung until the dizziness passed.

Picking up the scope, I fiddled with the focus until I saw them where I expected. A contingent of black-clad figures, gunmetal and chrome bright against the Lightbar-issued fatigues.

"Rostbane!" I called and pointed to the southwest. "Zero-three-hundred!"

"On it!" he shouted, not even bothering to correct me on his name. The speedbike revved to life and the man disappeared in a flash, weaving through the empty streets with dazzling speed.

I gaped, an eye-witness to the fact that JR was, indeed, *not* a speedbike rookie.

* * * * *

I felt the speedbike's approach before I heard it—a deep buzz resonating through my muscles. When it finally did enter earshot, the bike sounded strained. It sputtered, backfired, and sputtered again as if running out of gas.

JR burst into the plaza, hitting the water in a magnificent spray, two fins parting as the bike slowed. Water droplets coated the man's face and hair, clinging to his curls like gems. About halfway across, the bike died, its engine flooded. JR jumped off and staggered, one hand on the bike. The other scraped across his eyes to clear them of water. Fumbling with my PLRF, I focused on JR.

Eyelashes glittering wetly, he squinted into the sun and tucked several sodden strands of hair behind his ear. He stumbled through the mire, leaving behind a trail of red floating atop the water.

I zoomed in further. Blood seeped from the man's upper thigh. I tapped my comm anxiously.

"JR, you okay?"

Moments went by while I watched him fondle for his comm. Nothing came through. But of course it wouldn't. Where *was* his helmet?

"JR!" I shouted. "You okay?"

He heard me and glanced up. Nodded. Shook his head. Held his hands up in a dramatic shrug. His slog slowed. He doubled over, gasping for breath. Still hunched, he pointed behind him, then looked up again and ran his hand across his throat in a slicing motion.

"They're coming," he mouthed.

A loud boom made the water ripple. A mortar flew through the plaza and smacked against the far wall sending shards of concrete scattering. I whipped my head back to JR.

He struggled to his feet, water droplet spraying from his flailing, but he looked to be unharmed. *More unharmed,* I corrected myself, watching him flounder desperately through the water.

"He's not going to make it," I muttered. I could feel the CORPs soldiers only a handful of yards away. I tapped my comm again, "Rostbane's wounded! We need to help him!"

Mitchell's voice came over the comm, "Too dangerous. I won't risk any more men in this fool's errand."

Ames didn't respond. I could see the man standing on the top of a building at about my eight-o'clock. He scanned the plaza, his usual slack expression giving nothing away. I cursed. We'd set up this trap, done the worst of the work, yet when it came down to it, no one was going to help JR?

I knew what I had to do.

It was too high for me to jump down directly, so I scrambled down the ladder, slipping on the damp rungs. My haphazard descent almost succeeded, until both feet missed a rung at the same time. I threw my weight to the side, to avoid racking myself, grabbing hold of the pole at the last minute. But, I was no gymnast. There was no way I could throw a leg back onto the ladder.

Well, it was only twenty feet to the ground…

"Lilly, what the hell are you doing?" came Mitchell's voice through the comm.

"Getting my partner," I grunted, swinging hand-over-hand down the pole.

I let go at ten feet, more or less, and hit the watery plaza in a jarring crouch. My knees stung and dirty spray seeped around the edges of my face shield, but I was up and running before I could check myself for injuries.

Bullets whizzed above my head, and I hunched low, scanning for JR.

The man had slowed, panting. But there was no time to slow down, mechs already funneled in. This was too close.

The high pitched whine of our sniper rifles tickled my eardrums, more shots zipping through the already chaotic scene. *Great. Caught in a firefight. What fun…*

By the time I reached JR, he'd fallen to one knee, hand pressed against his wounded thigh.

"C'mon, man," I said, pulling his arm around my shoulder.

"You didn't have to," JR gasped while I half-carried/half-dragged him toward the edge of the plaza.

"Bullshit."

"Seriously, I had it..."

"Shut up."

A rumbling noise spread through the plaza. The water rippled again. Shouts drifted on the breeze. Mara's wall. The mechs froze in place. Those who were not dead looked around in confusion. I used this opportunity to haul JR onto the set of stairs at the first entrance to the plaza, the rubble wall we'd discovered.

More shots. More shouts. Our snipers had reloaded. Chaos erupted again, this time with the panicked edge of soldiers stomping around in water frothy with the blood of their slain companions.

We climbed up the slope of debris, me pulling the smaller man when he faltered. He fell onto the rocky incline, hands gripped tightly around his thigh.

"Go," he gasped, his face pale and his lips bloodless.

"No," I replied. "You got this." I gripped him under the arms and continued dragging.

"Rob, you stubborn bastard, just leave me!" He tried to claw his way out of my grip.

"I told you to shut up!" I snapped at him. "I'm not. Fucking. Leaving you."

A beam of energy, blue and unsettling, fizzed to our left, leaving a smoking gouge on the rock. I had felt its presence—a clean heat, so unlike the fires or the general humidity of the city. The smoke produced a chemical smell, burning my nostrils.

"Rob..." JR mumbled.

His Aurawave touched me.

I should run. He's not worth this.

"No!" I growled, no energy left to say more.

I shook my head to clear away the clouds. Even this wounded and close to unconsciousness, JR was trying to use his Skill to get me to leave him. Talk about a stubborn bastard.

With one final heave, I shoved JR down the other side, sheltering him in a damp pocket of rubble.

"Lilly!" Mitchell's voice came through the com again and I realized the sergeant had been yelling for some time. "Where the hell you going?"

I tucked down beside JR who moaned softly at the jostling. "Don't worry, Sarge," I said in a voice much calmer than I felt, "I got 'im. We're safe."

"No thanks to you, asshole," I added under my breath. I didn't care if Mitchell heard me. He deserved the insult.

I studied the wound on JR's leg. Something had scored a deep gash through JR's radlon suit all the way to his flesh, exposing muscle and bone. I looked away, queasy, then forced myself to look back. Whatever had gotten him had partially cauterized the wound, so I wasn't too worried about him bleeding out, but I removed my knife anyway. Cutting a strip from his ruined suit, I bound the wound hoping to keep it clean(ish) until we could get a hold of a med kit.

I knew I still had work to do, the commotion still rang on the other side of our hiding spot, but suddenly my body felt as if it were made of lead. I collapsed against the warm stone, trying to find a well of energy somewhere deep inside.

Maybe the plan was flawed. Maybe JR screwed up. Maybe *I* screwed up. Maybe…this is where we die…

* * * * *

I swam through a fog, my body lethargic and heavy.

"Where am I?" I tried to shout, but no sound came from my throat.

My comm buzzed, a piercing chirp through the fog.

"Lilly! Where the hell are you?"

My eyes shot open. I had dozed off.

"Uh, here, Sir," I slurred, slapping my helmet as if I could slap some cohesion into my thoughts.

"Thank Charger," Ames said, his tone shrill.

In the background mechs screamed, gunfire rattled across the plaza, and the weighty pulse of mech frequencies pressed against my senses.

"Mitchell's down," Ames continued, "Carson's down. Rostbane is…"

"Down…for now," I responded, checking JR's pulse.

Still breathing.

"Teague's down."

"The bombardier? Shit, Sir," I said.

Teague was supposed to block off the escape route from the plaza. From the tension in Ames's voice, I assumed he'd failed.

Listlessly, I heaved a breath. "What do we do?"

There was no immediate answer from the other side of the line.

I peered above the barrier, trying to pick out the sharpshooters we had left.

Bullets tore through the misty air, splintering wood and shattering stone as pandemonium churned in the plaza below. Mechs struggled in the knee-deep water, their movements sluggish under the weight of their armor. Some collapsed in sparking heaps as our snipers picked them off with ruthless precision. Through my range finder, I spotted one mech twisting aimlessly, its head jerking side to side, unable to pinpoint where death was coming from. It stumbled, then sank with a hiss into the murky depths. A small knot of survivors were trying to regroup, clustering like cornered animals in the shadow of a toppled monument.

Finally, Ames spoke, "This is your plan, Private."

I sighed, gripping the handle of my pistol and thinking about Mara's tiny silver bombs. That technology would be convenient right about now. The steady pounding of at least three sets of boots echoed up the street behind me.

"Robert!" came Mara's cry, as if summoned. "The mechs are fleeing from the southern district."

I turned to see Mara standing with two others I didn't recognize: A very dark-skinned, older man and a younger woman with wild eyes. From their stocky builds and the complete lack of superficial wounds, I guessed the new people were also Tanks.

"Mara! Charger's Beard, I'm glad to see you," I flashed an exhausted grin. "Bombardier's down. You got any more of those silver thingys?"

She nodded slowly.

"We have to blow the entrance." I pointed across the plaza.

She nodded again, setting her face in a determined smile. "Griffin, Sir, can we do this?" she asked her commander.

The man nodded with a wicked grin. "Oh yeah, we're wired. Let's go."

The three of them climbed gingerly up the rubble, testing each foothold to ensure it would hold their heavier frames.

"Rostbane's wounded," I said as they passed.

The other woman nodded. "I have a kit," she said in a husky voice.

"Brit, help the private," Lieutenant Griffin said to her. "We'll go on ahead."

"Aye, Sir," Brit said and lifted JR as if he were a child.

"Stay out of the water!" I called to the Tanks as I picked my way down the wall. "I've got to finish this."

"Roger!" the two shouted in unison.

Tapping the comm, I said to Ames, "Griffin and Dark from the Black

Cats are going to collapse the far street. Can the guys hang in a little longer?"

Ames responded with an affirmative. "Good choice, Lilly," Ames said with renewed energy. "We can do that."

"Good," I said, trying not to sound too winded. "I'm going to fry those fuckers!"

This is it, I thought to myself taking a deep breath. *We may just get out of here alive.*

* * * * *

Mechs were everywhere—my head, my bones, my blood, my very soul. I tried to turn inward, to ignore the overpowering hum of blood mixed with oil and focus on that distinct vibration of the power lines.

I placed my hands on the breaker box and felt for the energy—dormant, expectant. The lines clung to it, poised to fulfill their singular purpose: to let the current flow. I had felt the sensations earlier when the square was empty, but now that the press of mech bodies churned up the bloody water, their fear and confusion muddled my thoughts. The din from the constant fire of guns combined with the teeth-jarring clamor of mech technology made my head spin.

Grinding my teeth, I willed the dormant energy to make itself known. My scalp prickled.

There it is.

I breathed out a controlled whistle of air and slowly opened my eyes. This task was bigger than anything I'd ever done before.

An explosion rocked the square, bursting through my calm. I froze, every nerve on edge, bracing for impact. A cloud of dust rose across the square. As it dissipated, I saw a new pile of debris. I let out a stuttering breath. It was just the Black Cats, doing their thing. I thought of Mara, hoping she was all right, before I turned my attention back to the breaker box.

Ten meters away, the generator chugged and huffed, its familiar churning bringing me comfort. I gripped the large, hodge-podge breaker in both hands and flipped the switch.

Nothing happened.

I pulled myself up and looked out over the plaza. Chaos still reigned. Black smudges crawled up the walls of the ruined buildings—mechs trying to get at the snipers above. I tapped my comm urgently.

"Ames! Get everyone out. The power isn't coming."

Silence on the line. Was Ames still conscious? Or even alive?

"I'll give you sixty seconds," came the delayed reply. "Good luck."

"Luck, my ass," I grumbled. This operation required all my expertise, and more importantly, my Skill.

I checked the generator. As I suspected, it was running in good order. I traced the lines back to the breaker box. All connected.

"So, it's the switch," I muttered with a frown. Great.

Feeling around carefully within the breaker, I found it almost instantly. The connectors were not…well…connecting.

"Dammit!" I snarled, slamming my fist into the switch.

No amount of impact or jostling I did could move it those last few centimeters. I rummaged through my tool bag, pulling out a large screwdriver. It took me only a moment's contemplation to come to a decision. It was stupid. It was risky. But…at this point…it was the only way.

With a gulp and a silent prayer to Joanna Greysoft, patron saint of all savants, I slammed the screwdriver home. Power jumped toward the lines.

Time froze, or maybe I just did, unable to feel anything but the power coursing through the lines. Strong. Triumphant. A new kind of explosion engulfed Sky Plaza—not one of fire and powder, but one of energy. It lifted the hair on my arms and vibrated my teeth. A spark blossomed on the screwdriver, I could see it in my mind—blue, yellow, and red—and traveled toward my hand.

I'm not sure if I let go or if it threw me backward, but the next thing I knew I was on my back, muscles twitching, heart racing. A strong urge to fight the energy coursed through me, but instead I exhaled and let it flow through me. Out from my fingertips and the bottoms of my feet. Out from my head. Out from my heart.

As I lay there dazed, the commotion in the plaza subsided to a dull roar. The sky stared down at me, its facade a watery blue. I tried to move my head, but it felt like a bowling ball lying upon the ground, heavy and slippery.

Is this where I'll die?

A face floated into my vision. A man I hadn't seen before with disheveled hair the color of straw peppered with gray, smiled at me. He actually *smiled,* despite the mud smeared across his MOPP gear and the gash over his temple. I had never seen him before, and he wore no name or rank on his uniform.

"Private Lilly?" The man's voice sounded tinny and far-away.

I tried to nod but could only blink in response.

"Let's get you out of here."

He reached down, taking my limp hand and hauled me up. I managed to make my limbs work and gripped onto his arm for support. My legs wobbled like noodles. He gave me a moment to steady myself against a piece of concrete. I vomited, spewing MRE all down its face until I was panting and shaking. I wiped my face.

"Who the hell are you?" I asked, voice like gravel.

"Nic Saint Claire," he said, "from the Red Rat squad."

"Never heard of them." Though, from his accent, I could tell this man was also American.

"You okay?"

"Peachy," I croaked, with a pained chuckle. "Perfectly fine."

He led me by my elbow from the edge of the plaza.

"Why go through all this trouble for me?" I asked as we rounded a corner and came upon a packed open-top hovervan. "I'm not that important."

Saint Claire grinned. "Someone says otherwise."

Mara's head popped up, smiling, as she helped me into the van. Still trembling, I tried to smile back and practically fell on an unconscious JR. Someone had wrapped his leg better and given him an IV. I was relieved to see color returning to his cheeks.

"Mendez, we're good to go," Saint Claire shouted over the rising din.

"Okay, boys an' girls," came a light, female voice from the driver's seat, "Get ready to fly!"

The van rose above the buildings with a jarring heave. If my stomach hadn't already been empty, this would have done it. Mendez laughed, her wild auburn hair fanning out behind her.

"I had no idea hovercars did this!" I said in Mara's ear, gripping the rails with white knuckles.

Mara snorted. "Me neither," she said, though her strained expression softened when she saw the pallor of my skin. She ran her fingers along my aching jaw. "You seem off," she said. "Everything all right?"

I touched the back of her hand, grudgingly removing it from my face. Though her touch felt like fire on my skin, I kept hold of it anyway. I gave her a crooked grin.

"I'll live."

"I'm glad you survived," she said quietly.

"Me, too," I responded. And I really was. I wanted to sleep for a week or disappear into a hot bath…anything to shake the weight pressing on my chest. Others hadn't made it. Their absence clawed at my thoughts, hollowing out any real sense of relief. But then there was Mara—her hand in mine, grounding me. Despite the guilt gnawing at the edges of my heart, just for a moment I let myself feel the quiet, selfish gratitude of being here with her.

She rested her head on my shoulder as I peered out over the city.

The plaza churned with movement, a mass of black and chrome mechs. Skirmishes sputtered out, the soldiers leaving their dead piled in grim heaps. The remaining forces scuttled through the streets like frantic insects—some limped or bolted away, while others pressed forward, oblivious to the wreckage left behind.

Our disorganized forces retreated in every moving vehicle: hovercars, speedbikes, SMRT cars, flighted vehicles, and even on foot. We had done it. We had stalled the advance long enough to evacuate. We would survive, but we hadn't won.

Turning from the fray, I turned toward the city. Its heart still smoldered, the skeletal remains of crumbling 'scrapers looming overhead, their hollow windows staring vacantly into the chaos. Xi'an would need years—decades—to claw its way back to its former glory, if it ever could. For now, it was little more than a graveyard, home to several million wounded... and fifteen million ghosts.

Part Two

Lanzhou, China

- 6 -
C.E. 2253 February 19

A hub of industry, the city of Lanzhou oozed decay. Home to almost nine million people, its streets were thick with the stench of rusted metal and scorched plastic. Neon signs flickered feebly against the smog-choked skyline. In the distant past, the capital of the Gansu province had been called the Golden City, the locus between East and West. Now, a rotten shit hole, it was known as the Dark City.

Nestled between mountain ranges to the south and the north, Lanzhou's valley collected all the byproducts of its industry. The Yellow River, which wound through its center, slipped along as a putrid green waterway with bubbles of slime languidly rising on its surface to burst in an unpleasant spray of fumes and ichor.

A dark film of fine brown-red powder covered everything. No matter how tightly you kept your suits tied or how well you sealed your windows, it found its way inside—inside your house, your clothes, even beneath your fingernails. The haze lay thick and low upon the city, especially during the coldest days of winter. Even from our sixty-fourth floor window, we couldn't see farther than the nearest 'scrapers and smokestacks, and definitely not as far as the storied mountains. Many winter days here felt as dark as the nights.

It made my hometown, the slum city of The Sink, look like an island paradise.

Where Xi'an had been beautiful, Lanzhou was hideous.

Due to this, the inhabitants of the city left their homes as infrequently as possible. When they did, it was rarely during the worst days of winter. When it was during the worst days of winter, they dressed for the weather. My radlon suit remained mostly intact, though it had needed significant modifications due to the sky-silt clogging up its filtration system. Its color had long since morphed from its original dark gray to a greenish, reddish brown. Its visor was scratched and pitted; silt embedded into the grooves. Still, I hated to retire it for the cheap alternatives the locals used: insectile respirators with round, awkward goggles and dingy synthetic coveralls. They were uncomfortable and looked ridiculous.

Mara, on the other hand, gave up that concern long ago. She stalked beside me like a squat, hulking beetle. Very few things could hurt a Tank. Their cell composition, one-third atrinite, a tough metal only found within the cells of savants, made their skin thick like armor and their bones hard and dense. But, the one thing that always worried Tanks, was damage to their airways. They feared suffocation just as much as the rest of us.

"Hey Robert," Mara's echo-y voice piped over the comm, "You ever gonna to tell me why we're outside during the coldest hour of this moonless winter morning?"

She stopped, casting her gaze toward the haze as if she could will the sun to rise and bathe the city in its weak, filtered light. Though, it wouldn't add much warmth through the impenetrable fog anyway. Temp readings on my handheld said five degrees below freezing, warmer here on street level than higher up. The buildings radiated a kind of repulsive heat of their own, borne by industrial wastes pumped through the walls to the sewers below.

"Because we're desperate," I chuckled humorlessly. "We haven't had a decent haul in weeks."

A yellow-green steam rose from a sewer grate, and I caught the miasmatic tang of unidentifiable waste in the back of my throat despite my suit's filtration system. The first time a person smelled the city, they were lucky if they didn't hurl. I had not been so lucky.

Mara groaned. "This is a better fate than starvation?" She snorted. "Can't wait to get out of here."

I grunted in agreement. We'd been holed up here since the evacuation of Xi'an, eight months ago. Eight months of waiting, of listening, of scraping together a meager pile of resources and weaponry. Eight months of filtering our own urine for drinking water.

"Actually, it's not a food run, this time," I replied. "We need information."

Eight months had shed no light on Rose's agenda. Rumors abounded—cities bombed, savants in captivity, an elite super-army rampaging across the countryside, a secret biological project—but due to China's haphazard communication network, they remained just that. Whispers on the wind.

If we were lucky, the CORP had already turned its attention to other projects and forgotten about us. But, if I'd learned anything in my time here, we never got lucky.

"Wait," Mara said, stopping in the shadow of a dilapidated fountain, "you dragged me out of bed to chase another rumor?"

"My Lieutenant believes this is more than a rumor," I said, trying to sound as sympathetic as I could. "I hate it too, but if we can learn something —anything—of value, don't you think we should try."

She looked over at me, her expression unreadable beneath her mask. She sighed. "I suppose. So, do I get the deets, or what?"

I didn't know how to explain it, so I sent her the message instead. She looked down at her handheld.

TO PRIVATE ROBERT LILLY: I CAN HELP YOU FIND THE KEY. DONGFANGHONG PLAZA, GULOU RESIDENTIAL DISTRICT. 0600 HOURS, 19TH FEBRUARY. LOOK FOR A SIGN. REMEMBER, THEY CAN TAKE OUR HOMES AND OUR LIVES, BUT THEY CANNOT TAKE THE DREAM. WE DO NOT KNEEL.

"That's you?" she asked, cocking her head toward me.

"Unless you know another Private Robert Lilly in this army."

She shook her head. "I still don't understand it."

But I did.

Just when I'd felt ready to give up, the message reminded me. *We do not kneel.*

Thinking of all those who hadn't made it to Lanzhou, or who *had* made it, but were scarred like JR, I knew I had to keep fighting. I begged Ames to let me follow this lead. He'd been more than happy to allow it. He felt the pressure as much as I.

"You'll see," I said, hesitant to voice my suspicions lest I be wrong.

I led us down the cracked walkway, tiles once ivory and coral, now dingy yellow and putrid orange, toward Dongfanghong Plaza—a plaza long abandoned to time and silt. Grass once thrived here, filling the gaps between the stones with vibrant green. Now, those spaces had withered into patches of brown, marshy dirt—tiny wastelands of decay. The mud clung like quicksand, fine and relentless, tugging at my boots with every step as we squelched through the mire.

The streetlights glowed weakly through grime-encrusted globes. Only a third of them even functioned, casting deep shadows across the slimy ground. I scanned the plaza. Now that we were here, I wondered how I'd identify this mysterious informant. My hand rested on the handle of my pistol, just in case this was a trap. Mara clenched her fists.

Only one other person trod through the square, a heavily shrouded porter pushing a wagon of mildewed barrels and sodden crates, but I didn't think he was our guy, unless our informant had come up with a really cumbersome disguise.

One of the dead streetlights flickered on, shining brightly, while all the others began to dim in the growing dawn. It didn't look like the rest; it was older with only one bulb as opposed to five, and a saucer-shaped hood like a UFO from an old movie. It bathed the square in golden light.

I could hear Mara's surprised hiss crackled through my comm and we both had to shield our eyes from the brightness. A figure stood beneath the light, clothed in a gray hooded robe, one gloved hand on the light pole. The other beckoned to us.

"Well, that's not creepy at all," Mara said, voice low. She looked at me. "We going?"

I nodded As far as signs went, that was a pretty obvious one.

"Are you worried they'll try to kill us?"

"That's why I brought you."

Mara shrugged, then nodded. "Good enough for me."

The figure stopped us when we were about five feet away.

I breathed deeply and focused on them. I couldn't feel anything, save for the hum of the streetlights and the vague shadows of mechs moving about in the surrounding 'scrapers. I didn't detect any mods.

The figure spoke. The voice was smooth with a slight rasp at the end.

"Nǐ fǎnduì Lightbar ma?"

I shrugged, hands held up at my sides.

"Something about opposing Lightbar," Mara muttered.

"Oh, um…" I stammered. "Uh, yes, uh sir…or ma'am?" I said louder, wincing at the waver in my voice.

The figure tried again. "Then come. Not safe here," she said in English.

We followed, our steps hesitant. Mara gripped my arm and made sure to stay half a step ahead of me. I couldn't tell what she was thinking, but I knew she took her job as my bodyguard seriously.

The figure moved like a wraith into an alley and toward a small, metal door.

"You, check," she said to me.

"Check?" I asked.

With a huff, she grabbed my hand and placed it against the door. Even through my glove, I could feel the vibrations within. Standard electrical equipment, a corridor or server room. No mech presence.

"Safe?"

I nodded and she popped the door open and ducked in quickly. I followed, instructing Mara to take up the rear.

We entered a dim hallway full of steadily blinking LED lights. My silty visor did not help with the visibility, adjusting slowly to the low light. I should have cleaned the sensor. Computer equipment hummed. The shadowy figure navigated through the dark confidently. Every machine they touched brightened, illuminating the next few meters of the hall.

We emerged into a small room, overhead lights sparking to life as the figure entered. Filled with several beat-up couches, overturned crates acting as tables, and a server bank in one corner, the room would have seemed like a gamer hangout save for the suave blond man sitting on one of the couches. He wore a clean standard-issue MOPP suit and no mask, and he grinned at me like an old friend.

I'd heard nothing of Nic Saint Claire since he and his driver, the woman named Mendez, had dropped us off in Lanzhou directly following the assault on Xi'an. Even my searches on him through the army's thorough database had come up empty.

"Where the hell have you been?"

Saint Claire smiled. "A lot of places. Now, I'm in Lanzhou."

"I see that," I muttered.

"It's perfectly safe in here," Nic said, making a circle around his face and gesturing at my helmet.

We removed our respirators and tucking my helmet under my arm, I subconsciously ran a hand over my messy mop of hair. It was probably time for a trim.

"Ah, Americans," came a heavily accented women's voice behind me. "Friends of yours, Nic?"

I realized I'd lost track of the cloaked figure when I entered the room, too distracted with the appearance of my previous rescuer. Now I turned and staggered back in surprise.

Deep brown eyes studied at us under a pale, wrinkled brow. Wispy strands of black hair drifted around her face, having escaped her messy bun. She stood, hands serenely clasped in front of her and a light smile on her face. Even without the pressed suit or immaculate hairstyle, there was no mistaking her husky voice and confident demeanor.

I inclined my head to the older woman. "Tàitài Zhelan," I said, hoping I remembered the proper title of deference, "I saw you on the holo. I'm happy you survived."

She nodded sagely, though her throat tightened as she swallowed. "It is a mixed blessing," she replied with a heaviness in her voice. "I am happy to be able to fight another day."

I didn't know how to respond to that, so I went with the obvious, "Private Lilly, ma'am. And this is PFC Dark. I was…requested?"

"You are younger than I expected," she chuckled and looked at Saint Claire. "Are you sure this is the mind behind the Battle of Sky Plaza?"

I blushed, shuffling my boots on the dirty tile floor and wondering how Nic knew more about me than I him.

"It is, ma'am," Mara spoke up, stepping beside me. "I was there for it all."

Zhelan nodded again. "Very well, Private," she said. "I have a job for you, highly classified. If you'll take it."

I looked at Mara and she nudged me in the ribs for encouragement.

With a deep breath, I tried to flash a magnanimous smile. "It would be an honor, ma'am. What can I do for you?"

Zhelan returned with a weak smile, all the tragedy and hardship painted across her features. But her eyes held hope. "I am glad," she said, "I have a friend you need to meet."

* * * * *

I was disappointed, but also curious.

Zhelan hadn't directed us to a weapons cache or a secret bunker that would solve all our problems as I had hoped. Instead, she gave us a name and some GPS coordinates, then sent us away with a lot of questions.

Rom Query.

"What kind of a name is Rom Query, anyway?" JR scoffed.

He eased himself down onto one of the plastic benches in our makeshift Commons. The bunker around us was a patchwork of salvaged materials—corrugated metal walls, cracked plastic sheeting for windows, and a sagging ceiling reinforced with beams scavenged from the derelict building above. Flickering LED strips gave off pale blue light, barely enough to push back the shadows creeping from the corners and the faint hum of an overworked generator added to the ever-present sense of instability.

"Screw this cold weather," he said, leaning a cane against the rickety table.

"You sound like a damn geriatric," Mara said, smirking as she leaned back in the chair. "What's next? Complaining about your bunions? Dinner at four?"

JR shot Mara a dark a look. "Chemical rifle burns aren't exactly a spa treatment, you know. You try dragging half your leg through Sky Plaza and see how spry you feel."

"Oh, the war stories," she teased, resting her chin on her hand. "What was it like, old-timer? Did you walk uphill both ways?"

"You were there, genius! I was brilliant, by the way. If it weren't for my speedbike prowess, the battle would have never even started."

"Oh sure, Grandpa. Need me to knit you a blanket while you talk about the glory days?"

"You're hilarious," JR said flatly. "Remind me why I let you sit with us again?"

"Because you love me," she said, taking his cane and spinning it like a baton.

"Give that back before you break something!" JR snapped, reaching across the table. A glass rocked precariously. "Rob! Make her stop pestering me!"

I caught it before it spilled.

"Guys, cut it out!" I said, snatching the cane from Mara's hand. "We've been over this. It's not JR's fault our med equipment is crap. The medics have done their best."

Mara pouted while glaring at JR. "You just *had* to get dad involved, didn't you?"

I rolled my eyes. "I will not justify that with a response," I grumbled, realizing that's exactly what I had just done. Then I fixed a hard stare at JR. "However man, have you ever thought you're being maybe a wee bit dramatic?"

He grimaced. "Well, getting your leg almost shot off kind of changes your attitude about life. Do you realize how many liaisons I've had to turn down because I'm now a cripple?"

"Okay, now you're *definitely* being dramatic," Mara helped.

"You know, there's more to life than fucking," I told him.

"Yeah…like eating," JR mumbled. "But we can barely do that here, too."

"I meant friendship."

JR groaned. "With friends like you…"

Mara chuckled, but flashed me a secret smile, looking up through her dark eyelashes. "So, what about this Query guy?" she said, steering us back on track. "Do we trust Zhelan?"

"Definitely," I said without hesitation.

The others looked at me with wide, questioning eyes.

"So sue me," I continued, "but I like the woman. And something about her just feels…genuine."

Mara shrugged. "Works for me. And she thinks this…what are they? Savant? Mech? True?…is the key to taking down Lightbar?"

"I guess? No one really knows who this Query figure is or where they came from."

"But it's not like we have any alternative," JR added.

I nodded. "It's in Healey's hands now. I hope she makes the right decision."

* * * * *

Someone knocked on the flimsy metal door of my tiny bunk. Since JR was still milking his stay in the more comfortable medical quarters, I had this shoebox of a room all to myself. Clad only in my underwear, I stretched out on the narrow cot, balancing an electronic reader on my stomach.

"Come in," I called lazily, assuming it was JR. He or Mara were the only ones who ever bothered to visit me here, usually to harass me about something or, in JR's case, steal whatever snacks I'd managed to hoard.

The door creaked open, but instead of JR's cheesy grin, I was greeted by Staff Sergeant Mitchell's stone-faced glare.

My stomach dropped.

"Uh—sir!" I stammered, jerking upright and fumbling with the reader, which clattered to the floor.

Mitchell let out a gruff snort and stepped to the side, holding the door open. Behind him, Lieutenant Ames strode in, his expression unreadable.

Oh, great. Both of them.

Scrambling to my feet, I saluted hastily, pounding a closed fist to my bare chest. "S-sorry, Sir—uh, I wasn't expecting—"

"No kidding," Mitchell said, one eyebrow twitching upward as he took in my bare legs and the rumpled blanket tangled around my feet.

Ames folded his arms, gaze sweeping the room. His gray eyes sparkled. "Comfortable, are we?"

"I—uh—yes, I mean no, Sir," I sputtered, wishing the floor would open up and swallow me whole.

Mitchell sighed and ran a hand over his buzzed scalp. "Lilly, put on some pants. We need to talk."

"Right, of course, pants, yes, sir," I mumbled, snatching my fatigues from the back of a chair and nearly tripping over my own boots in the process.

As I yanked on my pants and tried to salvage a shred of dignity, Ames exchanged a look with Mitchell, his lips twitching as if he was fighting back a smirk. "Well, this is an unexpected twist," he said.

"Sir?" I asked him, glancing surreptitiously around the room for a shirt.

"Private Lilly," he continued with formality, "we would like to congratulate you on your promotion." He held out his hand and in it was a new patch for my suit.

"Wait—what?" I stared, dumbfounded.

"To sergeant," Mitchell said with a grumble.

I looked at the patch—three silver triangles nested inside of each other, a big difference from the stripes I currently wore.

"Sergeant?"

"Your performance at Xi'an, while a bit foolhardy, was solid. Not only did you come up with an effective plan, but you saved many fellow soldiers in the process. The officers have discussed it, and we believe that you would do well to lead your own squad."

"*Me?*" I knew I sounded like a complete idiot right now, but I hadn't expected a promotion this soon into my service—especially not while standing barefoot and shirtless in my messy bunk.

Ames nodded, "And, as sergeant, we have a new assignment for you."

Pressing my lips together in a tight line, I nodded. *Duty comes first.* "Whatever you need, Sir."

"It's unusual," Ames continued, "I assume that doesn't bother you?"

After all I had done so far with the army, I nodded. None of it had been usual.

"As you've noticed, we don't exactly have a full roster, so your squad needs to be small. But, you may choose your soldiers."

I gaped. They were going to let me pick my own squad? Had I won the army lottery or something? "Thank you, Sir," I said lamely.

"Since Dame Zhelan mentioned you directly, we want you to find this Rom Query person."

"Really, Sir?" I asked, "Wouldn't that be a better job for an ambassador? Or a diplomat?" I was neither.

Ames chuckled, responding to my unspoken thought. "As far as I'm concerned you are both. You've already managed to earn the respect of more than one senior officer," he looked at Mitchell who hesitantly grumbled in approval.

"Thank you, Sir," I inclined my head, finally taking the patch from his hands.

He laughed again, more heartily this time. "Lilly, you don't have to 'Sir' me in every other word—I know I outrank you. Just speak like a human, not a malfunctioning protocol bot."

"Yes, S—" I coughed. "Um, sorry."

"Meet us in the briefing room tomorrow at zero-eight-hundred hours." Ames continued. He shook my hand, "Looking forward to having you on board."

"Looking forward to being on board," I said, hoping the insecurity didn't show in my voice.

"Oh, and Lilly?" Ames said as the two turned to leave, "You will do great things." He winked at me. "Just remember to have some fun, too. You're too young to be so serious."

Says the Lieutenant who looks like he could be my older brother, I thought. Maybe Ames was speaking from experience.

The officers exited. I was left staring at my radlon suit hanging on the back of the door on a piece of rusty wire. Pulling off my old rank, I studied the suit's original color beneath the patch. We'd been through a lot together.

Ames words echoed in my head. Did he know something I didn't?

"Sergeant," I whispered to myself as I headed back to my bed. "Well, isn't that something." I switched off my reader and killed the lights.

When I woke up, would I be someone different?

- 7 -

C.E. 2253 February 20

"Dark," I said immediately. An obvious choice.

Swallowing hard, I looked around the assembled officers as they watched me expectantly. Ames and Mitchel were there, as expected, also Major Healey and several other officers. I recognized Lieutenant Griffin, the leader of Mara's squad, but not the others. Keeping my hands clasped behind my back, I tried not to let them see me trembling with nerves.

"She's one of my best bruisers," Griffin said, "Small enough to get into places where most of us can't and strong enough to do a lot of damage."

"That's why she would be an asset to this mission, Sir" I said, pumping as much confidence and machismo into my voice as I could. I still didn't feel it.

Fake it till you make it, Robert, I thought.

Griffin nodded. "Well said, Sergeant Lilly."

"Private Dark," Ames mumbled, entering information onto his handheld, "Who else?"

I hesitated for a moment. An information gathering session would benefit from a Sway, but would JR be up to the task? There was no one else I trusted as much. Plus, he owed me one.

"Rostbane."

"Can he hack it?" Mitchell asked. "Been whining about that leg for months."

I shrugged, "He'd better. We need someone like him and he's good at what he does."

Ames nodded approvingly. "This will be good for him. The kid needs a task." I snickered slightly. JR was going to hate me. "Who else?"

I had to admit I hadn't bothered to get to know many of the others well enough in my eight months here. The cynical part of my brain was already chastising me for getting too close to Mara and JR, at the expense of others. War could take people out of your life in an instant and I wasn't sure if I'd be able to deal with that kind of heartache.

"Ferryman. I'd like someone who can do some damage from a distance."

97

The man's Skill had been invaluable help during the Battle of Sky Plaza. When we'd all regrouped here in Lanzhou, I was happy to learn he'd survived.

"Ferryman's still in detention," Mitchell said.

Then, I remembered why. A new guy, Anderson, had made fun of his name. Ferryman retaliated by directing a flying tankard into Anderson's junk. The retaliation would have been overlooked, save for the fact that the tankard shattered, and a shard of glass opened up an artery. I still wasn't sure if Anderson had been released from medical.

"He needs an outlet for that anger," I said, "He's effective in tight situations. And he's scrappy," I said. "I'd be happy to have him on my team."

"And you can handle his temper?"

I nodded. JR probably could, if nothing else.

"Very good," Ames said. "You'll need a driver."

"Is Mendez back?" I asked. Her driving skills during the flight from Sky Plaza had impressed me.

One of the unnamed officers chuckled. "If you can convince her," he said.

I looked at him, raising an eyebrow in curiosity. "Sir?"

"Roberta Mendez is her own contractor," Ames said, "but I'm pretty sure I can convince her." He gave me a benign smile. "This assignment is right up her alley."

"Works for me," I said, grateful I didn't have to do the convincing myself. "What about Saint Claire?" I still had no idea of the man's rank or title, but his connection to the mayor would be a boon.

This time, Healey spoke, "Saint Claire has other responsibilities."

"Plus, he far outranks you," Mitchell added with a smirk. He may now respect me, but the man still didn't like me.

I cast my gaze downward to avoid rolling my eyes at my former sergeant.

"But I think this roster is enough," Ames said lightly, steering us back on track. "We don't want to startle our informant."

"Yes, Sir," I complied. Five people wouldn't be much if the mechs came after us, but at least these were five I could trust.

"Gather your team and get ready to leave at eighteen-hundred hours tonight," Healey said. "We need to move on this. Do you have any questions?"

A mission statement popped up on my handheld, and I read it quickly. The coordinates pointed to a warehouse in an unused industrial district on the south side of the city. The objective: meet with Query, find out what they know, and get out.

"No, Sir," I said. "Seems easy enough."

With a formal nod, Healey said, "Then you are dismissed."

"Also, Lilly," Ames added almost as an afterthought.

I stopped and turned back to the officers.

"Query could very well be a mech. Zhelan is known to not discriminate. Be careful."

"I will, Sir." And I meant it. Even if this person *was* on our side, I was still wary of mechs. And I was scared as hell.

* * * * *

JR and I shivered in our suits and masks as we waited near the garage where the army kept its less expensive vehicles.

"So, sergeant now, huh Rob?" JR said, his voice prodding.

"E-yup…"

"I don't have to salute you, do I? Charger Knows, I didn't pay any attention in army school."

I chuckled, "No."

"Good. Cuz I clearly already listened to you when you were a nobody. Title doesn't change any of that." Leave it to JR to both make me feel warm and fuzzy while also reminding me of my place in the world.

"Thanks buddy, glad you have such faith in me," I responded, sarcasm in my voice.

"So, I hear they promoted you?" Mara approached us smiling.

"Yeah. I guess I did something right, there in Xi'an."

She laughed. "I could've told ya that." She punched me in the shoulder, her fist like a sledge. I winced at the impact. "Congrats."

"For what?" A new voice came through dim haze.

"Robert's promotion," Mara said.

The other voice grunted as the fog revealed its owner. Ferryman skulked over. "Promoted? Shit. I never thought you'd be one to show initiative," he said, clapping me on the shoulder. "Well done."

"Thanks, Ferryman. You remember Dark and Rostbane?"

"I prefer JR," he said through gritted teeth.

Ferryman chuckled, "I hear ya. Ferryman is my father. Just Chet for me."

Chet. I held in my snicker, remembering Anderson's nut sack.

"Who we waitin' for?" Chet asked.

"The Zephyr."

A tall figure emerged from the gloom, slim and lithe. She was dressed, unlike the rest of us, in fashionable brown faux-leathers. A modern mask and set of goggles rested upon her face while a pilot's cap covered her head underneath a fur-fringed hood. I wondered how she kept her gear so clean. Or maybe she was just smart, getting clothes already in the color of the pollution.

"Ready to go boys? And girl…" she added with approval in her voice when she saw Mara.

"Squad," I said, testing out the word. When I decided I liked the term, I continued, "Mendez is going to be our escort."

Chet whistled and the woman snorted through her mask. "You only wish," she scolded him. "Let's do this."

"Shotgun!" JR called, but Mendez shook her head.

"That seat's for God," she said sternly. "A-K-A. no one sits up front but me."

We settled in for a forty-minute trip to the sound of JR's grumbling.

In the hovervan we removed our cumbersome masks, and I studied the faces of my team. Mara looked the same as always, black hair in a frizzy low ponytail, but JR was skinnier than I remembered and paler, his curly hair hidden by a tight beanie. The reddish-brown scraggle on Chet's chin had been poorly maintained, like my own beard. On the whole, we almost looked defeated. I think my first job as sergeant—or was it second?—would be to clean these bastards up.

Mendez on the other hand, shone like a beacon of composure, bordering dangerously on some sort of fashion sense. Angular goggles rested on her brow and her luxurious auburn curls had been pulled back into a neat braid. The fur of her hood connected to that of her collar, and I briefly wondered why the woman wasn't driving high-end hovercars for wealthy business magnates instead of shuttling around our ragtag team.

"Okay, Mendez," I began, "I'd like you to stay with the van in case we've got to get out quick."

"Of course, jefe," she said with a white-toothed grin.

"Mara and Chet," I looked between the two of them, "you'll be the muscle but *only* if things go south. You got it?"

They both nodded.

"I need to hear it," I said, giving Chet an especially hard stare.

"Yes, Sir," they said, and I caught a hit of amusement in Mara's voice.

She smiled at me, and it caught me off guard. Even though she outranked me the previous day, she seemed to have no problem falling into this new role. I wanted to tell her how grateful I was for her trust in me, but I didn't want to appear sniveling to the others. So, I just smiled back, taking a deep breath.

"Hey, lover boy," JR said, jamming his elbow into my ribs. "Rob!"

I whipped my head around to him, annoyed at him ruining my moment.

"What, JR?" I asked, annoyed.

"I was just asking what my job is," he glowered at me.

I waved my hand in a dismissive gesture. "Just do what you always do. Charm the pants off our contact."

JR narrowed his eyes. "I didn't know it was *that* kind of assignment," he said. "Otherwise, I'd've worn something nicer."

I rolled my eyes, but this time did *not* justify JR's words with a retort.

"So, do we trust this guy?" Mendez asked from the driver's seat.

"I guess," I replied. "Do we have a choice?"

"We always have a choice, niño," she said.

"Healey seems to think they're our only option," I shrugged, though I knew she couldn't see me. "So, I do the job."

"That's why you're a good soldier boy," she laughed deeply, "and why I would be a terrible one."

"But I thought you were…" Mara began.

"Charger's Beard, no way girl! I help out Healey. We are sisters at heart."

"So, *should* we trust this contact?" I asked, realizing Mendez may have further intel on the subject.

She clicked her tongue. "I wouldn't. But, as you said, Healey seems to think this is our only option. And I trust her. So, we will be cautious."

Chet made a grunt of agreement.

"Thank you, Mendez," I said, relieved that she had said what I could not.

JR snorted a laugh. I looked over to see him scrolling through something on his handheld. A bare breast, a set of legs.

"Are you looking at nudes?" I whispered to him.

Quickly, he turned off the screen, "Of course not!"

"Bullshit," I said, attempting to keep my voice low. Though Mara and Chet both watched us. "I need you to focus, man."

"Well, this is how I focus."

"Bullshit!" I snapped again. "This is serious, JR. If one of us slips up, we could blow the assignment or get someone killed."

"Not my fault you get to be in charge while I just get dragged out into this godforsaken dump before my leg is healed," he muttered, rubbing the back of his neck. "Gotta love risking life and limb again when I barely have half a limb left to spare."

"Well, isn't someone cranky today," Mara chimed in, leaning back in her seat with a sly grin.

JR shot her a look but didn't respond. Instead, his hand drifted to his cane, fingers tightening around it like a lifeline. The injury had clearly rattled him more than he let on, which was why he felt the need to mask that fear with sarcasm and distractions.

I glanced at both of them, weighing a response. JR's fear wasn't just about the mission—it was about whether he trusted himself to keep up. Discretely, I settled a hand on his knee and gave it a gentle squeeze. He looked at me, mouth open for another retort.

"I wouldn't have brought you on this mission if I thought you couldn't handle it," I muttered to him.

His eyes widened, but the tightness in his expression eased. I went to remove my hand, but he pushed it back down, covering it with his own.
I could almost hear Ames's voice in the back of my mind telling me that this is why he'd made me sergeant. Dammit, that bastard may just be onto something.

* * * * *

"Ahh, Lanzhou," JR said, staring out the window, "the city of factories."

I smiled inwardly. At least JR was feeling a little better. I hadn't been keen on pushing the squad through the Sway's foul mood.

He continued to narrate under his breath, "Big factories, small factories. Factories on the ruins of ancient villages. Factories in modern apartment complexes. Factories on top of factories. I'm so goddamn sick of *factories*!"

"Where we goin' anyway?" Chet asked

"Oh look, another factory," JR grumbled.

I followed the Sway's gaze. "Would guys you be surprised if I said it was a factory?" I asked with a chuckle, JR's light-hearted mood rubbing off on me.

Mara moaned, and Mendez said, "Looks like we're getting close."

However, unlike the industrial districts we'd recently passed, this one felt like a ghost town. No chemicals billowed out of the smokestacks and no lights glowed within the boxy shapes. Blackened, corroded infrastructure perched on the precarious bank of a dry riverbed, crumbling into the gray earth.

"Here?" JR asked, with a frown of disgust.

"Is what the coordinates say," Mendez replied, also trying to look at the factory from every angle.

"Is there an entrance or…do we have to bust our way through the walls?"

Mara laughed. "Won't be hard." She cracked her knuckles. "These buildings look ready to fall down anyway."

"Who would want to live here?" Chet asked.

"Mendez, are you sure you got the coordinates right?" JR prodded.

"Charger's Balls, with the questions!" I snapped, rubbing the bridge of my nose.

If I had known there would be this many questions, I may have reconsidered the promotion.

A flicker of red caught my attention.

"There," I said and pointed. "Left," I added when I remembered Mendez couldn't see me.

A light, the only one that shone in this district, illuminated a set of stairs leading into a dark hole below.

"Well, that's not terrifying at all," JR mumbled.

"You sure this is the place?" Mendez asked again.

"Did anyone see any other option?" I said, putting on my mask.

No one spoke.

"Then, this is as good a place as any."

"Greysoft's Blessing to you," Mendez said as we exited the vehicle.

I sighed. "We'll need more than blessings tonight," I muttered under my breath. "We're gonna need a miracle."

Mendez's laugh followed me into the dark night.

The stairs led to a dead-end and a heavy iron door, rusted shut.

"Well, this is great," JR muttered.

"Should I take it down?" Mara asked, pointing to the door.

Before I could answer, Chet said, "Look." He indicated a small speaker box off to one side. It had a single button.

I shrugged and pressed it.

It crackled to life, and a voice echoed from somewhere deep inside.

"Speak."

A frequency resonated deep within my belly. Mechs. Healey's fears were correct.

I swallowed around the nausea. My lips worked, but no sound came out.

"Oh, seriously, Rob?" JR grumbled and shoved past me. He leaned close to the box, his tone dropping into something smooth and steady, like silk over steel.

"We're not here to waste your time," he said, his voice carrying that practiced charm. "We know what Lightbar did at Xi'an. We saw it firsthand—the destruction, the loss, the lies."

Silence crackled on the line, tense and heavy.

He didn't wait for an answer. "Your enemies are our enemies. And we don't forget the people who've stood against them. Open the door, and we can prove it."

The air crackled—whether from the tension or JR's Aurawave, I couldn't tell. It rose in my throat like static, bitter and overwhelming, until I realized it wasn't mine. It was his. JR was pouring it on thick, a blade angled to press just enough without cutting.

The line went quiet again.

A loud click. The floor rumbled and clanked. Then, it started sinking. A sudden lurch. I whirled my arms to keep upright. Mara caught me by the elbow. Chet went down in a crouch, and JR fell on his ass, cane clattering across the floor. He cried out in a low, frustrated howl.

When the platform stuttered to a shaking halt, I reached down and helped JR up, handing back his cane to the litany of profanity spewing from his mouth. A dilapidated gate creaked open, disappearing into the wall.

"Come in," came a voice from the shadows.

Viridian eyes shown from the darkness, casting us in a pale, greenish glow. We shuffled forward, hands thrust out to catch any surprises. The air was moist, and it stank of damp earth and rusted metal. A heavy footfall landed on the heel of my boot, almost taking my shoe off. I stumbled, crashing into JR.

"Seriously, Rob?" JR grumbled, tapping his cane in front of him.

"Sorry," I muttered, trying to push Mara off my shoe.

She bumped into Chet. "The hell?" he snarled. "You trying to take me down?"

"For fuck's sake," she huffed. "I don't have night vision in my helm like you lot."

A tinny chuckle cut through the darkness. "I am remiss," the voice said. "I forget you nats cannot adjust your vision."

A breaker switch snapped, and sulfur lights buzzed on, casting the room in a bloody red glow. Their activation, a warm liquid coursing through my blood, boosted my confidence, until I felt the mech standing in front of us. It stopped me in my tracks, gasping.

Icy cold. A frozen river in the dead of winter. A whistle just beyond the edge of your hearing. Absent. This mech resonated at a frequency I could barely feel. Apparently, no frequency at all unsettled me more than massive waves of vibrations ever could.

The figure before us defied gender. Dressed in an impeccable pinstripe suit with matching bow tie and polished boots, their face betrayed the illusion of humanity—a smooth, hairless head with eyes the shifted from green to gold, unnervingly pink lips, and visible joints where the jaw met the skull—an unearthly blend of beauty and horror.

"I presume you are the ones Liu spoke of?" they asked, drawling out the words.

"I…Mayor Zhelan?" I stammered. "Yes. Probably. Are you Query?"

They nodded. "You may remove your masks. The air down here is perfectly safe, I assure you."

I looked at the others. They looked back at me. I noticed that my handheld no longer read an air quality warning. I nodded to my crew.

"Ah. Americans," the mech said when we had all removed our gear. "Long way from home."

"Yes. I'm S-Sergeant Robert Lilly," I said, tripping over the unfamiliar title.

"It's a pleasure to meet you, Sergeant Lilly," Query said.

"And you as well, Sir…um…"

"Mech," JR helped, giving a wide smile. "I've never seen one like you before." He sidled up to Query without hesitation, admiration dripping from his voice.

Query chuckled. "That's because there *is* no one like me, as far as I know. And, I prefer the term 'cyborg' if you please."

JR rose an eyebrow, still eying Query with appreciation. "Cyborg?" he asked.

"Yes," Query continued slowly, "'mech' just doesn't sound right for me. It feels…" They made a sound of disgust.

"This guy confuses me," Chet whispered into my ear. "Does he want to kill us or fuck us?"

I held back an amused snort. They confused me, too.

JR made a show of contemplating Query, putting his hand on his chin and everything. "Cyborg…." he said again. "You baffle us all. You seem human, but you're not. You wear fashion hundreds of years out of date, yet it looks as new as if it were made for you. You, my friend, are an enigma."

Query smiled, pink lips spreading in a too-wide grin. I think he was pleased. "Indeed," he said, looking over to the main who had paid him the compliment. "So kind of you to notice."

"Anyway, friend," I continued, for lack of a better title, "Dame Zhelan said you had some information for us?"

"I do and have decided I will share, thanks to this handsome fellow, here." Query made an odd gesture, circling his hand at the wrist and aiming two fingers at JR as if presenting him to an audience. "Please follow me."

We followed, despite my concerns. This person was a very mechy type of mech. A cyborg? I'd never heard the term used seriously before. Why would they want to help a bunch of savants?

"That was the weirdest conversation I've ever had," JR murmured to the group.

"I think they were flirting with you," Chet said back.

JR made a face as if scandalized, then he winked. "Or, maybe I was flirting with them."

He drifted away to engage Query in more small talk, a spring in his step. It seemed his confidence was returning. Well…at least one of us was having fun.

As Query led us through twisting hallways and up several flights of winding stairs, they talked. Their voice was expectant, excited, and a little bit desperate. I got the feeling this mech didn't often have visitors.

"I hope you nats will forgive me for what I am about to tell you, but I must say I never meant any harm…"

"People who say that usually do mean harm," Mara snorted under her breath.

Query heard her. "Well, to be fair, I did mean harm, but only to those who would harm us. You see, I am a scientist at heart. An engineer. A biologist. A Technomancer. I love to learn. To experiment. Energy fascinates me the most. Kinetic energy. Life-force energy. Electrical energy. I took up my research on kinetic energy since it was the least explored."

They stopped to take a breath, though I wasn't even sure this mech needed to.

"Kinetic energy can move anything, vehicles, power plants, rockslides, and when you combine it with potential energy—for instance gravity—it can do so many things."

"That doesn't sound ominous at all," Chet said to Query. "And trust me, I know what kinetic energy can do."

"Yes," Query said a light laugh in their voice, "I am sure you do, Kinetic."

That took Chet aback. He stopped. "How do you know what I am?"

The ceiling dipped, and Query had to duck their head to avoid hitting it on an exposed beam. "Oh, I know what you all are. These sensors, you know," they said as if it were the most natural thing in the world.

Chet made a harrumph, then fell in step beside Mara.

"I grew up in awareness under the shadow of The Third," Query continued, "I watched you being made. I watched you evolve. But…" I digress.

We'd been walking at an incline and now came upon a rusty staircase. The wobbly railing creaked under our hands, and the walls, streaked with grime and long-dried stains, whispered of decades of abandonment. Our footsteps echoed in the confined space, a rhythmic clatter softened only by the occasional drip of water seeping through unseen cracks.

"I oversaw the formation of the Triumvirate. Before that, anarchy reigned supreme. Nuclear weapons scorched the farmlands of America, mechs and savants fought bloody battles in the hills and on the plains. Fires raged across the European continent. And through it all, humanity survived. Though many of them—many of *us*—were changed."

"You saw The Third?" JR asked, syrup in his voice. "You must be wise."

Query scoffed. "I watched friends wither around me. Bandits raze new settlements to the ground. Livestock starve and die. If wisdom could come out of those sad times, then yes, I suppose I am wise."

Query stopped speaking suddenly, cocking their head as if waiting for a question.

"Okay…so?" JR asked. "Did you…try to do something?"

"Yes. I tried to save the world by getting rid of those who would hurt it."

As my brain worked to piece two-and-two together, JR already figured it out.

"You created the bombs," he said. His eyes widened, the whites and amber irises practically glowing in the low light.

"Yes. The Kinetic Energy Weapons Program, to be more specific."

Chet made a sharp, sputtering noise like someone choking mid-swallow. Mara clenched her fists. I put a gentle hand on her tight forearm trying to still her to inaction. We still didn't have the information we came here to get.

"I know, that was probably not what you wanted to hear, was it?" the mech said, sympathetically.

No one responded, but Mara's grip relaxed at my touch.

A final door stood before us, shiny steel, much newer than the rest of the building. Query pressed a hand to the keypad. A lock clicked and the heavy door swung open silently. We entered a server room that practically took up the entire ground floor of the former-factory.

Computing equipment swooped along curved wall in a gentle arc of comforting LEDs and gentle humming. A workstation jutted out on one side, an old-fashioned computer and monitor setup that was surprisingly immaculate.

Query took off one of their white gloves to reveal an equally white hand. It split into a dozen digits of various sizes which Query used to enter information on the computer in a rapid series of taps and clicks.

"I hope you'll believe me when I say," Query continued—though I didn't know what to believe anymore—"I never intended for my weapons to be used this way. It was never my goal to murder innocents or intimidate workers."

Mara's voice was tight with anger. "Hard to believe that after twenty million people are dead."

Query's tone turned sharp. "I didn't push the button. The powers that be had... different plans."

"Still doesn't make you innocent."

"Would you blame the inventor of the knife for every life it's taken?"

"That's not the same," Mara growled.

Query waved her off with a mechanical hand. "It doesn't matter. What's done is done. But maybe I can help undo it." Their voice softened. "I'd like to help you destroy this weapon."

Something about the tone—the sadness, the disgust—sent an uneasy prickle through my gut.

"There's something you soft bodies don't often understand about us."

I wondered if the "us" they referred to was mechs in general, or specifically the type of mech that Query was.

"We have lives, too. Friends. Families. Me? I... I have a daughter."

Chet nodded solemnly; the rest of us stayed silent.

"And when you see those you love suffer, you promise yourself you'll take steps—any steps—to make sure it never happens again."

Mara's shoulders tensed. "Wait," she said, stepping closer. "What are you doing?"

Query didn't react.

My heart thudded painfully in my chest.

"I have a bad feeling about this," Chet muttered, his eyes scanning for anything that wasn't tied down.

Query's voice dropped, almost trembling. "You seem like good people. I'm... I'm so sorry..."

"Sorry about what?" Mara demanded.

When Query didn't answer, she lunged, grabbing their throat and slamming them into the console.

"What. Did. You. Do?" she growled, punctuating each word with a strike to their chest.

A wave of nausea hit me like a freight train. My skin burned, my vision tunneled. I dropped to the floor, choking on the realization: this wasn't just nerves. Something was happening. Something was *wrong*.

Out of my star-speckled eyes, I saw Mara with both hands around Query's throat. The mech didn't attempt to escape. While Query didn't display any pain, their mechanical eyes darted back and forth. Mara's fingers strained, but even her strength could not crush this perfectly engineered mech body.

"Mara," I croaked as Query hit a button behind them. "Stop. Query's death will not help anything."

Glaring at me, she grudgingly released the mech. "I don't think I could kill him anyway," she mumbled, tossing him to the floor.

The curved wall slid slowly aside, revealing the world beyond: a great glassless panorama. The putrid smell of Lanzhou drifted through the now open hole, but the view outside the window dismayed me even more.

Mechs. Lots of them. They rolled up on curious vehicles which looked like several speedbikes bolted together. Their occupants clung to the sides, machine legs swinging, guns pointed outward. The whole contraption reminded me of a giant black insect, with hundreds of limbs and a dozen sets of deadly pincers.

"Fucking hell," Chet muttered, wrinkling his fox-like nose. He snapped the shield of his helmet shut.

"Rob?" JR asked, placing a hand on my shoulder. "What should we do?"

But I couldn't answer. I still trembled on the ground, trying to breathe away the static those mechs set off in my brain.

"I suggest you run," Query said softly.

A door slid open at the far side of the room.

"He ain't wrong, Lilly," Chet said, hauling me up with his Auranet.

The sudden feeling of being weightless but without any hands on me only served to disorient me further. I stumbled into Mara.

"Go," I said, looking between her and Chet. "Try to slow them down. JR, call Mendez."

The Sway swallowed, his gaunt face pale, and nodded. He jammed the button on his comm.

"Robert?" Mara asked, gripping my wrist in concern. "What are you going to do?"

"I'm going to deal with our friend, here," I said, trying to infuse my voice with cool rage. This dirty mech had betrayed us, and I wanted to make sure they remembered that.

With reluctant agreement, Mara and Chet slipped out the door.

I gave Query a hard look. I wanted to punch the mech in their smooth, alien face. I wanted to shoot them. I wanted to ask "why?" But, I could only glare as they watched me without moving.

"Rob," JR said, voice tight, "we need to get out of here."

"I can't," I ground out, my rage running through my veins like hot oil. I forced my sluggish thoughts to come up with some kind of revenge. Some retribution that Query would understand. "You go," I said. "Find Mendez. Get into the van."

"No," JR said, voice low. "You're *not* okay and I'm not leaving you with this *thing*."

I met his gaze. He held his cane in a white-knuckled grip, but his eyes burned with something raw and defiant. He didn't want to run, even if everything in his body screamed that he should.

I hesitated, reading the fear beneath his words but also the unshakable resolve.

"Fine," I said, forcing myself to stand straighter. An idea formed slowly. "You can help, but after that, we'll have to run."

He took a shaky breath, eyes flicking to his cane.

"And you can't do that if you're clinging to that thing."

His jaw tightened, and for a moment, I thought he'd snap back at me. But instead, he took a shaky breath and dropped the cane to the floor.

"Happy now?" he muttered, stepping closer to me. His legs wavered, but he didn't fall.

"Getting there," I replied, eying him for a moment. "Now, do what you do best."

He gave me a lopsided half-smile. "Charm the pants off our contact?"

I flashed him one back, my eyes sparkling. "Not that," I said, feeling better by the moment. "The other thing."

JR cocked his head.

"Make Query feel what we did in Xi'an."

His grin turned wicked. "Gladly."

He approached the mech, steps smooth, words like honey. "You said you didn't have a choice."

Query tilted their head, unblinking. "I did not."

JR took a final step forward, his Aurawave surrounding him in a stormy cloak of emotions—hot, alive, and full of rage. "We always have a choice," he echoed Mendez's earlier words, his voice low, laced with something sharp. "Let me enlighten you with the consequences of your choice."

The air grew thick and JR's Aurawave expanded outward, brushing against Query like an invisible tether. The mech stiffened, their golden eyes widening in response to whatever JR was imprinting.

I didn't need to hear what he muttered—his Wave carried all the weight of the last eight months: loss and fear, anger and defiance, and then, a desperate kind of hope followed by the bitter taste of betrayal. If Query was still even the tiniest bit human, he would feel these emotions in some deep, hidden place.

Sure enough, the cyborg ducked their head, cowering under the weight of JR's Aurawave. The lives lost. The weight on the minds of those left behind. Like us; the ones who had to pick up the pieces. JR forced Query to see the cost of their actions not through their eyes, but through their heart.

Query flinched, their many-jointed hand rising to their chest as if the Aurawave struck like an arrow. I gaped in wonder. Beneath the metal and synth, something human *did* resonate within Query. I could feel it, a gaping hollow within the pulse of electricity, but I couldn't identify it. Organic modifications were not my expertise.

"I'm s-s-s-sorry," Query stammered.

"Good," JR said, his voice steadier than I'd heard it in days. "Now help us fix this."

A new resolve pressed into Query's thin lips. They reached toward me with a lightning fast hand, taking hold of my wrist. Before I could think of pulling away, they pressed a cold, metallic datachip into my palm.

Leaning in close, pink lips grazing my ear, they repeated, "I'm sorry. They have my daughter. Someday, you'll understand. Now run!"

Then, the cyborg pushed me away and, grabbing JR by the elbow, I ran out into the cold, stinking night.

* * * * *

The sounds of chaos greeted us as we sprinted out into the night. The faint hum of mech engines and the rhythmic clank of metal feet reverberated off the surrounding walls, growing louder with each passing second. The air smelled of oil and ozone, the lingering scent of Lanzhou in the distance.

Mara had already torn through the first line of mech soldiers like a force of nature. I realized this was the first time I'd seen her fight—*really* fight—

and I found myself stopping to watch like a child. She whirled and kicked, taking about as many punches as she doled out. A vicious uppercut sent one mech soldier flying into a wall, its mechanical limbs crumpling on impact. She didn't stop, pivoting to slam her gloved fist into another's chest, leaving a fist-sized hole in its body armor.

"Eyes up!" Chet called as he emerged from cover, casually cracking his knuckles. "More incoming!" He nodded toward a new wave of mech soldiers spilling around the corner.

The mechs advanced with terrifying efficiency, their insectile transports gleaming under the dim light. As more of them dismounted, I saw the glint of weapons in their many hands. They moved in unison, a synchronized machine, advancing toward us with the cold precision of predators.

"Well, this is bloody fabulous," Chet said under his breath, though his calm demeanor betrayed none of the tension in the air.

He rolled his shoulders, then his neck, as if he were warming up for a morning jog instead of preparing for battle. He raised his hands. A large shipping container rocked atop its stack. With a jerk of his arms, Chet launched the crate into the air with a forceful thrust. It sailed toward the mech soldiers like a wingless plane. Crashing into the edge of the force, it tumbled a few times on the ground, taking out a dozen or so.

"Watch it!" came Mara's grunt through the comm. "That could've been me!"

"Sorry!" Chet said and massaged his shoulder. "Aim's still not great with big things like that."

The remaining mechs surged forward, stepping over their fallen comrades with relentless precision. Their weapons hummed, the sharp whine of charged energy filling the air. Mara darted into their ranks, dodging the first volley of gunfire with terrifying speed. She sent a mech flying into its partners with a roundhouse kick, then rolled under another, coming up behind them. Sparks erupted as she tore off a mech's arm and used it like a club, smashing it into another's head, caving in the helmet.

Chet tossed several barrels into the fray, his aim much better, knocking the mechs to the ground. He bit his lip as he focused on the scattered debris around him.

"We're going to get overrun at this rate," he said in the comm, his voice clipped.

I swallowed hard, scanning the crowd, my hand instinctively brushing against the comm clipped to my wrist. My chest heaved as the familiar static of battle churned in my gut, each pulse like a warning siren.

"Mendez, where are you?" I asked, the words tumbling from my mouth.

I took another lungful of foul air, coughing. I hadn't taken the time to seal my suit's helm, and t it was too late now. Despite Mara's and Chet's efforts, there were still too many mechs. I unsheathed my pistol.

"Mendez en route!" a voice piped over the comm. "What the hell have you gotten yourselves into?"

I pulled JR behind another large shipping container as a rain of rail gun fire peppered us. He fell to the ground, gasping and trembling.

"Fuck, Rob," he heaved, breathless. "I'm out of shape."

"Round is a shape," I replied on instinct which elicited a derisive snort from JR.

"Hey, friends!" my comm blared with a strange echo from the outside world. "Where are you?"

With a breath I stood and waved my arms frantically. Fortunately, Chet had taken down the mechs coming upon us, so Mendez was able to pull up right away. I hauled JR to his feet and pushed him into the hovervan.

"Chet! C'mon!" I shouted.

With one final toss, Chet dropped the detritus from his Auranet and jogged over, panting.

"We have to get Mara!" I said as I boarded the hovervan. I pointed toward the ruckus.

"In there? I'm surprised," Mendez's said in a tone indicating she was not surprised.

Slamming the comm button, I shouted, "Mara. Get ready!"

I sat in the open door of the van, silt from the hover jets surrounding me in a noxious cloud. Mara ran from the clot of mechs, glistening with what looked like oil or blood, or a combination of both. Some of her clothing was torn, and her mask had been knocked askew. She grabbed the runners of the van as we drove by, rotating in a half-circle as Mendez flipped a too-fast U-turn. I took her hand and helped drag her into the cab, hoping she didn't pull me *out* instead.

"You made it," JR said, an exhausted smile on his face.

"I made it," she said, pushing up her cracked goggles and wiping sticky, black soot from her eyes.

"You okay?" I asked her.

She nodded with cough. "Nothing that won't heal."

She touched the pink streak on her cheek with a wince. It ran into her hairline where the hair had been singed away. Blood seeped slowly. In a moment of foolish compassion, I wiped a thumb along her chin.

I must have looked worried, because she said, "Laser burn. I'm fine. But thanks." She whispered those last words so only I could hear.

"Hey lover boy," JR said, kicking me in the shin. "We're still being pursued."

Grunting, I put a hand to the stinging wound and looked out the van's rear window.

But JR was right. Mechs followed our van. Bullets ricocheted off our left quarter panel.

"Everyone get down," I commanded, retracting the window.

Crouching low myself, I stuck my laser pistol out the window and let off a few shots. Several mechs went down, leaving holes in their formation as their compatriots had to skirt the prone forms.

"Nice shot," Chet said, peering out next to me. "Need help?"

I nodded and Chet waved his fingers. A cloud of dust rose up until it formed a cyclone about as tall as a man. The van darted around a sharp corner, throwing him against the wall. The dust cloud fell. A rocket collided into an abandoned building, near where we had just been, showering us with dust.

"Where'd you learn to drive, Mendez?" Chet snapped, picking himself up.

"Suria!" she shot back with a laugh, referring to what had once been the continent of South America. "People were always shooting at us there, too!"

Suddenly, I had an idea.

"Can you do that again?" I asked Chet, who seemed even paler now.

He pressed his lips together with reluctance. "Aye. For a bit, anyway."

"Okay!" I called. "We're going to disorient the soldiers, then Mendez, can you pop us into the air like you did in Xi'an?"

"Sí, but it will leave us wide open."

"Understood," I replied. "Chet, go!"

He nodded. The dust rose once more.

"Mendez, on three. Chet, make the cloud thicker."

"One…" I counted, firing my gun into the cloud, not caring if I hit anything.

"Two…Denser Chet!" The cloud thickened.

Chet grunted. "Not gonna last long, Sarge. I'm spent."

"What we waiting for, Lilly?" Mendez asked, irritated.

"Three!" I shouted as Chet's hands wavered.

The hovervan lurched straight upward, jostling the others to the floor. The dust cloud sank in one curtain-dropping motion. The Kinetic had fallen unconscious.

As we rose, I noticed a lone a man behind us. A mech. He lead the pursuit on a one-wheeled speedcycle, his focus intent while all the others milled around in confusion. He wore no helmet, just a black mask obscuring his face. An ocular device glowed coldly—a clear, blue beacon in the fog, connected to his body armor by glowing conduit. His arms from the shoulder down were bare, save for the conduit running around them like veins. An uncomfortable resonance slid across my senses with a serpentine liquidity. A scanner, I realized.

He raised his gun.

I fired.

My shot, flew true, cutting through the mech's heavily modded shoulder. Burning through tissue and bone. His arm dropped to the ground and his gun with it, the last desperate shots scattering against the bottom of the van. He flopped like a rag doll from his speeder, pain and rage darkening his features.

Smog enveloped the van and the mech disappeared. We climbed until we emerged from the malevolent cloud. I sucked the fresh air into my lungs in grateful gasps, feeling the cold dryness burn my throat.
A ragged cough tore through me, doubling me over as I eased myself away from the window. My chest heaved, each gulp of air coming faster, shallower, and more desperate. It felt like trying to breathe through a straw, the walls of my throat closing in. My pulse thundered in my ears, drowning out everything else. Black spots bloomed at the edges of my vision, and this time, when the world started to shrink to a pinpoint, it didn't stop. The darkness swallowed me whole.

* * * * *

"Mara, girl, I hope you haven't ruined the interior of my car!" Mendez scolded, her voice far away.

Something pressed down on my face, suffocating me. I fumbled at it, panic gripping me once more. Rough hands enclosed over mine.

"Robert, it's fine. It's just oxygen," Mara said, gently pulling my hands away.

My eyes fluttered open and I blinked up at her. My head rested on something soft and warm that smelled like an oil repair shop. The van was still in motion, so I couldn't have been out for too long.

"Why would you ruin her car?" I asked hoarsely. My throat hurt.

"Because she's a mess!" Mendez laughed, nervous but also triumphant.

I realized who I was leaning on and, with a gasp, tried to sit up straighter. Mara held me down.

"It's okay," she hushed. "You've been through it. You can rest."

I closed my eyes again, hoping the oxygen mask obscured most of my awkward blush.

It didn't. She chuckled and waved off my embarrassment.

"Well, that was a dangerous waste of time," JR grumbled. He sat on the seat across from me, his hands gripping empty air where his cane used to be.

"We survived, at least," Mara said. She heaved a sigh.

JR made a sound with his tongue. "Last time I 'survived' something, look where I ended up!" He gestured wildly and flicked his fingers in air quotes around the word "survived."

"Rostbane, you're too young to be so curmudgeonly," I said with half a laugh that hurt my injured lungs.

JR harrumphed. "I hate it when you call me that."

I grinned beneath the mask. "I know."

He was right, of course. I winced. If I had a credit for every time JR was right… That had been too close. We'd escaped with our skins mostly intact, but I'd put my crew in danger. I hadn't prepared enough for things to go south. Sure, we knew the mission was risky, but none of us had expected a betrayal.

I glanced at Chet, still unconscious. "He okay?"

Mara nodded, "'Nets just need sleep after they exert themselves. He'll come around."

"And that Query guy…er…person…er cyborg…" JR continued as if he were in his own conversation, "what the hell was his deal, anyway?"

"They're a mech, a weapons manufacturer, and a traitor," Mara said, "Something broke in their brain—probably due to all the modifications— and they're probably also psychotic."

"But they had an Aura. I felt it," he shuddered. "Charger's Beard, I *touched* it. And it didn't feel right."

"Not right how?" I asked, taking another slow, deep breath and letting the cool oxygen infuse my lungs.

"Cold," JR said, his gaze far away. He'd taken up twisting his beanie between his hands. "Dead."

"Dead? How can an Aura feel dead?" Mara asked. "I thought when we died…" she trailed off with a shrug that bounced my head slightly. I blushed again but covered it with my next words.

"Query's a machine," I said, "Every part, save one."

"Which one?"

I thought back to that dark hole I felt when I sensed Query. "They're not like any other mech I've encountered," I began, chewing on my lip and trying to think. "With mechs, I can sense their mods and the processors beneath their skull, but their organic parts are just…there. Or not there? Shit…I don't even know what I'm saying," I finished with a mutter.

I closed my eyes, reaching my senses outward, past the walls of the van, and into the city streets. I sensed several nearby mechs.

I tried to explain my Skill to the others. "There are mechs nearby. I can visualize an arm, a leg, a nervous system—each of them belongs to a different person, but none of them are the shape of a whole person."

After a brief silence, Mara made an uncertain, "Mm-hmm." At least someone was humoring me.

I continued, "But with Query, an entire form filled my mind when I focused on them. Torso, limbs, internal mechanisms, a supercomputer for a brain. Everything. Except for that black hole…."

I opened my eyes. It was my turn to shrug. "It's like they're a bot but with an additional *something* that I cannot name."

"Maybe that's their Aura," JR mused. His hands had gone still, proof that this puzzle intrigued him.

"But I thought the CORPs couldn't do that," Mara said. Absently she brushed a piece of hair from my forehead as she looked down at me in puzzlement. "If they replace every organic part with a machine, that person no longer exists."

JR nodded. "I know I've read studies where scientists have tried. None of them succeeded."

"Could you do it with your Skill?" Mara asked me.

"Make a being who's all machine but with an Aura?" I sighed. "I doubt it, but even if I could, why would anyone want that?" I could still feel the shadow of Query's resonance, echoing through my mind.

"Immortality," JR said softly. "My father wanted that. Thank fuck he didn't achieve it."

"Query was old," I said. "Third World War-old. Maybe older."

"Means they've seen some shit," JR laughed. "You'd think they'd care more about the future."

That reminded me. I frantically patted the pockets of my suit. In the chaos, I had forgotten the device Query gave me. With a sigh of relief, I pulled out a small drive.

JR smirked. "Was wondering when you were gonna show that. You think that'll help us defeat Lightbar?"

"I hope so," I said as the hovervan pulled into the garage.

Flipping the van into PARK, Mendez turned around. "Wanna see what's on it?"

Reluctantly, I sat up from Mara's lap and removed the oxygen mask from her face. I debated saying "no," but one small part of me was still a rebellious private.

"Why not?" I placed the drive into her outstretched hand. The drive, like Query, felt weird. Like something I didn't really want to be around.

Mendez pressed the drive into the van's computer. The lights of the vehicle went dead, the engine stopped rumbling, and the door locks deactivated.

"Oops," she said, attempting to restart the van.

Dead.

"Shit!" she cursed.

JR looked worried. "What do we do now, boss?"

I shrugged, retrieving the drive from Mendez. All I wanted to do was roll into bed. My body ached, I sounded like death, and I was exhausted—physically and mentally. But I still had a team to command. "We have to report to the major and turn over this information…whatever it is."

"Can I shower first?" Mara asked, shedding soot and dried blood from her hair as she debarked. "Sir," she added with an awkward smile.

"Will we get in trouble for the van?" JR asked, unusually concerned about repercussions.

Mendez gave a sheepish smirk. "I'll deal with that. Mea culpa, anyway."

"Thank you, Mendez," I said, then turned to my team. "Go clean up and get some rest. We will debrief at zero-six-hundred tomorrow."

When my crew began to disperse, including Chet who shuffled away sleepily, I gripped Mendez's hand in a grateful shake.

"Glad to have you on board," I smiled at her. "I'm sure you'd rather be on more prestigious assignments."

She shrugged, her dark eyes twinkling. "I think, at this moment, I'm right where I need to be, niño. Nice work today," she finished, clapping me on the shoulder.

And for some reason, the praise of this mysterious Zephyr meant more at that moment than any praise from Ames or Healey. I had found my team.

- 8 -
C.E. 2253 February 21

The next morning, my squad gathered in the ops room, groggy and unrested. Sleep had eluded me entirely as my thoughts circled the Zetadrive Query gave me. Smooth and inscrutable, the device consumed my attention. Its kill program wiped the van's system, but why had Query given it to us? Was it another trap? A key? Or both?

As I handed the drive to Healey and recounted the mission, I could see concern etched on the officers' faces. Query's betrayal—and their strange, regretful apology—still weighed on me. Were they playing us? Or was there something genuine beneath their actions?

Healey broke into my spiraling thoughts with a surprising commendation: "Nice work, Sergeant Lilly. Your Lieutenant says you're quite skilled with computers. Care to take a stab at this one?"

I stared at the drive in her outstretched hand, my pulse quickening. There was nothing I wanted more than to crack it open and see what lay inside.

Eight hours later, I was regretting my decision.

The drive was my problem now, and, as JR so helpfully pointed out, I'd been the idiot who volunteered for it. Normally, I liked this kind of work—solitary, focused, tactile. But the stakes here were higher than ever. One wrong move could erase the data, kill the base's power, or, worst of all, summon mech shock troops straight to our door.

I shivered, recalling the lead mech at the factory. That dull black eye paired with the glowing blue monstrosity of his scanner still haunted me. His insignia marked him as a Hex—equivalent to our Captain. Serious business. The memory of his ocular scan crawling over my skin made me uneasy. I hadn't told anyone, but I was probably in some internal database now. If they found me, it wouldn't end well.

No time to dwell.

I had to deal with this drive before anything else.

Carefully, I removed the tiny screws and slid off the faceplate, revealing a standard circuit board—XC Compendium Flash storage, ionium processor, wireless transmitter, the usual suspects. But one component stood out: a cube-like metal box in the corner with a blinking red microlight. When I touched it, a sharp jolt shot through my arm. The red light blinked faster, angry. A power bank, I realized—a power bank with AI.

It wasn't just electricity that hit me; there was data, too. The shock carried a virus designed to shut down any system that tried to access the drive. The virus wouldn't just travel into my computer; it would possess it like a thinking being. That would be bad news.

I rummaged through my toolkit, searching for something to insulate the power bank. After sifting through screwdrivers, pliers, and ancient odds and ends, I found a thin scrap of rubber. Warming it in my hand, I stretched it carefully and wrapped it around the power source, avoiding the delicate wires and memory units.

I tapped the power bank again. No shock.
Exhaling slowly, I closed my eyes. The rest of the drive I could navigate by touch alone.

- 9 -

C.E. 2253 February 24

Three days later, I finally felt confident enough inserting the drive into my borrowed Digitally Enhanced Computer. I know the officers waited on me, but I had to make sure I didn't mech this up. It wouldn't do to kill the borrowed DEC, like I did with the van (see? I can learn).

Today, I ran out of excuses.

"Okay, let's see what you've got," I said to this frustrating piece of technology.

A knock on the door interrupted my big moment. I groaned. "What?" I asked, sourly.

"Rob," a voice came through the hollow metal. It was JR. "Are you still alive? Have you eaten? I have food."

I didn't answer. I didn't have time to socialize. Then, my stomach rumbled. How long ago had I eaten that meal bar? It had been today, hadn't it? The aroma of the food JR carried drifted through the crack in the door.

"Rob," JR said again, punctuating his call with a knock. "Rob. Rob. Rob."

Man, I was *really* hungry.

"Fine!" I growled, "You win. Come in."

JR entered, smirking like a maniacal kitten.

"You little sneak!" I scolded when I realized what he'd done. "You used your Aurawave to get me to let you in."

The other man chuckled. "Use the tools you're given. Also, we haven't seen you in three days. Mara is convinced you're dead, while Chet just thinks you're hiding in here jerking off."

I frowned. "With friends like you guys, who needs friends?" I grumbled.

He set a plate down on the small desk. At least he hadn't lied about food. He slammed a bottle of hot sauce next to the plate which contained of some reconstituted protein and brown gravy.

"I know how much you like this garbage." He wrinkled his nose at the sauce.

I grinned. It was kind of nice that my friends knew me.

"You've cracked this bastard already, right?" JR asked, eyes sparkling.

I shook my head. "I haven't even connected it yet."

"What?" he gaped. "So, you *have* been in here jerking off."

I rolled my eyes, fixating him with my grumpiest scowl. "No. My genius takes time."

"Three days' worth of time? How many sessions of wanking?"

"You know what?" I said around a mouthful of protein covered in spicy chili paste. "You do your job, and I'll do mine. I had to make sure it didn't shut the base down."

"Good data, I suppose. There you go being all reasonable again. When you gonna start it up?"

"Well, I was going to do it five minutes ago, but then I got unexpectedly interrupted. Thanks, by the way." I shook the bottle of sauce. "This makes the dish."

JR gave me a smirk and perched on the edge of my bed. "I could move in with you. Then, I'd always be around to interrupt."

"Greysoft help me," I moaned, though secretly I didn't hate the idea of bunking with JR again. He always made things interesting.

"Well, what are you waiting for you big lug? Let's see this shit!" He gestured animatedly at the computer.

"I see how it is," I grumbled and shoveled another large bite into my mouth.

I picked up the drive and, holding my breath, clicked it into the DEC. The screen waxed to life with its comforting, yellow-tinged welcome screen. The drive made no noise, but I could feel it initiating.

I kept my fingers on it just in case. If I felt a power surge, I'd have to remove it before it killed the DEC.

"You think it's going to do what it did to the va—"

"Shh!" I hissed. "Don't jinx it."

JR pshawed but stayed silent after that.

But the AI must not have detected any threat, because it didn't initialize. A paper-shaped file icon popped up on the screen with the word *TRANSFERRING*... below it. I exhaled a breath.

"That's good, right?" JR asked.

I held up my hand as I watched the progress creep along at a snail's pace.

How big was this file?

Five minutes went by, and it was still transferring.

"Can I talk yet?"

I shook my head at JR, eating left-handed. My right hand and my eyes remained glued to the DEC.

Finally, the bar reached one-hundred percent.

I clicked on the new icon. It opened a single notepad file.

"What in the actual fuck is that?" JR asked. "It looks like a rabbit."

I shook my head, pressing my fingers against the bridge of my nose. It wasn't just a rabbit—it was a message, taunting and ridiculous, staring back at me with an almost smug mystery. Charger's Beard, I hated riddles.

* * * * *

```
 ______________
|              |
|  CONGRATS    |
|  ROBERT!     |
|  NOW         |
|  FIND        |
|  CONTROL     |
|  __________  |
(\__/) | |
(•人•) | |
/     づ
```

C.E. 2253 March 18

Nearly a month had passed, and I was still buried in the endless labyrinth of data on the drive. Each layer unraveled into another, like peeling an infinite onion of data.

That mocking little bunny did not give in easily. Slowly, I unlocked bits of information, though much of it didn't seem immediately useful. Somehow, though, I didn't think Query would give me a drive loaded with a bunch of crap for no reason. It had to be related. I just had to figure out how.

Digging through the mountain of files, I started to notice connections—threads linking much of the data together. Some content, such as full topographical maps of China, Asia, Europe and even the UCCA, I passed directly to the officers, but other files seemed pointless. I couldn't tell if *Dr. Tam's Recipe for Perfect Shrimp Wantons* was an encoded message or a prank. From what I knew about the cyborg, it could go either way.

The most useful info, however, revolved around The Kinetic Energy Weapons Program, or KEWP. I found technical specs of the rods, historical documents on the program's inception, founder bios, and even bits about Query themself buried in the archives.

One particular project stopped me cold: *CIBRG. The Complete Integrated Brain-Robot Grouping*. The name alone was enough to set off alarms, but the file was frustratingly thin. All I found was a mission statement:

To create bodies for those who have none, thus preserving the human consciousness and extending life.

CIBRG…cyborg…Was Query themself a beneficiary of this program? Or were they the founder?

I kept returning to Mara's question. Could I make a robot with an Aura?

I mean, yes. I could build a robot. Robots already performed many mundane tasks: hauling trash, cleaning sewers, carting away the deceased.

The Aura part was trickier to replicate. Many savants used their Aura to power their Skills—Sways, Kinetics, maybe even me. But for all its uses, no one truly understood what an Aura was—or if it was even "Aura" at all.

AI technology couldn't compare. It was too rigid, too bound by rules. Human consciousness was unpredictable, chaotic, acting on whims no algorithm could anticipate or control—not for long, anyway. No AI had come close to matching the complexity and range of the human brain.

But if the CORPs had somehow found a way to meld a human consciousness with a mech body, immortals like Query would become commonplace. They'd be world leaders and CORP execs like Norman Rose. The implications were too huge to think about.

No, I thought, pacing my bunk. *That can never happen.*

- 11 -
C.E. 2253 March 19

I wanted to quit. Wanted to go back to my squad. I wasn't getting anywhere…

The officers, on the other hand, didn't seem to agree. I was commended by Ames who prioritized this job as my most important.

"Those who do not learn the lessons from history," he quoted some long-dead philosopher, "are doomed to repeat them."

I thought it a strange mentality from someone like the Lieutenant, who always seemed to be looking toward the future…

"Sounds like Ames is just repeating some bullshit he learned at the Academy," JR commented one day during lunch with the squad.

"What lessons are we supposed to learn from a super-secret weapon program sponsored by a bloodthirsty CORP?"

"Don't make bombs," Mara laughed, though with a hint of melancholy.

"What about this 'cyborg' program?" JR asked. "You think that's Query?"

"Seems likely, doesn't it?" I said.

"Maybe," JR continued, "but what is it, exactly? Are they putting a human brain in a machine? Or are they somehow downloading someone's mind into a computer?"

"I can't imagine either," Mara said, mischief lighting up her eyes as they locked on me. "Sure, you could make a robot with thighs like mine, but they'd never be warm—or know what to do with you."

She pressed her leg against mine, and my pulse raced, a jolt of heat shooting up my spine. I barely managed to keep my breath steady.

"Rob!" JR snapped, pulling me from my fantasy.

"Oh, uh, yeah," I sputtered. "The file didn't say. Honestly, I don't see how either is possible without killing the person."

"If it worked," Chet added, "would that person still be human?"

I chewed on a piece of stale bread while I thought.

"Well, what makes us human?" I asked, looking at each of my squad members individually.

"Our thoughts?" Chet asked. He levitated a fork off the table and flung it into a nearby wall where it stuck.

"Our squishy brain parts?" JR joked.

"Some nebulous concept of a soul?" Mendez asked, furrowing her brow.

"What about optimism? Belief in good nature?" I suggested.

"Nah," Mendez scoffed, "too many shit humans for that. How 'bout our senses? Our Skill?"

Chet shook his head, "That would make mechs and Trues not human. I think it's our will to survive. Our reasoning."

I turned to Mara who had been quiet until now. "What do you think?"

She shrugged, though a smile tugged at her lips. "Mine's dumb."

"No dumber than 'squishy brain parts,'" I said, raising an eyebrow at JR.

"Fine," she huffed, "What if our Aura is actually just our emotions?"

I met her gaze. My heart thumped. I cleared my throat.

"Maybe it's all of that," JR said, trying to lighten the mood.

I contemplated that, then nodded. "Our love of others."

My eyes flicked toward Mara. She looked away, a faint blush coloring her cheeks, and tucked a lock of hair behind her ear.

"Our leader's quite the romántico," Mendez joked, tapping my leg with her foot.

Chet grunted with a wicked smirk. "More like a pushover." He shoved me.

"I think…Rob may be hiding some feelings," JR teased, nudging me with a wink.

Mara's eyes narrowed. "Hey, leave Robert alone. He's one of the good ones. Unlike most of this lot." She gestured around the Commons. "He's genuine and honest. If any of you think you're better than him, stand up now. We'll go." She made a fist.

Her dark glare silenced the group, who shifted awkwardly. No one looked at her.

She smiled, one again all sweetness. "I thought so. Carry on."

I fidgeted awkwardly. No one had ever defended me like that—or so openly, without hesitation. Not like Mara had.

- 12 -
C.E. 2253 March 20

KEWP K-Force Rods Schematics, the screen read.

"Well, now that's something," I muttered, scrolling through the file on my handheld as the smell of burnt oil and chili stung my nose.

"Nice place you picked, Mitchell," JR said, leaning back and balancing his chair on two legs. "Is it extra if we get food poisoning?"

Mitchel grunted as he slid into the seat next to him, his broad shoulders almost knocking over the stack of cheap napkins on the table. "Beats eating out of ration packs," he said, looking at the stained menu hungrily.

He'd heard my squad complaining about the food at the base and, in a rare moment of charity, invited us to his favorite noodle house.

"Plus, I know the owner. Food's good," he finished.

"Ah…you *know* the owner," JR said waggling his eyebrows at Mitchell, though the man's gruff expression cut short any further detailed questions.

"What are you looking at, Robert?" Mara asked, leaning close and glancing over my shoulder. Even in this dive, I could smell her hair over the scents of cooked food, clean and musky.

The blueprint on my screen showed a weapon—massive, intricate, and terrifying. We didn't have the resources to build something like this. But would we, if we could? Our army used weapons just as much as any other, but did we really want to cause destruction on such a massive scale?

A warped chair leg creaked as I shifted in my seat, trying to balance on the uneven flooring. Across the table, JR tapped his fingers on the scratched surface, glancing toward the kitchen where a pot clattered loudly. "Food's taking forever," he grumbled.

"Probably a good thing," Mara said, eying the grease-streaked table warily. "I'm not convinced this place passes health inspections." She wrinkled her nose.

Normally, I lived for this banter, but right now something heavier weighed on me.

"Are we really gonna talk food safety right now?" I asked, glancing between them before gesturing at the schematic on my handheld. "This is the kind of thing that could level an entire city and we're sitting here debating appetizers."

"That doesn't sound half bad," Mitchell growled from the corner, hunched over a chipped glass stein of cheap beer. "Burn those fuckers—burn them all."

While I could understand the sergeant's reasoning—nerve damage from the Battle of Sky Plaza had made him extra cranky of late—I was glad he wasn't the one in charge. Somehow, that solution seemed a bit…premature.

A faint hiss sounded from the kitchen, and I caught a glimpse of an elderly cook pulling a wok off the flame, the scent of charred garlic wafting over to our table. JR leaned back, staring at the ceiling, his expression tight. "What's there to debate? It's not like we can make those things, anyway."

"No, but if we get a hold of them, we should use them," Chet said, his gravelly voice muffled by the sound of clattering bowls as the server brought our food. "The only thing that festering turd of a CEO will understand is violence and power. We need to show them we have some."

"Seriously, Chet?" Mara snapped. "That would make us no better than him."

"A bold statement coming from someone with the ability to crush just about anyone's skull," JR shot back, wincing as his elbow stuck to the table.

"I'm not a single-minded murder-machine," she retorted, wiping her chopsticks on the sleeve of her dark jacket. "Just because I can kill at will, it doesn't mean I want to. I have a conscience, you know."

"She's got a point," I said, shoveling noodle soup into my mouth. Mitchell was right, the food here was surprisingly good.

JR gestured to his leg, to Mitchell, and then to the general area. "After all that has happened," he said to Mara, "you think we shouldn't use the rods against Lightbar?"

"I dunno," she drew out her words, "should we destroy a city and wipe out a population just to kill several thousand CORP soldiers? Does that sound right to you?"

"What if we could take out Rose himself?" I said.

Mara froze, chopsticks poised over her bowl. "Do you really think sacrificing millions of lives to take out one is a good trade?"

"Absolutely," Chet said, not missing a beat. Mitchell nodded over his noodle bowl, steam curling around his face.

"I'm just saying, if it came down to it," I chewed thoughtfully, "as long as Rose lives, he has the potential to cause the deaths of even more millions. It might be the only way to stop him."

"But we don't know he'd do that," Mara protested. "Maybe Xi'an was a one-off."

Mitchell slammed a hand on the table, rattling the bowls and splashing broth across the table. "A one-off? Are you kidding me? You've seen what they're capable of! You think Rose won't do it again the second he gets the urge?"

"And what about all the people he already killed?" Chet added. "Where's their justice?"

JR flinched, using the whole stack of napkins to clean the space around his bowl. "Can we not talk about this? I'm trying to eat."

"Well, that's convenient," Mara said, flashing JR a dark look. "You always have something to say. About everything. Every fight, every choice, every meal in this dump. But now, when it actually matters? You'd rather *eat*?" She made a sound of disgust.

"What do you want me to say, Mara?"

"I want you to say you don't agree with this madness. That this path of reasoning is insane."

JR shrugged, tone quiet but cutting, "What if I don't disagree?"

She stared at him in disbelief. "Of course you don't. When it comes down to it, you all," she waved around the table as if she were shaking droplets of something gross from her fingertips, "would just as well watch the world burn if it meant proving you're the biggest, baddest bastards around."

"It's not that simple—"

She cut him off, "No, it's exactly that simple. Men and their egos, always chasing vengeance like it'll make you whole again. Like it'll *fix* everything."

"That's not it," I said, "it's not about vengeance. It's about securing the future."

I placed a hand on Mara's forearm, but she snatched it away.

"I'm disappointed in you, Robert," she hissed. "I can't believe you're entertaining this idea."

She stood abruptly, her chair scraping against the uneven floor. She jabbed a finger at Mitchell. "Will murdering millions of innocent people secure a future you *actually* want to live in?"

He growled, throwing his chopsticks into the empty bowl. "They're not innocent. They're complicit—every last one of them. They prop up the system."

"They're just trying to survive," Mara retorted, her hands trembling as she leaned on the sticky table. "You'd sacrifice children, families—people who had no choice—just to get at Rose?"

"It's called war, little girl," Mitchell snapped. "You want to play hero, fine. But heroes don't win wars. Violence does."

A shadow passed over Mara's face, her features pinched in anger. I'd seen what happened when you made a Tank angry. "I'd choose your next words carefully," she snarled at him.

JR glanced between Mitchell and Mara, his face pale. "Guys," he said, a low warning. "Just let it go."

But Mitchell sat back in his chair, crossing his arms. A smug smile crept on his face. "Go ahead," he prodded Mara, "show me that violence can win this battle."

The shadow faded. "I can't sit here and listen to this," she dropping her volume, voice trembling. "I'm going to find Mendez. I'm sure *she'll* see sense."

Then, she turned and stormed out of the noodle house, the door slamming shut behind her.

JR looked at me, his expression oddly sympathetic. "You gonna just let her go like that?"

Cool air from the HVAC ruffled my hair as I stepped into the hallway. Mara stood a few paces away, leaning against the chipped wall, arms were crossed tightly over her chest.

She didn't look at me as I approached, the sound of my boots on the tile floor breaking the silence.

"You didn't have to leave," I said, my voice softer now.

She glanced at me, her eyes glinting in the lamplight. "Didn't I?"

I rubbed the back of my neck, unsure what to say. The argument still churned in my head. "I just… I'm trying to look at the bigger picture here."

"The bigger picture," she echoed, her tone laced with bitterness. "That's what people always say when they want to justify doing something terrible."

I frowned. "It's not about justifying. It's about survival. If Rose lives, he'll keep killing."

"And if we do this, we're no better than him," she shot back. "What's the point of surviving if we lose what little humanity we have left?"

Her words stung, but I couldn't back down. "You saw Xi'an," I said quietly. "But you didn't see the body count—" My voice broke off, the memory cutting through me.

Mara stepped closer, her expression softening. "Robert…"

I realized how close she was when I felt her hand brush mine. Her touch was light and hesitant, but it sent a jolt up my arm.

"You're not like Mitchell or Chet, or even JR," she said, her voice barely above a whisper. "You care. That's what makes you a good leader."

I blinked, caught off guard. "A good leader?"

She smiled, small but genuine, and took another step closer. "Yeah. Even if you're a pain in the ass sometimes."

Her fingers lingered on mine, and for a moment, the air between us felt charged, electric.

"Mara…" I began, but I didn't know how to finish the sentence.

She tilted her head, her eyes searching mine. "You could take a break occasionally, you know. Let someone else carry the weight for a bit."

"I don't have time for breaks," I said automatically, the words tumbling out before I could stop them.

Her smile faded, replaced by a look of quiet disappointment. "You always say that."

I swallowed hard, feeling the weight of her gaze. "I mean… I can't afford to let my guard down. Not now."

She stepped back, crossing her arms again. "Right. Of course. Always the mission."

"Mara, I didn't mean—"

"It's fine, Robert," she said, cutting me off. "Go back inside. I'll be fine."

I hesitated, the words I wanted to say caught in my throat. Finally, I nodded and turned away, the regret already settling in my chest as I walked back toward the noodle house.

- 13 -
C.E. 2253 March 23

The room had become my prison. It kept everyone away while I worked, leaving me alone with my thoughts, my shame, my embarrassment, and my DEC. After the botched attempt at being flirted with, I couldn't bear to see Mara again. I was afraid I'd ruined our friendship, our professional relationship, and killed any chance of something more.

I ignored the knocks on my door. The pounding fists. The clang of something metallic. The shouts and expletives from JR. It all blurred together until that asshole started flash-messaging me on my handheld.

ROB, WHAT THE HELL? ARE YOU DEAD?

I stared at the message, feeling the familiar ache in my chest. I can't even get away from him, can I?

NO, NOT DEAD. WORKING.

THAT'S IT?

YEAH.

BULLSHIT.

JR had no idea what this was like. Back in the day, he was a socialite—a fuckboi. He was used to charming the pants off anyone he wanted, being a Sway. Me? I was awkward with women, especially Mara. How was I supposed to navigate this? My head screamed one thing, but my heart said another.

I wasn't planning on having a family, but a child was coming—well, after this long, he'd already been born—so I felt obligated. That was why I was stuck in this mess to begin with—working for a future I wasn't sure I believed in, trying to pay a debt I didn't know how to erase. The army wasn't the answer, not when finance was a joke and comms were all but nonexistent. I couldn't even see if Constance was getting paid, and no one could tell me anything.

And now Mara. I felt like I was drowning in a sea of what-ifs, trapped between a promise I'd made and feelings I couldn't ignore.

The door rattled again, this time louder, more insistent. The metallic clang of whatever JR had thrown at it only strengthened my resolve to hide and work.

Then my handheld pinged again.

ROB YOU NEED TO COME GET DINNER.

I'M NOT HUNGRY.

ROB

...

ROB

...

ROBROBROBRBROBROBRO…HEY! WHEN I STRING YOUR NAME TOGETHER IT SPELLS 'BRO'!

I groaned. JR, always the pain in the ass. He couldn't understand what was going on in my head right now. Not the commitment to Constance, the future I thought I'd build with her, or the pull I felt every time Mara was near. Hell, he didn't even have to worry about being stuck in a crummy little base with no way to communicate with the outside world. He'd made it clear. No one waited for him on the other side.

JR. DON'T EVER CALL ME BRO.

IF YOU DON'T COME HAVE DINNER WITH ME, I WILL ONLY EVER CALL YOU BRO FROM NOW ON.

BRO.

BRO.

BRO.

That was it.

DAMMIT, JR! …FINE! I'M COMING.

GOOD. MEET ME IN THE COMMONS IN 5.

MAKE IT 30. I NEED A SHOWER.

GOOD CALL. WOULDN'T WANT YOU TO STINK ME OUT.

I reluctantly shoved my handheld aside and stood. At least I could escape my own mind for a bit, even if it meant dealing with JR's relentless teasing.

I made my way to the door but paused. A moment of hesitation gripped me. The feelings for Mara hadn't faded. If anything, they had only intensified, swelling up like the quiet buzz I get before something big happens. I wanted to push them away, to focus on my duties, my fiancée AND the life I had planned. But here I was, stuck.

The next time Mara comes to me, I thought, would I run away again, like a coward?

With a deep breath, I pushed the door open, the weight of my thoughts trailing behind me like a heavy shadow.

* * * * *

"When was the last time you left your room for more than a piss break?" JR chided.

I dragged a chair over with my foot and sat down heavily. "Dunno, but the moderately warm water and pitiful soap chips were almost worth it," I grunted.

"Mara say she hasn't seen you since Noodlegate 2253."

Mara. I shook the thought off and snorted, "That's what you guys are calling it? Noodlegate?"

"It seems to fit. No one's been the same since. You've been locked away, Mara's been skulking around, and Chet and Mitchell are going on pretending none of it ever happened."

"Well, what do you want me to do about it?"

He shrugged. "We're your team. Well, except Mitchell. Why don't you figure something out?"

"JR," I huffed, "I don't need this. I still have the rest of Query's information to go through."

"Well, I say we find some bathtub gin and all get fucked up," his eyes sparkled.

"Freg, no," I snorted.

The *last* thing I wanted to do was get drunk with Mara and all the guilt and desire building up in my brain.

"I get it, though. This place sucks but…" I trailed off, unsure what I wanted to tell JR.

"Or, you could just go ask her," JR continued.

I blushed and again kept silent. My ears were on fire, and I couldn't look into the other man's eyes.

"Wait a second…." he goaded, "Did you already do it?"

"NO!" I snapped, blushing harder. Heat spread from my collarbone all the way to my hairline.

"Why not?"

"Because," I stressed, "I'm supposed to get married, JR."

The other man waved his hand in a dismissive gesture. "It's military tradition, Rob. You go off to war, you fuck a deployed eight, but Jodie fucks your girl back home. When you return, you both pretend like none of it ever happened."

"Hey! Mara's more than an eight." I glared at JR.

"Oh, so you *do* want to fuck her."

I ignored him.

"Fine. Fuck another nine then, or even a ten, though with those standards you'd be lucky to get anyone. Either way, we've been away from home for near a year, living in claustrophobic quarters with people we'd never have chosen to stream with in real life. We may die anytime. Might as well have fun before we do."

I grumbled something about war not being about having fun, but JR wasn't buying it.

"When was the last time you even touched another human?" he asked and grabbed my bare forearm.

I jerked it away, uncomfortable. That touch initiated feelings I'd been trying to suppress for too many days, and that was a *problem*. I wasn't even into men like JR was, but still…it had been a bit.

"No," I said, unsure if I was trying to convince him or myself, "I can't do that."

The younger man clicked his tongue, "How many near-death experiences have you had so far?"

"Well, that's an odd segue." I frowned, "Only two."

"What about the time with the mech patrol outside of their camp at Xi'an?"

"Okay, fine, three. What's your point?"

"That's two or three more than most people in the UCCA," JR reminded me. "Do you really want to die a year celibate?"

I sighed, brushing a loose lock of hair from my eye. "It's just not possible, JR. On so many levels."

"Not with that attitude is isn't. You want some help or…"

"NO."

He rolled his eyes. "She's totally interested in you, by the way."

I made a dismissive grunt.

"Don't be stupid, Rob. A blind idiot could've told you that. Hell, even Chet can see it."

I huffed.

He grinned, flicking his eyes toward the door. "Now's your chance."

Mara entered, carrying a tray of food. When she saw us, her face lit up with a smile.

"I gotta get back," I muttered, standing up and rushing toward the door.

"You're a jerk, Rob!" JR called after me. "And a cowardly idiot!"

Mara flashed me a confused look.

"Sorry," I said as I passed.

The light in her eyes dimmed to disappointment and her shoulders sagged just slightly. However, I didn't think it could compare to the disappointment I currently felt in myself.

- 14 -
C.E. 2253 April 12

```
 ___________
|           |
|  CARPE    |
|  DIEM     |
|  MEANS    |
|  SEIZE    |
|  THE      |
|  DAY!     |
|________   |
 (\__/) ||
 (•ㅅ•) ||
 /    づ
```

* * * * *

"There's that bunny again, " I said to myself with a deep frown.

The last three weeks had been a blur of work, loneliness, and gnawing discontent. I'd been chasing this bunny and its stupid riddles until my eyes crossed, at the expense of most everything else. I didn't need it taunting me about my lack of a social life on top of everything else.

This time, though, the bunny came with a file. While I waited for it to load—painfully slow—I mulled over my situation. I'd forced myself to stop hiding in my room, joining JR and the squad for meals at least once a day. I could even talk to Mara without blushing like an idiot or tripping over my words.

Her reserved demeanor wasn't, and that gave me hope. Maybe I hadn't wrecked everything. Maybe we could still be friends. Friends. Was that really all I wanted? My skin prickled. I kept telling myself the feelings would fade.

They didn't. The loneliness and panic clawed at me more often now, sharp and unrelenting. I reminded myself that what I was doing was for the greater good—that I didn't matter. But the words were never comforting. I continued to buzz with arousal and a looming anticipation. Maybe I was going crazy.

The file finally loaded. I opened it with a click.

KEWP CONTROL: ACTIVATION AND DEACTIVATION, the simple report read.

"Control?" I muttered to myself, pondering that stupid rabbit. Then, it hit me. Control…I skimmed the short text on how to access and control the KEWP rods.

I jumped up with a whoop, pumping my fist in the air.

"Yes!" I shouted, then stopped for breath, thanking Charger and Greysoft and all the Greats that no one had passed by to witness my temporary insanity.

On the fourth read-through, I noticed a footnote: *"Congratulations Sergeant Robert Lilly of New Colorado. You are the nat after my own heart. I hope you can use this information to the benefit of all—mechs, savants, everyone. I also hope someday you'll forgive me. Signed, Rom Query."*

So, Query *had* intended to give us the information. Had they planned to betray us, too, or did that come later? I didn't know what to believe when it came to the cyborg, but what I did know was that I just uncovered something big.

In addition to activation and deactivation codes, the document also included the location of the main KEWP Control Center. *This* was what we had been seeking. *This* could turn the tide of the war.

I had to tell the officers…no, first I had to tell my *friends*.

In my excitement I forgot my embarrassment. I forgot my insecurity. I forgot everything except for the fact that I was the baddest-assed hacker in the entirety of the army. I sent messages to JR and Mara on my handheld, being too excited to spend time searching the complex. I don't know if I should have been concerned that they both answered immediately, or that they did so even though it was now well after midnight.

I FOUND SOMETHING!!!

MARA: I NEVER DOUBTED YOU FOR A SECOND

JR: I MIGHT HAVE. ;-)

REALLY, JR? :-\

JR: DRINKS ON YOU THEN?

UH…I DON'T HAVE ANYTHING EXCEPT WATER

MARA: I DO. WE WILL BE BY IN 10

JR: WE WILL?

MARA: YES, JR. WE WILL.

JR: OKAY THEN…C U SOON

We drank until the clocks blinked 0300 hours, and then we continued drinking.

"Shouldn't you be presenting this info to the big badges?" JR slurred, hanging off my bed upside down.

"I dunno how you don't hurl like that," Mara laughed, tossing a pillow into the man's stomach.

He made a dramatic gagging noise, chucking away the pillow. "I will if you keep doing that." Languidly, he slid off the bed and held out his hand. "We got any more of that hooch?"

"Here," I tossed a clear, stoppered bottle at JR.

The booze inside was a murky, white-ish clear with a flavor profile somewhere between battery acid and rubbing alcohol, with a finish that reminded me of an old boot. But it got us drunk.

"Where'd you get this stuff, anyway?" I asked Mara, who'd draped herself across my lap as we sat on the floor.

She winked up at me, taking a swig from another bottle. "A girl can't give away *all* her secrets," she paused for effect, "but it was Mendez." She snickered. "All the good shit always comes from Mendez."

"Not sure I'd consider this 'the good shit'," I joked, tilting the bottle back and forth, watching the particulates float by.

We continued to drink until the room grew fuzzy and a burning heat infused my cheeks.

At some point JR passed out on my bed.

At some point, I found Mara straddling my lap. We'd run out of coherent topics to talk about some time ago, and now we just laughed. Giddy. Nervous. Wasted. She wrapped her arms around my neck, and I cupped her backside, enjoying her weight against my legs. Her face was only inches from mine.

I inhaled the scent of her, her vodka-heavy breath warm against my mouth.

At some point, I kissed her…or she kissed me…it didn't matter.

Her lips were soft, but her kiss demanding. I slid my fingers up below the hem of her tank top, her skin as hot as her kiss. She took hold of my hair and pressed my face into hers.

"We should probably get some sleep," she said breathlessly once we'd disengaged, though she kept her lips close to my ear.

"JR's bogarting the bed." I tilted my head to his snoring form.

"There are other beds in this place, you know." Her tongue slid out of her mouth, and she gave a sultry wink.

Before I could answer, she hauled me up, practically dragging me from my room.

We arrived at her bunk, across the empty Commons, and she pushed me against the wall, her hard body making me grow hard as well. I had to lean down to kiss her, taking her lower lip between my teeth.

She chuckled.

"What?" I asked, sliding my hands further up her tank top.

"You're not gonna hurt me, you know. Even if you do fancy yourself a big brute."

"Oh yeah?" I laughed, shoving her away and onto the bed, pinning her with my bulk.

She squealed, and allowed it, though I knew she could've broken me in half if she wanted.

"I like it rough," she said, voice husky. Then grabbed the back of my neck and pulled me into a bruising kiss.

I ground my pelvis against her, tongue intertwining with hers. Then I broke away, flicking my tongue over her chin, her neck, her collarbone.

At some point we removed our clothes, shedding them with the rest of our inhibitions. I caressed her smooth skin. Her hard muscles. Her ample breasts. She pulled me down onto her and the rest of the night was lost to sensation.

We never got any sleep.

- 15 -
C.E. 2253 April 13

I woke up in a pitch-black room, wrapped in warmth. The bed felt smaller than I remembered. As I rolled onto my back, a single, terrible drumbeat pounded through my skull. My legs jerked involuntarily, and someone groaned beside me. I froze.

Sitting up was a mistake—the pressure in my head seared through my optic nerve, forcing me back down. Slowly, tentatively, I reached out a hand. My fingers brushed over smooth skin, tracing a path along a curve I knew all too well: high, dipping low, then rising again.

My chest tightened as the realization hit. I had just spend the night with the woman I admired, feared, and—if I was honest—desired.

What's done is done, I thought, swallowing hard. Though I'd crossed more lines than I cared to count, only the faintest pang of regret stirred within me. Maybe JR had been right—war had its own set of rules, and morality was just another casualty.

Mara sighed softly beside me. The lump in my throat grew. Had I just made a terrible mistake? The idea of fleeing crossed my mind, but I forced myself to stay. Running would only make things worse—for her, for me, for whatever fragile connection we still had.

What's done is done, I repeated to myself. We had both chosen this, and I would live with it. Even though the fear lingered, coiled and heavy, so did something else. Something dangerously close to satisfaction.

Mara rolled over, her warm figure pressing against my own. Her shoulder came close to my mouth. I kissed her softly, trailing my lips over its curve, then I bit her, hard. She moaned, burying her face into my chest.

"Fuck," she groaned, covering her eyes with an arm.

"I think we might have overdone it."

Mara's dry chuckle reverberated against my ribs.

"So, how much alcohol does it take to get a Tank drunk, anyway?"

"About as much as I had yesterday," she drawled.

I snorted. "Less for me, though I feel like I had as much as you."

She laughed and poked me in the ribs. "S'what you get trying to keep up with a Tank."

I snorted and tried to turn over. My stomach heaved in great waves. Fearing I would vomit, I slid awkwardly out of the bed and stumbled to the small sink Mara had in her room. Resting one hand against the cool concrete wall, I splashed cold water on my face. It ran down my chin, landing like ice on my bare chest. I gasped.

Mara laughed behind me.

"What?" I asked.

"Your ass."

I looked at her, "What about my ass?"

She made a suggestively appreciative whistle.

Heat coursed up my neck, burning my cheeks. I tried to hide the blush on my pale skin, but watching her just made it worse.

She hugged the blanket against herself with half-lidded eyes, a smile tugging at her lips. The crest of her breasts was only just visible: soft, tan, flawless. Her muscular leg hung over the edge, with a calf that should have its own zip code. A strand of hair fell across her cheek, disappearing into her cleavage. Her chest heaved in steady breaths to counteract the hungover daze.

"You are poetically stunning," I muttered, growing aroused once more.

She made an amused snort. "And now you're a poet?"

Her eyes hadn't left my naked form, and I was now very aware of the rise beneath my awkwardly positioned hands.

"You gonna go address the officers," she asked me, gaze flicking toward my hands, "or do you want to take care of that first?"

"I should go…" I muttered, watching hungrily as Mara 'accidentally' let the blanket slip. "Nah. Fuck it."

Removing my hands, I marched back to the bed in all my glory, with a cheesy grin on my face.

"I can talk to the officers tomorrow," I told her as I slipped under the blankets once more. "We're not done here."

C.E. 2253 April 14

When we'd finally had our fill of hangovers and the pleasures of the flesh, I brought the information to Major Healey and Lieutenant Ames. Sure, I may have fudged the timeline just slightly, but I really didn't need my senior officers to know about the rager that took me a full day to recover from.

As a non-commissioned officer, Ames invited me to sit in on the convergence of the Military Council while they discussed their plan. I was advised not to speak unless I had something pertinent and well thought-out to say. *If I speak at all,* I thought to myself as I stared in awe at all the decorated military figures in my wake, *it will most definitely be pertinent. And extremely well thought-out.*

Lieutenant Ames opened the formal discussion. "One of my men, Sergeant Lilly, has obtained the location of the control center for Lightbar's Kinetic Energy Weapons Program. It is not at Lightbar's HQ as we suspected, but in a secret underground location east of here."

An enthusiastic smattering of applause followed this declaration, and I wanted to sink further into my seat when I realized they were partly clapping for me.

"If we can gain access to this control center, it could turn the tide of this war," Healey said. Her hands fluttered for a moment before clasping tightly in her lap, as if to keep them still. "It is now time for us to decide on a course of action."

"We could level Lightbar's corporate HQ with these!" one officer exclaimed.

"And murder millions of innocents?" another responded. "Would you have us turn into that which we oppose?"

Ames nodded, his misty eyes flicking toward me. "That is a dangerous path to tread," he warned, "for, once on it, we will not be able to turn back."

The room devolved into argumentative chatter. Two officers stood up and began shouting across the room.

"They've done worse to us! To their own people, even!"

"But Hong Kong Island is more than just Lightbar's HQ!"

"Yeah, some of our own people are there!"

"Saint Claire is already investigating it!"

I groaned inwardly, remembering the argument in the ramen shop. This could become Noodlegate all over again.

Amidst this commotion, a figure slipped into the room, unnoticed by everyone but me. I didn't recognize her, but the geometric green eagle insignia on her worn but neatly pressed uniform marked her as a general. I caught her eye as I scrambled to stand. She smiled gently and gave me an appreciative nod. As she passed others with measured steps, they quieted and hastened to their feet. By the time she reached the front, everyone stood like statues save for one angrily blubbering petty officer.

We all saluted as one.

"At ease, soldiers," the woman said, removing her cap to reveal short brown hair.

Everyone sat down.

"For those of you who may not know me," she began, looking directly at me but not sternly, "I am General Amelia Mazet."

A smattering of gasps and unsettled mutters ran through the room.

"Do not worry, officers. News of my visit here was not widely circulated."

I turned to the guy next to me, another sergeant by the insignia on his uniform, and asked, "Have you heard of General Mazet?"

He shook his head and shrugged.

"I am here from our outpost in Tianjin," Mazet continued.

Tianjin? Much of my data hunt this last month had been spent reviewing maps of China, but I did not remember any city called Tianjin. I did vaguely recall a note in one map that pointed to the underwater ruins of Tianjin. Had that been one of the coastal cities flooded after The Third's nukes warmed the planet enough to melt the ice caps?

"In light of the Xi'an tragedy, we must ensure it will never happen again. I am here to help lead the next phase of the plan based on some information discovered by one Sergeant Lilly."

There was my name again. This time, I *did* slouch in my seat, but the woman saw me anyway and waved her hand. I rose more slowly than I thought possible and stood with an uncomfortable smile plastered on my face.

"I want to personally thank the sergeant for his hard work and dedication to our cause…"

She paused, and I wondered if she expected me to say something. I cleared my throat. "Just doing my duty, Sir," I said, less confidently than I'd have liked.

But the general just gave me a firm nod and a benign smile. I

"This information is both useful and dangerous," Mazet continued.

As the eyes drifted away from me, I sank back into my seat.

"We need to proceed with care to keep the CORP's eyes off us. While it may seem like nothing is happening on this side of the continent, I can confirm that the east is in turmoil."

Lieutenant Griffin raised a hand with two fingers pressed together. "Do we know Lightbar's plan?" he asked, when Mazet indicated he could speak.

She shook her head. "The only chatter we've been able to glean is that they are still looking for the leaders of the rebellion." Her lips thinned as she continued, "They've ramped up surveillance in every sector, but so far, no arrests—just a lot of intimidation tactics and public broadcasts trying to smoke them out."

"That includes us," Healey said.

Mazet nodded again.

"We've done well remaining in the shadows after Xi'an, but the time for hiding is over. The people of China cannot live with what has been done. They are resisting—forming their own cells and organizing against the oppression. Several cities have already seen standoffs with CORP troops. Local officials have publicly declared that they no longer wish to remain under the control of a Western corporation. This nation is teetering on the edge of a fight for democracy."

Another mutter ran through the officers, some stared in shock while others nodded knowingly. I was part of the 'shocked' camp. While we marinated in the stench of Lanzhou, a country-wide conflict had been brewing. And I had no idea.

"So, how do we fit in?" Griffin asked.

"We need a contingent of volunteers to join up with the larger cause, the Citizen's Army of China. Together, we can storm the KEWP Control Center and shut this program down," Mazet said.

Several officers stood up proclaiming their expertise on infiltration, warfare, ballistics and all manner of disciplines. Mazet and Healey scanned over the crowd, watching with neutral expressions. Something tickled inside my gut, and I found my legs straightening to stand, as if raised by a Sway's persuasiveness.

In almost slow motion, I raised my hand, two fingers extended upward, pressed close together. Stepping out into the aisle so I could be seen by the general, I looked her in the eye.

"Sir!" I said, "I volunteer my squad for this mission."

Mazet smiled and even Healey quirked a small one of her own. Ames nodding approvingly. Mitchell scowled, as usual.

"Very well, Robert Lilly, formerly of the Street Dogs," she said to the shocked silence of the rest of the officers, "you can lead the charge."

Suddenly, a feeling of dread ran through me. I'd done it now. The enormity of what I'd volunteered for hit me like a blow to the chest. Did she really mean it? Me?

For a fleeting second, I hoped she'd change her mind. Surely, someone else was more qualified. More experienced. But her steady gaze left no room for doubt.

I had been chosen.

And I had no idea if I was ready.

- 17 -
C.E. 2253 April 15

"We're going where?" JR asked incredulously as I briefed my squad in the Commons the following day.

"The Jing-Jin-Ji," I repeated. "The east coast of China."

"But more importantly," Mara added, "away from this polluted gǒu cāo de city."

I remembered that particular Mandarin slang from my time in Xi'an. It referred to doing something inappropriate with one's dog.

"Such a mouth for a lady," JR mock-scolded.

Mara wrinkled her nose. "Don't see any ladies here," she punched JR in the shoulder, making him wince, "just a handful of assholes."

I chuckled. Leave it to Mara and JR to lighten the mood when I currently felt like a wound-up ball of tension.

"And you're going to *lead* something?" JR asked me. "I mean... something bigger than just this handful of assholes?"

I shrugged, trying not to make it a big deal. "Apparently Ames said some nice things about me to Mazet..."

"That guy totally has a crush on you!" JR egged.

"Why's everything gotta be about sex to you?" I sighed, embarrassed.

"What else is there?"

I shook my head. "Can I do it?" I asked quietly, afraid to voice my doubt too loudly, lest it be true.

"Absolutely!" Mara said.

"Probably," JR said at the same time.

Chet just shrugged. "If not you, then who? Some other ingrate?"

I laughed, a high-pitched, nervous sound. "Thanks for the vote of confidence, guys. But seriously, you think we can trust this information?"

Mendez leaned back in her chair, her polished boots finding their place on the table with deliberate ease. She tapped her fingers on the armrest, her voice calm and steady. "You know what I say..."

"Don't trust anything," I filled in, a heavy pit in my stomach.

"Sí, but also, this—sometimes, you don't get perfect answers. You get choices and you trust yourself to make the right one."

"But what if it's the wrong one?" JR asked, his tone uncharacteristically serious.

Mendez shrugged. "Always a possibility. But think of the adventure. Or better yet, think of the difference it'll make."

"Besides," Mara added, "do you think Query would have made you go through all that just to have you uncover false information?"

I nodded, hesitantly. "I suppose not. Charger's Beard, I wish I could get in touch with Zhelan or Saint Claire to confirm everything…"

JR blew air noisily through his lips. "From what I understand about that Saint Claire guy, he tends to show up when he's needed. If he's MIA, we probably don't need him."

"There's truth in his words," Mendez said, flashing a grin at JR. "Trust the timing, Lilly. Trust the process. But always," she leaned forward, her boots thudding to the ground as she emphasized her point, "be mindful. Don't rush in blind. Keep your squad close and your instincts sharp."

Mendez's words lingered in the air, heavy with a truth I didn't want to admit. *Trust the timing. Trust the process.* Easy for her to say. She wasn't the one being asked to lead a dangerous mission. *Be mindful*—what did that even mean in a place where the line between caution and cowardice was razor-thin? My instincts hadn't exactly been flawless lately, and the weight of her calm certainty felt like a mountain pressing on my chest.

Outwardly, I managed a nod, though it felt more automatic than intentional. "Mindful, right," I said, my voice stiff, trying to sound as steady as Mendez looked. "I'll keep that in mind when we're deep in the heart of Lightbar territory."

The corner of her mouth twitched, just enough to tell me she wasn't buying my attempt at bravado. "You'll be fine," she said.

I wasn't sure if she genuinely believed that or if she just wanted me to believe it, but either way, it didn't matter. I was the one who had to stand at the front of this thing and hope for the best.

"Either way," I said to my squad, "Pack your things. We need to be ready to leave when the officers tell us too."

Ames entered the Commons, and my squad stood. I turned in surprise.

"Sir!" I saluted sharply.

"At ease, Sergeant," Ames said with a chuckle. I noticed a change on his lapel. Where before he sported the double blue pentagon with underlying line of a Lieutenant, he now wore a red square framed by a diamond.

"Congratulations, Captain," I said and smiled.

Ames smiled back and nodded briskly, scanning over my squad. "Remind me to get you an office when we move." He chuckled, holding out his hand.

"What?" I asked in disbelief.

In his palm was a new badge—triple triangles, now with a silver stripe below it.

"You'll need a bigger team to carry out this mission," he said, pressing the badge into my palm, "Staff sergeant, Lilly."

"Th-thank you, Sir. But…" I took a shaky breath, "I've hardly done anything. Do I deserve this?"

"Healey seems to think so," he said.

"And the Major ain't quick with her commendations," JR pointed out, then coughed, "said respectfully, Sir." He eyed Ames sheepishly and I wondered what the Lieutenant—no, Captain—had done to earn JR's respect. He was about as stingy with that as Healey was with her praise.

He flicked his eyes to JR with a smirk. "And I agree with Healey," he finished.

I grinned like a child. What was that spark of fire in my breast?

It must be pride. Maybe I could do this, after all.

"Your new additions will be introduced when we get where we're going. Be prepared to leave in two weeks' time. Looking forward to this next chapter, *Staff Sergeant* Lilly." He emphasized my title, while I just stood there like an idiot.

"Staff Sergeant," Mara echoed once Ames left, giving me a wink. "You want to show me what that new title has to offer?"

"Well, we do have some time…" I smirked with a raise of my eyebrows and a flick of my gaze toward the door. "I'll meet you in ten."

Then, I scurried toward said door before my blush could give me away, to the whistles and suggestive jeering of my squad.

- 18 -
C.E. 2253 May 3-5

I could barely contain my excitement when the day came to finally leave the desolate heart of the country and go to the Jing-Jin-Ji, the hub of the east. We'd all had enough of Lanzhou's putrid air, the sky-silt, and the thin brown crust on every surface.

"Mmm…I'm looking forward to clean clothes," Mara said, tone dripping with something close to lust.

"Clean bed sheets," JR echoed, hefting his bag over his shoulder.

"Like your bed sheets are *ever* clean," I teased him, chucking a duffel bag to Chet and eliciting a hearty laugh from the Kinetic.

"Hey!" JR snapped. "I could say the same about you. Apparently dustboys also know how to have fun."

I shut him up with a dark look.

"Just get to the boat," I muttered, shoving him away. "I need to review our route."

Once we'd boarded, I scanned the deployment document.

The CORP presence grew thicker as one traveled east, so planes and hovervehicles were out of the question—China's airspace belonged solely to Lightbar. And since it would be hard to conceal an entire company of soldiers caravaning through the center, we had split up into three platoons of two or three squads, each platoon taking a different route through the high deserts and skirting the fertile middle. On the first leg, we planned to sail north on the Yellow River, or Huang He as the locals called it.

I'd never ridden in a water-boat before, and I found the whole process rather disconcerting at first. The miasmatic river slapped against the hull, occasionally splashing over the rails to run across the deck. Our boots skid on the slime it left behind. More than one soldier was left with a wet, sore ass when the boat shifted around an island of debris. Most of us got seasick, the stench of past meals rivaling the reek of the river itself.

As we left the city behind, the river grew cleaner and less putrid. It still retained its yellowish-brown color, and I learned it came from the loess sediment the river carried. Fortunately, the cool spring breeze diffused the fetid stink. By the third day, we removed our masks on the deck, which greatly improved morale, especially after the constant smother of Lanzhou's air.

My squad shared a craft with Lieutenant Griffin and half the members of the Black Cats, which were all men save for Mara, Mendez, and the other Tank I'd met in Xi'an. I think her name was Brit. The rest of the Cats followed with Ames, Healey, and the Green Dragon squad.

One night, in an attempt to bond with other members of the army, I reluctantly agreed to have dinner with the guys. As we sat shoving instant beef noodles into our mouths, Chet clicked his tongue at me.

"She's into you hard, you know," he said.

"Who?" I asked.

"Don't be an idiot, Robert," Chet grunted at me. "Dark."

"Really?" I lifted the bowl to my face, trying to conceal my awkward blush.

"Igen, yes," nodded Károly Mezei, a Tank with the Black Cats. "Yes. You should—what do you Americans say?—go get it on."

I almost spit my noodles.

JR, even though he already knew everything about me and Mara, wouldn't be left out. "Yeah. I hear it's a ride. Anyone ever been with a Tank?"

I bit my tongue.

"No," Chet continued, oblivious to JR's mischievous smirk. "But I hear they're so strong that when they climax, they'll break your dick off!"

Mezei and the others hooted with laughter.

"Who's breaking dicks now?" came Mara's voice from the doorway of the cabin. She and Mendez looked smug as they showed bottles of something clear to the group.

Chet's eyes widened. I did my best to melt into the chair, refusing eye contact with either of the women.

JR, however, had no discretion…or maybe he just liked the drama. "Mara, Chet here claims your pussy will break a man's dick off when you come. You know…because you're so strong."

Mara was silent for a moment too long. I couldn't see her face, but I braced myself for the inevitable sound of someone getting broken. There was going to be paperwork.

Instead, both women burst into breathless laughter. Finally, Mara caught enough air to speak, addressing the room. "It's definitely stronger than your right hand, Ferryman. Which, I'm sure is all you've gotten in a very long time."

Mendez slammed the bottles down on the table. "My girl and I will be drinking the good stuff on the bridge. You gentlemen can join us if any of you feel up to the task." She waggled a finger at Griffin who sat at the end of the table with an amused smirk on his angular face.

"Dang son," he muttered on the way out, throwing his coat over his shoulders with practiced grace and winking at Chet. "You may want to get some cream for that burn."

I wanted to expire with humiliation…or at least sink through the hull to become entombed in the fine silt of the Yellow River. I couldn't identify with the level of lechery of these boys, and even though Mendez said it was an open invitation, I had to admit I didn't feel up for the task.

"You guys are an embarrassment to our gender," I said with a long-suffering sigh and finished my noodles in annoyed silence.

C.E. 2253 May 7

Pillars of rock reached toward the heavens. Their narrowing peaks clustered together like so many trees. The sky hung low, a pale blue, scattered with wisps of clouds. The locals called this area the Stone Forest, and now I understood why. The river wound through the mountains and the rocks stretched upward and outward as far as my eyes could see. They were bare stone of a yellowish-tan, with varying color bands running horizontally through them and had remained the same for millennia, out here in this remote location, holding up the sky.

This was another first for me. I had never been so close to such a large natural wonder. In theory, New Colorado had mountains, but the haze blanketed them more often than not. Even when they were visible, the pollution softened their outlines, turning them into a surreal memory of the mountains of old. Once upon a time, I'd read how important they were for Colorado's recreational community, but now no one visited anymore. What's the appeal of acres of dead trees, their thin, gray skeletons pointing skyward, accusatory fingers to our violence and neglect? The Stone Forest on the other hand, made me feel precarious and insignificant—as if humans were just a blip on the incomprehensible timeline of Earth.

In this remote river valley, it was all nature. Plants and leaves emerged after a long winter, giving the stark landscape splashes of brilliant green. I drew a deep breath and could smell the vegetation on the slight river breeze. I didn't exactly find it a pleasant odor, but then again, growing things had never been very present in my world. I supposed I'd get used to it, just as I'd gotten used to the stench of The Sink or Lanzhou. Every place had their own personality.

The boat crept along the river, propelled by the sluggish current and barely any electric power. Sails flapped noisily overhead, and a flag flew from the tallest mast, marking us as a commerce vehicle. We stopped at every checkpoint for "inspection" where Lieutenant Griffin and Captain Ames made up some lies, while the rest of us waited anxiously in the darkened cargo hold, hoping not to be discovered. After nearly a week, the crews' light-hearted moods began to dissolve.

For me, though, views like these eased that tension. It was easy to get lost among the towering spires or in the endless sky. I took another breath feeling almost content.

"They call that peak 'Qu Yuan Asks Heaven,'" JR said, coming up next to me and pointing at one of the larger stone towers in the distance.

I ignored him. It had been two days since the incident at dinner and I hadn't quite forgiven him for his role in the awkwardness. Mara said she didn't care, but I did.

"Then that one is 'The Goddess Looks at the Moon.'" He pointed again.

"How do you know all this?" I turned a curious eye on him, my annoyance temporarily overshadowed.

The man looked at me plainly. "Don't you want to know where you're going before you get there?"

"Hadn't occurred to me," I said shortly. Then, since I'd opened a line of communication, I couldn't help but say, "Why'd you have to tell Mara about our shit-talking?"

JR didn't seem surprised at my change in subject. "Would you have your squad, or another squad for that matter, disrespect one of your soldiers?"

"Do you have to answer every question with another question?" I snapped, even though I knew he had a point.

JR shrugged. "What do you want me to say?"

I sighed. "I don't know. What do you want *me* to say?"

He stared over the railing for a moment, silently chewing on a lip. Then, he pulled out a slim cigar and lit it, taking several exploratory puffs.

"Where the hell'd you get that?" I asked him.

"Traded Mezei for it. It's not bad." He passed it to me.

Inhaling the spicy smoke, I coughed but decided I liked it. I took another drag.

"I baited them," JR said without preamble.

"You did?"

"Shit yeah, I did," he responded, though there was no bravado in his voice. "Doesn't matter if she's your lover. You shouldn't let your people talk like that."

Suddenly I felt the weight of my leadership press down on my shoulders. I should have stepped in. Should have said something so JR didn't have to. I took one last drag of the roll-up before giving it back.

"It's an odd world," I muttered, not looking at JR, "where you're somehow a better person than me."

JR cocked his head, holding the cigar between two fingers, looking like he should be on a far fancier boat. "Seriously, Rob," he said with mock offense, "you've spent all these months thinking I was a *bad* person?"

I shrugged. "Well, you know, son of a mobster and all…"

"There's a reason why I'm here rather than running my father's company."

I sighed. "Fair point. And, next time I'll intervene."

"You better," he said to me with a smirk. "Or I'll make it even more uncomfortable. You have no idea."

"Oh, I have an idea," I said, giving him a shove. Then, I clapped his shoulder and threw an arm around him. "You know, Rostbane, you're kinda all right."

JR rolled his eyes. "You know, Rob, I hate it when you call me that."

Though, he chuckled all the same.

- 20 -
C.E. 2253 May 13

My platoon camped for a week in the Yin Shan mountains outside Ordos, a rare patch of green in a world that had forgotten what green looked like. Our tents were small and almost cartoonishly bright against the landscape, though they blended well enough into the scrubby, hardscrabble vegetation. Camping was an entirely new experience for me—where I came from, no one willingly slept outside. The very idea of pitching a tent seemed absurd.

I heard that the forests of distant Candalaska offered real wilderness—towering pines, untouched rivers, even clean air—but those were luxuries only for people who could afford the trip, where most of us could not. Natural spaces like that were whispers of the past, left unprotected long enough for pollution to seep in and choke the life out of them. What survived the industrial boom and apathetic leadership had been scorched during The Third, turning entire regions into poisoned wastelands.

Even long before the Third, the leadership of the UCCA had stopped caring about the preservation of wilderness areas. They cared about cities —'city' was literally in our country's name—and tech, and the advancement of the one-percent. For people like me, raised as consumers, the cities were our everything: crowded, chaotic, polluted, but at least they had beds, running water, and walls to keep the chaos out. When you grew up in places like that, the thought of being outside, exposed, made your skin crawl.

Besides, what lay beyond the cities wasn't worth the risk. The Third had seen to that. The gaps between urban centers were vast, barren wastelands, carved out by old battles and forgotten by everyone else. Take the great swath of dead in the middle of our country, the Uninhabitable Wastes…no one went there unless they wanted to vanish. It was different here, however. Ordos was a bright, vibrant town, friendly to savants though scant on amenities.

Running water sounds mighty good right now, I thought as I splashed my face with what remained in my wash basin. A gel-fuel puck warmed my small tent, and I sat hunched over, the glow of my tablet causing my eyes to water. It had been the first time I'd gotten to read in peace, without JR, Chet or someone else peering over my shoulder. My stomach fluttered. There was a lot of information to digest.

A soft scratch on the canvas signaled Mara's entrance. She crawled through the open flap, a dark shape against the moonlit night. Her warm chin brushed against my cheek as she nuzzled close to kiss my forehead.

"You okay?" Mara asked softly, settling in close and trailing her fingers up my spine.

Sparks shot through me, momentarily scattering my thoughts. I set down my tab, forcing myself to focus.

"I don't know," I said with an exasperated sigh. My voice came out heavier than I intended. "I'm worried about the next leg of our journey… and my role in the upcoming campaign."

She kissed me, light and lingering, on the cheek this time. Then, wrapping her arm around my shoulder, she pressed her warmth into me. "You'll do fine," she said, her voice steady, like she really believed it.

I wanted to believe it, too. For a moment, I let myself lean into her, soaking in her reassurance.

"Plus," she added with a small smile, "we'll all be with you."

I nodded, giving her hand a gentle squeeze. But my eyes drifted back to the message glowing on my tab, the words that had consumed me ever since I read them.

"Jacked some bandwidth from the town today," I began hesitantly. "Finally got a message from Constance."

Mara's eyebrows rose slightly. "How'd that go?"

I shrugged, my throat tightening.

"This feels weird to talk about," I muttered. "She's my fiancée, after all. And we're not exactly…" I trailed off, unsure how to finish the sentence. Mara already knew.

"Then don't," she said, her tone calm, free of malice or bitterness. "You don't owe me any explanation."

Her understanding both comforted and stung. I bit down on my lip, torn between wanting to confide in her and wanting to bury the emotions clawing at my chest. If I didn't talk to her, who would I? JR wasn't exactly equipped for this kind of conversation.

"No, it's fine," I said, though my voice wavered. "My son, Sam, was born in December. And I wasn't there."

The weight of the words crushed me as they left my mouth. My chest tightened, a flood of emotions surging at once—regret, shame, and an overwhelming ache of love for someone I'd never even met.

"I feel…awful," I admitted, barely above a whisper. "He's out there, a piece of me, and I wasn't there to see him come into this world. I should've been. I wanted to be."

Mara's fingers tightened on my hand, grounding me, even as her expression remained steady, a quiet understanding in her eyes.

"But," I added, voice trembling with another emotion I couldn't quite name, "I'm also…happy? I mean, I have a son. That's something, right? A life created in the middle of all this chaos. I kind of can't wait to meet him."

I met her gaze, desperate for her to understand the contradiction tearing me apart. "It doesn't make sense, does it? To feel all of this at once?"

She smiled faintly, brushing her thumb over my knuckles. "Of course it does. You're human, Robert. It's love. It's messy. But messy doesn't mean wrong."

Her words struck something deep within me. I turned back to the tab, re-reading the message like it could somehow offer me absolution.

"I'm also happy to be here with you," I said finally, glancing at her. "I need you to know that."

"I do," she replied, her earnest tone tearing me open, making me feel vulnerable and full of longing.

I stared into her eyes which reflected the weak orange flame. "Wanna get messy?" I asked.

A smile tugged at her lips. She shifted, straddling my lap and turning her body to face mine. I pulled her close and breathed in her scent, woodsmoke and pine intermingled with unwashed bodies and the faint aroma of weak beer. Her softness made my head grow light and her lips engulfed mine.

For one night, the worries of the future and regrets of the past faded, leaving our warmth, her scent, and the fleeting illusion that this—the two of us together—was enough to hold the world at bay.

- 21 -
C.E. 2253 May 16

The next stop, Hohhot or the "Blue City" as the ancient Mongolians called it —blue representing sky and eternity—sat lonely and prone on a wide grassland that seemed to stretch on forever under a sky as vivid as a sapphire. A key shipping port on the Yellow River, Hohhot served as a hub between eastern China and the western desert lands.

The city had seen several battles in the last few months as the CORPs and Chinese resistance vied for control. The resistance had won—for now. Plumes of smoke could still be seen from the eastern district. Even during the increasing winds, the area bustled with recovery efforts, its streets alive with the clang of salvaged metal, the shouts of laborers, and the steady hum of machinery as survivors worked to rebuild what had been lost.

We camped in the countryside, among a cluster of hill valleys. Weary from a day of travel in bumpy, hot over-land vans, we stumbled out into the camp, our legs stiff and our clothes clinging to us with sweat, eager for any hint of shade to cut through the stifling heat. The winds were no help, sandblasting us with dust churned up from the northern steppes.

"Tell me again why we had to take the four-hour detour north?" JR shouted, wiping sticky locks of hair from his forehead, only to leave smudges of dirt behind instead.

"Wasn't for the scenery," Chet said with his usual dry chuckle, hood pulled tight around his head. "Nothing out there but sparse desert and ruins."

The ruins he referred to were what remained of Baotou, an old industrial city in Inner Mongolia. Once a thriving hub of steelworks and rare-earth mineral processing, it had been abandoned long ago after the failure of the Baogang Tailings Dam, which caused widespread environmental contamination.

"The Badekar Monastery was nice though," Mara added, wincing as she downed the last of a warm water bottle. Wind whipped at the loose strands of her hair.

Still inhabited by a small handful of monks, the monastery had stood as a striking contrast to the beige, rock-strewn landscape. With its squat,

160

white-washed buildings and their colorful awnings, unchanged for hundreds of years, its serene presence offered a refuge from the surrounding dust. Sadly, even the cheery monastery wasn't immune to the changing environment. The desert had taken its toll on the complex, eroding the greenery with the inevitable stubbornness of nature. The skeletons of dead willow trees stood sentry over the silent buildings, and those still living held onto their clusters of gray-green leaves like a child with a fistful of candy.

We slipped into the officers' tent, trying to scrub the sediment from our eyes. The cloud of brown had come upon us suddenly, gusts of wind picking up sand and dead grass in swirling eddies. The canvas of the circular tent flapped in an echoing thrum, but its shape and low height kept the foundation sturdy even as the winds roared around us.

My head pounded from the pressure, and I crunched the grit between my teeth.

"All I know," I said in a low voice, "is that I'm thoroughly sick of the desert."

Mara snorted. "Well, when this is over, we can curl up in your tent and sleep for a week," she whispered to me, "or…until the officers make us get up and leave."

I bumped her shoulder with mine as we stood at attention with the rest of the squad, a grin threatening to break out on my lips. However, that grin fled the moment Captain Ames arrived.

He shouldered his way through the assembled soldiers, not unkindly but with a steady resolve. His face was grim, misty gray eyes even more unfocused than usual. Behind him trailed a soldier—ragged, pale, and moving stiffly. His right arm hung at his side, wrapped in a makeshift sling, the pale skin around it marred with the telltale discoloration of bruising. A shallow cut ran across his forehead, blood congealing in the hairline, but it was his eyes that caught my attention—distant and haunted.

"Soldiers," Ames began, his voice steady but laced with a gravity that made the air feel thicker, "we lost the Red Boar squad today."

A hushed murmur spread through the gathered soldiers. The shock settled into silence as those present processed the news.

"They were ahead of us scouting and ran into the shock troops we were trying to avoid. The Cats managed to rout them, but the mechs had already done irrevocable damage," Ames continued. "Sergeant Granger here is the only one who made it out."

The sergeant nodded, his gray face a grim mask.

"We can't just let this go," Mezei said, his voice tight, eyes flicking to Granger. "Shouldn't we track them down, make them pay for this?"

Ames fixed him with a tired but firm stare. "We haven't the manpower for revenge. Not every battle is ours to fight. Some things, we leave behind."

Mezei growled, but didn't argue.

Griffin spoke up from the front row. "We have a bigger fight ahead. We keep our focus. One stray squad won't derail us."

Ames nodded, his gaze sweeping the room. "We need to move carefully through the next leg of our journey. The Jing-Jin-Ji is still a long way off, and we're not clear of the danger yet."

The murmurs of agreement were cut short as the soldiers began to break apart. I caught Ames' sleeve, pulling him aside.

"Sir?" I said, my voice soft but determined.

Ames turned to me, his face drawn, older than his years. It was the look of a man who had seen too much, too soon.

"Did you know this would happen?" I asked. "Is that why we were rerouted? Did you know about the attack?"

Ames shook his head, his tired eyes flickering with the faintest hint of something else—regret, maybe. "Yes to the first part. No to the second. The attack happened after I rerouted us." His voice softened, eyes distant again. "I tried to stop it. I saw it, but comms were down in the desert. I sent the Cats, but... they were too late."

My stomach dropped as understanding settled in. "You saw it? But how?"

His lips curled in a tired smile. "I'm a Timeseer, Lilly."

I blinked, trying to process the weight of his words. "You can see the future?"

Ames looked away, as if the idea itself troubled him.

"Yes."

"So, do we win? Is China…safe?"

He shook his head. "I can't say. The future is fluid. I am able to see glimpses, but it's not clear. The farther out I look, the more outcomes I see. One small change can throw everything off course. So, I can't trust just my Skill. I trust my people."

I stared at him, a wave of frustration crashing over me. "But that doesn't help us now. I need something more than… uncertainty."

Ames placed a hand on my shoulder, his grip firm but filled with something gentler—concern and even a trace of pride. "You'll be fine, Lilly. You're strong. You've got this." His voice dropped. "I've seen it. You're a good soldier. A good leader."

Those words felt like a lifeline I could barely reach. I nodded, unable to hide the unease still gnawing at me. "Thank you, Sir. I hope I can come to believe you."

He smiled lightly. "You will," he said with a wink. Then he added with a hesitant cough, "I'd appreciate it if you kept this to yourself. The more who know, the more questions I'll get. Questions I can't answer."

I nodded quickly, understanding the weight of his request. "Of course, Sir. You have my word."

Ames saluted wearily, the motion almost automatic. "You're a good man, Lilly. You *will* make a difference. Dismissed."

The praise was unexpected, and I couldn't help the blush that crept up my neck. But was it enough to wash away fear and the weight of this mission as it settled deeper into my bones?

- 22 -
C.E. 2253 May 25

The next leg took us even longer. We transitioned from desert to forest, the mountains reducing our speed to a crawl. The crew traversed through narrow deer tracks, stopping at first in the region of Ulanqab, among colorful yurts and miles of verdant grassland, then spending a week in the mists of Haituo Mountain, and finally arriving at the Huairou District.

"Did you know," I told JR one evening as we relaxed in our beds, "that this bunker used to be a tourist center—back in the days of international travel, I mean."

JR smirked, "Did you actually do your research this time?"

I tossed a sesame cluster at him from the bag I was eating. "I do learn *some* things," I retorted. "I can even tell you guys about its attraction."

"Oh yeah?" he said, pulling the cluster from the folds of his T-shirt and popping it in his mouth. "Then, spill."

"The Great Wall…" I began and my squad rolled over on their mats, fixing me with their rapt attention.

The Great Wall, one of the longest human-created structures in the world, stretched all the way across the northern edge of China—from Hushan, Liaoning in the east to Jiayuguan Pass in the west. Technically, our route had us skirting this wall since Lanzhou, but we saw no evidence of it until now. Many segments had crumbled in the dry desert air, and shifting sands had subsumed others. Archaeologist had deemed it a magnificent feat of ancient Chinese engineering.

In this mild wet region, we finally could understand why. The wall stood as majestic as ever, an imposing forty feet high. Begun by the ancient Qin dynasty, it grew over one-thousand and eight-hundred years, continually added to by many rulers and dynasties, to hold off invasions of the northern tribes. As massive as it was, however, its effectiveness was hotly debated, even now.

"Still an impressive view," Mara said, her tone wistful. "I wish we could get a closer look at it."

"How do you guys feel about sneaking out tonight?" I asked suddenly, surprising even myself.

"Really, Rob?" JR asked, one eyebrow creeping toward his hairline. "Aren't you supposed to be a responsible leader?"

I shrugged, shoving another sesame cluster into my mouth. "Fine, let's call it team-building activity."

"I like your style, niño," Mendez laughed. "I'm in."

"Why not?" Chet scoffed. "We ain't doin' nothin' else."

Mara settled her dark eyes on me, her grin evil. "Where we going?"

I pointed in the direction of the wall. "Up there."

The squad's eyes widened, but no one declined.

"I'll bring booze," Mara said, pulling a half-full bottle from her bag.

Mendez pushed herself up into a sitting position, shrugging on her brown jacket. "That's not enough. Come girlie," she said to Mara, "we'll get more and meet the boys up there. That is," she said, directing a scolding glare at each one of us, "if you can keep your tasteless comments to yourself."

I made a zipping motion with my hand across my lips then grinned. I'd already learned what happened when you made a classy Zephyr mad.

* * * * *

I stood with JR and Chet, leaning against the rough stones of the Great Wall of China. We watched the lights of the compound and the city of Jing-Jin-Ji far beyond. The megacity lit up the sky in a glowing halo on the horizon, even though mountains and rivers still stood between us. Beyond Jing-Jin-Ji, lost to sight, lay the ocean. A vast, dark expanse I couldn't even begin to comprehend.

"Can you believe we're here?" JR asked, his voice dreamy. "Who in the UCCA can say they've stood on a Chinese monument that's thousands of years old?"

I shrugged. Constance would never believe it. Not that she'd understand even if she did. Taking a deep breath, I asked the guys, "Do you miss your families?"

"What's family?" JR replied. He crossed his arms over the short stone wall and lay his head on them.

"You know…parents, siblings, kids. That kind of thing."

JR scoffed. "I know what family is, you scraphead. Just sayin'…. I don't have any. My parents are rich, even in terms of mech families, which means they care for nothing but the moola. All ill-gotten, obviously. Stolen and dragged from the hands of the dead—savant and mech alike."

When Chet and I stared at him, he frowned.

"What? I won't pretend they were righteous. They're shit bags like all the elite. When my father died three years ago, I one-hundred percent tried to waste all my inherited blood money. Of course, my mother disowned me. My siblings rejected me. My brother Kai took over the biz, and my friends, well it turns out they weren't really my friends. I joined the army because I had nowhere else to go but prison. Was hoping it might just kill me."

"Yikes," I said. "I see." Though I didn't, not really. "I always thought being rich would solve all my problems," I continued, feeling like I owed JR a better response. "Didn't think about how it would only cause more."

"Well..." JR said with a snort. "What about you, Chet? Don't you have like... kids or something?"

Chet lit a cigarette. "One kid. He's..." he counted on his fingers, "three years old. Have a wife, too. We're happy."

"Then why'd you join up?" JR asked. "Gimme one."

Chet placed the package of cigarettes in JR's hand. "Needed the cash."

"That's it?"

He grunted an affirmative.

"I'm glad we had this talk," JR replied with a roll of his eyes, lighting his own cigarette. "What about you, Rob? Any change of heart?"

Before I could answer JR's awkward question, the crunch of boots on the stone stairs crackled through the air. Mara and Mendez arrived, carrying two clear bottles.

"How do you two always find booze?" JR asked, eying it warily.

Mendez laughed with her husky voice. "We use our feminine wiles."

"Whatcha guys talking about?" Mara asked.

"Our families," I said. "Speaking of which, I don't know anything about yours."

Mara snorted. "That's because it's not a good story, Robert."

"Humor us," JR goaded. "It's not like we're going anywhere. And Chet's story sucked."

The Kinetic just grunted again with an apathetic shrug, but still refused elaborate.

Mara sighed and took a large swig from the bottle. "Grew up in the New York Metro Complex in a group home. Eventually, I was four or five I think, some Trues adopted me. No idea who my bio-parents are."

I raised an eyebrow. "None?"

She passed the bottle to JR. "None."

JR's eyes widened. "Was it horrible?"

She shrugged. "The Trues were nice enough people, I guess. But I also had to pretend to be True. Didn't work out well though," she added with a snort. "All I wanted to do was fight. I was so angry."

I placed a hand on her shoulder. "I'm sorry, Mara."

She shook her head. "Don't be. I got out. Joined the army the first chance I got. And now, somehow, things are marginally better."

JR scoffed and passed me the bottle.

The liquid set fire to my insides, sliding down my throat like molten metal. I coughed. "Tastes like jet fuel," I wheeze, handing the bottle to Mendez. "What about you?"

I looked on expectantly, but at the same time wondered if she'd even answer. The woman was a league above the rest of us—a decade older and not exactly part of the army. Yet she'd stuck around. I still didn't quite understand the reason.

The woman smiled with white teeth. "You think living in the UCCA is hard. Try being from Suria. It's *almost* functional anarchy," she continued. "Neither the CORPs nor the cartels can control the whole of it. But, you know how I said 'almost?' Well…sometimes it works. And sometimes it kills everyone you love."

She gave us a moment to digest all of that, her demeanor serious. Then, threw one arm around Mara and the other around me.

"Boys and girl, you are all the family I need," she finished with a grin.

When we'd finally killed the bottle, the five of us made our unsteady way back toward the compound.

"I have to admit," JR shouted, stumbling drunkenly down the eroded stairs, "this seemed like a better idea when I was sober."

A brick crumbled under his heel, and he grabbed at the sleeve of my T-shirt for support. His weight dragged on my own drunken stagger, and I pulled away, only to land sharply on my ass.

I grunted and shoved the man away, who ran, laughing and slipping, down the decline.

"You okay?" Mara asked, pulling me up with a strong grip.

I nodded, feeling the finality of this last reprieve.

"What's up?" she asked when I didn't speak.

"Next time we stop, we'll be in the Jing-Jin-Ji," I said with a sigh. "Then, the real work will begin."

"Mm-hmm," she agreed with me, "quite the sobering thought. At least for those who are not sober." She snickered.

"Hey Mara?"

"Yeah?"

"Back in Ordos when you said, 'love is messy,' did you mean…?"

"That I wanted to get messy?" she interrupted with a smirk. "Yes."

The weight of those words slammed into my drunken mind. I gaped and tried to stammer something out, but my throat constricted with all the things I wanted to say.

"I love you, Robert," she continued. "I know I shouldn't. Or…I'm not supposed to. Or whatever. But…the fact of the matter is—"

"I love you, too," I interrupted.

I'd said those words before, to Constance, the day I left for China. They didn't feel the same then as they did now. Then, they'd felt like the end. But this…

This felt like the beginning.

"You don't have to say it, just because I did," Mara said, her gaze soft. "I know you have—"

But suddenly, I was kissing her hard. Her grip tightened, crushing my fingers, and she kissed back.

"Fuck it," I said when we'd pulled apart for breath. "I mean it. I really do."

She kissed me again, pushing me against the ancient wall.

It would be some time before we returned. My drunken friends didn't even notice.

Part Three

Jing-Jin-Ji, China

- 23 -
C.E. 2253 June 6

As we came upon the city of Jing-Jin-Ji, I saw two things I had never seen before: The Pacific Ocean and the largest city in the world.

The Jing-Jin-Ji, or the JJJ as locals called it, formed during the prosperous year of 2054 with the merging of three ancient cities: Beijing, Tianjin, and Shijiazhuang. Subsequently, the name adopted by this new supercity included elements of all three original cities.

The neighborhoods on the outskirts of the JJJ clung to the western edge of the Tianfang Mountains like a colony of fungi in a rainbow of colors: reds, browns, and yellows. As our hovervan slowly navigated the paved, winding roads, we passed many speedbikes and foot-pedaled carts, the primary forms of transpo in this part of the city.

A sharp whistle pierced the air. A hovercar whizzed by, sleek and chrome with blackened windows, looking out of place in this warren of old-world apartment buildings.

"What the hell was that?" I asked, watching the sexy vehicle zip around too quickly for the narrow roads.

"Zhōngxīn jūmín. Center dwellers," JR explained. "And rich ones, at that."

The residents barely took note of the disruption, not even bothering to lift their heads as the car swooped around a corner.

"Who are the center dwellers?" I asked.

He rolled his eyes. "The money that lives on the other side of the wall. Though I'm not sure if all of them are as baller as our hovercar friend over there. As opposed to those who live in this part of the city, who are mostly farm and factory workers. The two rarely mix…something about not getting along."

I nodded. "I can identify," I said, studying their attire, which practically transported me back to the centuries-old, and now lost, city of Beijing.

"Yeah, I hear it's different on the other side of the wall. The JJJ Sea Wall that is."

"China really likes their walls, don't they?" Chet drawled in his gravelly voice. He lit a cigarette.

171

"Ferryman!" Mendez shouted from the driver's seat, "You get rid of that poison this instant, or I'll throw you out of the van myself!"

Chet grunted in exasperation but tossed it into a nearby puddle anyway. No one wanted to find out how Mendez intended to enact her threat.

"Bloody heathen," Mendez muttered, "If you're so intent on killing yourself, why not wait until we're in an actual battle?"

"Hey!" I returned, "Don't say that. I need every one of my soldiers!"

Captain Ames chuckled.

I brought my thoughts back to the sea wall, trying to catch more than a glimpse of the gray-brown ribbon to the east.

"How big is the JJJ, anyway? I can't see anything in this maze of roads and towering buildings.

"Not sure anyone really knows," JR continued, "I mean, Beijing was big even two-hundred years ago. It was a megacity before we really even had megacities," JR said.

"It's also the oldest city in China, right?" I boasted, trying to show him that I'd done my research this time.

"Some say so," Ames said, "though not everyone agrees."

JR snorted, "Not much is left of the old city, per se. A lot of shit has happened since then. Our lovely capitalism has allowed pollution to run unchecked."

"And you Americans loved those nukes in The Third," Mendez added with a scolding click of her tongue.

Chet laughed dryly, "We did have the most, after all."

"I thought China escaped much of the war," Mara said, frowning as she glanced down at her handheld.

"Mostly," Ames began, "but the coastline suffered. Secondary effects of climate change are a bitch. The Republic of California may be the only place where the old beaches still survive. Though they're dry now."

The RoC, as we called it back home, consumed the entire west coast following The Third. Their government initiated the construction of a massive sea wall to hold back the rising sea water, a result of massive global warming. Of course, they used the most prevalent source of free labor at the time—savant POWs.

"I've heard rumors of original beaches enclosed in glass cases. But I doubt that," I said.

"They exist," the captain sighed, "I've seen them."

"How?" JR asked, eyes wide. "The RoC is protected like a fortress. Savants don't get in or out. Believe me, I've tried."

"Oh, they can get in," Ames's voice came as if from far away, "but they rarely get out. Those of us that do are few."

"No way!" I gasped. "You're pulling our wires."

Ames shook his head.

"So, you're really from the RoC?" Mara asked.

"I am."

"Then, you must be from one of the sea wall internment camps?"

He nodded, his eyes growing sad.

"How'd you get out?" Chet asked. "I didn't think it possible."

"It was…difficult," Ames said, "many who tried ended up dead or recaptured. My brothers…" He shook his head as if trying to dislodge an unpleasant memory. "Never mind."

A knot formed in my stomach. Growing up in The Sink had been hard, but at least I had been given the choice to leave. Those who grew up in the RoC's savant internment camps didn't get that choice.

"I'm so sorry, Sir," I said to my captain, giving him an apologetic nod.

"Thank you," the man replied, though his bottom lip trembled, and his normally misty eyes shone more than usual.

At this moment, he looked more like an unsure young man, rather than the captain I knew him to be. I licked my lips, trying to think of something more reassuring to say.

"We're at the wall," Mendez said, pulling the van into a pay-by-the-day parking garage.

Ames brushed invisible lint off his jacket and stared purposefully out the window where the roads ended next to a high stone wall, his demeanor changing back to that of a captain.

"Let's get moving," he commanded.

Open-air elevators or the more manual ladders and staircases, wended their way up the wall's sheer face. We took an elevator, clinging to the handrails with white knuckles, since its enclosure seemed ready to rattle apart at the merest hint of a breeze.

"Anyone afraid of heights?" JR asked, looking around at the group. "Anyone?"

We all shook our heads.

"Good," he practically squeaked, but I noticed he avoided looking down.

Once we surmounted the wall, I gaped at the vast expanse of water stretched out in front of us. The gentle sound of waves lapping against the far side was almost soothing, but the sheer thirty-meter drop shattered any sense of safety.

"This used to be a bay?" I asked, glancing at Ames.

He nodded. "Much of the land here was less than a hundred meters above sea level, so when the water rose, it submerged everything."

"Now they just call this whole area the Bohai Sea," JR added, gripping the lip of the wall and staring at the far horizon. "See the scrapers in the lowlands?" He pointed to the skinny islands standing tall amongst the swells. "The people just built upward on existing frames."

"Like the New York Metro Complex," Mara marveled, her curious grin taking in the scenery.

"I've never been there," I mumbled as our water taxi arrived. "I've never been most places," I snorted, trying to poke fun at my own sheltered upbringing.

"Remind me to take you sightseeing when we get home," JR teased, and we all piled into the taxi.

"This place is prettier than the Metro Complex though," Mara said, "These buildings have ocean front property. Not the dirty back alley canals I grew up with."

I glanced at her in surprise and made a face. "Shit. Has everyone lived somewhere more interesting than The Sink?" I asked no one in particular.

Chet coughed. "No," he said shortly, "Slum-born and slum-raised, myself." He slapped a heavy hand on my shoulder. "I'm with ya."

I winced but smiled weakly. Chet, however, didn't seem to notice as he stared at the ocean. Maybe he was thinking about his kid.

Mustering up my courage, I stared out the window as we drove. Serpentine skyways and nu-maglev tracks crisscrossed overhead connecting the various buildings together. Water and air-based taxis zipped around us, in a chaotic ebb and flow.

"How the heck do these guys not collide with each other?" Chet asked with a whistle. I noticed he went for another cigarette, but then quickly slipped it back in its package before Mendez could yell at him again.

"Unspoken rules," JR said. "Though it doesn't always work."

He pointed out the window to an accident between a water taxi and what looked like a cargo vehicle. Crates floated in the water surrounded by shattered wood and a swirling rainbow slick of spilled fuel, while emergency workers scurried about.

"Well, that doesn't make me feel great," I muttered, but JR just gave me a pat on the back in solidarity.

"We'll be fine," he breathed closed to my ear. "Mendez is a good driver."

As we navigated through the tall urban islands, we passed shorter floating neighborhoods, only five to ten stories high. They bobbed and twisted but never floated away from each other, due to the tethers that attached them to the underwater ruins. As we traveled east, we came across free-floating neighborhoods, maneuvering between the 'scrapers propelled by underwater turbo engines.

"They say these were built by the CORPs," Captain Ames said, pointing to a particularly large one being tossed about in the swells. "They're based on the technology that keeps Londyn City herself afloat."

My jaw dropped. "I thought no one has heard from Londyn City in fifty years?"

Ames shrugged. "The Queen and her cabinet broke away from mainland United Kingdom during The Third and the Irish takeover that followed. Some say Londyn City sank, but others believe it's out there somewhere… like the Lost City of Atlantis."

"Either way, the technology clearly works," JR said gesturing around us. "At least at this small scale."

"We're coming upon our base on Tianjin Island," Ames said, gesturing to one skinny 'scraper, standing derelict and gently swaying near the mouth of the ancient bay.

"That's it?" JR asked incredulously. "I thought Tianjin was a whole city."

"It used to be," Ames said, "but it was too close to the coast and had to be abandoned. This is all that remains."

"Sacred Rabbit Island," Mendez said, reading the navscreen. "That the place, boss?"

"Yes," Ames continued, "originally, it was meant to be an urban housing project, but that died when Lightbar took over China's industry and deemed it 'too far away, and too small' to be commercially viable. Now, it's just a small community of fisheries."

JR laughed, "So, we're gonna be fishermen?" He made a face to look like the lips of a fish.

Ames shot him with an unamused grimace. "It is also the secret ops center of the Citizen's Army, you scraphead."

"A sub-aquatic military base?" Mara's asked, a look of terror flashing briefly on her face.

"Good ol' military ingenuity," Chet muttered, though his appreciative glance showed that he was impressed.

Mara just shook her head, jaw tight. I placed two fingers on her shoulder blade in attempted comfort, and she leaned back slightly with a sigh. I didn't know what Mara was afraid of, but part of me was glad I could help.

General Mazet herself escorted us from the taxi and onto the cluster of ramshackle docks that made up Tianjin Island. They were mostly sturdy, but I could still feel the faint rocking beneath my feet. Suddenly, I was glad all that time on the Yellow River had given me some form of sea legs.

We followed her down a set of stairs and into the belly of the 'scraper. Though they had once been carpeted, only a few straggly red threads remained as evidence, clinging to cracks in the worn plywood. Dim sodium lights flickered at uneven intervals, the space between almost completely dark. Mazet held up a flashlight, but the glow barely reached the end of our column.

"Don't be alarmed if you see water on some of these floors," she warned. "Leaks spring up here and there, but I can assure you, the center section is quite safe. When we do spring a leak, the water crews work quickly."

"Oh great," Mara mumbled, her hand tightening on my upper arm.

"Are there any windows in this thing?" JR asked, "You know…I think it would be pretty cool to see out…"

"No!" Mara snapped. "No windows…and if there are windows, don't tell me about them." She squeezed my arm tighter.

I grunted in pain, twitching my arm. Turning over my shoulder I whispered, "You wanna save the bruises for when we're alone?"

"Sorry," she replied, "I just…really…hate water."

"Can't you swim?"

"Nuh-uh," she said emphatically, "Tanks don't float. We're too dense."

I'd never thought about that before, but I supposed it made sense. With so much of a Tank's body-water content replaced with metal, I could see how that would reduce buoyancy.

"Well, you can show the rest of us the window later…Sir," JR whispered into the back of Mazet's head.

I gave the man a back-handed swat. "Don't speak to greater officers unless spoken to," I hissed at him, "unless you want to make me look bad."

But, the general just chuckled and JR flashed me a smug grin.

My boot plunged into several inches of water, and I was grateful for Mazet's warning. However, when Mara's feet followed she let go to flail her arms about.

"Shit. Shit. Shit. Shit," she cursed.

I managed to grab a wrist before she broke my nose. "You're fine," I soothed. "It's shallow."

Letting out an unsatisfied groan, Mara followed it with a shaky breath. "Sorry," she muttered again, sloshing along behind me.

Finally, Mazet brought us to large metal bulkhead.

"Watch your step," she said, pointing to the lip of the door, which sat above the floor by a foot. Once through the door, we found ourselves standing on a slick, dripping grate that hung precariously over a sheer drop of at least a hundred meters. Far below, dark water rippled faintly, its surface disturbed by unseen currents.

"Nope," Mara said.

"Come on, Mara," I encouraged, "it'll be fine."

"Do you see this flimsy thing? There is no way it'll hold me."

Mazet looked puzzled. "It'll hold a Tank, Private Dark. I mean, we've got more weight on it right now."

She gestured to the five of us, then jumped up and down. The grate shook, but only slightly.

"Besides," JR said, "what do you plan to do? Just wait on that side until the meeting is done?"

Mara scowled. "Fine," she sighed. "But you guys go across first. I'll follow."

Ames chuckled and shook his head in defeat, but Mazet nodded, a slight smile teasing at her lips.

She entered some information on a keypad, scanning her handprint and her retina. The far door hissed open like an air lock. I brushed my fingers along the door frame.

"Don't worry," I turned to Mara once the others had left, "this doorway has so much tech in it—sensory equipment, regulating mechanisms, water-sensing alarms—that there's no way water's getting in here." I couldn't help but whistle. "This is one serious door!"

"Okay, nerd, c'mon," JR said, dragging me by a belt loop. "Let the lady cross in peace."

Mara gave JR another scowl and a huff but followed me through the bulkhead.

I couldn't help but stare.

"This must take up the entire floor of the 'scraper," JR said, looking around in awe.

"Just about," Ames smiled.

We entered a large room dominated by high-tech computer systems. Servers, big screens, holo projectors, and control panels lined the walls and filled crowded islands scattered across the floor. In one corner, a makeshift lounge offered couches, tables, and even a few fake plants. People darted between workstations, tapping frantically or whispering in small clusters. Major Healey and Lieutenant Griffin stood nearby with the Black Cats.

The far end was obscured by cubicles, but faint rustling hinted at more activity—voices murmuring and equipment humming. Screens and a central holoviz displayed sectors of the city: urban islands, a floating commerce center, an outskirts neighborhood, and Tianjin Island itself.

When I finally stopped gawking, Mara appeared beside me, pale and still catching her breath.

"Charger's Balls, Mara," JR whispered, "You'd better hope the army doesn't intend for us to bunk here."

Mara snorted in response, "Agreed. I may not survive the night."
Mazet gazed purposefully at our group, silencing our banter. "Welcome to the War Room," she announced.

- 24 -
C.E. 2253 June 7-8

Fortunately, the officers did not require us to live in the underwater army HQ. Instead, they gave us one of the houseboats that bobbed on the perimeter of the island. Even Mara approved of the accommodations, though I noticed she stayed well away from the open-air, wrap-around deck.

We sat in our new small-but-functional common room, waiting for Mazet to arrive and give us our orders. LED strips cast a steady glow across the mix of worn but comfortable seating: a scuffed leather couch, a few cushioned chairs, and a low table with a tarnished chrome finish. The faint hum of the boat's generator filtered through the walls, accompanied by the occasional creak of the hull, and a holo-projector cast a crisp map of the surrounding islands, its blue glow reflected in the polished metal of the table. I could smell the salt in the air along with freshly brewed tea—courtesy of JR—and the heady aroma of fish frying in a nearby stall. These touches contributed to the chaotically cozy atmosphere of the quirky houseboat. Compared to our quarters in Lanzhou, it was practically heaven.

To outward appearances, this island was home to a colony of blue-collar workers, mostly fishers and water porters, though we'd been warned to be careful as pirate sightings had grown more frequently in the previous months.

"This neighborhood is made up of primarily Chinese citizens," Mazet began when we all had our tea. "You will need a cover to explain why five white people are suddenly living here." She handed me a thin tab with a series of document links glowing yellow.

"Four white and one brown," Mendez asserted. "I'm from the Suria. We know what sun feels like."

"If you're brown, then I'm at least a dark beige," Mara joked, indicating her darker complexion.

Ames shook his head at the insubordination and gave us a stern glance, though only Mendez seemed to notice.

She chuckled, "I suppose the point here is that we do not look Han."

"Or like most of the other ethnicities in China, of which there are many,"

JR added, raising a finger scoldingly.

Mazet clapped her hands, bringing our focus back to her. "I have given Sergeant Lilly all the information there," she gestured to my tab. "However, in short, you are a group of college students on an exchange program from the UCCA. You're here to learn ocean health monitoring and deep-sea fishing," she continued, without missing a beat.

"College student? You think I look that good?" Mendez fluffed her curly hair.

"No, Mendez," JR said with a wink and an eyebrow waggle, "You look even better."

"Thank you," Mendez smiled, and touched JR on the nose. "I think I'll keep you. Even though you're a Sway."

"You're welcome." JR grinned and made a dramatic bow where he sat.

"Shee-it," Chet snickered, "you two have a line for everything, don'tcha?"

"Soldiers, pay attention," Ames chided. "You'd think the army is desperate, putting up with you jokers."

Though, he didn't exactly seem cross with our antics. Like me, I'm sure he enjoyed seeing the crew in a lighter mood after the difficult journey from Lanzhou.

"Regardless," Mazet continued, without missing a beat, "I will warn you to be careful. While some of the inhabitants on the island are sympathizers with the resistance, we cannot trust the confidence of everyone. And you never know who you're talking to..."

While she spoke, something strange happened to the general. I blinked hard and even then, it took my brain several extra seconds to process what it had seen. Her complexion changed from pinkish pale to golden bronze and her hair grew long and black. The features of her face morphed and elongated, cheekbones and chin becoming fine and pronounced, nose widening, and eyes tilting. *Now* she looked Han.

"What the...?" Chet muttered.

"You're a Grifter?" Mendez said with surprise. "This is good stuff!"

"Hey, Mendez," JR said with a cheesy smile. "How do you know when you're talking to a Grifter?"

I smiled. I'd heard this one before. "You don't."

Mazet allowed the crew a moment to laugh, then nodded. "As Private Rostbane pointed out, you never know when you're talking to one, so always be mindful. Since Grifters can change how your brain interprets our appearance, it's customized to each person, making us very hard to ferret out."

"So…is that what you really look like, Sir?" Mara asked. She leaned forward in her chair, studying the general. "I've never met a Grifter before…that I know of."

Mazet chuckled but shook her head.

"Then how do we know what you really look like?"

She smiled. "You don't."

JR pointed at Mara in silent mockery, and she shot him a dark glare.

"Anyway," Mazet continued, only slightly put off by the interruptions, "we've been gathering intelligence at this base for a while now and are starting to put our plans into action. While you've been in Lanzhou, we've been dispensing wùdǎo xiǎoduì, or misdirection squads, to sow unrest across China. Their instruction is to keep Lightbar guessing on where we will strike."

"Impressive, Sir," I said, "you all have been busy."

She nodded. "Now, thanks to you Lilly, it is time to act. Tomorrow, the rest of your squad will join you, and you will begin preparing for your next assignment. In the meantime, get some rest, enjoy the scenery, and eat the fish—trust me, you will not be disappointed."

"Yes, Sir," we all said, standing up to see the general out.

Once she'd left, the crew went out to try the recommended fish, and Mazet was right. It was delicious.

"Well, Mazet is not what I'd expect of a general," Mara said, licking grease from her fingertips.

"I like her," Mendez agreed. "It's good to see more women in positions of kicking ass!"

The two shared a laugh and I felt myself nodding along. "She does seem singular," I added with hesitation, "but I'm worried she's putting too much faith in me."

"What do you mean?" Mara asked.

I sighed. "All I did was hack a chip. Any knucklehead with a basic knowledge of computer systems could do that. What if I got the wrong information?"

"Rob, Rob, Rob," JR muttered, picking the fish apart with his chopsticks in an almost dainty display of manners, "don't you know? *I'm* a knucklehead with a basic knowledge of computer systems, but I'm pretty sure I couldn't have done *that*."

Mara made a sound of agreement. "You've done exactly what was expected of you—and then some. That's not something to brush off."

"Yeah," Chet said, swirling the beer around the bottom of his Styrofoam cup. "You've gotten us this far. No one else has done that, either. You're not just okay, you're necessary."

The words sank in, settling some of the tension in my chest. I glanced around at my team and nodded. "Thanks, guys."

JR popped a piece of fish into his mouth and pointed his chopsticks at me. "Just don't let it go to your head, boss. Remember who taught you how to fix your comm the night you fried it."

Laughter broke through the lingering seriousness, and I allowed myself to relax. If they believed in me, maybe I could too.

But I didn't, not really, which became apparent the next day when I met the rest of my squad. The five guarded expressions and the way they glanced at me but didn't quite meet my eyes indicated that these soldiers clearly weren't sold on me either.

Regardless, I put on a large, official smile and waited in the War Room with the rest of my crew for the officers to arrive and introduce us. Once the pleasantries had been completed, Ames began without preamble.

"Sergeant Cheng Duan," he said and gestured, "formerly of the Golden Nimbus division."

A man came forward with slow, deliberate steps. Much shorter than me but just as muscular, he had a square jaw with light stubble across his chin and cheeks, and a buzz cut so short I could see his scalp. He gave me a severe nod and, only after a stern look from Ames, a half-hearted salute.

"Cheng will be your second in command. If you need to split your squad, he's your guy."

Cheng said something in Mandarin, frowning deeply.

"I'm sorry," I said lamely, "do you speak English?"

Despite JR's tutelage, so far I'd only picked up individual words spoken slowly. I could order a noodle bowl, ask where the bathroom was and—of course—order a beer. None of that helped now though, and I felt like the poster boy for "idiot American."

Cheng sighed and crossed his thick arms. "I said," he drawled as if speaking to a child, "I am at your service."

"Right," I cleared my throat, trying to cover up my nervousness. "Welcome to the Street Dogs. I'm happy to have you."

Cheng replied again in Mandarin and nodded. One of the soldiers behind him snickered.

"Yeah, um, thank you, too," I replied, even though I knew *that word*, and Cheng had most definitely not said it.

Internally, my mind raced. Cheng must know more English than that. The officers wouldn't assign me a second-in-command with whom I couldn't communicate, would they?

Ames also gave a side-eye to the insubordination but didn't mention it. "Your savants," he continued. "First, Mister Han Niu."

A large man stepped forward. Towering over even me, he performed an energetic salute.

"Sir. They call me The Ox, Sir." He quirked a lopsided smile. "I am enthusiastic to work with you."

"Enthusiastic?" Mara muttered, "Does he mean excited?"

"Shit!" JR said at the same time, but much louder. "What the hell did your mother feed you?"

"My grandmother," The Ox grinned, "fed me rice and," he paused for dramatic effect looking at each of us in turn, "more rice. We ate *a lot* of rice."

Mara snickered and even JR managed a smirk. "Must've been some rice," I heard him whisper to Chet who just snorted back.

I released a breath. After the introduction to Cheng, I silently thanked Greysoft for giving me this cheerful giant.

"The Ox?" I chuckled. "I can see that. You're a Tank?"

He nodded, his top knot bobbing. "Yes, Sir."

Then, he stepped back and Ames introduced Ru Wei as our Spark.

Ru gave me a curt nod, his wiry frame coiled with quiet energy. He kept his hands tucked into the pockets of his jumpsuit, and his eyes flickered briefly to Cheng before returning to me, his expression passive. He muttered something in Mandarin barely louder than a murmur, then looked to Cheng for confirmation.

I opened my mouth to say something encouraging but hesitated, unsure of how to bridge the gap. When Ru's salute came at Cheng's slight nod, it was sloppy—more of a half-hearted gesture than anything formal—and I couldn't help but feel a pang of frustration.

But I forced a smile. It felt thin, brittle, and awkward. "Right... guess we'll figure this out," I muttered under my breath, more to myself than anyone else.

I gave Ru an equally half-hearted salute and he scurried back to the group.

"Lastly," Ames said, who'd been watching this whole interaction with composure, "we have Yaozu Jin, an Auraseer."

"An Auraseer," I said slowly, suppressing a shudder.

Though they were common enough in the savant world, I had never felt comfortable when they were around. My mother was one, and she could always tell when I was lying, just from the shifting colors of my Aura—a thing I could never control. I could tell Yaozu was sizing me up as well, the way she stared just up and over my left shoulder, despite her diminutive height.

"Welc—"

"I don't waste time with pleasantries," she said flatly, her voice icy and dismissive. "We're here to fight, not make friends…Sir."

She tacked that final word on with an edge like steel, then turned her attention to the room as if the conversation had already been forgotten.

I looked over at Ames, trying not to let him hear the tremor in my voice. "Three savants?" I asked quietly.

He nodded.

"Then what is Cheng?"

"True Human," Ames said, loud enough for my squad behind me to hear him.

"A True?"

"Sir, I heard they abstained from these types of conflicts. They don't trust us or something?" Mara said, taking a bold step forward.

Yet again, she'd asked the question I wasn't sure I could. Greysoft bless her.

"Yes, Private Dark," Ames explained, sternly but not angrily. "It is a correct understanding that True Humans are inherently distrustful of both mechs and savants. However, here in China, they have more freedoms than in the UCCA and thus, they have as much interest in this conflict as the rest of us.

"Thank you, Sir," Mara said demurely, lowering her head in acknowledgment. For the headstrong, brash woman that Mara was, I respected her ability to play the part she'd been assigned.

I only wished I could do as well as her. Already, I felt as if I was drowning in a sea of leadership I'd been thrown into against my will. I couldn't imagine anything that could be more awkward.

Until meeting my last squad member, that is.

"Finally," Ames said, his lip twitched as if uncertain if he should continue, "Jun Li, your mech."

"My wha—?" I said as the last woman stepped up.

She was the smallest of them all—I guessed just over five feet—and had an almost sweet face and wispy ponytail. I had thought she just wore a high-tech backpack, until it unfolded to reveal four mechanical arms, attached to the shoulder joints of her human arms.

"Heh-llo!" Chet spat, taking a step backward in surprise. "Well, that's…different."

"Different?" JR snapped. "She just made arms come out of her…

arms!" A wave of unease settled on me from his Aurawave.

"That's typically what mechs do, my little grapefruit," Mendez said, tugging on a lock of JR's curly hair and letting it snap back in place. Her deep gemstone eyes danced in secret amusement and JR's Aurawave faded.

"Don't worry," Ames said, his voice soft but firm. "She's got full control."

Jun gave a small, polite bow, the mechanical arms retracting smoothly against her back. "I'm... used to surprise," she said, her voice a little shy, though her eyes held an edge of pride. "But you have questions... I answer them."

Chet scratched the back of his neck, still clearly thrown. "Yeah. Ah… I'll pass on the questions for now. I'll just be over here... not staring."

I couldn't help the nervous laugh that escaped me. Jun's calm demeanor made me feel a little better, but I wasn't sure how I'd get used to working alongside someone with arms like that.

Ames waited silently for us to take it all in.

"As you hopefully realize by now," he finally said, "this war is not just about savants. It affects everyone who works and lives in China. Mods, Skills or neither, the CORPs have proven they don't differentiate, and we shall do the same. Are we clear?"

My squad nodded slowly and the new additions even more slowly.

"Sergeant Lilly, *are we clear*?" Ames asked again, his gray eyes boring into mine.

"Yes, Sir!" I replied, scouring my brain for a positive affirmation. "We should welcome all who wish to fight Lightbar."

Ames smiled with approval, and I let out my held-in breath.

A silent moment followed.

"Well?" Ames prompted. "Any orders for your squad?"

I began to stammer. Mendez touched me on the shoulder, leaning close to my ear. "Invite them to dinner, niño," she whispered.

"Yes, right," I muttered. "I want everyone to meet in the common room of our quarters for dinner tomorrow, eighteen-hundred sharp. Until then, get settled in."

A chorus of "Yes, Sir!" (and one rogue "Yes, boss" from JR) followed.

Ames nodded and called us all to be dismissed.

I had to hand it to my squad—my original squad. We'd all grown up with the mindset of the UCCA, where savants were the good guys and mechs the bad. Yet, no one cursed or uttered a slur. All-in-all, they had taken the introductions in stride. Much better than I had, if I'm being honest.

Confidence blossomed again in my breast. We would get through this. We *would*, no matter what. We were a team. We were all a team.

I left the War Room trailing the others, and JR fell back to join me. Turning to me, he whispered close to my ear, "Quite a squad you have there, boss. Do you even need me?"

"Of course I need you, clutterhead," I responded from the corner of my mouth. "We're 'bros' remember? I wouldn't dream of doing this without you." I paused. "Unless, of course, you don't want to come."

JR opened his mouth.

"But don't you dare say 'no'."

The other man smirked. "Well, I was going to say, 'You'll always have my gun,' but…I can't shoot for shit."

I flicked his arm with the back of my flat hand. "Shut up. I'm trying to keep it together here."

"Never!" He winked, prodding me in the ribs.

I smiled to myself, "What would I *ever* do without you, Rostbane?"

"Rostbane was my father," he responded in a light tone though there was an edge to it, "I'm just JR."

I waved my hand in a dismissive gesture. "Nah. You much *more* than just JR. Now let's get to work. We have a mission to prepare for."

"I thought you said we had the day?"

I blew air through my lips, "We do. But, since you need extra target practice…"

"Aw c'mon, Rob!" JR moaned. "I can learn to shoot tomorrow! I was thinking we could hit the bar…let off some steam."

"And miss a prime opportunity to improve that shit aim?"

"Fine…Your Majesty," JR said with a deep bow. "But every time I hit the target you owe me a beer."

I gave him a long, hard look, trying not to let the strain show and quirked an evil smile. "Piece of cake. What would you ever do without me?" I countered.

"Get drunk," he grunted but clapped an arm around my shoulders anyway.

- 25 -
C.E. 2253 June 9

The next evening during dinner, four pairs of dark eyes and one of icy blue bore into me. Yaozu, the Auraseer, had been dissecting me with her gaze since the moment we'd met, her focus unrelenting. Cheng's glare was different—not sharp, but heavy, weighted with a brooding intensity that made me feel like I was under interrogation. His silence wasn't idle; it was the silence of a man sizing up someone he wasn't sure he could trust.

JR, ever the extrovert, noticed the tension. His Aurawave pressed against mine, warm and insistent, as he cracked jokes and laughed too loud trying to bridge the gap between us and our new squad mates. I shoved the good vibes away. I wasn't ready to let go of the disapproving stares or the gnawing insecurity curling in my chest. I needed to sit with them, to stare my inadequacies in the face, no matter how much it hurt.

Mendez jumped in, firing off teasing jabs at JR, her tone light and whip-sharp. Normally, I would've laughed, but even their playful banter couldn't cut through the oppressive weight hanging over the table. The unspoken verdict seemed clear: I wasn't enough. Not yet. My shoulders tightened under the pressure of it, but I refused to look away from their judgment.

Pull it together, I thought to myself, hand tightening around the cup in front of me. *The squad looks to you for leadership*. But the problem was… I still didn't feel like a leader.

Mara leaned in as we passed around mugs of locally brewed beer—the general's peace offering. Her hand brushed mine briefly, squeezing just enough to draw my attention.

"Give them time," she murmured, her voice low enough for only me to hear. "We're the outsiders here, Robert. It's not just about us being American. They've fought and bled for this land, and now we're stepping in, acting like we know better. They'll come around—eventually."

Her smile was small but genuine, and for a moment, it anchored me. I nodded, forcing the corners of my mouth to twitch upward in return. It wasn't much, but it was something.

Just as I was beginning to think I might survive the night, Yaozu spoke.

"Well, Sergeant Lilly," she said, her voice smooth and deliberate, each syllable drawn out as though she were testing my name on her tongue, "you have a plan for us, yet?"

She tucked a strand of dark hair behind her ear, smoothing a hand against her tight bun. Her bright gaze didn't waver.

"You can just call me Lilly," I interjected.

"Or boss," JR winked.

"Rostbane…" I began to threaten, but JR pretended not to notice.

"You have a plan?" Yaozu pressed, undeterred.

"Don't be so impatient, Yu Jie," The Ox replied before I could. He must have had some familiarity with the woman, since he used what I presumed was a nickname. "It's only our first day."

Yaozu swiveled her gaze to meet his. "Technically, that was yesterday. Today is our *second* day. Sergeant Lilly should have a plan."

"Don't worry. He's our leader." The Ox said as if that answered all her questions. He patted her hand.

"I was," I said, clearing my throat, "I *am* waiting for the official announcement before deciding on a course of action. Does that satisfy your question?"

It didn't.

"Why wait?" Yaozu sounded unconvinced. "Every day Lightbar soldiers kill our people. Are we sitting around to do nothing? Do you even care?"

She stared just over my left shoulder. I brushed at it, subconsciously trying to wipe her eyes from my Aura. Not that it had any effect. I could tell, however, that whatever she saw, she didn't like.

"I'm sure Mazet and your officers are analyzing the situation as we speak," I continued.

"Tā sīhū méiyǒu nàme zìxìn," she said, looking between her compatriots. Jun and Ru nodded in agreement. Cheng even smiled his approval.

But Mara winced.

"You understood that?" I asked her in a low tone.

She nodded, directing a glare toward Yaozu. "It was *not* complimentary."

The pit dropped into my stomach, and I wanted to quit the table. To flee. Instead, I shoved a dumpling in my mouth as I tried to figure out what to say

The three chattered together in quiet voices, their words quick and clipped. Jun giggled behind her hand, her eyes darting toward me with a spark of amusement. Ru snorted and made a sharp, dismissive noise, his lips quirking in a smirk. My jaw tightened, and a flush of heat climbed the back of my neck.

"I have an idea," I said, crossing my arms over the table and leaning forward, hoping to project intensity. "If you're going to talk about me, how about we do it in English? Kay?"

"Yu Jie. Nǐ yīdìng bùyào huáiyí tā!" The Ox chided Yaozu when they ignored me.

A heated argument erupted among the five of them, voices overlapping in a chaotic clash of words. The Ox stood, towering over the others, broad shoulders taut and fists clenching at his sides. Frustration burned in his eyes, and though he could flatten the others in a physical brawl, this verbal sparring was getting the better of him. His booming retorts were met with quick, cutting jabs and he stammered, growing increasingly irate.

"Uh, boss?" JR nudged me with his elbow. "Should we step in and say something?"

Mendez leaned back in her chair, propping a knee against the table. "Dunno about you, but I'm enjoying the show."

I looked between JR and Mara. "Do either of *you* want to step in?" I asked. "You probably know more about what they're saying."

Mara shook her head. "Nope. Too fast for me." She cracked her knuckles, "But, if it gets any worse, I could always deck someone. Doubt anyone would need a translation for my right hook."

JR chuckled, "Or—I could do it all gently-like."

A soothing wave of contentment washed over me, but an angry flash of Yaozu's gaze snapped me out of it. Seems this crew already knew Sways too well.

JR shrugged and I sighed.

"So, we're just going to sit here and let this happen?" Chet asked, studying the group as he slurped noodles from a bowl.

Suddenly, The Ox slammed his hand on the table, rattling glasses and bowls. "Nín de zǔxiān tīng dào nín zhèyàng shuō huì gǎnjué rúhé, Yaozu?" he shouted.

I leaned back in surprise as beer splashed across the table. This time, I recognized the word "zǔxiān", or ancestors. Highly revered in China's culture, ancestors were not brought up unless things were getting *serious*.

"Tāmen huì juéde xiūchǐ," Cheng spat as he stood to face The Ox, tipping over a chair. "Měiguó rén shì yīgè shībài zhě!"

"That's it, I'm punching someone," Mara muttered, her face twisting into an expression of irritated frustration.

She stood as well, approaching Cheng with slow, menacing steps.

"No punching!" I scolded, but Mara wasn't paying attention.

She shoved Cheng, just hard enough to make him stagger backward.

"We gonna to have a problem here, jūnshì?" she spat.

I knew that one too, sergeant. But, Mara wasn't using it in deference.

Cheng glared at her and said something I didn't catch, but from the look on Mara's face, I knew it wasn't an apology.

"You've heard of the Battle of Sky Plaza," she said. It wasn't a question.

Cheng frowned, and though she was shorter than the sergeant, her aggressive stance and low tone gave her an imposing presence. "Well, he was responsible for that."

"Hey! I helped," JR interjected. I nudged the man to be quiet.

"So, you *will* give him respect," Mara continued, bringing her face close to his, "or I'll knock that glare off your face so hard, your *zǔxiān* will feel it."

The fire drained Cheng's stance and he finally turned toward me with only the shadow of a scowl left on his lips.

"My apologies, Sir," he said, still ignoring my preferred title.

He made a bow, so low as to be almost mocking, and turned to leave. A dagger-filled glance hit Mara. "Jiàn nǚrén," he said under his breath.

"You know I am!" Mara called back at him, eyes narrowed.

Yaozu and Ru rose to follow, their bows more subdued, and Jun hesitated before bowing last, hers the most hesitant of all.

When everyone had left, The Ox righted Cheng's chair and took a seat. His complexion had returned to its normal tan and the smile lines appeared around his eyes.

"Do not worry, Sir," he said and patted my forearm with an embarrassed chuckle. "They know their duty and will not shrink from it. If you learn Mandarin, maybe they will trust you. I'll teach." He attempted a conciliatory smile.

"Good luck," JR blew air from his cheeks. "I've been working on that for almost a year."

"Except, your attention span is about five minutes." Mara's tone was teasing, but the tension still lingered in her neck and shoulders.

"So, you gonna tell us what they said that pissed you off so much?" Chet asked The Ox.

"Do you really want to know?" Mara asked me, concern creasing her brow. She sat, placing a hand on my knee. For the thousandth time, I thanked Greysoft she'd stuck around, though I still didn't understand why.

I opened my mouth to say "no," but the words stuck in my throat. Though, I already knew the other half of my squad didn't like me, as their leader I needed to know how much. I didn't have the luxury of being in the dark anymore.

"Yes," I finally said, "as long as it doesn't ruin everything for you all to find that I really don't know what the hell I'm doing."

Chet chuckled into his mug, "None of us know what the hell we're doing."

"Except me," Mendez goaded, "I fly things."

I looked at The Ox, "And you?"

He shrugged. "I liked you when I met you. You're strong. And uncomfortable in your role as leader. You're the best kind."

I doubted that. Maybe The Ox didn't understand the meaning of "uncomfortable."

"And Boss?" JR said, nudging me, "We'll follow you regardless. It's not like anyone else here wants to make the decisions."

Mendez laughed, "The Snack has it right. Charger's Beard, I wouldn't want your job!"

"Plus, we kinda like you," JR flashed me a white-toothed smile. I felt a warm wave of reassurance drift over me. That scamp was using his Aurawave again! This time, however, I let it run its course, giving me the boost I needed to continue this conversation.

I blushed and changed the subject before Mara could make me more embarrassed. "Okay so lay it on me. What do the others think of me?"

Pink tinged The Ox's cheeks. "They think you're incompetent and a coward."

"And an idiot," JR added.

"It was probably Yaozu," Mara said, "Auraseers always make me uncomfortable."

Auraseers, there was a reason the CORPs in my home country used them to ferret out revolutionaries. They were able to read deeper into your psyche, oftentimes knowing things that you didn't even know about yourself. They undressed you, in an emotional sense, stripping away every dream, every lie, and every suppressed feeling stored behind your mental walls.

I disliked them because they usually were right.

"Oh, and Cheng called you a loser."

"Damn," I said, "but I suppose she's not entirely wrong. Sure, I'm frightened of what's to come—who wouldn't be? But me, a coward? Seriously?" I made a distasteful sound.

"Don't feel too bad," Mara consoled me, "he called me a bitch."

"Wow," I continued, "but if it makes you guys feel better, I wouldn't back down from this war even if Charger himself told me to stop."

The Ox's smile widened, eyes crinkling even further. "That's what I like to hear," he said. "I think you'll do fine."

"Thanks." I smiled weakly, making a mental note to take him up on the lessons as soon as possible.

"That is," he continued, his grin becoming mischievous, "if you can keep up with me." He patted one of the kegs.

"Oh, so you're not leaving with the rest?" I asked, looking at the door where the others had exited.

The Ox shook his head. "What kind of soldier would I be if I left you to take on this challenge alone? There's beer to drink."

"He's right," Mara smiled, refilling my glass, "we've been given an order."

"We have?" Chet asked.

Mara nudged me with her knee under the table. She flashed a purposeful look to the rest of my squad.

"Right," I said, though I didn't really feel like drinking beer with anyone except my own miserable self. However, The Ox had put good faith in me, and I didn't want to jeopardize that now. "I order you all to get drunk!"

Mendez laughed. "Now, that's an order even I can get behind," she said, raising her glass in a toast. "To our fearless leader!"

After that, the six of us drank beer until we couldn't see straight. I suppose that's one way to get over your fears and insecurities…

C.E. 2253 June 10

…that is, until the hangover sets in.

The next morning, I found out firsthand why our officers didn't like it when their soldiers drank. The claustrophobic heat in the War Room made my stomach churn. I bit back the bile rising in my throat for the third time, while trying to focus on the presentation.

People sat or perched on all available surfaces and even more stood in clusters across the expansive floor. The HVAC churned, trying to cool a room filled with this many bodies. I could feel the fans' vibrations deep in my bones, but the nearest vent was at least five feet away and the press of bodies absorbed whatever cool air it might've pushed out.

Many of my squad mates were in a similar state and stood sullenly, save for Mendez, who'd managed to convince us that she was sloshed, while also retaining her decorum. As she was at least a decade older than us, I wondered if that was some of the wisdom age imparted on a person.

Two groups sat at the front of the room: A group of Chinese officers led by a grizzled older gentleman and our officers—Mazet (who looked like she did when I met her), Healey, Ames, Griffin, and a new lieutenant whose name I could never remember. Richards? Ripley? Ryan? It hadn't mattered, since Ames didn't seem to mind me bypassing the lieutenant for all my requests. The now-captain only upheld ceremony while others were watching.

Mitchell had opted to stay behind in Lanzhou. He claimed it was due to his sustained injuries from Xi'an, but the crew speculated that it had more to do with the owner of a particular noodle shop…either way, the old sergeant had done his time and deserved a bit of a break. I just hoped Cheng would come around and prove to be as effected as Mitchell—I mean, their attitudes were already the same and neither seemed to like me.

Besides the groups that had traveled with us from Lanzhou, the remainder of the assembly was made up of Chinese men and women. I guessed they were the rebels we'd heard about for the past year.

Finally, Mazet cleared her throat and ordered us to begin. A tall Chinese man with salt-and-pepper hair stepped forward and said in a deep voice,

"Tīng wǒ shuō!"

"Hear me out," Mara whispered in my ear.

Since his insignia was unique, I assumed he was a general.

The rumble of voices fell silent.

"Greetings officers and soldiers of the Citizen's Army," Mazet said, hand clasped behind her back. "Thank you all for being here. Let's get right down to business. First…" she gestured and the holoviz blinked to life in the middle of the room.

Three figures stared back: Major Healey, Captain Ames, and…me? I wanted to hide behind my squad, but I made sure to straighten my shoulders anyway.

"We would like to welcome the American platoon from our western company." Mazet introduced each of us in turn then continued, "These individuals are the ones who uncovered the coordinates to the control center for Lightbar's Kinetic Energy Weapons." Low muttering went around the room and a few of the nearby eyes looked at me in surprise.

Fortunately, the holoviz shifted to display drone footage of a single hill in a countryside I did not recognize. I contemplated the image as it rotated.

"That's the KEWP Control Center?" JR whispered incredulously. "Where's the door? Where's the tech?"

I shrugged, focusing on the dark green, conical trees that dotted its surface. The footage zoomed in on a single pillar of rock that protruded straight from the top, narrow base growing wider as it went up.

"Okay," JR continued, "that's *definitely* not a secret base. It looks more like…"

"A cartoon caveman's club," I interjected before JR could make the obvious phallic comparison and embarrass me to everyone in our vicinity.

"It's actually Chengde Qingchui Mountain," The Ox whispered in my other ear, completely missing JR's reference.

The footage zoomed in further and I could barely see the faint ghost of a broadcasting antenna protruding from the top of the pillar.

The Ox made a surprised, "Oh!" beside me and JR cut short a snort of laughter.

"Well, obvs," JR snickered, implying the idea was anything but obvious.

"An antenna that tall can probably send a signal a long way," I said, trying to at least steer our chatter toward business.

The older Chinese man, who'd called us to attention earlier, now spoke up. "I am General Qian of the Sacred Cloud Army," he gave a small, formal bow of introduction then continued. "We have been monitoring the location and can confirm the Americans' coordinates. Sightings of Lightbar patrols and an increase in transmission activity indicate this is, indeed, a central communication hub for a larger operation."

The officers at the front nodded in agreement, their faces serious.

"It is well-concealed and heavily fortified," Qian went on, his tone steely. "After careful deliberation, General Mazet and I have agreed it is in our best interest to combine our forces to take this base down together. You will notice integrated squads of American and Chinese soldiers, working side-by-side. I trust you will be able to cooperate, as General Mazet and I have, to ensure the success of this mission."

I tried not to wince, though the statement felt too close to home after the previous evening.

Mazet fiddled with some controls and the holo of Chengdu Mountain vanished, replaced by a map of the area, covered in colorful lines. She began to explain.

"Company two-four-two will be charged with diversion and decimation. The Black Cats and Steel Pistols will hold the perimeter in the mountains to the south and the north. These squads will keep enemy forces busy with pointless skirmishes and harrying attacks, using guerrilla tactics. You'll be outnumbered."

"Just how we like it!" Mezei shouted from the corner of the room and the other Tanks pumped their fists in enthusiastic agreement.

Mara scoffed. "Kind of glad I got out of that squad," she muttered to me, "bunch of viscous animals."

I snickered. "So, what does that make you?"

She winked, sliding close enough to run a hand down my buttocks. "A *luscious* animal," she purred, almost making me snort in surprise.

I bit the inside of my cheek hard as I felt an enticing tingle run up my legs. Squeezing my eyes shut and snapping them open again, I diverted my focus to the X and O marks drawn across the map.

"We need them to think there's more of us than there are," Griffin was saying, "which means…heavy casualties are encouraged."

Whoops broke out from the Black Cats, followed by other voices across the floor.

"This will ensure the enemy's focus is divided," Mazet said, "and most importantly, not on the mountain itself."

Qian continued the explanation. "Soldiers under the Sacred Cloud have been installed throughout the nearby towns and cities to spread misinformation about our forces, heightening the terror of your attacks."

This time, the room remained quiet as the gravity of this mission sunk in.

Mazet spoke again, "The Street Dogs and Green Dragons will be responsible for taking the control center."

While I already knew this was what I signed up for, I tried to keep my breathing steady as Mazet continued her briefing.

"Dragons will cover the rear, keeping attention diverted and only as a last resort, attacking the center."

The holo changed one more time, depicting a single figure standing among a crowd. His face blinked slightly in surprise when I realized the person…was me. And not an image of me, but a recording. Of me. Standing with my mouth agape and a befuddled look on his face.

I snapped my mouth shut and Mazet spoke again. "Sergeant Lilly, if you please?"

She motioned me up to the front of the room. Chewing on my cheek and heart pounding in my ears, I approached, trying not to shove over any soldiers on my way up.

"Sergeant Lilly will lead the Street Dogs into the mountain and find the main command console, turning the weapons back on Lightbar's HQ or disabling them altogether," Mazet said, once I'd joined her at the podium.

"Cut off the head of the snake!" someone shouted in accented English, though I couldn't tell who it was.

"Disable them!" someone else shouted. "We're not monsters!" I realized it was Mara.

I looked at her, but she wouldn't meet my gaze. I already knew her stance on the bombs and, after my travels through China, I now almost agreed with her. These people had faces…had *lives*…a fact that became clearer with every town I visited.

Mazet raised a hand, calming the voices before a full-on argument broke out.

"This is not an open forum!" Mazet scolded and the room dropped into silence. "We are leaving this decision to Sergeant Lilly and his commanding officers," she said, "Trust them to make the right choice based on the circumstances."

The sweat froze on my brow, and for a moment, I forgot how to breathe. *My* decision? I looked at Ames, and the captain gave me a firm nod. His confidence in me had never wavered, but mine had.

I popped a weak smile to the congregation, grasping my clammy hands tighter behind my back and hoping I didn't look as pathetic as I felt.

"Do you want to say anything encouraging?" she whispered after my silence stretched too long.

I cleared my throat. "We got this!" I said lamely. The Americans laughed and even Healey looked amused.

"Yes we do," Mazet smiled, "Thank you, Sergeant."

I nodded once and slunk back through the crowd avoiding eye-contact as much as possible.

"Well, that was terrifying," I whispered to Mara.

"We got this!" JR prodded me in the ribs.

"I hate you," I bantered back.

Mara snorted.

"Thank you, General," Qian Gen said, with his hands clasped behind his back. "If you permit me an indulgence, I would explain. Five hundred years ago, our country was subjugated by the English and after centuries of resistance, we were able to throw off that rule. But we made a mistake, and the new government was weak and beset by consumerism. We allowed the corporations to gain a foothold and overtake us. No longer. The people are going to take over them."

The Chinese soldiers in the room applauded politely. The Americans just looked confused. Did we need more reasons to destroy the CORPs? I know I didn't…the destruction at Xi'an and the following broadcast were enough reasons for me to want to kill Rose a thousand times over.

"We will be setting out in one week's time, during the Dark Moon."

One week. I had a week to force myself to face the fears that had plagued me since my promotion to sergeant—to cast away the uncertainty, the crushing weight of responsibility, and the worry that I wasn't enough. I was sure I had done harder things, though I couldn't think of what.

When the time came, would I be able to detach myself enough to make the hard choices, no matter how much it hurt?

* * * * *

"You Americans are so funny," The Ox said in his heavily accented English.

That evening, five of us clustered around the common room table—all Americans, plus Mendez—for our first Mandarin lesson from Niu, even though JR and Mara were far more advanced in the language. Regardless, I appreciated everyone's support.

"Why ever would you say that?" JR asked with an attempted dramatic flip of his knife. He dropped it and everyone laughed.

"What is it means, 'We got this?'"

"It means um, like…" I stammered. How did one explain your slang without using other slang to do it? Words were not my strong suit.

"Wŏmen néng zuò dào. But add a 'fuck yeah!' at the end," Mara helped with a smile.

"Ha!" The Ox said, almost spitting out his beer. "You see, I learn from you, too. And you are right, boss," he said, slapping me on the shoulder blade with a hand like a sledge. "We can tā mā de do this!"

Coughing, I sputtered.

"Boss," JR teased and turned to The Ox, "See? Has a good ring to it, doesn't it?"

"Remind me to slug you later," I muttered to JR, but the slick Sway just gave me a languid grin and went back to his drink.

"Niu, what is this Dark Moon?" I asked The Ox, trying to distract myself from JR's antics.

The Tank smiled, "Americans call it the New Moon. We believe it is a good time for beginnings. Starting the operation at that time will bring luck to the endeavor."

"Good omens," Chet said in his gravelly voice. "I like the sound of that." He gave me a wink.

Nodding back, I tried to hold on to that hope into the evening, but found myself staying up way too late, pacing about my room.

"Shit is getting real," I muttered to myself. "Shit is getting real, and you are falling apart. Stop that!" I snapped at my racing heart, pounding on my chest and wiping my sweaty palms on my pants for the millionth time.

I drew cold water from the small sink and splashed it across my face. It stung my eyes and tasted slightly salty, invoking a feeling of nostalgia for a beach I'd never visited.

"I just need a plan." All good missions started with a plan.

Many bad ones did too....I thought back to the debacle at Query's compound and winced. I thought about the fate of the Council and the casualties in Sky plaza. The ruined city of Xi'an. Tears tickled the corners of my eyes, and I scrubbed at my face in frustration.

"This time will be different," I said. "This is *not* the time to break down."

"Who ya' talking to?" JR asked, striding into my room.

Mara followed.

I turned my face away. "Don't you guys know how to knock?" I couldn't bear even JR and Mara seeing me like this.

"Rob, we know better than to knock." JR said with a chuckle.

"Yeah, then you'd just lock the door," Mara confirmed.

They were right. "Dammit! You two officially know me too well," I attempted a snarl, but it mostly came out tired. "What are you doing in here?"

"We're staging an intervention," JR continued. "We can hear you stomping and muttering across the entire boat. Both Mendez and Chet have proposed that Mara knock you out so we can all get some sleep."

"Though Mendez did suggest I could do it with booze," Mara laughed.

"Shit…I'm sorry." I flopped onto the bed.

The two sat down next to me, one on each side. This really was an intervention.

"Rob, what's going on?" JR asked.

There, in front of my two closest friends, I broke down, burying my face in my hands. "I don't know what to do…" I groaned. "This mission… the decision…there's so much pressure. Why was *I* chosen for it?"

"Because Ames and Healey believe in you," Mara said.

"Why not the Black Cats? They're mostly Tanks and tough as fuck."

"They don't have a you," she replied.

"Besides, most of them are as dumb as rocks, which may be an insult to the rocks," JR added.

He yelped as Mara slapped the back of his head.

"What?" he whispered to her.

"Not helping!" she snapped back.

I groaned again. "Still, I don't know if I can do it. What if I screw up?"

"We'll have to find another way," JR interrupted. Warm reassurance washed over me. My shoulders sagged and I took a deep, cleansing breath, releasing a muttered curse at the end of it.

"JR, you're a prick," I mumbled. "Stop it."

"It's working though isn't it?" He raised his eyebrows. "I know you want to do a good job. And you will. Hell, you've already done incredible things."

I snorted. "Like what?"

"Seriously, Rob. Don't make me do this. I hate pep talks."

I couldn't help but tease him. "Well, you *are* the one who got the pep talk Skill. So, pep away."

JR rolled his eyes. "Fine. You hacked the mechin' awful datachip we got from that whack-job cyborg. You literally locked yourself in your bunk for days to get it done."

"Yeah," I grumbled. "I think that's the definition of insanity."

"You managed to make me respect you," JR continued.

I gave him a hard look. "Now I know *that's* the definition of insanity."

"No," Mara said sternly. "That's called dedication. Ever since I met you, you've been focused on doing the right thing. You care less about duty or honor and more about people."

I blushed. "I mean it's not…"

"Look," Mara continued, "when I was in the brig in Xi'an, no one else bothered to visit me. Not even the officers who'd put me there. *You* cared. If it weren't for you—I don't know where I would be—but it wouldn't be here."

"And I probably would've been killed a long time ago," JR joked.

"You may not feel like a leader, but whether you like it or not, you are," she said. "You believed in something when you got here. No matter what you say, I don't think it was really for money or glory. Maybe you don't see it, but I did. The minute we made eye contact, I knew you were a leader. Ames saw it. And Healey. Now Mazet does, too."

"You're right," I mumbled to Mara. "I don't see it."

"The good ones never do," JR said. "But what I see?" He paused, giving me that sharp, unapologetic look he'd perfected over the years. "What I see is a scared, self-righteous bastard who'd rather bury his head in a datachip than be here."

I stared at JR, his words hitting harder than I wanted to admit. My gut twisted, and I opened my mouth to snap back, but nothing came out. He wasn't wrong. I *hated* that he wasn't wrong.

"Can you stop being fucking right, for a change?" I growled at him.

JR smirked, leaning back like he'd just won a game only he knew we were playing. "Not in my skill set, boss," he said, crossing his arms, "but we need that self-righteous bastard to take the damn lead. We're all with you."

"Just, look in the mirror," Mara said with a kiss on my cheek. "Eventually, you'll see what I see."

"And until then," JR bumped me with his shoulder, "you'll stumble along, and we'll be here to cover for you."

For once, I didn't argue. I just nodded, letting their words settle like the first light in a very long night.

- 27 -
C.E. 2253 June 16
2200 hours

"Alrighty, boys and girls," our pilot's velvety voice floated through the cabin of the hovervan. "We're about twenty kilometers from touch down."

The day we headed to the KEWP Command Center marked my first full year in China. Following the altercation between Mara and Cheng, an uneasy truce had settled over my squad. On the plus side, after realizing Mara knew enough Mandarin to call them out, no one threw shade in front of me again. I could not control what they said behind my back, but I would take the victories I was given, however small.

It unsettled me more than I wanted to admit that I didn't seem like a competent leader. Charger's Balls, I was only twenty-four, doing the best I could. I'd had one great idea—breaking a mech force at a key moment and saving rebels in Xi'an—and a lucky tip that led me to the city's former mayor. Those two moments earned me a promotion, maybe too soon. Ames saw something in me, though I had no idea what it was. Chewing on the inside of my lip, I resolved to try harder—to fake it if I had to—and hopefully complete this mission without getting anyone killed.

We sat in silence in the dim cab of the hovervan, the faces of my crew bathed by the ambient light of the retreating city. General Qian had outfitted us in the latest high-tech gear, much fancier than my previous set. The sleek black helmet of my new radlon suit contained a slew of sensory equipment, monitoring both my vitals and the environment around me. To a regular person, these monitoring systems were indispensable, but I found the constant activity distracting.

We each carried an energy pistol as well as a mechanical revolver, in case Ru needed to fry everything with his Skill, along with several blades of choice. Handhelds, strapped to our forearms, contained all the info we'd need for this job and comm units connected us with each other as well as Captain Ames, who accompanied the Green Dragons in our cover fire.

I watched my squad, trying to gauge the temperature of the crew. Mara stared out the window, ever alert, scanning the blackness beyond, and JR slouched, though the rapid tapping of his foot belied his feigned indifference.

201

Chet, as usual, wore his perpetually bored grimace.

The others were harder to read, besides The Ox who had an almost silly smile on his face as if he was looking forward to this task. Ru and Jun held their faces in matching blank masks, their chests rising slowly with their breaths and Yaozu continued to scrutinize us. Her unsettling blue eyes practically glowed in the dimness and darted between us, becoming unfocused. I pushed all the confidence I could into my Aura, hoping she wouldn't see how nervous I was.

I had no idea about Cheng. He'd spent the entire ride so far with his eyes closed. I'd have thought he was sleeping, save for the deliberate shifting movements and the fiddling with his gear. He must have felt my gaze on him, for he suddenly opened his eyes, studying me.

"Sergeant Lilly, we have a plan?" he asked.

"Yes," I replied.

"You going to tell us? Or do we read your mind?"

"Of course," I said, in an attempt not to stammer over my words. I'd been waiting for the right time, but I feel like I may have waited too long. "I was just…waiting until you finished your nap," I finished dryly trying to cover up my blunder.

He narrowed his eyes at me, frown deepening, but only said, "I'm listening."

Good pivot, I told myself when I caught Jun's smile from the corner of my eye. *I got this. I've totally got this.*

Mara also smiled, making a fist and punching me in the thigh lightly. I flinched. Even a light blow from a Tank still stung.

"Okay, listen up," I said in a low voice, "when we get to the prairie, we split in two groups—Alpha and Beta—to take advantage of the scrub and boulders to both sides of the track. Alpha with me: Rostbane, Yaozu, Ru, and Dark. Beta with Cheng: Niu, Ferryman, Jun. There will be guards…"

I pulled up a small holo of the Taihang Mountain Range and the awkward rock pillar right in the center. The officers had marked off a glowing yellow area as the entrance to the control center.

"…here and here. Yaozu, you'll be on the lookout for Alpha. Jun…"

I paused. I'd read the profiles of all my crew and knew what Jun's mods could do, but the ingrained distrust of mechs still made me balk. Was she trustworthy?

"With respect, Sir, my sensors can see things like Yu Jie can," she said, tilting her head at Yaozu.

I nodded in understanding. "Then you can help identify the guards but only get involved in the fighting as a last resort. Same with you, Yaozu. We need our eyes."

I glanced at the Auraseer and was surprised to find a slight smile on her face as she nodded along with my plan.

"Dark, Rostbane, Niu, Ferryman, I want you four to neutralize the guards—quickly and quietly. We don't want them calling for backup. Once we make it to the door, I'll unlock it."

I paused as The Ox was quietly translating. So far everyone nodded.

"We have to make it to the door without a brawl," I stressed. "Whoever's inside must *not* know we're coming."

Ru said something in Mandarin.

"He says he could spike the door if needed." The Ox translated.

"Only as a last resort. That'll draw a lot of attention." I knew Sparks and their unpredictable temperament. In terms of making a scene, I trusted them least of all.

The Ox relayed the message. Ru shook his head but shrugged.

"Mendez will remain with the vehicle. If we are not back by dawn, leave us."

"Really?" she asked from the front seat. I could tell by her tone; she didn't like the idea.

"Yes." I nodded for the squad to see my confidence, even though I was terrified. "We'll find the emergency escape tunnel if we have to."

Mendez groaned an assent.

"Any questions?"

"Sergeant Lilly," Cheng began slowly, "you run stealth mission before?"

Well, that question took me by surprise. "Not as such, no," I replied truthfully. The Auraseer would know if I lied. "Do you have some concerns?"

Cheng shrugged. "Americans like you. They go in with, as you say, guns blazing. Not so good for stealth, yes?"

"Do I really seem like the guns-blazing type?" I asked, looking directly at JR.

The Sway just snorted but shook his head.

"Good," I continued. "Because that's not my plan."

"What we do in case of failure?" Cheng prodded, catching me off guard again. "Do you have a backup plan?"

"Get the hell out, I guess," I said with a shrug. No, I did not have a backup plan. That might've been a good idea.

"We should set a rendezvous point in case we get separated," Mara said, flicking a glance at me. "If you think that would be wise, Sir." She gave me a small wink.

"Uh…yes. Great idea," I said. Spinning around the three-dimensional map of the area, I pointed at a large boulder several yards away, standing alone. "There. Everyone got it?"

A series of nods responded.

"But…we're not going to fail," JR said with projected confidence, "or get separated. We got this."

Cheng didn't seem convinced. "You know this will be dangerous mission, yes?"

Would this guy just shut up! "I do," I confirmed. "If you are too scared," I continued acidly, "feel free to stay in the van."

"I am not scared," Cheng said slowly. "I am cautious. And you should be, too."

His words stung more than I wanted to admit, but I shoved the feeling aside. There wasn't time to dwell on personal grudges or bruised egos—not when everything was riding on this mission. I really hoped, when this was all done, he and I would be able to sit down and resolve our differences.

As the hovervan settled quietly in a copse of small, lush trees, I steeled myself for the task.

"Okay, it's go time!" I said as the door to the van slid open.

We exited the van as quietly as possible, though its whirring engines already sounded too loud.

"Alpha Squad moving into position," I spoke into my comm, keeping my voice low.

"Roger that. And good luck, Sergeant Lilly," Ames answered, his voice crackling through the distortion. It sounded calm, but I knew better.

"Beta Squad moving into position," Cheng echoed me. His squad crouched low in the grass, their movements precise and soundless, awaiting further orders.

I gripped my pistol tightly against my side and adjusted my visor. The darkness was almost suffocating—no moonlight to guide us, only the faint glow of the JJJ casting an orange halo over the distant mountains. The air was damp and heavy, clinging to us like a warning.

Ahead of me, Yaozu raised three fingers to her left and two to her right. Alpha Squad had one more guard to handle than Beta Squad—just as expected.

"All right. Everyone move out," I ordered into the comm, my voice steady despite the tightness in my chest.

Beta Squad moved, The Ox taking point with the others following in a disciplined line. They vanished into the shadows, leaving only the faint rustle of leaves behind.

I lead my team north, over a small berm and through a tangle of underbrush.

"Three mechs. Ten meters ahead." Yaozu said through the comm, our helmets muffling the sound. "One's laying down. Maybe asleep. But hidden."

I nodded and motioned for Mara to circle around, approaching the first guard from the back.

"Boss," JR whispered into the comm, "I got the second one."

I nodded, and JR set off down the track, not bothering to cover up his movements. His mumbled words drifted through the comm, though I couldn't make them out.

I turned back to the first guard. He held an automatic rifle in his silver hands, face covered by a black respirator. A shadow slipped from the trees, small frame turned in on itself. Mara had to stand on her toes to get her arms around the mech's neck, but she did it so quickly they had no time to react. The mech went down. Then, Mara stomped, and I felt the inaudible shriek of dying tech rattle through my bones.

"Took out the transmitter," Mara said through the comm, her voice hushed.

"Good call," I whispered back, following Yaozu to the third guard.

Meanwhile, JR spoke to the second guard who stood frozen, head cocked, listening to whatever lies JR was spewing. He flipped up his visor, bringing his face close to the guard's and whispered something in their ear. They dropped their gun, JR catching it before it could hit the ground. Then, he jammed it under the guard's chin and eased him. A flash of blue light. The skin-tingling hiss of an energy weapon. JR stood up, tucking the extra pistol into his belt and wiping his hands.

"Well," JR said into the comm, a trembling undertone to his voice, "that's one shot I didn't miss."

I suppressed a shudder, crouching down further into the scrubby plants, unable to decide which was more unsettling—Mara's violence, or JR's deadly persuasion.

"One meter," Yaozu said, pointing to the prone guard.

I pulled out my knife and groped for the mech. I felt for the cold metal of their shoulder and rolled them over. But they sat up before I could act. Violet eyes, illuminated by some inner fire, met mine and filled with fear. I froze, knife pressed to her throat, unable to drive it home. She had long lashes and wore makeup to complement her eyes. For a moment, she was not a mech or a guard but simply a person.

My hesitation allowed her to recover, and she reached up, grabbing my neck in her mechanical hand and squeezing tight. The vibrations in that hand made my teeth chatter, and I gasped for breath. I lost my grip on the knife.

Ru slapped the mech's helmet and disabled her mods with a directed pulse of his EMP. The hand snapped open, and I slouched, panting. Before I could recover, Ru snatched my knife off the ground and plunged it into the mech's open visor five times. Blood splashed across his helm and mine. Her lower body writhed for escape. She gurgled until all the life bled away.

Casually, Ru wiped the knife on the dead mech's uniform, and I trembled, trying to get my churning stomach under control. Sure, I'd killed lots of mechs so far, but none so close. None so—personal.

"Thanks," I croaked to Ru, snapping open my visor to try and get more air. "Even though I told you to wait with Yaozu," I muttered, though didn't think he'd understand me.

"Precaution," he said, without emotion.

"Don't trust me?" I asked him, staring hard at the visor of his helmet, wishing I could see his eyes.

He just gave me a shrug, holding up his bloody hands.

I sighed. "Let's keep moving," I said, sending a questioning glance at Yaozu.

She nodded, confirming my suspicion that none of our targets would be getting up. We met at the entrance, and if I hadn't felt the heavy tech hum inside the mountain, I would have never guessed this blank rock face led to anything but more rock. Beta squad joined us moments later and I gave Cheng a questioning thumbs-up sign. He slapped his hand against his helmet and made a sigh I could hear through the comm but returned the gesture with a note of sarcasm.

I turned my focus to the doorway, removing my glove and caressing the edges with sensitive fingertips. My inspection proved that the door was not made of rock, but of textured metal cleverly disguised to blend in with the surrounding mountain.

"No visible openings, ports, or scanners," I recorded in my comm, "but it's wired. I can feel it."

"Boss," JR said, and pressed something smooth into my palm.

A chipped badge, slightly bent and splattered with blood.

"Good job. Now where the hell do I put it?"

I looked at the others and everyone shrugged or stared at me blankly through their visors.

"I need a card reader, or a lock, or…*something*," I snapped, groping blindly in the dark.

My heart raced and my head still felt light from earlier. *Think, Robert, think!* I chided myself. I'd never met a door I couldn't unlock.

"Boss, movement ahead," Chet warned through the comm.

Sure enough, dark shapes and flashes of light in the distance indicated a fight—the Green Dragons watching our back. However, one shape broke off from the fray, running toward us.

"I need more time," I ground out.

"Copy that," he responded.

A small rock rose from the ground and flew away. It slammed into the head of a patrolling guard like a bullet. I didn't hear the crunch, but I could imagine what it would sound like. The shadowy figure fell. They did not rise.

I still couldn't find the opening. Panicking now I resisted the urge to ask, once again, for a solution. I was the leader. I *had* to figure this out. I took a deep breath, closed my eyes, and traced the threads of energy. Something thrummed through the soles of my feet.

I felt a tap on my shoulder. It was Ru, who was pointing to where I stood.

I was getting to that, I thought with irritation. Nonetheless, I placed my palm on the ground and found a panel. With a click, it slid open, and a panel rose from the floor.

I pressed the ID against the scanner.

GENETIC SAMPLE REQUIRED, it read.

"Damn it," I muttered. "Fucking two-factor authorization." I looked at Mara. "We need a…sample from JR's guard."

I attempted to sound confident, though my voice cracked at the end, when I realized I was commanding Mara to dismember a dead guy.

She nodded, but Ru grabbed her arm. "Wait."

He looked at me, his dark eyes sparkling, then at the panel. Reluctantly, I gave the Spark a nod. Trust went both ways.

"Everyone back," I said. "He's gonna blow it."

We crammed against the far side of the doorway, pressing into the shadows as much as possible. A spine-tingling fizzle crawled across my skin, as if my limbs had fallen asleep and were waking up all at once. The glow on the card reader dimmed, power bleeding from it like a life force. Ru caught the console as it fell back into the earth, lowering it down with a muffled click. The door drifted open, and I jammed my revolver into the crack to keep it from closing.

"Jun? Yaozu?" I asked, motioning to the door with my head.

"We should be able to enter unimpeded," Yaozu confirmed.

Even unlocked, it took both The Ox and Mara to force the heavy powerless door open. Every scrape of the mechanisms sounded too loud. It set my nerves on edge. Security devices, maglocks and alarms sat dead on the door's open edge.

I silently cursed myself. I had been too preoccupied with getting the door open to think about the sensors. Ru's EMP, controlled with a finesse I hadn't expected, had taken care of everything at once.

"Nice work," I said and flashed him an encouraging smile.

He returned with a single, confident nod.

I entered first, stretching my senses for active tech.

It was as if the building swallowed the last remnants of the moon's ambient light. The hallway was darker even than outside. My visor's night vision struggled to adjust, flickering faint outlines of walls and shadows. Then it hit me—a thrumming hum, low and insistent, vibrating in my chest and the hollow of my skull. The tech here was alive and dense. Cameras. Servers. Computers. Mechs.

Holding up my hand for the others to wait, I slowed my breathing, letting the noise flood me. The harmless signals—the HVAC systems, overhead lights, background currents—rolled off like static. My focus narrowed, searching instead for the sharp edges: laser trip wires, active security mechs.

The visor wasn't enough. I pushed it up to my forehead, the cool air brushing my brow. Eyes squinting into the blackness, I trusted the signals under my skin more than the tech strapped to my face.

Left. A camera.

Tapping Chet's shoulder, I pointed at a round globe with the faintest glint of red in its glass orb. The 'Net twisted his hand, and the unit exploded into thousands of glass shards. He shepherded them gently to the floor with only the barest tinkle.

Right. Tripwire.

I touched Ru and gestured at the small round disc at ankle-level about a meter away. He slid along the wall until he was able to send his EMP radiating through its wires. The weapon buzzed with a low frequency and went dead.

"Guard," Jun said with the barest whisper, pointing toward an auxiliary hallway. She waved a single finger, while her mech hands gripped twin knives.

I gave her a nod to take care of it. She disappeared down the hallway, surprisingly lithe for being part machine. A moment of silence later, she returned, a ruddy reflection on the blades of her knives. We continued on.

"Two men, ten o'clock," Yaozu said, tugging me back into the shadows.

I nudged The Ox ahead. He took one down with an elbow to their face, and the other by collapsing their windpipe.

I thanked Greysoft for Query's map, which I'd loaded onto my handheld. Otherwise, I'd have gotten us hopelessly lost in this warren of tunnels, supply closets, and server alcoves. The map led us to the final turn. Just ahead, a heavy, reinforced door loomed in the dim corridor, the faint hum of tech spilling out from behind it. My squad froze, weapons poised, breaths shallow.

Yaozu held up both hands. All fingers splayed wide on the right, thumb and forefinger jutting out on the left. I motioned silently, directing Mara and The Ox to take point, their steps impossibly light for such heavy hitters. Behind them, Chet rolled a small rock between his fingers, the promise of precise destruction. Jun twirled a blade in her mech-hand, its edges glinting in the dim light, while the rest of us readied pistols.

Inside that room, seven occupants sat in their semi-circle of desks—unaware of the storm about to break through their door.

I glanced at Ru. Sparks like him could turn the tide of a battle in seconds—or fry everything within a hundred meters. His nerves were steady now, but I'd seen what happened when that control slipped. If Ru lost it here, we wouldn't just lose the mission. We'd lose everything.

I raised a hand, signaling a hold, and whispered into the comm, "Ready up. Quick and clean. On my mark."
This was it. No second chances.

2300 hours

Everyone's eyes were on me. I nodded. Time to move.

I activated the touch sensor. The door swished open, quiet as a breath. None of the occupants turned. That was a good sign.

Mara and The Ox slid into position, low and fast. But Chet's rock flew too soon, catching number three sharply behind her ear. I cursed as the mech's head slammed against the control panel with a sickening thud.

The room exploded into action. The Ox reached his target, number one, and even with the man's reinforced titanium spinal plates, the Tank snapped his neck like a chicken bone. Mara lunged toward her mark, number two, but he wheeled out of the way, flinging himself into a metal cabinet and pulling the door closed. She slammed a fist against it, but it was wedged shut.

With a growl, she whirled on a secondary target, number five, knocking the considerable bulk of flesh and machine from her chair. She thrust a knee into the woman's chest, while her fist pummeled her the ocular sending up a shower of sparks that lit up Mara's face like a firework.

Meanwhile, Jun Li crawled spider-like at number four, wrapping her human arms around the man's mouth, holding in his warning shout. Two of her mech arms slashed at his throat in a brutal dual-knife display, spraying blood in a long gout across the controls.

JR fired multiple shots into the room, but managed to miss number six completely, covering the screens and consoles with smoking holes. Aiming my own laser pistol, I took him down with one shot, silently berating JR's aim. But, maybe I shouldn't blame him. *He* had to practice. For me, the gun just told me exactly where to shoot. Hard to miss that way.

Somehow, number seven had made it to her feet. She stood at a far console, tapping furiously on the touchpad.

Why is she not dead yet?

"Someone get her!" I shouted a second later, raising my pistol.

She turned at my shout. JR made an annoyed growl, his energy pistol fizzing out for a recharge. When number seven saw us, she gaped. We must have looked like demons—armored, snarling, and covered in blood.

I fired into her open mouth.

Her head rocked back, and she teetered, slumping onto the control pad.

I rushed over, shoving her to the floor. Though it hummed with a boot-up sequence, the computer hadn't sent any outgoing transmissions.

"Thank Greysoft," I muttered, jamming in a sleep command. Then, I looked at Cheng. "Wasn't she supposed to be yours?" I asked, making sure he understood the implication of my words.

He shrugged, holding his gun at the floor. "Rifled jammed," he said shortly.

"Bullshit," I growled. "That's not a rifle…and energy doesn't jam."

The other man just shrugged and flashed me an annoyed expression of his own. "Gun no work."

I scowled, stepping closer to Cheng, the tension between us palpable. "Gun no work? Fine," I snapped, "this one does." I pushed my own gun against his chest, letting go without caring if he caught it.

Cheng opened his mouth, but I raised a hand, cutting him off. "We're not here to screw around. We have a job to finish."

I turned to the console, forcing myself to refocus. Behind me, JR muttered about blood on his visor, but I tuned him out. We didn't have time to bicker.

"Jun, check the closet," I barked, pointing toward the small alcove.

"Niu, help her. Mara, seal the door. JR, sweep the bodies and double-check the gear. We're not done here."

"Wait," Yaozu intoned, deliberately scanning around the room. She had on the deep, piercing stare of an Auraseer looking for someone hidden. "Number eight," she said, a hint of embarrassment in her voice.

"There's an eighth person here?" I asked, incredulous Then from the corner of my eye I noticed the slowly spinning chair at the edge of the room. Someone had left, and quickly.

"Not here," Yaozu answered. "That way." She pointed at a dark indent behind the chair. Scanning through the plans for this base on my ocular, I found the spot. A hallway led deeper into the mountain toward a washroom, server room, and emergency exit.

"Shit! How could you have missed one, Yaozu?" I snarled at her.

She flinched. "I'm sorry…. I didn't see…. the walls underground…" she stammered, the cold composure replaced by trembling fear. "I can find…"

I took a breath to keep from shouting. "Fine," I said through clenched teeth, "Cheng and Mara, go with her. Let's hope this operative just had to piss."

The other two options could make things far harder for us.

"Copy," the three assented, though Mara gave me a worried backward glance.

I grabbed her hand. Neither Tank wore a helmet—they didn't really need it—just a set of ocular glasses and a comm clipped to one ear. Pulling off my own helm, I leaned in as if I were going to kiss her but instead whispered close to her ear.

"Be careful. Something's not right."

She craned her neck to look me in the eye. "I always am," she breathed against my lips, though I could feel the nervous twitch in her arms. I knew neither Yaozu nor Cheng could hurt her, but I worried, nonetheless.

Turning my attention to the rest of the squad, I snapped, "What the hell are you waiting for?" I pointed at the cabinet. "Christmas?"

"It's locked," JR said without amusement.

"Sorry, Boss," the Ox replied with that goofy apologetic grin. "No problem."

With a crunch and metallic clatter, he ripped off the door and dropped it to the ground.

I traced my fingers over the keyboard of the nearest computer, waking it up from sleep. The screen flickered to life, displaying a labyrinth of menus and commands. Ignoring the standard navigation, I accessed the system's core functions, searching for the launch control protocols.

"Boss?" JR said uncertainly. His voice seemed far away. "We have an…issue."

"Take care of it, Rostbane," I ground out, not turning around. I couldn't find the outlink, and time was running out. I focused all my attention on the computer, pinging the missile hangar, hundreds—thousands—of miles away.

UNDELIVERABLE.

What?

"Boss," JR said again.

I ignored him and tried again.

UNDELIVERABLE.

"Charger's Balls!" I cursed under my breath. Why did the pings keep getting deflected?

"Sergeant Lilly?" The Ox said.

I continued to ignore them and tried one last time.

UNDELIVERABLE.

"Robert. ROB!" JR snapped.

Finally, I ripped my eyes away from the computer with a frustrated growl. "What?!"

"You need to take a look at this."

I stomped over, even as warning bells something screamed in my head.

The mech was curled in the closet, his wheeled lower half sticking into the air, wheel spinning slowly. He held something in his shaking hand. I couldn't quite tell what it was, only that it had a large dial on its face, a switch in the middle.

"Liánmǐn," the man muttered, tears in his eyes.

"What?" I snapped.

"He asks for mercy," The Ox translated.

I felt toward the device in the man's hands. A cold, darkness blossomed before my rib cage. A sound like splintering wood and a pain in my chest followed, the sense of loss leaving me gasping. I knew exactly what the man held.

"Drop the detonator," I said, biting back the tremble in my voice.

But he just shook his head, repeating the word for mercy, knuckles growing white with the force of his grip. He wouldn't look me in the eyes.

Suppressing a surge of nausea, I pulled the trigger, hitting the man in the forehead. The sound of the shot reverberating through the cabinet tore at me. The man slumped to the floor, detonator tumbling from lifeless hands. I released a shaky breath.

Mercy. In standard warfare, the Geneva Conventions emphasized humane treatment of the hors de combat. The face of the dead guard from outside gave me an accusatory glare. But not at the expense of my own people. Not at the expense of the mission.

JR watched me turn, shock and revulsion rippling from him in gentle waves. Chet let out a humorless chuckle, masking his own discomfort. The rest remained stoic, but I sensed their unease.

I remembered Major Healey's words.

"This is not the time for mercy," I said, my voice cold, making sure to look at each of them in turn. "Make sure you remember that. Remember Xi'an."

Five pale faces nodded back.

I gave my attention back to the control panel, determined to complete our objective, even as the weight of my actions pressed heavily on my conscience. Agonizing seconds passed by as I watched the *Connecting* icon spin.

CONNECTION UNAVAILABLE. PING ATTEMPTS EXCEEDED. COMMENCING EMERGENCY SHUT DOWN.

"No!" I shouted, slamming both fists on the console in agitation. The desktop touchscreen cracked, spider-like fractures crawling across its surface.

"Boss?" Chet asked me in a low voice. He placed his hand on my shoulder. "Do you hear that?" He pointed up.

"Hear what?"

A faint metallic scratching. I looked toward the ceiling. A shadow drifted over the vent, then a panel popped loose—the sharp crunch of metal, a crash. JR grunted as the corner of the vent clipped his head as it fell. He crumpled.

We stood frozen in surprise. Even Chet, the quickest of us all, only managed a half-raised hand in defense. Something small and dark descended through the open hole, its trajectory almost languid. I don't know if I heard or felt the ticking of the device, but pain seared through my body like fire. So much potential energy in such a small package.

"Ox," I managed to choke out and pointed at the device, which ticked down the seconds. "Bomb!"

At that word, the squad burst into action.

The Ox launched himself at my feet, bowling me over as he curled his massive form around the bomb. Chet and I went down in a tangle of arms and legs. We scrambled for cover, but there wasn't much to hide behind, save for the bolted-down chairs.

The too-familiar tingling of Ru's EMP trickled through my pain, intensifying to the sensation of razorblades dragging across my skin. The computers behind me popped and fizzled as the EMP fried their internals. My ocular croaked, losing power. I ripped the comm's from my head, its death rattle shooting daggers through my eardrums and covered my head.

A muffled boom launched The Ox across the room, slamming him into a bay of computers, which exploded in a shower of flaming shards. Shrapnel pelted us and darkness fell on the control room, as deep as the bottom of a mineshaft. I stretched my eyes wide, despite the throbbing in my head, but couldn't make out anything.

A deep, bone-aching silence followed the explosion, save for the ringing in my ears. No other sounds rang, no buzz of lights or hum of servers, and no electric pulses reverberated through my nerves. A distinct odor lingered in the air—burnt hair and chemical smoke. Dead. All our tech, and theirs too, had been toasted by Ru's EMP.

My whole body felt numb and heavy.

A sudden, jangling crash shattered the silence, followed by the unmistakable sounds of a struggle—grunts, the scrape of metal against metal, a heavy thud. A brief flicker of light illuminated the scene: Jun stood over a fallen mech, three of her four mechanical arms gleaming faintly in the dim light cast from the fourth, which held a bright blue flame. The dead mech lay at her feet with twisted limbs, one human hand reaching for escape, and a dark pool spreading around their head.

The Ox groaned, a low rumble that broke the stunned silence. He pushed himself up, shaking off debris. "Everybody…good?" he coughed, his voice strained but steady.

I nodded, though I wasn't sure he could see me, and a chorus of assents followed from everyone but JR, who still lay unconscious on the floor.

"Thanks to you," I said, through a tight throat, untangling myself from Chet.

The Ox managed a grim smile, wiping soot from his face. "Just doing my job."

As if he hadn't just taken a bomb to the gut, The Ox crouched down beside JR like a protective beast. I pulled out my gyro-powered flashlight and wound it up. Dim light radiated over JR's sheet-white face.

"He'll be all right," The Ox said.

He held something under JR's nose, and the Sway's eyes fluttered open. Blood ran through his golden hair, but the cut was superficial. I released a strained breath.

"Where the hell is your helmet?" I muttered, holding a canteen to his lips.

"Where's yours?" he slurred back.

Ru suddenly appeared by my side, his hawk-like face scrunched in agitation. "More!" he urged with tired breaths and pointed to the door.

"More…?" I breathed, but then I felt them.

"They are no dangerous now," Ru continued, "but soon."

Based on the scale of Ru's EMP, I gathered it had disabled those mechs, too. For now. It wouldn't take long for at least some of them to be back up and running.

"We're boned," I said to my squad without another thought. "We need to go."

"What…?" JR mumbled, his voice thick and groggy. "Go where?"

"I got you, buddy," The Ox encouraged, dragging JR to his feet. "What about you, Boss?"

I turned to Chet, buried half-deep inside an open computer panel and rummaging with something. His own flashlight emitted a dull yellow glow, illuminating the wires that spilled out around him.

"Go ahead," I said. "We'll follow."

The four of them made their silent way to the door.

"Ferryman," I said, "we need to go."

"Just a little insurance," he muttered.

I nudged his leg with my toe. "We can't contact the launcher. I already tried."

"Not the kind of insurance I was talking about," he replied, voice muffled around the light wedged between his teeth. "If you keep the hall clear, I'll follow soon."

This was no time to argue, though it pained me to leave one of my squad behind, even by his own wish. I kept him in my sight until the blackness of the hallway engulfed me.

Several yards down the hallway, I ran into something very solid and dropped my flashlight. It skittered across the floor, spinning until it settled its light against the far wall. I took a step backward, but someone grabbed my arm, yanking me close. The grip did not feel friendly. I thrust up a knee, impacting something far too solid to be human flesh.

Pain and shock lanced through my leg.

A mech in power armor.

I cursed through my teeth, struggling to pull my arm away.

The emergency lights flared on, stinging my eyes, the sulfur bulbs rumbling in deep bass notes. A bloody red glow down traveled down the hallway, revealing a line of mechs behind my captor, twenty in all, in various states of functionality. Some writhed on the ground, while others remained locked in place, only able to scowl angrily in my direction.

My captor gasped and again, I tried to pull away. Then, my eyes met his, and I assumed a similarly baffled expression. I recognized this man.

"You?" he grunted.

Close-cropped hair, stern expression, dead ocular unit hanging from a strap around his neck. The officer who'd scanned me in Lanzhou. He'd managed to free himself from his power armor, but one arm—half-modded from elbow to shoulder—hung uselessly at his side. The name on his jacket read Tristan.

"Me," I ground out, trying to think of a way to escape.

He threw himself into me. We tumbled to the ground, his half-meched right arm pressing down on my throat. I struggled to get him off, but even out of his armor, he was not small. His body weight alone rivaled my own, and his additional mods made him even heavier.

I grabbed the cold metal arm, trying to free my airway. He shifted just enough for me to wedge my arm between us. Slowly, I drew air in through my nose, pressing my lips together. I refused to give him the satisfaction of gasping.

He flailed on top of me, trying to get purchase, but his toes just slid across the smooth linoleum floor. Jerking his shoulder toward my face, he tried to use his dead mech arm to pin me, while his human arm sought leverage without releasing me from its grip. I fought to kick him off but only managed to paw at empty air.

Using my unbound hand, I pushed at his arm but from this angle, my pathetic attempts were ineffective. He slammed his forehead into mine. Stars danced across my vision. Fighting back the dizziness, I clawed at his face, keeping him from head-butting me a second time, but only barely. His hot breath wafted across my cheek, and the gnashing of his teeth sounded like the clicks of a giant beetle. He shifted, falling more heavily against me, and pressing down on my throat once more. The tenuous grasp I had on breath vanished.

"Sarge!" Chet called from behind.

I twisted my head just in time to see a knife flying towards me. I grabbed it from the air before it could cut me or fall into my enemy's hand.

With dark spots speckling my vision, I slashed at the mech's head. The knife made contact on the first blow, and the man roared. Blood sprayed out, the hot, viscous fluid clinging to my skin like a living thing.

Sacrificing balance to clutch at his face, Tristan fell forward, his head slamming against mine. The reek of hot copper coating my lips, made my stomach churn. I wrestled myself out from under the man before I could choke on my own vomit.

Chet helped me roll the struggling mech to one side. I rose to my hands and knees, choking and spitting out blood and sour bile. Chet dragged me to my feet. His revolver discharged over my shoulder. The crack sent a spike of pain through my ear.

I scanned the hallway. The deep sulfur glow from the S-lights disoriented me. Was the room spinning or was I? Blackness pulsed at the edges of my vision. Blood pounded in my skull. I placed a hand against the wall to steady myself, even as Chet tugged on the straps of my suit.

"Gotta go, Boss!" he urged, voice muffled beneath the ringing in my ears. He shot at another mech who was dragging himself toward us with one hand. "Not many shots in these mechanical poppers."

We skirted the grasping limbs of other soldiers barreling down the hallway. At some point, the ground must have turned to liquid—or I was suffering from a concussion—because I stumbled over nothing, spinning on my heel, then getting my legs tied beneath me.

"We have to keep moving," Chet said, pushing at me. "Still more."

Something tangled around my foot, and I finished the progression of my fall. I traced cable to the final soldier in the column—a bright wire, reflecting the deep red of the sulfur lights connected to his arm.

"Fuuuuck," Chet grunted, "that's Razorwire!"

Oh no, I thought. I'd only heard of this weapon on the HV, but never seen it, which had me assuming it was too cumbersome to use. They called it a new kind of monofilament, supposedly charged with energy to separate a person's cells. Fortunately, my thick boots offered some resistance as the wire pulled taut.

I kicked my leg in erratic panic, the hallway whirling around me. Dragging myself away, I attempted to dislodge the wire, but it only grew more tangled. Chet fired at the mech holding it, but his gun just clicked—the last bullet having left the chamber just seconds before—into a different mech.

"I need your gun!" he shouted to me as I flailed in a panic.

But I just raised my hands in defeat. I'd given my gun to Cheng but hadn't taken his. The wire bit into my boot, the song of the weapon floating through my mind.

Such a pretty song for such a deadly weapon, the idle part of my brain mused while the realistic part was still freaking out about losing a foot. I yanked my leg again.

The wire released its tension, uncoiling in one smooth motion. I just barely managed to turn my head and avoid kneeing myself in the teeth. I rolled away, knocking the back of my head against the floor, and coming to rest against a pair of boots.

"Robert!" Mara shouted, nudging me with her toe. "You gotta get up."

She held a barely conscious Cheng draped over her shoulders with a bandage around his upper thigh. It glistened black under the crimson lights.

"Finally got that son-of-a-mech," Chet panted, wiggling his fingers to indicate how he uncoiled the wire without touching it. Lines etched his face, the fatigue from over-using his Skill setting in.

"Thank Greysoft," I muttered while Chet and Mara helped pull me up. I still had both my feet. "Let's go."

We met up with JR and the others at the entrance, barreling through the doors and out into the starry night. I took stock of my squad.

"Yaozu?" I asked.

Mara shook her head. "I don't know," she heaved a breath. "Everything went dark. Mechs attacked us. Cheng…got shot."

"Rendezvous," Cheng mumbled behind Mara's back.

"Yes," I said, setting my resolve against the goosebumps prickling against my skin. "We go there. That's where we said we'd meet."

I absently scratched at my arm through my sleeve, but when the itching only got worse, I confirmed my biggest fear.

"More soldiers are coming," I shouted at my team. "We need to get outta here!"

"Sarge," Chet said, touching my shoulder. "I think it's time." He held up a small remote with a half-crazed smirk on his lips.

"What's this?"

That smirk widened, fully crazy now. "Our insurance."

I felt the click of the detonator—a thuddy, far-away pop, deep in my bones.

"Run!" I shouted at my squad.

Then, an explosion rocked the complex, the shock wave throwing us forward on unsteady feet.

- 28 -
C.E. 2253 June 17
0100 hours

Mara, black fatigues glistening under the cold light of the sparse starry sky, crouched over Cheng. The man lay motionless in the dirt, his face a bloodless pale. We'd run almost two miles into the dense forest before the adrenaline from the scuffle faded, slowing our steps. Now we rested, tucked into a small copse of fragrant, stunted trees. The location would have been peaceful were it not for the muffled *krump* of explosions and the *tat-tat-tat* of mag-gunfire in the distance—the misdirection squads at work.

"Where the hell is she!" I growled, shaking our one working comm, an ancient thing that had somehow managed to survive Ru's EMP. Yaozu still hadn't arrived, and there was no sign of Mendez.

"Boss," The Ox said, pointing at Cheng.

"One minute," I said, trying the comm again. What I didn't say was that my attempts at reaching Mendez were just an excuse. Someone else could have done it just as well, but I didn't want to face the reality of my wounded second.

Jun shoved past me, no attempt at deference in her haste. She carried strips of cloth and antiseptic in four of her hands from her portable med kit. She checked Cheng's wound, redoing the tourniquet on his leg. Concern creased her pale face, eyes shining almost white in the starlight. She cooed to him in soft Mandarin.

Cheng didn't respond, his chest rising with the only faintest breaths. Blood soaked his pants, and now the ground he lay on, as it streamed from the hole in his thigh. Finally, I uncurled myself from where I hunched over the comm and approached Mara, who sat with her hands in her lap and her shoulders hunched.

"What happened?"

She shook her head, wiping her shining face with the back of her hand, leaving a streak of blood in place of tears.

"It was so fast. One minute, we were alone in a hallway and the next surrounded by ten mechs. We tried to get to the exit, but it was chaos. I took them all down, but not before..." She gestured toward Cheng.

"Robert, I have some concerns," she continued, uncoiling herself with obvious effort. "Come."

Once we were away from the others, she leaned close. "There was no one there," she said, voice low.

"What do you mean, 'no one there?'"

"I mean," she said, rubbing her hand across her collarbone with a wince, "where Yaozu took us to look for that last operative…we didn't find anyone. But…"

"But what?"

"When the lights went down, I lost track of them. I think they turned down a different hallway than I did. I caught back up with Cheng during the scuffle, but he'd already been injured."

The sweat dried cold on my skin, but a red-hot cannonball dropped in my stomach. "You think Cheng had some other agenda?" I asked. "You don't think he…" I trailed off, unable to say what I was thinking.

But Mara picked up on it anyway. "No. I don't think he killed Yaozu," she said. "At least I hope not."

I shook my head. "I'll put it in my report," I said. "There's nothing else we can do."

Mara nodded, her expression unsettled and movements stiff.

"You okay?" I asked her.

"Yeah I'm fine," she said, stretching her shoulders back. "Got shot."

My heart caught in my throat. "How many times?" I snapped, trying to search her clothes for fresh bloodstains.

She wrinkled her nose. "Three…maybe four. Or more…" She shook her head. "Not sure. But I'm not a fan of it," she finished with a dry chuckle.

"Are you bleeding?" I took a protective step toward her, brushing her hand from her shoulder.

"I'm *fine*," she insisted. Pulling back the collar of her jacket, she showed me the beginnings of a large bruise marring her flawless skin. "Go help Cheng."

I gave her a frustrated huff but understood her point. I nodded.

"If we hadn't been separated," she said to my retreating back, "maybe I could've saved them…."

I froze, turning to her. She hunched and cradled one arm against her chest. Despite her defined musculature, right now she looked more like a lost teenager than a mech-killing Tank. My heart seized, and the weight of leadership so precariously balanced on my weary shoulders bore down like a massive boulder. I wanted to turn inside out, or melt into the ground, or do anything besides cause her grief.

"It's not your fault," I said, putting a gentle hand on her shoulder. "It's mine. If I hadn't sent you guys on a wild goose chase…"

Suddenly, her lost look hardened into one of determination. She clenched her jaw, growing serious. "No, Robert. We're not gonna do this."

"Do what?"

"Compete for blame." She took a shuddering breath and straightened her shoulders. "We have a situation to get through. We need you *here*. Not in the past."

I staggered from the physical blow of her words. She knew me well. Knew I'd dwell on what I couldn't change, even when things I could change were staring me in the face. Cupping her cheek in my hand, I wiped the blood from her chin.

"You're right," I said softly, bringing my face close. "I hate it, but I love you."

She flashed a devious smile and gave me the barest peck on the lips before pushing me away. "Me too. Now go check on your sergeant," she said.

Reluctantly, I flopped onto the ground beside Cheng, pressing into his neck. His pulse fluttered, weak and thready. His breathing was ragged.

"How is he?" I asked Jun, who was wiping ineffectually at the blood on his clothes.

She shrugged. "Not a medic," she said. "But he *need* be okay."

"Cheng," I said, feeling totally helpless, "it's gonna be—"

He drew in a sharp gasp. His eyes flew open, staring directly into mine, wild and desperate.

"Chāo jí bái, nǐ méiyǒu líkāi wǒ…Xièxiè," he croaked.

"What?" I asked as he held my forearm in a claw-like grip.

I recognized the slur "super white" (he'd called me that before) and "thank you," but not the phrase in between.

"Cheng? Nǐ shuō shénme?" I asked him what was wrong—the first phrase The Ox had taught me.

Instead of repeating his earlier statement, Cheng gurgled, "Duìbùqǐ (I'm sorry)."

His dark, glassy eyes lost focus, and his grip on my arm weakened. He coughed, blood staining his lips.

"Jun, what did he say?"

But the mech ignored me, muttering something under her breath, touching his hand, his arm, his face.

"Niu, Dark," I cried, "what did he say?"

Cheng's grip fell from my arm. He took one gurgling breath, then another. No third breath came.

"No," I whispered, "no, no, no. Cheng, wake up! I need…"

I needed him to not die, but with his final breath, he defied even that order.

I shook him, searching for a pulse again. His nostrils flared. He took half a breath, then his body went limp.

"Méiyǒu! (No)" Jun cried, jostling his shoulders along with me. When he didn't respond, she beat on his chest, repeating the cry louder.

The Ox staggered over, picking up Jun with obvious effort and pulling her away from the body. "Mèi mei," he hushed into her ear, "he goes on to his next story."

I knelt beside Cheng's lifeless form, the reality of his death pressing against me. How was I supposed to bear this burden? All the hopes I'd harbored for reconciling our differences, the frustration I'd felt over his opposition, the resentment I'd allowed to fester—all of it evaporated, leaving only a profound sense of loss. I gasped for breath, but the air had been stolen from my lungs. My throat constricted tighter than it had been beneath Tristan's weight. In this moment, I realized how trivial our conflicts had been in the face of such finality. Regret gnawed at me, a relentless ache that I knew would linger for a long while.

Mara leaned in close. "Cheng was," she said with a pause to get her trembling voice under control, "thanking you for not leaving him back there."

"And what was he apologizing for?"

Mara just shrugged.

"Look!" JR said in an urgent whisper. "What the hell is that?"

A dark form staggered toward us, the sounds of cracking branches and rustling leaves following in their wake.

"Yaozu!" The Ox cried, rushing up to the woman. He ushered her toward the group, though I monitored their procession with a wary eye.

Once the light hit her face, I saw a bruise spreading over half of it— from her eyes to her jaw.

"Mechs," the woman gasped. Her suit was torn, and she was missing her helmet, comm, and pistol. "Too many!"

She made a dramatic moan, putting her hand to her forehead, and rambled out a string of Mandarin to Niu.

"She says they got separated in the dark," The Ox translated, "and soldiers ambushed them. They knocked her out."

I nodded, studying her. Red-rimmed eyes, large bruise, hunched posture, trembling hands: it looked like she'd been through hell.

"She said she managed to just get out before the first bomb took down the control center."

"Well, we're fortunate she did," I replied, though the words rang hollow. "Niu, give her the rundown."

"Yes, Boss," The Ox said, flopping gratefully to the ground.

Moments later, the comm crackled.

"Lilly?" The voice came through distorted and choppy, "Were the hell are you, niño?"

"Mendez!" Chet spoke into the comm, hugging it to his chest. "We're two-point-three miles due east of the drop-off location. Give or take a few feet."

I shot Chet a questioning look.

"What?" he said. "I can estimate."

"We'll see," I gave a skeptical mutter back, though was quickly disproved when Mendez came flying through the trees.

"Thank Greysoft!" JR grumbled, bandage on his head. "My comm unit still isn't functional. Damn Spark."

Ru shot JR a glare but threw up his hands as if to say: *it's my nature.*

I ran to the edge of the glade, waving my flashlight overhead. Chet followed and used his Auranet to ping the van's windshield with tiny rocks.

The van stopped parallel to us, door sliding open.

My squad piled in, but Jun stopped. "We cannot leave him," she said.

"But we…" I glanced back in the trees, "we don't have time to get him."

"No. She's right boss," The Ox said, the only one left on the ground besides me and Jun. "His soul must be allowed to go."

He spoke with his jaw set in a manner I hadn't seen before.

"I will get him."

It wasn't a question, but I nodded my permission anyway. I knew I wouldn't win this fight.

"What in the name of Greysoft happened, boys and girls?" Mendez scolded, once The Ox and Cheng's body were safely aboard. "I've been trying to reach you for the last hour!"

"Cheng's dead." The voice that left my lips felt heavy and lifeless.

I rubbed the place where he'd gripped my arm with his last breaths. *Charger's Beard,* I could still feel his fingers lingering there.

"What?" Mendez snapped. "How?"

"Mag bullet to the thigh. Bled out." The last words came out as a croak, my tongue like sandpaper.

"Ay, nada!" she swore. "You should have called me earlier!"

"I *tried*," I snarled, frustration boiling over, "but Ru's EMP fried nearly everything!"

Mendez scoffed, processing the information the rest of us had already been sitting with. "Ay, Sparks," she muttered, then uttered a string of Spanish so savage, even I flinched. She slammed a palm on the van's control wheel. I'd never seen the Zephyr so angry.

A fourth bomb went off, huge this time, shock wave making the windows rattle, even as far away as we were.

"What the hell did you do, Ferryman?" I growled at the 'Net, rerouting my anger toward another target.

But Chet didn't seem to care. He gave me a wicked smirk. "You weren't the only one who had some tech survive Ru. My charge worked."

"Your charge for what?" Mara asked, peering at the man.

"A Matryoshka bomb. Mezei taught me. They get bigger until everyone's dead. Fun, isn't it?"

I shook my head. Fun was not the word I'd use. "You're a sick man, Ferryman, you know that?"

"Ha!" he said, a boisterous, gravelly laugh scrunching his craggy face. "Like you're any better, Lilly," he said. "I saw the look in your eyes when you cut that tā mā de mech captain in his big, ugly face."

"Maybe you're right," I snarled, "but this is not the time to measure dicks."

I knew I shouldn't be angry at my squad, but the weight of our failure and Cheng's death pressed down on me, and I lashed out, unable to contain the storm of guilt and rage within.

The person you should really be angry at is yourself, Robert, I thought. I tried to push that nagging voice away, but it lingered, growing like a Matryoshka.

I was in charge. I was the one who let Cheng die.

0600 hours

The captain greeted me with a face as solemn as my own when I entered his office after a few fitful hours of sleep. I felt like shit. On top of my raging headache and throbbing limbs, my heart was heavy. We had failed in our mission. One of my soldiers was dead.

"Not every mission goes as planned," Ames said as I stood in silence trying to keep the quiver from my lip. "Destroying the KEWP control center hurt the CORPs for now. Maybe they won't have another way to activate the rods."

"I doubt that, Sir," I replied. "It would be pretty stupid for them to not have backup controls."

Ames shrugged, "Perhaps. But this at least gives us time to figure out other ways to hurt them."

"Permission to speak freely, Sir?"

"Granted," Ames replied, noticing the rigidity of my arms. "At ease, Lilly."

I slumped. "Cheng's death…. What do I do about it?"

"Have a funeral service."

"That's it?"

"Death happens, Lilly. I lost twelve soldiers in the Battle of Sky Plaza. You saved most of your squad with minimal injuries. That is commendable."

"But I—it's my fault, Sir," I pressed, practically looking for a reprimand. "We—we weren't on the best of terms. I didn't trust him. Sent him into danger."

Ames pressed his lips into a thin line, rubbing the bridge of his nose. "I read the reports. Yours, Dark's, Niu's. All of them. Cheng wasn't being cooperative. You did what you had to."

"But… we don't *know* he wasn't… It's my fault," I repeated. "I—my decisions—they weren't that of a leader. I didn't deserve that promotion."

"But they were," he sighed. The shadows under his eyes were dark, proof that he had a stressful night as well. "You're a leader, and you made decisions. Thus…" He held up his hands. "Not every decision you make under fire is going to be easy or correct. It *will* be quick and based on your instincts and your subconscious emotions. You know the priorities—your people first, the mission second, safety third. You did what you had to and kept the casualties to a minimum."

I huffed, eyes downcast. "I just wish I could've kept the casualties to zero."

Ames made a non-committal gesture, "Even if he'd loved you, it could not have prevented his death."

"Wait, what?"

"I Saw it happen."

"You knew Cheng would die?"

"Sort of. I knew you two wouldn't get along. But it was put-up-or-shut-up time for Cheng. He already had a history of being difficult with officers." Ames sighed. "I saw two possible outcomes. Either, you figured out how to get along, or Cheng died."

I gaped. "You willingly sent a man to his death?"

The captain's face grew sad, his eyes distant. "I willingly send men and women to their deaths every day. But, death is only one possible outcome of our choices."

"I…don't understand, Sir."

He held up his hands. "The future is like a blank canvas. If I know the artist, I can deduce what the painting may look like, but I don't know the artist's thoughts. They may choose a color they don't often work with, or they might stick with what they know. Every one of us is the artist of our own destiny. We can choose to be the same—thus, my prediction comes to pass—or we can choose to grow. When that occurs, many surprising things can happen, proving me wrong." He smiled. "And when all I see is tragedy, I love being proven wrong."

I nodded, though my heart still thumped its sorrowful song.

Ames smiled then, his eyes haunting. "Of all the possible outcomes I Saw, you carried out the best one. As I knew you would."

"How…" I began with a shaky voice, picking at a hangnail, "how do I keep moving forward?"

"Put one foot in front of the other. It's one of the burdens of leadership. You'll never get used to losing a soldier."

"But I…."

"There is still work to do, Sergeant. We have a corporation to topple. The Citizen's Army *will* find a way."

"Did you See this, too?" I asked him.

Ames chuckled, "Don't ask questions when you're afraid of the answer."

I shuffled my feet. Even though Ames couldn't read my mind, he'd gotten that one right. I *was* afraid.

Since arriving in China, this mission had been my first taste of real failure —and the first death under my command. As I chewed on Ames' advice, Cheng's final words floated into my mind: *"thank you"* and *"I'm sorry."*

Would I ever know what Cheng had been sorry for? Or was that just one more secret that died with him?

"You will need a new sergeant," the captain continued, changing the subject.

"Okay," I said, wary of his mischievous grin, "who've you got for me?"

"We don't have anyone to spare," he continued, "so you'll need to promote one of your soldiers."

"Yes, Sir. Which one?"

Ames shrugged. "You know your people better than I do. Who would you choose?"

Chewing on my lip, I asked, "Will the squad hate me if I choose the wrong person?"

"Does it matter? You are their commander, and you operate under the officers' demands. They swore an oath to follow you."

Sighing, I knew he was right, though my own authority discomfited me. Ames had the final say, but his reliance on my judgment was daunting.

JR was the obvious choice. Being a Sway made him naturally suited for leadership. He could use his Aurawave to back up his commands. But, while he was only a couple years my junior, he acted even younger and still hadn't really abandoned his reckless partyboi mentality. Besides, I always felt a little gross when JR used his Aurawave. No, he was not yet ready.

Chet? His confident, no-nonsense attitude appealed to me. He always seemed to know what he was doing and didn't hesitate to jump into action. I had come to like the guy, but if I were being honest, he wasn't very charismatic. Also, I suspected he may be a little crazy. I worried that authority would go to his head.

The Ox had interest in leading, and Jun and Ru were far too young— plus I still didn't really know how much English the latter two *actually* spoke. And Mendez was a contractor, she'd made that clear from the get-go. Which left…Mara.

"Dark?" I asked, already knowing it was the right choice.

Ames laughed, "I knew I'd promoted you for a reason. Would you like to tell her, or should I?"

I thought for a moment. While I'd love to be the one to tell her, I figured she was less likely to punch Ames. "Can you do it, Sir? If you don't mind. I'm not sure she'll be…happy…with the information."

"Consider it done," Ames chuckled. "I'll probably be able to see the punch coming, anyway."

I gaped at my captain. Had he just made the same joke I'd made to myself? "Thank you, Sir," I said. "And I wish you health in your endeavor."

Ames clapped my shoulder in dismissal. "Yes, definitely picked the right person."

Whoever he was talking about didn't matter. I hoped I'd live up to his praise.

- 29 -
C.E. 2253 June 18

We burned Cheng's body as the first light of dawn crept over the horizon. The flames danced and flickered over the floating pyre, consuming the remains of my second-in-command and casting long shadows that twisted their fingers into my heart. The acrid scent of burning flesh and chemical fuel packets filled the air, a stark reminder of the fragility of life in these tumultuous times. Small buns, cones of incense, and ghost paper—inscribed with symbols of wealth and prosperity—cluttered a small table.

The squad stood in somber silence, each taking turns dropping their piece of paper into a small urn. I placed my paper last, contemplating fate and futures. The Chinese believed the spirits of the dead continued to dwell in the natural world and thus could influence the fate of the living. But Ames talked about choices, of the paths we carve through our decisions. Cheng had made his choice in those mountains, but would that choice still dictate our future, or would we be able to move forward?

Jun flicked a flame from her mechanical hand and set the paper alight. I watched it burn, my eyes flicking between the ritual urn and the man on the pyre, taking my questions to the spirit world, or somewhere into the ether, leaving more practical questions lingering.

Following the service, we gathered in the common room of our houseboat, surrounded by dumplings, buns, rice dishes, and soup. As near as I could tell, Jun and The Ox had spent the better part of a day and night cooking, with other members of the squad stepping in to help for an hour or two.

I admired their dedication, whether it was for Cheng, the rest of us, or a little bit of both, they seemed to be in a better mood at the end of it. And, we got to benefit from their efforts. I allowed my questions to resurface, watching my crew pile food into their mouths as if they hadn't eaten in months.

I was loathe to interrupt the shared trauma-bonding among the squad, but at some point, we had to get down to business.

"Okay," I said, my voice rough, "it's time to have the hard conversation."

Everyone froze, JR with a dumpling halfway to his mouth. "Great," he muttered, setting the dumpling down and leaning back, arms crossed in front of him, "here comes Mister Buzzkill."

I gave JR the most deadpan look I could muster, then turned to the rest of my team. "Buzzes aside, let's talk about what went wrong at the control center. Here are the facts: Yaozu miscounted the enemy. One slipped away, presumably sounding an alarm. Cheng's pistol jammed, or so he claimed. We split the squad. Yaozu almost got left behind and Cheng's dead. Thoughts?"

Chet, ever the blunt instrument, spoke first. "Maybe Cheng was setting you up, Boss. He was difficult enough. Could've been looking to make you fail."

Jun flashed Chet a hostile glare and The Ox shook his head. "I know Cheng wasn't trusting. But a traitor? No. He was loyal to the cause."

"Maybe he was trying to play the hero?" Mara asked with a shrug. "Everyone wants to be a hero."

"I don't," JR said flippantly, returning to the dumpling with gusto. "I just want to enjoy myself."

"Rostbane," I snapped. "Enough!"

JR slouched into his chair, and I immediately regretted my tone. I knew he was just trying to inject levity into a tense situation, but I needed my squad to take this seriously.

"Yaozu," I said and turned to her where she sat, hunched and small, a cup of hot tea clutched in her delicate hands. "You got separated. How?"

Though her hands trembled, she sat up, giving me her icy blue stare. "It was dark," she said.

"What?" Mara snapped. "What'd I do?"

She gave a lazy roll of her eyes. "Not you. The light. Out." She sliced the air with her hand.

"Oh," Mara blushed and turned her attention to a very interesting puddle of soy sauce in her bowl.

"I lost them," Yaozu continued. "Tried to find…" she shrugged.

"You can't see Auras in the dark?" I asked, brow furrowing.

She huffed, as if she was explaining a simple task to a child. "I saw Auras. They were the enemy."

"So, you can't tell the difference between a mech and a Tank?" Chet said, eyes narrowing.

Yaozu frowned and took a long sip of her tea. "Let me ask you something, 'Net," she said instead of answering his question. "When dark happened…could you a throw rock and hit target?"

"No. But my Skill needs my sight."

"Really?"

"I don't fuckin' know!" Chet growled. "I've never been dunked in solid darkness before."

"Neither have I," Yaozu drawled, her voice as icy as her stare, "and by the time I knew what happened, someone hit me in the face. For all I know it could have been the Tank."

Mara scowled. "It was dark," she said, emotionless, "but I don't think it was me."

I made a frustrated sigh.

"Maybe we shouldn't have split the party," JR added, his voice quiet. "Or…"

"Or people should've done their fuckin' job," Chet snarled. He leaned forward, elbows on the table. "We can't afford mistakes—"

"Or egos," I interrupted. I'd thought about this a lot over the past two days, and my squad's conversation had awoken a truth in me. "Bottom line —we still don't trust each other. And that can't happen."

Everyone froze, side conversations ceased, and each member of my squad set down their chopsticks, their glasses of tea or beer, or their food. They watched me with one mind.

"How do we fix that?" Mendez asked, speaking for the first time.

"From now on," I said, setting my jaw resolutely and steeling myself for a proclamation I knew they would all hate, "we are going to do everything together. Eat, sleep, train—"

"Shit?" JR added, wrinkling his nose.

I sighed, but allowed myself a mischievous smirk, "Not yet, Rostbane. But, if you all can't figure out how to get along, we may have to go that route."

The Ox chuckled and even Mara grinned.

"Fine," Yaozu said, "what does that look like?"

"Well, you tell me," I said to my squad, leaning back in my chair and crossing my arms behind my head.

A heavy silence settled over the table, but it wasn't the brittle kind that came before a fight. It was the kind that meant they were thinking, weighing my words, considering the impossible—trust.

Then Mendez exhaled through her nose and nodded. "Alright. We try it."

Yaozu followed with a shrug. "Can't be worse than what we're doing now."

One by one, they gave their agreement—some grumbling, some

reluctant, but all in. Even JR, though he made a point of muttering something about shared toothbrushes under his breath.

I let out a slow breath, surprised at the warmth creeping into my chest. This wasn't a promise that everything would be fine. It wasn't even close. But it was a start.

And sometimes, a start was enough.

* * * * *

What it looked like was everyone moving into a single houseboat, cramming into tiny rooms, bunking on the floor, cooking together, drilling together. That evening, we sat around the holoviz, chatting or reading, or making fun of the ridiculous newscasters. I had to admit that this transition had gone smoother than I expected, and I finally allowed myself a speck of hope.

That is, until the holoviz shrieked with a skimmed broadcast of urgent importance.

"Uh, boss," JR said, eyes fixed on the HV, "I think you'll want to see this."

I looked up from the after-action report I was reading—Niu's—to see the *COMMUNICATION INTERCEPTED* banner flashing across the screen.

"What is it this time?" I sighed, steeling myself for another new tragedy.

JR hit *accept* on the controls and the show came to life.

Two faces appeared in the image, both mechs. The first, a man of indeterminate age with an unnatural pallor and neat suit, sat in an easy chair with his legs crossed at the ankles. The colors of his eyes shifted with the changing lights behind him.

The other man, clad in a navy uniform with a bandage over one eye, lounged in his chair. His mechanical arm idly toyed with an energy pistol, and he cast a cocky smirk toward the camera.

"Shit," I muttered, "that's Tristan."

"That guy?" JR asked pointing at the military man. "Yeah. Apparently he's the hero of the hour."

The screen blinked to a set of stats as text scrolled across the bottom:

AFTER-ACTION INTERVIEW WITH HEX TRISTAN OF LIGHTBAR UNIT GAMMA-7XF12. PRESENTED TO YOU BY GUY BAUDELAIRE, HOST.

Date: 2253 June 17
Location: Chengde Qingchui Mountain
Deaths: 26

Casualties: 6

"Good evening Mech World!" the host began, his voice tinny and artificial.

I groaned.

Guy Baudelaire, a flamboyant HV personality, usually conducted interviews with politicians I didn't know and celebrities I didn't care about. What was he doing interviewing a military captain?

He gestured magnanimously and continued, "Welcome to *your* show where we cover all the most *important* news in the Triumvirate."

More text drifted across the screen as he spoke.

TONIGHT: THE CONFLICT IN CHINA CONTINUES.

"For a year now, our beloved Lightbar Industries has been fighting a bitter war against the genetic freaks. Freaks who would see all the comforts of technology destroyed and return the country to the Luddites. The Luddites! You know, those pre-war anti-tech nutjobs who protested cybernetic modification."

"Genetic freaks," Mara grumbled. "If I had a credit for every time I heard that..."

"You'd still be a freak," JR laughed bitterly.

Mara wrinkled her nose. "But not a Luddite. Those ancient anti-cybernetic activists were just as crazy as mechs! Present company excepted, I suppose," she said, looking at Jun.

But the mech just shrugged. "I am crazy," she said, the hint of a smile tugging at her lip, "crazy good."

She used one of her mech arms to snatch a peanut from a bowl, flick it into the air, and catch it in her mouth. Then, with a precise twist of her fingers, she shuffled a deck of cards one-handed, sending them into a perfect bridge. "And crazy entertaining."

"Tonight, I have a very special interview for you," the HV host continued. "Hex Tristan of the company GAMMA-7XF12 managed to survive a brutal, unprovoked attack while on patrol in the Chengde Qingchui Mountains. These savant "soldiers" tried to take on our own security troopers and destroy them. The gall! The arrogance! Clearly when the heretic Greysoft set about manipulating their DNA, she didn't code them with any abundance of brains..."

"JR," I interrupted the screening, "Do we need to see how many ways this guy can insult savants?"

He shrugged. "That's the entertaining part, right?"

"So, Captain Tristan, you pride yourself in your ability to neutralize the savant menace, is that right?"

"I've killed my fair share of savants," the Hex said, half smile on his lips.

The Ox snorted, settling in on the couch. "More like fair share of rumors," he muttered.

"How does it feel? Glorious? Thrilling? Or do you feel bad for them—like you're killing a child or animal?"

"What the *hell* is that supposed to mean?" Mendez snarled, throwing a peanut at the HV.

"It's war," he drawled, looking bored. "What more can I say? Unless you've been there, you can't possibly understand."

"Man, is this guy the poster child for toxic masculinity or what?" Mara asked, giving Mendez a nudge. "I wonder if it's just an act or if he's really that arrogant?"

"He really that arrogant," Jun said. "Father trained with him as a teen. Then died when Tristan refused retreat."

I looked at Jun in surprise. Guess that explained why she fought with the resistance now.

"Humor us," Guy prodded. "What exactly happened in those mountains?"

Tristan thought for a moment. "We were inspecting a distress call from a research facility. Thought it was just a tripped alarm or smoke detector fail, but instead we come face-to-face with the savages."

"Tell us more, Mr. Tristan," Guy prodded, "For those in the audience, what *happened?*"

"Matryoshka bombs. Serious business, those."

"Is that how you got that injury?" Guy gestured vaguely at Tristan's eye.

Tristan rubbed his head and pointed to the bandage, "Oh you mean this? Yeah, hurt like a bloody bitch. I knew there was no saving it. But, it doesn't matter about me. I'm the Captain. It's my job to help my soldiers."

"Language, Mr. Tristan!" Guy Baudelaire interjected, "You're on national holovision, after all. Why don't you just start from the beginning?"

Chet gave me an encouraging slap on the arm. "Didja see him avoid the answer?" he chuckled. "Can't admit that a 'savage freaky savant' got the best of him."

I rolled my eyes at him.

"At least you still have two!" he continued and pointed at me with his fingers in the shape of a gun.

Tristan sighed dramatically but began the story. "The gene-freaks had a Spark with them. Fried the whole facility and my soldiers too. I hate those guys. Why don't we have more tech to stop them? Anyway, I had to dump my own armor which cost me two months' pay! Bleedin' tossmongers, the lot of them."

"While we are all very sad to lose our tech," Guy made a sympathetic clicking with his tongue, "we must remember tech can be replaced. Lives cannot. Tell us about some of the survivors. The public cares deeply for the lives of each and every one of our valiant men and women who spend their days fighting the savant menace."

"For what they did to Cheng, I'll show them 'menace,'" The Ox said, slamming a fist into his palm and startling half the squad with the noise.

Tristan shook his head, "Yeah, yeah, yeah. Try talking about how much the public cares to Wraith and Excelsior as I dragged them, complaining all the way, toward an Emergency Exit. Got out three others, too. Minister, Pyro, and Phase. It was more difficult to pull them from their technological mire—damn outdated mods! As I keep saying, all soldiers should be equipped with quick release toggles, so they don't become trapped by their own bricked tech. But who listens? No one!"

"Terrifying business, that. I can't imagine losing my own mods! They're like my children."

Tristan scoffed, "You shouldn't get so dependent on them, you know. Wraith and Minister had it worse than the rest of us. Wraith couldn't get rid of her leg, so she dragged it all the way to the E-Exit. Minister was practically blind, more blind than me, as his ocular mods were frizzled. Maybe that's where the savants had it right. Tech can turn on you in an instant."

The interviewer looked uncomfortable at that last remark. He fidgeted for a moment until changing the subject. "Tell us about the bombs. Matryoshka bombs sound dreadful."

Tristan shrugged. "Dreadful is an understatement. Weak soldiers are terrified by them (but I wasn't). They're no mere 'crack-and-boom' bombs. They're smart. They've got life-sensing technology. They keep getting bigger until all heartbeats in their sensor radius are extinguished. Even the E-Exit, with its heavy metal door, wouldn't have protected us for long."

"How big were these explosions? Like baby elephant farts, sonic boom, or California Sea Wall earthquake big?"

"What the heck does that mean?" JR muttered, echoed a moment later by Tristan.

He made a grimace. "I have no idea what you just said, but they were mechin' big. I swear the passage was about to collapse, pebbles and dust everywhere. The E-Exit door cracked in half like one of your fancy biscuits."

"Then what happened?" Guy asked, "I'm literally on the edge of my seat! Get the camera in here. The audience needs to see this!" A brief image flashed of the correspondent's bobbling ass, hanging half-off his chair.

"I hate these shows," I groaned, and JR chuckled.

Tristan looked equally annoyed as he waited for the tom-foolery to end. "I don't think my soldiers understood the urgency of the bombs. Damn young mechs, they think they're invincible with all their tech. I had to keep prodding them down the corridor even with the blood streaming down my face."

"You sure are brave, Mr. Tristan," Guy said, voice dripping with sensuality. "Any advice for our viewers on how to be even a tenth as brave as you?"

Tristan grunted, "Suck less."

"Right…" Guy sniffed, then continued prodding, "I hear that Private Phase is one of those in training for a special job. Got one o' those new wire weapon thingies."

"Razorwire," Tristan snorted in disgust. "You wanna talk about a useless weapon? The son of a savant couldn't reel it in after the Spark killed the current. Tripped me up right awkward. Luckily, the electrocurrent was gone or I'd be getting foot mods now, too. The Razorwire program is a sham."

I shuddered again at the thought of that. Sham or not, it had certainly been scary at the time.

"Well, it clearly didn't do him any good in this situation," Guy laughed nervously.

The Hex snorted, "At least it didn't cause him to become a melted pile of scrap...this time. You wanna know the true hero of the day? Excelsior. He's a beefy man and was able to pound the E-Exit door right out of its frame. Otherwise, that jammed son-of-a-savant would have trapped us. Thank Mirabel he still had the strength left."

Guy let out a long breath as if he had been holding it in for Tristan's whole story. "That's quite the story. Then you got free with no further harm?"

Tristan grunted. "Not hardly. We were almost buried in dirt and the dead scrub of the mountains. We had to tunnel through the debris, up a hill covered in loose earth and scree. My soldiers didn't like the slope that greeted us on the other side. Wraith whined about her clunky leg and how she was going to fall. But what other options did we have? Couldn't go back."

"What did you do?"

"I shoved her. No time to deliberate on the finer points of hill descent with bombs licking at your asshole."

Guy gasped, "You did that to your own soldier?"

"He did a lot worse, too, during the battle of Sky Plaza," Jun muttered, a disgusted look on her face.

"They gotta learn to do what's needed to survive. The rest followed without complaint. It was either risk scrapes and bruises from the fall or be incinerated by the Matryoshka. I didn't quite make it before the last blast went off, though."

"That must have been terrifying for you," Guy urged.

Tristan shrugged. "Didn't have much chance to think at that time. As I guided my soldiers over the hill, the force hit me full in the face. I was thrown backwards."

"What did the explosion look like?"

"It was an angry mushroom billowing up into the night air: an undulating cloud of black smoke and orange fire."

"And that injury. You said you were injured before the bombs?" Guy asked, even though Tristan never actually said.

At this point Tristan spat. "A savant freak—a big, blond guy with a crazy glint in his eye."

"Hey, Rob, that's you!" JR gasped, pointing at a picture that appeared in the top right corner of the screen—the scan from Lanzhou—though something was off about it.

I scoffed. "That picture makes me look like a monster." Artists or AI had gone wild on my visage, giving me glowing red eyes and a slavering grin.

"I dunno, I think it's kind of hot," Mara murmured in my ear. She slid her hand into mine, giving it a gentle squeeze. A wave of heat rushed up my neck.

Tristan continued, "He put a knife right in my face. Don't let the old stories fool you. Analog weapons still hurt. Never grapple with a Luddite if you can help it, especially when all your tech is dead."

"I assume that means you let him get away?"

Tristan laughed—a grinding, gravelly sound that held no humor, "Yeah. Figured I'd go easy on him this time. What's one eye among friends?" When Guy opened his mouth for another surprised question, Tristan cut him off. "No, you clutterhead! I didn't let him get away! That beastlyman gideon savant traitor ran like a chicken shit."

He turned his eye directly to the camera with a baleful glare. "I'm looking for you, Sergeant Lilly," he said with venom, "and when I find you, I'll be taking more than just your eye."

A chill ran down my spine, but I forced myself to stay still, my breath slow and steady. The others were watching me, waiting for a reaction.

I sat up straighter on the couch and broke the surprised silence. "Guess we'd better be ready for him," I said, my voice steadier than I felt, "and if he thinks I'm gonna make it easy…well, he's in for a big surprise."

"Fuck yeah he is!" JR said, and suddenly I felt a warmth that bolstered me into confidence.

The rest of the squad must have felt it too. They cheered and hollered, patting me on the shoulder, or lifting their glasses in a toast. I kept the confident grin plastered on my face, long after the feeling had waned, because deep down, I knew this wasn't just about me.

Whatever was coming, I wasn't sure any of us would be ready for it.

- 30 -

C.E. 2253 June 19

As I had expected, Mara was none too happy with her new promotion when Ames officially delivered it to her. To her credit, though, she didn't punch him or even storm from the room. She accepted it gracefully and with determination.

Though, she still wouldn't look me in the eyes.

"The officers made right choice," The Ox said during our lesson, later that day. He looked intently at Mara. "You will make good replacement for Cheng. Not the best replacement, but good."

"Oh?" I cocked my head at the Tank. "Who would be the best?"

"Me," he said with a wink of his eye.

Mara scoffed, "You only say that because you think you're stronger."

The Ox laughed, "Boss here's a new word." He smiled mischievously as he continued to stare at Mara, "Míngxiǎn."

"It means 'obviously,'" Mara said with a scowl. Then she turned to The Ox. "You wanna prove it?"

"Zǒng shì." (A word I understood. It meant "always." Niu's lessons were working.)

She put her elbow on the table with her hand up, "Okay then. Let's settle this like adults."

The Ox waggled his eyebrows and took her grip. "You mean like Tanks?" he chuckled. "On three. Boss, you count…in Mandarin," he added with a smirk.

"Ugh. You really are determined to teach me something, huh?"

The Ox just smiled.

"Okay," I began, "ready?"

"Zhǔnbèi," they said at once.

I laughed. The competition between these two was strong.

I began to count: "Yī, èr…" and, taking a deep breath, "sān!"

Their grips locked, muscles tensing. I saw each grimace as they fought for the advantage. Initially, there was not much movement. I had watched a lot of arm-wrestling on holoviz as a child, including the mech-armed ones, so I knew what they were doing. *Saving energy for the push.* The two Tanks looked peaceful as they smirked at each other, as if this was easy or something.

The rest of us waited in tense silence. I watched disapprovingly as JR leaned over to whisper with Chet and Mendez. They smiled and pulled out their handhelds.

Even though Mara was physically smaller than The Ox, she was also scrappy and clever. Her arm wasn't as bulky as Niu's, but it was more centered on the table. More bent at the elbow. His was straighter. She leaned back slowly, almost imperceptibly. In fact, I would not have noticed it, except her eyes flicked to me, and the barest hint of a smile drifted across her lips.

Her wrist hinged forward, and The Ox's surprised eyebrow-raise indicated she was gaining the upper hand. Mara's jaw clenched and she took one slow breath through her nose. Niu stuck his tongue between his teeth even as his arm tilted to the left. Mara leaned in the same direction.

Seconds later, a loud *thunk* resonated through the room as The Ox's wrist bent backward and slammed onto the table, leaving a dent in the thick metal. His fingers opened, and he emitted a good-natured growl of defeat. JR discreetly slipped a flask to Mendez, while Chet rolled three cigarettes across the table with a frown. Mendez took them with a wicked smirk.

"Side bets?" I whispered to her.

She shrugged. "We all gotta have some fun, no?"

I shook my head at the three, and gave them what I hoped was a reproachful glare.

Their return giggles indicated that I failed.

"So how do you say, 'eat your words' in Mandarin?" Mara asked, a triumphant smile wide on her lips. Her chest heaved, and she shook out her wrist.

The Ox massaged his hand but seemed in good spirits. "I'm not sure what that means, but I think the word for 'show off' is 'American.'"

"Ouch," JR joked but I laughed. He wasn't wrong.

"You wanna go next, boss?" he asked me.

Looking at Mara, I stuck out my tongue.

"Only if she wants my job."

She met my eyes before realizing she was mad at me. I flashed a congenial grin. She furrowed her brow before sighing in defeat and smiling once more.

"Hell no. That's one promotion I won't accept."

Just then, my handheld beeped. A message brightened the screen.

* * * * *

* * * * *

A link for a file replaced the message. I stared at it for a long moment, a realization materializing. I'd seen this file once before on the drive from Query. At the time, I'd written it off as a Red Herring. Hesitantly, I clicked on *Dr. Tam's Recipe for Perfect Shrimp Wontons*, hoping for more than just a dinner recommendation.

* * * * *

For posterity, I would like to note here that Staff Sergeant Robert Lilly, while usually a bumbling fool, occasionally finds something useful. Well, in this case, I had 'useful' handed to me, and it was *quite* useful. After reviewing the file, I rushed to contact Ames.

I barely had time to process what I'd found before the officers convened in the War Room, someone pulling strings to make sure this meeting happened. Whether that was a good or bad thing, I couldn't say yet. But if I was going to make my case, I needed backup, so I took JR with me.

"Okay tell me, what's the dealie-o?" JR asked, as we headed into the underwater command center, his voice light but his shoulders tense.

"The officers are divided," I explained. "Mazet wants to hit Lightbar where it hurts most."

"Ah. Their HQ," JR surmised, referring to the large spire located on Hong Kong Island.

I nodded. "But General Qian is not willing to risk the Sacred Cloud Army or the civilians in Hong Kong without more intel."

"Of which we have jack-diddly," JR gave a humorless laugh.

"Until now."

He paused to look at me, his hand on a damp wall. "What do you mean?"

I exhaled. "I got a coded message that basically implies we can crack not only the Island's defenses, but Lightbar Spire itself."

JR gaped. "Rob, that's huge!" He threw up his hands. "Hong Kong Island is practically one of the most secure towns in the world, up there with the RoC."

"Yep," I agreed, thinking of the mountainous fortress, surrounded by water and blanketed by aerial surveillance.

I suspected Query was behind the message, but I had no clear confirmation. And frankly, we were out of time. Every moment wasted was another moment for Lightbar to regroup and retaliate. This was the only shot we had.

Convincing the officers wouldn't be easy. Ames would listen, but Qian? If I wanted to keep this war moving in our favor, I had to use everything at my disposal, including JR's Aurawave. Was it a dirty trick? Sure. Could it get both of us in serious trouble? Probably. But it was a risk worth taking.

By the time we arrived in the War Room, the officers were already there, faces grim.

"Lilly, Rostbane," Ames said when he noticed us standing respectfully at the door, "please join us."

I ducked instinctively, a prickling unease settling over me. I'd never seen them all so quiet. So solemn. The small holoscreen at Mazet's right elbow caught my attention. Red letters scrolled across the screen:

BREAKING NEWS: LANZHOU LEVELED. MILLIONS DEAD.

We already wasted too much time.

"The rods?" I asked the officers and Ames nodded.

I stared in horror at the smoking ruins, memories of Xi'an slammed into me—charred streets, the sickly-sweet odor of smoke and decay. My nose itched. My body screamed to run, to yell, to do anything, but I stood frozen.

Mitchell was in Lanzhou.

The thought hit like a fist to the stomach. A hundred-plus American soldiers of the Citizen's Army. Query.

JR's fingers brushed the back of my hand, and I resisted the urge to grab it—if for nothing else than to hold onto something familiar that wasn't death and destruction.

Mitchell. Query. The mission.

I grabbed the back of a chair and lowered myself into it as casually as possible, but my hands trembled. If Query had been caught in the attack, the responsibility of decoding the message would fall to me or other tech-wizards. And we would be far less likely to succeed. Had we just lost our only hope?

JR flopped down beside me, far less controlled. His emotions hit me in waves—fear, revulsion, horror. At this moment, I regretted bringing the Sway. Maybe he'd been right—he wasn't cut out for soldiering.

"Rostbane," Ames said quietly, looking at the man with a gentle frown, "You may want to tone that Aurawave down a little."

JR, pale from crown to lips, swallowed hard and nodded stiffly, "Yes, Sir." He squeezed his eyes shut and I felt the fear recede. "Sorry, Sir."

The silence dragged on. Taking a breath, I studied the holoviz.

"How long ago?" I asked.

"As far as we can tell…three hours," Mazet said, jaw tight.

"Before we agreed to meet."

"Yes," Ames confirmed.

That was… something. Maybe Query hadn't been in the city when the bombs fell. Maybe.

Mazet exhaled sharply and turned to me. "Sergeant Lilly, you had something to present?"

I forced my brain to work, to push past the horror. In a stammering breath, I explained what I had found.

"The datachip Query gave us contained more intel than I could process at the time," I began. "Some files seemed useless, but I think that was their way of encoding sensitive data so it couldn't be skimmed by the CORPs. Today I got a—a notification from (I assume) the cyborg about one such file."

I piped something onto a second holoscreen from my handheld, *Dr. Tam's Perfect Shrimp Ramen Recipe* blinked open. I navigated to the embedded code.

"See these signatures here…and here?" I pointed to several anomalies. "They could unravel the information in the file and provide the real data but…"

"We need the cipher," JR finished.

I nodded. "Without the cipher, cracking the code could take months."

"And we don't have months," Mazet sighed.

"So how do we know Query's not just trying to betray us like last time?" Griffin asked, his angular face creased with barely-contained rage.

I hesitated, then leaned back in my chair. "We don't."

JR cleared his throat, "But right now, it's our only option."

I gestured to the holoscreen. "And after what just happened, we may have even fewer options than before."

Most of the officers nodded, except General Qian. His face remained unreadable. Finally, he spoke.

"This cyborg…how do we find them?"

I swallowed. "Has anyone we know come out of Lanzhou?"

Silence.

JR tensed. "Are we looking? Or are those people just lost to us?" His voice cracked at the end.

Qian sighed. "Savants don't have a lot of mobility right now, as I'm sure you two are aware," he said blandly. "We have some contacts but so far no messages have been returned."

I rubbed my eyes and looked pleadingly at Ames. If anyone knew of available options, it would be the Timeseer. But when he met my gaze, his misty eyes were sharp, alert. He raised his hands.

"All we can do is wait. A solution will present itself," he said vaguely. "In the meantime, Lilly, I suggest you begin working on that data."

I nodded, swallowing the lump in my throat.

"A solution will present itself," I repeated, trying to quell my anxiety. I said it like a prayer, clinging to the words. But deep down, I hoped the solution didn't wait too long. Otherwise, there wouldn't be much of a China to save…

* * * * *

Tense silence filled the walk up the stairs from the War Room.

We'd laid out everything—the encrypted file, the slim chance we had to crack it, the possibility that Query had left us a way in. The officers listened, made their calculations, and handed me the job. But none of it could drown out the horror of Lanzhou. Millions dead. A city wiped off the map. It sat like a weight on my chest, but there was something else…something heavier…hanging behind JR's slouched posture.

Finally, he stopped, pulling me into a dim side hallway. Musty air tickled my nostrils and soggy floorboards squelched under our feet. I resisted the urge to recoil, though I tensed anyway, in case JR was planning to shank me or something.

"Rob," JR began in a low voice, frowning.

"Rostbane," I replied formally, slightly intimidated by JR's tone.

"You know I hate that name," he spat.

"I'm still your commander," I tried to keep my voice even, though irritation was beginning to bubble in my gut, "especially when you talk to me like this."

"I'm not talking to you as my commander, right now," the other man snapped, "I'm talking to you as my *friend*."

I made a face. "Okay, fine. Let's pretend I'm not your commander for a moment. What can I do for you, friend?"

"Why did Mara get the promotion?"

"Oh, for the love of Greysoft," I muttered. "Do we really have to do this now?"

"Yes," JR said, his breaths shaky. "You're my friend. My *best* friend. Don't you think I deserve an explanation?"

I sighed. "You're also my soldier. And as such, I don't owe you any explanation."

Turning on a heel, he paced in front of me. "Right. Humor me?" His eyes pleaded with me, frustration and hopelessness warring on his features.

Gritting my teeth, I forced myself to maintain eye contact with JR. "The officers determined her to be the best fit."

"But she doesn't want it! Any idiot can see that."

"It doesn't matter what she wants. She accepted it, and so should you."

JR's face was filled with anguish. "You know as well as I do that the position of sergeant should have gone to me. I mean, *what the fuck else* is my Skill good for in this army?"

"Your time will come, Rostbane." I tried to reassure him, though I felt anything but magnanimous.

"Why can't my time come *now?* I need to be useful!"

Doubt nagged in the back of my mind. Maybe I *had* made the wrong choice.

"Enough, JR!" I growled. "That's *not* the way to get me on your side."

The man scowled, but the feeling faded.

I took a slow breath. How do you tell your soldier he's too immature to lead? Shit, how do you tell your *friend?*

When I didn't reply, JR continued, "C'mon, Rob. You know I'm a dumpster fire when it comes to being a soldier. I've screwed up on every mission we've had. I think you just take me along because you feel bad for me. I'm a liability."

He pounded his fist against the wall, resting his forehead against the peeling paint. A tsunami of doubt, anger, pity, and self-loathing slammed into me, an almost tangible wave. I felt this as fiercely as I'd felt JR's breakdown in Xi'an when the council had been executed.

My resolve flagged. I slouched against the wall.

Snap out of it, Robert. I told myself, allowing all the emotions, JR's emotions, to bleed away. What replaced them was rage. *My* rage.

"Fine! If you want to be insubordinate, question your commander's judgment, and use your Skill against me, then let me tell you the hard answer," I shouted at him. "You're too unpredictable. You're indecisive, spoiled, impulsive, flippant, and your aim is terrible!"

A hot red blush spread up JR's neck and across his cheeks. He screwed his face into a snarl…and took a swing at me.

Anticipating this move, I grabbed his wrist mid-swing. Placing my other hand on his shoulder, I slammed him against the wall. The air whooshed from his lungs. As much as I wanted to hit the guy, I just pinned him there, one arm above his head my elbow on his chest.

He struggled against my grasp, but I was larger and stronger. Finally, I felt his tension melt. He sagged against my grip, his fist uncurling.

I took a deep breath.

He did too.

Calm nudged at the corners of my mind. I knew this was also from JR, but I allowed it to settle over me like a blanket.

Then, JR's face moved toward mine. I could smell sweat, whiskey, and a hint of gun oil over the murky waters in which we stood.

I pulled back, startled, letting him go.

"JR!" I scolded. "We are *not* that kind of friends!"

The other man sighed. "I know. Was just hoping…"

"Look," I said, my anger all but drained, "you can't do this stuff."

I gestured ambiguously.

"It could land you brig time."

He refused to meet my gaze. The sheen on his cheeks shimmered in the dim light from the hallway.

"Look, I'm sorry," I said, feeling sympathy for my friend. "This war has taken a toll on everyone. I understand what you're feeling."

He grunted, still staring at his muck-splattered boots.

"You are not a liability," I continued in a gentler tone. "I wouldn't have put you in my squad if I believed that."

"But I…" JR wiped his face with the sleeve of his T-shirt.

"But nothin'! You're a soldier. *My* soldier. And *dammit,* I believe in you!"

He looked up at me. "Rob, you're so full of shit."

"I'm not," I sighed. "You're good at a lot of things. A jack-of-all-trades —speedbike racing, tech wizardry, that martial arts thing you do. You make friends with everybody, you think fast, and you've got this way of coming at problems sideways that actually works. Not many people can say that."

He nodded, chewing on a lip thoughtfully. "You're not gonna tell anyone about this, are you?"

"Of course not! We're 'bros' remember?"

JR snorted. "Rob, you are so turn-of-the-millennium."

I smiled and gave his shoulder a squeeze, punching his chest firmly. "We synced now?"

JR staggered and grinned. "We're synced," he agreed.

For the first time since stepping into that War Room, I felt a little bit lighter, even though the weight of what came next still loomed on the horizon.

31

C.E. 2253 June 20

The next morning, a dark cloud hung over the breakfast table waiting. We ate in silence, waiting for something to happen. Rubbing the crust from my eyes, I nursed a very hot, very strong cup of coffee in both hands. I'd stayed up till dawn, digging through the code of the mystery file. But I couldn't find anything—every cipher I knew or found on the infonet was useless in decoding the data. I hunched into myself, yawning hugely.

"We hear anything yet?" Jun asked me, holding a similar cup of coffee.

I checked my handheld.

"Nope," I said.

"I *hate* this," JR snapped, slamming a hand on the table and rattling my coffee cup.

"Same," Mara replied, while pacing another circuit around our small living room.

I braced myself for JR or Mendez to joke about her wearing a hole in the floor, but the first seemed preoccupied cleaning nonexistent dirt from his fingernails and the latter stared vacantly into her coffee.

"I still can't believe it happened," Chet muttered, taking a long drag on a cigarette.

Technically, he wasn't supposed to smoke in here, but no one seemed to care enough to complain.

"Of course it happen," Ru snarled bitterly.

"But the residents," Mara said with a huff. "They didn't do anything to Rose. Were just trying to live their lives…"

"Angry white men in power hate everyone, even themselves."

I snorted.

The Spark flinched at the sound. "Sorry, Sir," he said hastily.

"Don't be," I sighed. "You're right."

The door of our flat opened with a loud swish. The Ox stormed in with a goofy, slightly crazed smile on his lips. In his arms he carried a large jug of pale yellow liquid.

Slamming it down on the table, he declared, "Today, we drink!"

Tilting my head at his dramatic entrance, I furrowed my brow. "A bit early to drink, don't you think?"

He flicked on the holoviz, "With most due respect, boss," he began, his initial frenzy cooled a bit, "today, it is not too early."

"That gōngjī yīyàng de rénzào zhìzhàng Rose visits Lanzhou today. To say statement," Ru said, his face scrunched up as if he'd just eaten something sour.

"That what—?" I asked.

The Ox smiled though his eyes remained sad. "Good lesson for you. It means 'rooster-like artificial moron.'"

JR stifled a snicker in his hand. I shot him a glare even while biting off my own chuckle.

"Okay, so Rose is making a statement," I repeated. "I suppose we should watch it, huh?"

I never understand why politicians always visited disaster sites. It was one thing to try and understand the destruction, another thing to offer aid and comfort the grieving, but to publicize your reaction on national holoviz made no sense. Especially when you were the one that called the bombs down in the first place.

I found the whole thing despicable.

Several of my squad reluctantly nodded and Mendez made a sound of disgust. "I hate that man," she muttered.

The Ox also nodded but added, "Not just watch it. When he says something stupid, we drink."

"A drinking game?" I asked.

JR's grin grew wicked. "I like your style, Niu. What's this?"

"Baiju or Du Kang," he said. "Made it myself. Very strong."

"I thought baiju was clear?" Mara asked, tilting the jug so very yellow liquid reflected the light.

Jun chuckled and said something in Mandarin I didn't hear. Using all six of her arms, she handed out napkins.

Mara shrugged. "She says the impurities will make us stronger," she said, though her tone was skeptical.

She twisted off the cap and took a swig, wincing. Her face bunched up as she tried to swallow.

"Well, I dunno about stronger, but still stuff'll definitely make you drunk."

I cut short my laugh as a news show began to play. The cameras panned over the still-smoking ruins of Lanzhou under that green-brown sky. Moving away from the city, the lenses focused on a hover convoy gently settling at the outskirts near a ruined Buddhist temple. Protesters stood between the convoy and the temple, holding signs and peace flags—rainbow edges fluttering in the thick breeze. Some of these protesters had burns or other injuries, indicating their proximity to the city as the bombs fell. I shuddered. The Ox handed me the bottle.

"We also drink any time something makes us want to cry," he explained. "For what can cure your melancholy better than Du Kang?"

Mara snorted. "So, you chugging the bottle first? Or am I?"

The Ox made a shrugging motion with both hands. "Your choice. I have more where that came from."

Mara grabbed the bottle and chugged till the fumes made her gag. She slammed it back onto the table. "Next?"

On the HV, security guards streamed from the convoy. They made a path for Rose, shoving the protesters aside with long batons. An old woman tripped, falling backwards into her fellows. Immediately they scattered to give her space to stand.

I contemplated the juxtaposition of compassion and violence. Gripping the bottle of baiju in both hands, I pressed it to my lips. The odor hit me first, pungent and cloying. Forcing myself to breathe, I allowed the yellowish liquid to slip across my tongue, smacking into my taste buds harder than a Tank's punch.

I coughed, my throat closing against the brew like a quick-lubed exit door. Baiju sprayed through the stand-alone holoimage and splattered against the wall behind me. *"Shit,"* I cursed, "that tastes like feet." Now I knew why Jun had distributed napkins.

The Ox roared with laughter. Jun and Ru snickered more politely.

I cast a suspicious glance at him. "Are you sure you didn't accidentally marinate your unwashed socks in grain alcohol?"

He slapped me on the back, making me cough further. "A few more sips and soon you'll feel the euphoria in your bones!"

I rolled my eyes. "Not sure you understand the meaning of 'euphoria,'" I said, dabbing the concoction off my chin. "But I'll give it a try."

I tried again. Swallowing my pride, I took another sip, more carefully this time. This time, the liquid went down with only minor gagging, warming my belly. I suppose once you got over the near-rotten fruit funk, it probably wasn't so bad…maybe.

By now, the guards were holding back the protesters, guns at the ready. Norman Rose rolled down the path between the guards and over to a makeshift dais at the temple. His large belly protruded as if he'd swallowed a balloon, and his skin glowed a sickly beige in the greenish pallor of the morning. On the dais lay two scorched objects: a bulbous-ended rod and a large, ornate bell with a crack running up one side.

Rose said something in Mandarin.

"What's he say?" I asked The Ox, "I didn't get any of that."

He shook his head. "That was completely unintelligible."

Yaozu nodded in agreement, "I *think* he meant, something like, 'Chinese citizens, I'm sorry for your loss.' But we don't say that to each other."

Rose picked up the objects. The Ox clucked his tongue. "Those are sacred things," he explained, "a prayer bell and Dorje, or 'thunderbolt'."

"Wǒ jiǎnzhí bù néng xiāngxìn tā de ěxīn de shǒu zhēnggè fùgài zài tāmen shàngmiàn," Jun said, chugging two large gulps of baiju. Surprising myself, I realized I understood that one. She said: *I can't believe his disgusting hands are all over them.*

Ru laughed bitterly, "Look at the idiot! He's holding them in the wrong hands!"

Indeed. Rose clenched the bell awkwardly in his right hand, trying to ring it, while waving the Dorje like a fool with his left.

"You ring the bell to for protection from the gods. The Dorje means enlightenment," The Ox continued.

"A little late for that," Chet muttered. "That bell ain't gonna ring again."

Jun snorted. "Him. Never enlightenment," she said bitterly in English.

Rose rang the bell.

A harsh metallic rattle sang once, then fell silent. Niu, Ru, and Jun all flinched at the noise and passed the bottle amongst themselves.

Rose spoke. "Friends, citizens, and distinguished viewers, I come to you proud of the response to this unspeakable tragedy."

Mendez made a sound of disgust again, louder this time. "I hate his voice. Does that count as something stupid?" The Ox smiled wryly and passed the bottle to her.

"*Dios mio!*" Mendez exclaimed, and held the bottle out to JR.

The young man eyed it warily.

"I did it," Mendez said through another cough. "Now you have to share my pain."

JR shrugged and took a sip. He, too, choked on the brew but was at least able to do so without completely misting us in baiju. Several fat droplets ran down his chin.

He gasped for breath. "I don't know what's worse…the man on the HV or this tā mā de drink," he muttered, wiping his chin.

"This bomb," Rose continued in a clipped, measured pace that sounded too loud even though our volume was turned down low, "was very devastating in terms of…bombs."

Drink.

"We mourn with the citizens of Lanzhou even though they knew what they were getting into."

"I'm sure that fruit peddler we met in the square was definitely aware they'd be bombed in five months," Mara scoffed, her eyes narrow slits.

Drink.

"I am here today to talk about accountability. What you have here is two sides coming together, violently. Coming together with clubs, and it was violent."

Drink.

"And what two sides were these? Mechs and savants?" A reporter yelled from the crowd.

"You had one side; you can call them savants—I just heard you call them savants."

Drink.

"They attacked our missile defense scientists violently and without provocation."

"Yeah. Not like he bombed any of our cities first," Ru muttered.

Drink.

"They are bad guys…these savants…bad, bad, bad guys."

Drink.

My face burned. Was it rage at Rose's grotesquely over-simplified, lie-ridden speech? Or was it the fire of baiju?

"And to eliminate bad guys and send a message, we—as Lightbar—must do what we must. The wonderful citizens of Lanzhou knew this. They were happy to give their lives to eliminate the savant menace."

Drink.

The Ox whistled. In a low, calm voice, he said, "I'm sure my zǔmǔ would think differently. She would never give her long life to a tyrant such as you!" His eyes remained dry, a fire burning within them, but the lines on his face deepened.

I looked over at him, surprised by his openness. Jun put her hand on his shoulder and Mara mumbled: "Xīwàng nǐ jiānqiáng yīdiǎn er." *I hope you can be strong.*

This exchange caused me to miss several lines of Rose's speech, but I decided it didn't matter. The man said nothing of substance, anyway.

"In terms of a real catastrophe," he was continuing, "like the Third World War where Europe was almost obliterated, and billions of lives lost… How many people have died here? Four…five…million?"

Chet rolled his eyes as he lit a cigarette. "Not a real catastrophe, my robotic ass," he said.

Drink.

"But as a nation, we are a national family now. It is our job to always protect, care for, and…make love to each other…"

"Make love to each other?" The Ox laughed. "He speaks English almost as bad as he speaks Chinese!"

JR snorted, wiggling his eyebrows in Rose's direction. His cheeks were flushed with baiju, and his speech slurred. "Maybe that's why Rose is so angry…probably hasn't fucked anything in decades."

"Except the Chinese people," Mara replied dryly, "repeatedly."

Drink.

"Yes, I'm sure even that muscle can atrophy," Ru added.

"His *deck* is so small, it's more like a patio!" Chet laughed.

Drink.

My head was growing light. I was having a hard time focusing on the HV—everything was tinged with the yellow of baiju.

Suddenly, a tiny drone circled Rose's head, landing with a *plink* nearby. Up popped an image of Zhelan. The dignified woman stood stoically, hands clasped in front of her.

"Hello, Rose," the holoimage said.

Rose looked at her confused, unsure why his moment was being interrupted. "Well, I'm going off-script here," he mumbled. Then, with a wave of his hand, a guard stomped on the tiny holo-drone. "F**K You, Zhelan!" He screamed, the HV network automatically bleeping out his profanity.

Drink.

Then the drone did something I'd never seen before. It replicated. Two drones took its place. Two more images of Zhelan.

The CEO continued to curse, but the only sound that came through our speakers was the voice of Zhelan.

"Rose, you will hear my message."

Two more guards crushed the drones, others shouted wordlessly to each other. From where each drone died, they doubled, producing four images of Zhelan.

"I think you will find, Rose jiào 'Xiānshēng," the four of her continued, without missing a beat, "the citizens of China will not let you get away with your tyranny any longer."

The guards crushed those, too.

Eight drones. Eight Zhelans.

Rose wheeled in a frenzy, attempting to snuff out the charismatic woman's image, but with every machine destroyed, two took its place.

Sixteen drones. Then thirty-two.

Wordlessly, my squad and I exchanged glances. *Drink. Drink. Drink.*

Soon a slew of images surrounded Rose, the guards, and even the protesters, each one staring at the CEO with cool anger.

"When the people are not heard," the holoimages said with sixty-four mouths, "They will find a way to fight back."

Then the image shimmered and changed, the holos melding together to form a black-and-white image of five bodies hung upside down from a girder. The text below appeared in both Chinese and English and read, *Benito Mussolini, April 28, 1945, Piazzale Loreto, Milan, Italy.*

"Those who do not learn the lessons of history," the voice-over continued, "are doomed to repeat them."

The baiju sat forgotten in my shaking fingers.

The next image was low-qual—a bearded man dressed in black with a rope around his neck. Surrounding him were others in dark hoods. One held the rope. A banner in Arabic was frozen on the screen. More text appeared below: *Saddam Hussein, December 30, 2006, Camp Justice, Baghdad, Iraq.*

Someone pulled the baiju from my hands, then put it back.

Drink.

Burning eyes fixated on the holo, I drank again.

Another image: a man in khaki fatigues, frizzy hair standing out in all directions. People grabbed at his clothing. He had a bullet wound in his forehead, still fresh and dripping blood. This text read: *Muammar Gadafi, October 20, 2011, Sirte, Libya.*

"All it takes is a spark," Zhelan's voice drifted over the silent crowd.

Resolve hardening, I clenched my hands into fists, rage bubbling in my gut. *We could do this, too,* I thought to myself.

The last display, a shaky video, captured another leader's final moments with the caption: *Chancellor Hector Valtras, August 3, 2132, Plaza Libertad, Neo-Buenos Aires, South American Federation.*

In this video, they'd pulled no punches. The dictator's once-impeccable uniform was torn and bloodied by the furious citizens who had dragged him across Plaza Libertad. Smoke and neon lights flickered over the scene, casting jagged shadows on the graffiti-streaked statues behind him—

monuments he had built to glorify his own rule.

He fell to his knees, hands raised in a final, trembling plea. Then, the crowd bore down, hiding him from view. Moments later, they dispersed, leaving his battered body sprawled on the cracked pavement, his golden insignia trampled underfoot, in the plaza where he'd given his first victory speech.

"We shall not suffer a tyrant's rule."

Static overwhelmed the news show. Zhelan's last words resonated within my skull, even though we could hear Rose again through the speakers, shouting and cursing.

"My camera man. Where is my camera man? And my producer? Cut the vid! Cut it!" A pause of fuzzy silence, and then, "You're fired!"

We killed the bottle as the picture went dead.

All it takes is a spark.

32

C.E. 2253 June 21

"Hey boss!" someone shouted from the common room of our apartment.

A struggle erupted—metal clanged, something heavy crashed against the wall of the houseboat, and then a sharp, mechanical whir sliced through the air.

Prying open my sleep encrusted eyes, I tried to wrap my throbbing head around the commotion. Laser pistol? Its hum reverberated through the walls, churning my already unsettled stomach.

"Oh shit! A laser pistol!" I muttered, suddenly alert.

Jumping out of bed in my briefs, I tripped over clothes and boots. The room spun around me, and my blurry vision struggling to focus. I rushed from the room, though it was more of a stumbling lurch, my hand trailing along the wall to keep myself upright.

"What the hell?" I snapped when I saw the disaster that was our common area.

Overturned chairs, scattered handhelds, and a shattered beverage carafe littered the floor. Coffee pooled around the shards of glass, turning the floor into a sticky mess. Chet stood on one end of the room, both arms outstretched and palms facing away from him, as if pushing against an invisible wall. JR held a laser pistol in both trembling hands, his face sheet-white, pointing the barrel at a third figure pressed against the far wall, pale pink hands above their head. Rom Query wore a neutral expression, but nonetheless their eyes darted between the two aggressors.

"I meant no harm," the cyborg placated in an even tone.

Due to their digitized voice, I had no idea whether they were scared or annoyed, but they looked less put-together than the last time I'd encountered them, suit torn and char marks across their bald head. One leg dragged across the floor, twisted at an odd angle.

"Query?" I asked, lowering my raspy voice an octave to try and gain control. "What the hell are you doing here?"

I looked toward Chet and JR. The former made a face, hands still raised. "Want me to let him go, boss?" he asked.

I shook my head, giving him a wave to say, *"wait."*

I approached JR cautiously, arms up. The Sway had still not lowered his gun, and from his vicious glare, I didn't think he would anytime soon. Gently, I gripped the gun, uncurling his fingers, though my eyes remained locked with his. JR scowled, releasing his bottom lip from between his teeth, his fury and fear buzzing about him like insects, but he let me take it. I flicked on the safety and tried to tuck it into my waistband, realizing I was still only in my underwear. Awkwardly, I clamped the pistol beneath my arm.

I turned to Query and straightened my shoulders, while I tried to fix the cyborg with an authoritative glower.

"You'd better have a damn good reason to show up here," I said to him with a menacing step forward, "after what you did in Lanzhou."

Query gave a frustrated sigh, "If you tell your man to release me, I'd be happy to talk like civilized humans."

"And why should we trust you?"

By this point Mara, Mendez, and the rest of the crew had made their way into the common room. Several other members of the squad were just as hungover as me, and they all eyed the scene with wary glances. Mara clenched her fists, shoulders hunched as if ready for a fight, but Mendez held a calming hand against her arm, the Zephyr as unflappable as ever.

"Because you're running out of options," Query replied, plainly.

"That's a poor excuse," JR snarled beside me. "With that rationale, he might as well be telling us all to go jump off a bridge."

I sighed, now very aware of my state of undress.

The cyborg made a frustrated gesture with his eyes, which looked like an attempted eye roll. "Very well," they said, "what if I told you I have the information you need to get into Lightbar Spire on Hong Kong Island."

I staggered. "Well," I said, brain kicking into overdrive, "that changes things. Chet, how long can you hold them?"

The 'Net made a show of yawning. "Long enough for you to get dressed." He winked.

"Good," I said, eyes raking over my squad. "Everyone take five to get yourselves presentable. Then, we'll see what this *cyborg* has to say."

* * * * *

It took me closer to ten minutes to get dressed, put away JR's gun, splash water on my face, and make my way to the common room. Someone had set up a chair for Chet, and now the Kinetic sat with a sheen of sweat on his forehead, one elbow propped on his knee and his hand in a *'stop'* gesture. Every time Query even twitched, Chet flicked his wrist like a conductor and pinned the cyborg back against the wall.

"You can relax now," I said to him.

With a breath he lowered his arm, face drawn, but expression unreadable. I took a seat next to JR who, from what I could tell, hadn't taken his eyes off Query since they'd arrived. The rest of my squad sat in a tense, silent standoff with the cyborg. The Ox kept his expression neutral, though both Ru and Jun glared at Query with open hostility. Yaozu stared at the floor, slight frown on her lips.

"You sure I can't fry him, boss?" Ru muttered to me, his eyelid twitching with agitation.

"No, Ru," I replied. "He's fine…for now."

The man sighed but gave a curt nod in response. He got up to pace off his energy.

My squad had cleaned up the mess, righted the chairs, and brewed a fresh pot of coffee. I poured myself a cup with a grateful sigh, turning my attention to Query who hadn't moved, despite being released.

The cyborg's posture was tilted, due to their broken leg. Their head snapped to the left occasionally due to a glitch in their processor. They raised their sharp eyebrows at me, as if waiting for permission. I gestured to an empty chair, wondering if the cyborg even needed to sit.

"Thank you," Query said gratefully, limping toward the chair with jerky movements.

I took a deep breath. "You don't look well," I said. "Did you get into trouble?"

Query gave a sardonic snort. "The last twenty-four hours have not been kind to me."

"I assume you came from Lanzhou?"

Query nodded.

"Is it really as bad as the holos say?" Mara asked, fixing the cyborg with a hard stare.

"Worse," Query replied, "depending on which news station you watch."

I frowned and even Mara slumped in her chair.

"I'm sorry," I said.

They waved their hand. "Nothing you could have done. I've survived bombs before. Many others…were not so lucky."

The Ox lowered his eyes, taking one hand in the other in a silent prayer.

"I assume you got my message, Robert?" Query continued.

"I did. Makes bloody little sense," I scoffed. "Why this? And why now?"

Query shrugged, a jerky motion rippling through their mangled body. "I had hoped it wouldn't come to this. I had hoped we could disable or destroy the rods, thus ending the conflict."

"But we failed," JR said bitterly. "If you had just given us the info on Hong Kong earlier…" he stood up, voice tone rising, "we could have prevented—"

I put a hand on his arm. "JR, chill."

"Chill?" he snapped at me. "I spent *months* in the medical ward with other soldiers who'd been injured in Xi'an, some who will never fight again. They were my friends! Some stayed in Lanzhou, a supposed safe space, and they died for it. Why the hell would I want to just *chill?*"

"JR," I said again, more forcefully. I stood to look him in the eyes. "*Sit down.*"

I pushed against his chest and the man folded, sinking into the chair and curling into himself. No one else tried to defend him, but the expression on several faces told me they wanted to. I had to remember that many members of my squad had friends—and in Niu's case, family—in Lanzhou, so I could probably stand to be a bit more sympathetic.

"I know. I'm sorry," I told JR, lowering my voice again. "This tragedy has affected us all. But right now, we can't dwell on the past. If Query can help us ensure that nothing like this ever happens again, I'm willing to listen to what they have to say."

"Chengdu mountain was not your fault," Query said. They tossed a datachip across the table. It was also singed—just enough that I could see the tiny circuit board inside. "I found this in the wreckage of the Control Center."

"Is this the cipher to the encryption?" I asked, turning the chip over in my hands. No energy tickled my senses, the chip as inert as every other.

Query shook their head. "No," they said, pointing to themself, "*that* cipher is me. This chip is…just a small piece of validation for Sergeant Lilly."

"Wait…" Chet said, "since the bombing of Lanzhou you've had time to go from there, to here, with a detour at the wreckage of the KEWP control center? That journey took us almost two months. How'd you do it?"

"That's not important," Query said with another frustrated wave of their hand. "What matters is that I came here as quickly as I could. At first, I didn't *want* to help you do what you're about to do. The price is almost too high to be worth it. But after Lanzhou, I cannot toe the line any longer."

"What do you mean?" I asked.

They spoke again, though I only caught every third word, talking about things like "duty," "love," and "regret." The speed of their speech increased, as if Query could dump all their feelings—if they had any—into a datadrive like the one that rested on the table.

"Enough!" I finally snapped. "What does any of this have to do with Lightbar Spire?"

The cyborg ceased their ramble with an almost surprised expression and blinked, as if resetting their internal processor.
"For that, my dear friends, I will need to go back to the beginning and talk about my first love," Query said, settling back in their chair. "Naira."

Part Four

Hong Kong Island, China

- 33 -
C.E. 2253 June 21
Query's Story

Naira and I met at the Eurasian Neuroscience and Physioengineering Conference in Xi'an, 2232. She was brilliant—sharp as a scalpel, relentless, and confident in a way that made you forget she came from a dying people.

Her ancestors had fought the rising tides, five million Bangladeshi survivors pushing inland, trying to outrun the water swallowing their home. But the land didn't want them either. Mountains, deserts, poisoned air, and war-torn tribes crushed them from all sides. Disease seeped into their DNA like ink in water. Three generations later, they were barely holding on—less than a million left, their bodies betraying them before they reached thirty.

And yet, Naira wasn't bitter. She was hopeful. She believed cybernetics and gene modification could save her people. That *she* could save them. Her theory struck something in me—something old and aching, buried deep in the circuits where my heart should have been. It felt like…déjà vu. As if I'd had the same idea once, in another life, before I became…this.

I wanted to help her. Maybe because I believed in her dream. Maybe because I needed a dream of my own.

But we were running out of time.

Naira was dying. Her spine was collapsing in on itself. Her organs failing. Her joints turning to dust. Twenty years old, and she had five left—if she was lucky. But I kept working. Sending her updates over telenet. Watching her slip away through a glass screen.

She was everything to me. The child I never had. The sibling I never knew. The companion I would never love. Watching her waste away was unbearable. I started to wonder if I'd shut myself down when she was gone. I'd lived lifetimes already, but none of them felt as real as the one with her in it.

And then—a breakthrough.

We had been working on a way to fuse cybernetics with organic matter —not crude, clunky implants, not the grotesque half-measures the corporations peddled, but something seamless. A perfect merger. A way to encase a fragile human soul in something stronger. If it worked, it would be revolutionary.

If it worked, maybe Naira wouldn't have to die.

* * * * *

"Wait…" JR cut in, brow furrowed. "Is that what you are?"

Query shook their head. "I am a machine. Inside and out."

"An AI?"

My stomach twisted. I leaned forward, pulse hammering. If a computer had evolved this far, if it could think, reason, and feel, then the whole human race was in danger. Being savant, mech, or True wouldn't matter anymore.

"No." Query's voice was steady, but something about it felt…weighted. "I was human once. I know this beyond a shadow of a doubt. My consciousness tells me so. I have…fears."

"Morals?" JR asked quietly.

Query nodded. "Regrets. Emotions. *Dreams.*"

Mara squinted at them, skeptical. "So, what happened to you? I mean, the human you?"

Query shrugged—an odd, deliberate motion. Their shoulder plates shifted in sequence, *clack-clack-clack*, like something unfurling beneath the surface. "I do not know." Their voice softened. "My storage drives are full. Databases, records, schematics. But my memories? They are only shadows. Echoes with the faint taste of humanity."

I swallowed hard. "This breakthrough…" My fingers curled against my knee, itching to reach out, to touch Query's metal body, to test it for myself. The information I could glean from an entirely robotic body…

I still didn't believe them. *Couldn't.*

Query's head tilted slightly. "I'm getting to that." Their voice remained steady, but something about their posture shifted, like a machine recalibrating. "My project, the Complete Integrated Brain Robot Grouping —shortened to CIBRG—was well underway."

"I read about that in the drive," I cut in, barely able to contain my excitement. If Query had been the one to mastermind it, I had a million and one questions.

Their slitted eyes narrowed. "Will you let me finish?" Their voice didn't waver, but irritation dripped through the precision of their tone.

I held up my hands in surrender. "Sorry." I grunted, trying not to sound too sheepish. "Go on."

Query regarded me for a moment before continuing. "Anyway, we had already developed the synthetic cerebrospinal fluid necessary to keep the brain alive on modified oxygen levels. The next challenge: connecting the brain to the heart. One cannot survive without the other."

"What about fake hearts?" JR piped up. "They've been doing those for years."

Query's head twitched sharply. Definitely irritated now. "Yes, yes, yes —but an artificial heart wouldn't work. The CSF needed organic cells produced by the real heart to circulate efficiently." Their fingers tapped against the table—a metallic clink. "Besides, I believe the heart is more than just another organ. It is the center of our love."

The words hung between us for a moment.

Love. Coming from a machine, it should have sounded ridiculous. But something about the way Query said it, like it was an immutable fact, sent a shiver down my spine.

"The breakthrough," they continued, "came from my discovery of Nu-blood: a combination of perfluorocarbons, optimized oxygenic compounds, adapted-CSFs, and a few other proprietary secrets. Pump this into the heart, integrate the lungs for total oxygen absorption, and you create super-organs in a highly efficient closed system."

I leaned back, gripping my knees. *Logic and love.* The two things that make us human.

Query might be onto something.

They settled back into the chair, mimicking a very human pose, though the stiffness in their limbs made it clear they were still learning. Their synthetic gaze flicked between us before they continued their story.

* * * * *

At first, I hesitated. Nu-blood had never been tested on a human. But Naira —stubborn, brilliant Naira—volunteered.

Her body had already shut down: connective tissue fried, nerves dead, muscles atrophied. But her brain—her glorious, sharp, untouchable brain— remained active, fighting against the inevitable.

Still, I wavered.

"I could never do this to you, Mèi mèi," I told her. "What if you die?"

She gave me a tired smile, her voice steady despite the frailty of her flesh. "Daÿita, beloved, I'm going to die anyway."

With that realization, I consented. To do otherwise would have been to deny a dying woman her final wish.

The procedure lasted twenty-four grueling hours. Another seven days of a medically induced coma to let her body adapt. And then—

She woke.

A complete success. Unlike my own transformation, Naira remembered who she was. Every memory, every thought, every trace of her humanity remained intact. This was it. The solution to her people's suffering. The key to my own missing past.

But the joy was short-lived.

Like vultures scenting fresh blood, the CORPs descended under the guise of sponsorship. Lightbar was the first to support my research, though I knew that bloated, decaying parasite, Sir Norman Rose, just wanted the technology for himself. 'The Fountain of Youth,' he called it. The miracle cure that would save a man who had spent decades indulging in excess, only to fear the consequences of his own gluttony.

I refused. I had already made the mistake of putting my kinetic weapon research in the wrong hands. I wouldn't make it again. But Naira…

She wanted to believe.

"Maybe if we share it, they'll leave us alone," she said.

I scoffed. "You really think that's how this works?"

I'd seen conflict. War. Greed. I already knew how these stories ended.

Even if we gave them the research, they'd never leave us alone. Tests and studies, labs and medical facilities—that would be our life until my circuitry burned out and her brain finally failed.

This technology did not belong in corporate hands. So, I destroyed it.

Encrypted every file, burned every physical copy, wiped every server. Maybe I was being idealistic. I thought that maybe if there was nothing left, Lightbar would move on.

I was wrong.

On June 14th, 2252, they came for us. They didn't just take Naira— they took Mayor Zhelan, the entire Xi'an Council, every official who had dared to champion our research.

And then the rods fell.

Xi'an burned. Leveled.

All because of our arrogance in believing we could change the world.

* * * * *

"So, when you said you'd survived bombs before…" JR began.

Query nodded. "I was in Xi'an when the rods fell. Among other things."

"Your own research—used against you." JR let out a sharp, bitter laugh. "That's irony, right there."

Query shook their head. "No. That's consequence." Their voice wavered, the first true crack in their machine-like detachment. "Xi'an. Lanzhou. This is all my fault."

They hesitated. A flicker of something unreadable passed over their face.

"Maybe I should have turned you over to them. Or kept the data from you. Would the war have been different?"

Silence settled over the squad like thick, suffocating fog.

"No," Query continued, more certain this time. "That was not the answer. Someone must stop the violence."

Chet let out a slow, dry whistle. The sound deafening in the quiet common room.

"Why are you telling us this?" I pressed. "What do you expect *us* to do about it?"

Query lifted their pink, synthetic hand, typing something into a datapad. "I sent you to the missile control center for a reason." They looked up, meeting my gaze with eerie precision. "I want you to rescue Naira from Hong Kong Island…if you can."

Naira.

Query spoke it with such reverence that I felt the weight of the name settle in my chest. She wasn't just tech. She was a person. And she was loved.

"If we can?" I asked, chewing on my lip. I could understand Query's love—at least to an extent. I brushed my fingers against Mara's thigh, my touch feather-light. A tremor ran through my hand.

Query made a sound—a long, low vibration. Something like a sigh, but too unnatural, too mechanical.

"She may not go with you," they said, their face falling. "Rose has sold her some very strong lies—that she'd be helping people, *saving* people, if she worked with him. He has bought her loyalty in the form of high-end technology, grants, and employees to work on this *advancement*, as he calls it."

Mara gave a dry snort. "Bet I know whose 'advancement' he's seeking." She wrinkled her nose. "His own," she spat when Chet gave her a curious glance.

Query nodded.

"What if we can't convince her to come with us?" JR asked. "Do we use force or what?"

"Kill her," Query replied, their voice like ice.

Mara gaped.

"Kill her?" Mendez asked with wide eyes, speaking for the first time. "Seems a bit extreme, no?"

"It does not," the cyborg continued without emotion. "I know my beloved. Once she gets an idea in her head, she will not release it. If you cannot convince her to leave with you and give up this silly pursuit of CIBRG technology, then she will never do so if forced. And the one thing that upsets me more than Rose using our technology for his own personal gain, it's knowing that the woman I love will deliver it freely into his hands."

"If you love her so much, why kill her?" JR asked. "Why not just…I dunno…lock her in a tower or something?"

"Because that works *so well*," Mara snorted and even I had to roll my eyes at that statement.

Query nodded, pink eyes pulsing as they surveyed the room.

"This technology is dangerous. No matter what I, or my love, believes, if it is given to men like Rose, it will never be used for good. It—she—will become a political pawn, exploited, and endlessly fought over. And worse, it could be used on nats. People with powers like yours."

My stomach twisted.

"Savants," someone breathed, though I couldn't see who had spoken.

The pieces clicked together—the CIBRG project, the nearly indestructible mech-humans, the experiments. Would the technology work on us? Could it preserve our Skills while turning us into machines?

I clenched my fists. *Of course* they wanted this tech. And *of course,* they'd turn it into something monstrous. When has corporate greed ever brought about anything good?

"While your intentions were benign, my friend," JR said, his voice low but charged, "your actions caused this. The bombs. The war. Do you feel good about that?"

The words landed like a blow.

Query shook their head. "All I ever wanted was to help my fellow humans."

The rawness in their voice was unsettling. A machine shouldn't sound like that. Clearly, they wanted to grieve, didn't have the capacity.

I studied Query—this thing that claimed to once have been a person, who had lived long enough to see their own good intentions turn to ash. I pitied them.

And yet…I was furious.

"This could create a whole new breed of mech. A more dangerous one. Did that ever occur to you?" My voice was edged with something I couldn't quite name.

"That would make us weapons," The Ox said, clearing his throat in clarification, "*CORPs weapons.*"

Query's pink eyes flickered. "The arrogance of intelligence," they murmured. "We understood the morality of it, in theory. But Naira and I… we never truly believed our work could lead to war."

They looked at me then, and for the first time, I saw it.

Regret.

Not in their face or their mechanical pink eyes, but in the way they held themselves. In the way their voice faltered.

"So, will you help me?"

I inhaled slowly. "What will you give us for this rescue?"

"Anything you want," Query said. "Security codes, underground routes, military bases... Any information I have is at your disposal."

The room fell quiet. The squad was waiting, watching Query. Watching me.

Did I trust the cyborg?

They had betrayed us before. Yet, they had also given us more information about Lightbar than all our spies put together. If we used this data correctly—

We could win this war.

Query also watched me, a slight tilt to their head. Their fingers curled against the table, metal scraping softly against the surface.

"Okay. I will help you," I said, my tone grave. "Because you're right, we don't have any other options."

- 34 -
C.E. 2253 June 28

"I hate sitting around," JR moped to me, spinning lazy circles in my desk chair.

A week had passed since Query arrived, and Tianjin Island was a frenzy of activity. With the cyborg's help, we cracked the intel file, exposing Hong Kong Island's defenses. The brass made their decision: we were going in. Troop mobilization had begun—training drills, war simulations, nonstop strategizing.

But for us lower-tier soldiers, it was mostly waiting. Regular duty, routine patrols, and too much time to think.

Too much time for me to run the plan over in my mind, checking and rechecking every detail. Ames had given me the full battle plan for my squad, and the weight of it gnawed at me. The others thought our only goal was to extract Naira, but I knew the bigger play. It killed me to keep it from them, especially Mara and JR, but I'd received strict orders.

The officers knew as well as I how dangerous the mission would be, and they needed us to be all in. This wasn't the time for hesitation, over-thinking, or regrets. I envied my squad's ignorance, because for me, one wrong move or one loose word could cause everything to unravel.

JR groaned loudly, tipping the chair back when I didn't answer right away. "Seriously, how long do you think they'll keep us waiting?"

"Why don't you charge your laser pistol and practice shooting?" I suggested, pulling the tool tray from my worktable. "Those bobbers are not going to hit themselves."

He made a noise of disgust. "I'm tired of pezzing tiny floating targets. They are too unpredictable."

"Like an enemy," I said, my tone flat. "How else do you intend to get better?"

"I was just hoping the enemy would walk onto my gun."

I snorted. "You are insufferably lazy, you know that?"

JR turned to me, pupils dilated by the spins, shaking his head. "I'm not *lazy.* I just have a different set of talents." He raised his eyebrows seductively.

270

I snorted in response and turned to my project, trying to tune out the Sway. As cantankerous as he was acting, I could tell he was in a marginally good mood. Both he and Chet had been promoted to Private First Class, and the accolade placated him.

"What's that you're working on, anyway?"

"A data ring," I mumbled, microdriver wedged between my teeth. "Found it on a dead mech in Lanzhou."

JR made a sound, "Mm-hmm. *Found.*"

I scoffed. "I didn't kill him, if that's what you're wondering. He was already dead, but the ring still had enough power to call to me."

The ring had become my pet project. A distraction. Something to focus on instead of my growing unease about everything else. In addition to the coming battle, I thought endlessly about Constance and silence from her side going on for weeks now. Not one damn message. But, I hadn't bothered to reach out either. Didn't know if I could face her, not when every time I thought about her, I came face-to-face with the uncertain, confused man I'd become.

I thought about Sam…. He didn't deserve a father who spent more time killing than bonding. Was I meant to be his hero or a distant, useless shadow? Sometimes, I wondered if it wouldn't be easier to disappear, and if he'd be better off if I were gone. Mara had mentioned doing just that when this was all over, but was that an escape or a cop-out? And how the hell would I ever explain it to him?

"Sorry son. I abandoned you for someone else, because life with you in it was too hard to face."

No, I couldn't tell him that. But hell, I couldn't keep living like this either.

"What's it do?" JR asked, watching me tinker with the ring.

"It stores data."

It wasn't a lie, but it wasn't everything. What I didn't say was that this was the only damn thing keeping me tethered to something that made sense.

JR groaned. "No shit. I got that from the name. What I meant was: what are *you* going to do with it?"

I shrugged. "Probably wipe it and upload all the data from Query. Then I'll give it to Sam. May be useful to the kid someday."

"Whoa, wait a sec," JR stammered, "doesn't that data belong to the army? Isn't that like stealing?"

I let out a dry laugh, my shoulders stiffening as I looked at him. "It's not *like* stealing, JR. It *is* stealing."

His mouth dropped open, and he didn't respond. Good. I didn't want to hear it anymore.

I paused in my tinkering, tool suspended in the air. "Besides, you of all people should understand. Weren't you part of the underground?"

"Doesn't mean I have no morals," JR muttered but I ignored him.

"Data is one of the most powerful things us savants have. We don't always have the numbers or the weapons, but knowledge can be more dangerous than either of those things. Never let data slip away. You got it?"

He nodded, a mischievous smile playing on his lips. "I get what you're saying. That's deep, Rob. I think I can use that concept when the war is over…if we survive that is."

If we survive. The words echoed in my head. Well, there was also that.

The assault on Hong Kong Island was still a risky gamble. We had information, but no plan could account for every variable. Death was as certain as the blood that would spill.

"Don't be such a pile of scrap, JR," I reassured him, trying to push the unease aside. "We'll be fine."

"I still don't see why that sticks us here, just cooling our jetpacks," JR pouted once more.

"Like I told the squad in our briefing, we are not going in until the Rebirth of the Moon festival, which is still months away. It's the biggest Chinese festival of the twenty-third century. You're the history nerd here, you get why it is so important"

"Sure, sure. It's how China celebrates the end of The Third. But I don't see why we should ruin everyone's holiday with an assault."

"There will be lots of people celebrating. Lots of people means lots of chaos. Fireworks. Pyrotechnics…shrimp wontons."

My mouth watered at the thought. The last time I'd attended the Rebirth of the Moon celebration in Lanzhou felt like a lifetime ago. Mara and I had snuck out of the bunker, pretending the world hadn't fallen apart, if only for a night. The street food, the costumes, the smell of life and celebration amidst that disgusting city—it was intoxicating.

By the end of The Third, the world had been a wasteland. Massive smoke clouds encircled the earth. The moon, in her silvery splendor, had also disappeared. When the smoke finally cleared weeks later, the moon also reemerged, a cause for rejoicing here in China. Of course, the Chinese rejoiced with food— and lots of it.

"Ugh," JR scoffed, "I still can't believe you didn't bring me any of those wontons."

"You could've come with us. Besides, we brought you New-Moon Cakes. That's the real specialty of the festival," I said in defense. "Why are you still grumpy about this a year later?"

"Because, you know how much I love food! Those New-Moon Cakes were good. It's a shame this time we'll be too busy killin' to pick up any."

I laughed, the absurdity of his words cutting through the tension. Only JR would find something so mundane to complain about during a war.

"How about this," I said, pausing to give him a pointed look, "when this is all over, I promise I'll find you some shrimp wontons."

"And New-Moon Cakes?" he asked, eyes sparkling.

"Did I hear something about New-Moon Cakes?" Mara's voice came from the doorway. She stepped into the room, her usual confident stride unmistakable. "Mmm….I could go for some of those right now." She hugged me from behind, kissing my ear.

I jerked away instinctively, though I couldn't deny the hunger that surged in me at the feel of her.

"Mara!" I snapped. "Here?"

She glanced over at JR and chuckled, "I thought you only pretended not to know when the officers were around."

JR groaned. "Yeah, but, like, do you have to do this right in front of me?" He made a sound of disgust. "Keeping secrets is already hard enough."

Mara laughed as she squeezed my shoulder. "Like the secret between you and Mendez?"

"What?" I almost squeaked but caught myself and coughed instead.

JR's eyes went wide, "I'm not…" His shock washed over both of us.

Mara snorted, "Don't lie, JR, you'll only implicate yourself further."

He stammered incoherently, while Mara's amused smile softened. Then, her face shifted, becoming unexpectedly tender. "Well, it seems like you're doing a decent job of keeping it on the D-L if even Robert didn't know."

"Well, Rob is kinda oblivious, so…" JR shrugged with a wave of his hands.

"Hey!" I snapped.

"Don't worry, qīn, you've been preoccupied with other things," Mara said, smoothing my sweaty hair from my forehead.

"Like destroying the world," I muttered.

"And by the way JR, no one cares." She winked at the red-faced man. She glanced at the data ring on my table. "That thing work yet?"

I nodded, slipping the ring onto my finger. It expanded, fitting perfectly. I could feel the processor humming, bytes of data running over my skin like static electricity. The ring was a reminder of everything I had failed to do, and everything I still couldn't fix.

"Someday Sam will have it."

"So, he has your Skill?" JR asked, having recovered enough from Mara's observation.

I shrugged, a bitter smile tugging at my lips. "I sure hope so…"

What I didn't say was that I hoped Sam didn't inherit Constance's True blood. That would be the final betrayal, wouldn't it?

I mentally slapped myself. *Enough of this self-loathing.* Enough of the past. There was only now, and the fight ahead.

I stood up quickly, ready to shake off the dark thoughts. "We should shoot some bobbers. Let's go."

"Gladly," Mara laughed.

JR just groaned.

- 35 -
C.E. 2253 July 8

The constant rumble of thunder could be mistaken for distant bombs, were it not for the summer rain that pounded against the walls. Wind and waves pitched the houseboat back and forth, my stomach pitching along with it. I languished on the couch in the common room, queasy and weak from vomiting. New Colorado hardly ever got rain, though we had wind aplenty. However, this particular combination, along with the raging sea, was a new kind of nightmare for this landlocked boy.

I staggered and heaved in front of The Ox, Chet, and JR, none of whom seemed to be suffering as much as me. Chet snickered after my latest trip to the toilet.

"It's relative happiness, boss," he said, even though he looked a little green himself. "As long as you're not the most miserable son-of-a-mech in the room, you're doing good."

I rolled my eyes, taking a tiny bite of a salty cracker and hoping it stayed down this time. A muffled knock sounded at the door. The Ox opened it.

"I'm looking for Staff Sergeant Lilly," the man said. He wore a soaked beige trench coat, hood pulled up, though sodden locks of hair still stuck to his forehead.

I took to my feet unsteadily, approaching the man with suspicion. It was the smile that I noticed first—confident, precise, and white.

"Nic Saint Claire?" I asked just as a gust of wind blew stinging rain into the room, slapping me in the face. "Get in here before you soak the whole house!"

He nodded, slipping inside and latching the door with one fluid motion. The Ox dusted rain from his tight T-shirt, and I wiped my face with the hem of mine.

"It's good to see you again," Saint Claire said, pulling off his sodden coat and hanging it on a peg. "Congrats on the promotion."

I noticed he was out of uniform, instead clad in dark blue denim pants, beat-up brown work boots, and a polo shirt with a purple and yellow logo on its breast.

"*Promotions*," I said flatly, too ill to care about platitudes. "What are you doing here, Saint Claire?"

"Just 'Nic' is fine. Titles are only necessary when I'm playing army."

"Playing army?" I said with a shake of my head. "Whatever. What can I do for you?"

Nic eyed the coffee pot on the counter, bubbling with a fresh pot someone had recently made. "Well, I could use a beverage."

I gave him an irritated sigh but waved toward the pot anyway. "Help yourself."

The boat made another rolling heave, and I staggered, catching the back of a chair and placing myself in it before I could fall on the floor.

"Who the hell is this guy?" Chet asked, glancing at JR. "Do we know him?"

JR shook his head, grimacing at Nic, and The Ox just shrugged.

"Guys," I said to the three men who'd now gathered around the table either sitting or standing next to me. "This is Nic Saint Claire. He's um," I coughed, eyes settling on the sandy-haired man, "what do you actually do for the army? What's your position?"

Nic laughed. "Oh, I am not enlisted."

"An officer then?" Chet asked.

He shook his head. "Strictly speaking, I'm not with the army at all. Consider me more of a consultant."

"Like Mendez?" The Ox said with a smile.

Nic had poured himself a cup of coffee and now took the last unoccupied seat at the table, leaving JR standing stiffly at my right shoulder. He gripped the back of my chair; I felt his fingers digging into my shoulder blade. His Aurawave simmered in my belly, replacing the nausea with something sharper—unease.

"Less hands-on, I'd say," Nic continued.

"Would you just tell us who the fuck you are?" JR snapped, his composure cracking.

What was making him so nervous?

Nic didn't react to the outburst. He took a slow sip of coffee, then finally said, "Second Chief of Spec-Ops."

I felt JR's grip tighten on my chair. I processed the words. Spec-Ops? That logo…had I seen it before?

Then it hit me, like one of Lightbar's rods slamming down. I stiffened, forcing myself not to push back from the table. "You're with the CORPs."

JR's hand flew toward his laser pistol, but I caught his wrist before he could draw. Across from us, Nic didn't flinch, though I saw the subtle shift

—his weight adjusting, his muscles coiling. Preparing.

"You're sharp," he said, trying to diffuse the situation with an awkward smile.

"Do the officers know?" JR asked, clearly rattled and not thinking straight.

"Of course, the officers know," I tried to reassure my friend.

They had let Nic into the army last year. And he was here now, in this room, which meant one of two things—either they trusted him, or they thought they could use him. The officers of the Citizen's Army may be a lot of things, but one thing they weren't, was sloppy.

But Nic didn't confirm or deny it. Instead, he took another sip of coffee and said, "I work for a smaller company. One of the CORPs, yes, but not all of us agree with the Triumvirate."

"So, you're a mech?" I asked, even though I knew it was a dumb question. Nic didn't strike me as someone who'd buy into a lot of commercial tech.

He shook his head.

"A True, then?"

Nic didn't answer.

Silence stretched.

"But you can't be…" JR exhaled sharply.

The man smiled, "The world is not so black-and-white, Private…" he peered at JR's name badge, "Rostbane. You know, I knew someone of that name back home. You wouldn't happen to be related to Aron Rostbane, would you?"

The question caught JR off guard. He blinked at the man, then said acidly, "He was my father."

"Quite the influence in The Sink," Nic continued conversationally, "for better or for worse. I take it you have your father's Skill?"

JR swallowed hard. I could feel his anger bubbling over as he clenched his hands into fists. He nodded slowly and said, "I'm not him. I don't condone the things he did."

Nic shrugged as if he had no opinion one way or the other. "We do what we can to survive. My sons are in The Sink right now. My eldest is a Sway like you."

Nic's son was a Sway? I hadn't felt any Aurawaves from him like I could from JR. Either the man was better at controlling it, or he didn't share a Skill with his son. I hoped it was the latter. I didn't need another person affecting my emotions, especially if I couldn't tell when they were doing it.

"Well, hopefully he doesn't make the same choices my father did. My brother is bad enough. The Sink doesn't need another like him." JR locked eyes with Nic, challenging the older man.

I cleared my throat. "So, whose side are you on anyway?"

"Neither," Nic chuckled, "and both. Right now, mechs and savants fight to maintain the status quo—the subjugation of one group for the advancement of the other. But if any of us are to survive, change must happen. Can you remember a time before the Tech Divide?"

"Of course not," I said, rubbing my temples.

Nic referred to the ideological split of the twenty-first century—tech versus genetics. Human augmentations started with prosthetics, then advanced to DNA manipulation. The key difference? Gene mods were passed down through generations, while mech upgrades had to be repurchased. The capitalist government's choice was obvious. Rich men stayed rich when people kept on paying.

"No one does," Chet added. "That was more than two-hundred years ago."

"True," Nic replied, "but our ancestors knew another way. They understood what it meant to work together. They understood equality."

I snorted.

"Bullshit," JR scoffed. "If they cared about equality, they wouldn't have created the divide in the first place. Humans have always found reasons to fight—gender, skin color, sexual orientation. We just trade one -ism for another, over and over and over."

I was raised to believe that the mechs of the UCCA despised us as much as we despised them. We were too different, after all. The Triumvirate and its ruling CORPs were *not* our friends. After The Third, they had claimed they wanted to rebuild the West, but all they really did was consolidate power, build megacorps, and sell more shit. When they couldn't sell to or breed out savants—when our abilities just kept getting stronger—they hunted us instead.

It was even more dangerous these days. Our existence depended on whether the Triumvirate decided to "reclaim our streets" on any given day. In The Sink, the cartels kept us marginally safe, but their goodwill could turn on a whim. In a sense, they were much like the Triumvirate, much like the mechs—as detached and unfeeling as a hunk of cold metal.

My opinion had begun to shift since I'd been in China. I thought of Jun, drinking baiju, laughing, wailing over Cheng's death. She was as human as the rest of us. And just as vulnerable. Her mods didn't change any of that.

I took a trembling sip of coffee, immediately realizing that had been a mistake. My stomach heaved again, and I had to resist the urge to gag.

"Saint Claire," I said formally, "as much as I'd love to sit here and debate philosophy with you, I'm currently locked in a battle to keep the contents of my stomach inside, and I'd rather not lose. Do you actually have something relevant to tell me, or are you just trying to waste my time?"

Nic crossed his arms and leaned back in his chair. "There's something you need to know, Sergeant. There's been a leak."

I tensed at the word, my gut twisting. I didn't need this right now. Not on top of everything else. "What do you mean?" I asked, cautious.

"The enemy's been too precise lately," Nic said. "They move before we do. Hit supply lines before we get boots on the ground. It's happened too often to be just bad luck."

I exhaled sharply. "You saying there's a mole?"

Nic nodded.

JR stiffened behind me. "That's a hell of an accusation."

"And an accurate one, too. Someone's feeding Lightbar intel. And given how your last mission played out, I have reason to believe they're close to you."

My stomach churned, and not from seasickness this time. I saw Cheng's face in my mind's eye—pale, bloodless, anguished.

"I'm sorry," he'd said…

I kept my voice measured. "You're not the first to suggest there's a traitor. We thought it might be Cheng." I gave Niu an apologetic grimace, he narrowed his eyes in response. "But he's dead now."

Nic held my gaze. "And yet the intel still leaks."

That implication hit like a punch to the ribs. I clenched my jaw, glancing at JR, who had gone utterly still. Our eyes met and I knew he suspected as I did. If it wasn't Cheng…then that meant…

Yaozu.

It had to be.

She was the only one left unaccounted for when things went south. The only one who'd gone missing, conveniently turning up later, battered, scared, with a half-baked story about survival. The squad believed her. I *wanted* to believe her—*needed* to for the sake of my squad—but doubt hung over me like a cloud.

"Shit," JR muttered under his breath. "She's been with us this whole time."

"Who?" Chet asked, glancing at The Ox, who just shrugged.

"We can't make assumptions," I said, dismissing Chet's question. My mind was already picking apart memories, replaying moments I hadn't thought twice about before. "I need proof."

Nic studied me. "I can't give you names—I don't have them—but I do know this: a particular officer wants your squad off the board. And they're getting help from the inside."

I exhaled slowly, the weight of it settling over me. I trusted my squad with my life. If one of them has been sharpening the knife meant for my back…. Shit. How many more betrayals could I take?

"If you know next to nothing, why tell me?" I sighed, the weight of everything bearing down.

Nic smirked, though it didn't reach his eyes. "Because, I need you to know that while there are those out there who would see you fail, we are also looking out for you."

"Looking out for me?" I asked.

At one time, I was a nobody private from a nobody squad but now… the implications of Nic's words rippled through the air. I looked at my men. The Ox gave me a wide smile, Chet grinned, and even JR seemed to relax behind me. Well, I wasn't a nobody now. Though still unsure of exactly *what* I was, at least I knew I wasn't alone.

Nic gave a slow nod, as if choosing his next words carefully. "Not every company in the Coalition backs the mechs. Mine doesn't. For now, we have to play by the Triumvirate's rules, but in the shadows, we make our own." He winked. "One day we will show our hand. Then, all hell will break loose."

He pushed his stool back and set the empty coffee cup on the table. As he did, something small and metallic slid from his sleeve. It hit the table with a soft, ringing clink and spun once before settling beside the cup. A dull, steel dog tag, worn at the edges. An embossed fist, knuckles raised skyward, glinted in the dim light.

"We'll need good people on our side," Nic finished with gravity. "I hope you are one of them."

I squinted at the tag. My heart jolted, though I couldn't say exactly why. Something about the symbol gnawed at me, deep in my chest. It blurred my vision. So much so that it hurt to look at. I wanted to push it away, but my hands stayed frozen at my sides.

Nic watched me as he shrugged on his coat, his movements casual. "Thank you for your hospitality," he said, voice light. "But now I really must get going."

I stood as well, my gaze still snagged on the table. "Thanks for the warning, Saint Claire," I muttered, mind racing.

He gave a business-like nod, turned toward the door, and placed his hand on the handle.

"Wait," I said, finally dragging my eyes from the table. "What is your company, by the way?"

"HumanSource," he said with a knowing smile. He twisted the handle and stepped into the gale.

I didn't move. The rain pattered on the rooftop like static. Slowly, I reached down and picked up the tag. The imprinted metal sent a jolt up my arm.

The coin's edges bit into my palm as I closed my fingers around it and slipped it into my pocket. No one else said anything, but the look of curiosity on their faces said enough.

Human. Like us. Like them.

C.E. 2253 July 9

"Rob, we need to talk about this, *now!*" JR hissed at me, tugging on my arm.

"Not here," I muttered, eying the quiet common room.

Chet dozed on a couch, reading tablet propped over his face to block the light. Jun and Ru were locked into that VR game they spent all their free time on, and Mara vacantly watched bubbles rise to the surface of her beer.

I knew what JR wanted to talk about—he'd been trying to get me alone since Saint Claire's visit the previous day. But I didn't want to talk about it. I feared voicing the concerns would make them real, and if they were real, I'd have to do something about them. Mara met my eyes, and I knew she'd caught me staring. I gave her an apologetic smile. Eyes dancing, she stood and walked over to where I sat at the table, contemplating yet another battle plan.

"You've got that look again, Robert," she said, her voice a gentle purr from the dozen beers she'd drank that day.

She rubbed her hands on the outside of my arms, and I leaned against her.

"What look?"

"The look that something's bothering you."

"Because something *is* bothering him," JR said urgently.

Mara flicked her eyes to the man, who sat at the edge of his seat, as jittery as a Spark, then looked at me again and raised a knowing eyebrow.

"Need some fresh air?" she asked.

I had wanted to tell her—I trusted her above everyone else—but hadn't known how to do so without sounding crazy.

I smiled. "Sounds like a plan." I nodded toward JR, then tilted my head toward the door.

"Oh, thank Charger," JR muttered. "This is a miracle."

"Miracle?" Mara asked him, pulling a handful of beers from the outdoor cooler—Niu's latest 'cure' for the squad's recent bored sobriety.

They followed me along the boat's wrap-around porch, where I led them to a set of benches. The slight breeze blew cool after yesterday's violent storm, bringing fresh scents from the ocean, which shone from the light of the setting sun like sheet of orange glass.

"Getting this tight-lipped, stuffy bastard to talk about his problems, rather than just ignoring them and hoping they'll go away. *That's* a miracle," JR replied.

Mara snorted. She opened each bottle with her teeth—a popular party trick among Tanks—and spat the caps into an empty barrel.

"So, what's the scoop, Sarge?" she asked me with a mischievous grin.

I sighed and took a long pull of my beer, wishing I hadn't even started this conversation.

"Yaozu's been betraying us," JR blurted, as if those words had been banging at the back of his teeth for days, just waiting to get out.

"What?" Mara snapped, sliding to the edge of her seat.

"We *don't know* that for sure," I said quickly, slapping a hand against JR's chest.

The man grunted. "But who else could it be? Saint Claire said we had a mole."

"Wait…rewind," Mara said, holding up a hand. "Nic told you this? When did you talk to him?"

I told her about the previous day's visit.

She nodded slowly. "So, you think Yaozu's the mole because I lost her in the chaos at the control center?"

"Has to be," JR said. "She was the only one unaccounted for."

Mara furrowed her brow, resting her inquisitive gaze on me. "So, what are we gonna do about it?"

"Get rid of her. Immediately."

"We can't just kill her, JR." I shot him a glare. "This isn't the mafia."

He rolled his eyes. "I *know* that. I meant remove her. Tell Ames. Tell *someone.*"

"It's not that easy," I said dryly. "You know that as well as I."

"Well, we can't wait. If she's been leaking intel, she's probably still doing it. She could be feeding them our battle plans right now!" JR stood up to pace along the lengths of the deck.

"We don't know that."

"We don't *not* know it either," he insisted.

"Look," Mara said calmly, peeling the label off her empty beer bottle. "We already doubted Cheng, and we lost him. Yaozu barely made it out of that place alive. If you start pointing fingers with nothing to back it up, you'll tear the squad apart before we even hit the battlefield."

"Why do you think I didn't want to talk about this?" I gave JR a stern look and ran a hand through my hair. "On the one hand, if she's innocent, we'll still have to find the problem. On the other, if she *is* the mole, then we're walking into a trap."

"Then, let's eliminate the obvious threat, first," JR insisted. "Maybe we *should* just kill her."

"JR," Mara scolded, "we don't just go around killing people for some assumption! What do *you* think we should do, Robert?"

I drummed my fingers against the nearby crate. "I…guess…I could talk to her?"

"Talk? That's your plan?" JR spat.

"Yeah. And if she gives me a reason to doubt her, then we'll do more than talk."

Mara chewed her lip thoughtfully, as if weighing me. "It's a good start, I suppose."

JR nodded, jaw tight. "Fine but choose your words carefully. The last person you need doubting you is Yaozu."

"Hey guys, whatcha—?" Chet's voice came from behind us. "Wait… Yaozu?" he asked, poking his head around the corner. "What about Yaozu?"

"Nothing," I waved him off and distracted his attention by eying the beers in his hand. "You sharing those?"

Chet narrowed his eyes. "Was gonna…before you got all shifty and secretive," he said, taking a seat on a crate across from me.

"It was just, like, battle strategy and such," JR said, waving a dismissive hand. "Hella boring sergeant garbage."

I looked at JR. The tension had fled from his shoulders, like a rubber band snapping back into shape. A wave of contentment washed over me, smoothing out the lines in Chet's skeptical face.

"Let's talk about something more interesting," JR said, his eyes twinkling, "like how you and Jun slipped away for a 'walk in the rain' last night." He elbowed Chet in the ribs.

The Kinetic laughed, flashing crooked teeth. "It was more than a walk, if you know what I mean." He licked his lips. "Those metal fingers are surprisingly delicate."

I threw up my hands. "Dammit! Is *everyone* in this squad fucking someone?"

"Not sure about Ru," JR said. "Though, I think he has a virtual girlfriend or some shit."

Even Mara laughed now, giving me a peck on the temple. "It's not like we have much else to do right now." She stood up, taking two of my fingers in her hand and giving me a suggestive grin.

"Well, that's my cue!" I said with too much bravado and stood up. As Mara led me away, I made a mental note to thank the two of them for saving me from an awkward exchange with Chet. That is, if I remembered anything after an evening with Mara.

- 37 -
C.E. 2253 July 11

I found Yaozu in the supply barge, cataloging a crate of new laser pistols. Her handheld beeped as she scanned a gun, confirming its functionality, then placed it into a second crate. The overhead lights flickered, the barge bobbing against the gentle waves. The hum of the generators filled the space between us.

She didn't look up. "Something you need, Sarge?"

I clenched my fists, rolling my shoulders before stepping forward. "Yeah. We need to talk."

A shadow shifted against the far wall—Chet. He leaned against the bulkhead, arms crossed, boot propped against the metal plating. Watching.

I exhaled sharply and flicked him a stern glare. "Alone."

Chet didn't move. "Nah, I think I'll stick around. Y'know, squad morale or some shit like that."

I spent one more long moment looking at Chet, but decided it wasn't worth my efforts to make him leave. Yaozu would either be forthcoming, or she wouldn't. Chet's presence wouldn't change that.

Yaozu forced a laugh. "The hell is this about?"

"This rescue mission is not gonna be easy," I said slowly. "I need to know where everyone stands."

"Stands?" she asked, looking down at her feet.

"I need to know if you're with me," I said, biting back the frustration in my voice.

She scoffed. "Seriously? You question my loyalty now?"

Her eyes flicked to Chet, looking for backup, but he stayed silent, studying her.

"You disappeared at the KEWP control center," I said. "No one saw you go down. No one saw you get back up. You got any insight on that?"

Yaozu's jaw tightened. "Already told you. I went unconscious. Woke up in the dark. Barely got out alive. Don't know anything else."

She gave me a plaintive look, as if daring me to doubt her.

Then Chet chuckled, low and rough. "Really, Yaozu? Do you think we're that fucking stupid?"

Her gaze snapped to him. "Excuse me?"

"You got knocked out at the perfect moment," Chet continued. "Didn't see Cheng get shot. Lost track of Mara. Then, you appear at the eleventh hour with only a black eye and a story of how you escaped the mechs *and* the bombs." He tilted his head. "Pretty convenient, don't you think?"

Yaozu's grip tightened around the pistol in her hands. "I don't need to explain myself to you." She looked at me. "Or you," she continued, her gaze dark.

"No," I replied, "you don't. But if you want my trust, you'll tell me the truth."

"Already did." She glared at me.

Chet grinned. "If you're so sure," he said, drawling it out, "we could call JR. He'd cut through all this bullshit real quick." He pulled out his handheld.

Yaozu went stiff, fingers tightening so hard on the pistol that, if she were a Tank, it would have shattered. Her breath caught in her throat.

"You wouldn't," she said, looking at me. Her voice trembled, a second of panic flashing in her ice-blue eyes. Then, her jaw clenched, and it was gone, replaced by a cold glare. "Only weak commanders would use a Sway against their own soldier."

I flinched at the comment, heat rising to my cheeks. I set my jaw tight for a retort.

Chet raised his eyebrows and spoke before I could. "Why not? If you're telling the truth, you got nothing to hide, right?"

Yaozu wheeled on him. "You're not putting that shit in my head!" she shouted.

He smirked, slow and satisfied. "Touched a nerve, did I?"

"Ferryman, enough," I snapped, holding up a hand before things escalated further. I turned to Yaozu. "No one's Swaying you."

Chet let out a disappointed huff, but I ignored him, watching Yaozu instead. The tension in her shoulders. The darting of her eyes. She was breathing too fast for someone who was just 'offended.'

"You're acting real guilty right now," Chet said with a shrug. "Just sayin'."

"Or maybe I just not enjoy being bullied by my my fellow," she snarled. "Suggesting coercion. *Questioning me like I'm criminal.*"

Chet spread his hands. "Hey, I'm not the one making myself look suspicious."

She took a sharp breath. "Fuck this." Her gaze flicked to mine. "I'm an Auraseer," she said through her teeth. "We good at sneaking. And we *know* things about people. Things they don't say out loud. Maybe you should watch out for me."

She shoved past us, stalking away and letting the veiled threat hang in the air.

I allowed her to go, reeling from the confrontation. For a moment, I'd forgotten that fact about Yaozu. Forgotten that she could see my truth through my Aura, know the emotion of my heart. What did she see in me that I wasn't willing to admit to myself?

Chet clicked his tongue, shaking his head. "You gonna tell me what's up now, Boss?" he asked. "Why you're questioning her loyalty and not Mara's?"

"No."

"I hope it's not just because Mara's your lover."

"It's because I'm not sure if I'm just being paranoid," I said flatly. "Or if we have a real problem on our hands."

Chet shrugged. "Well, I'm still with you, Boss. Even if you're being a cagey fucking bastard. And, if I do find out it's a problem…these won't hesitate to solve it." He held up his hands and cracked his knuckles, the loud pops like gunshots in the enclosed space.
The way he'd watched Yaozu's back, gaze burning from his craggy face, gave me no doubt he meant it, too.

* * * * *

Ames barely looked up as I stepped into his quarters. The captain sat hunched over his desk, tapping through a holographic display filled with logistical reports, casualty numbers, and the latest intelligence. His expression was as sharp and tired as ever.

"If this is about the new op orders, direct your questions to Ripley," Ames said without preamble. "I can't help you."

"It's not. I need to talk to you about something else."

Ames exhaled through his nose and shut off the display. He gestured to the chair across from him. "Then sit. Talk."

I hesitated, not used to such coldness from my captain. Finally, I obeyed, sinking into a seat.

"I need Yaozu out of my squad," I said.

Ames's brows lifted slightly. "And why's that?"

Since my confrontation earlier that day, I had already run the conversation through my head a dozen times, rehearsing my argument. But now that I was here, the words felt thin.

"She was unaccounted for at the KEWP control center," I started, "and we almost left her behind. But also, we missed that employee because of *her* mistake. How do I know the distress call wasn't because of that, too?"

"That's just speculation."

My jaw tightened. "I already talked to you about Cheng. But I didn't tell you everything. Sir, he apologized right before he died. *Apologized.* I can't help but keep wondering, 'what for?'. Some of my squad thought he was the one who leaked the distress call, rather than it being just bad luck. Then, Saint Claire shows up saying he thinks I have a mole in my squad and information keeps leaking…"

Ames let out a sharp breath through his nose. "Saint Claire's always chasing ghosts. I wouldn't put stock in his warnings."

"But Yaozu…. She disappeared right before everything went to shit. Don't you think that's too convenient?"

The captain shrugged. "If I analyzed every split decision or abnormal reaction that happened during war, I wouldn't have time for anything else."

I sighed, noticing I'd hunched in on myself, confidence bleeding from me as if from an open wound. I squared my shoulders once more. "Well, I confronted her about it. She got defensive. Real defensive."

"She's been through a lot. And now this," Ames said flatly. "Most people would get defensive if you accused them of selling out their squad."

I leaned forward. "Chet brought up using JR to get the truth out of her, and she lost it. Wasn't just that she was offended. She was scared."

Ames studied me, his expression unreadable.

"You really think she's the mole Saint Claire told you about?" he asked, voice measured.

I nodded.

"Do you have proof. Comm records? More unaccounted-for disappearances?"

"No, sir."

Ames sighed and rubbed a hand down his face. "Then I can't remove her."

I stiffened. "Sir—"

"I don't make decisions on suspicions alone," Ames scolded. "And neither should you."

I flinched at his tone.

The man's gray eyes softened, and he leaned on the desk. "Look, I'm sorry, but if I pull her without evidence, it sends the wrong message. It makes us look lazy. Arrogant. And most of all, unjust. If anything destroys trust faster, it's the sense that some people are punished without cause while others act without consequence. And without trust, well, you can say goodbye to unit cohesion. You should know that."

My fingers dug into my knees. "I do. But if I'm right—"

"If you're right," Ames said, "then you'll find proof. And when you do, I'll deal with her myself."

My throat felt tight. "And until then?"

Ames held my gaze.

"Keep her close. Keep an eye on her."

A heavy silence hung between us, and a cold lump formed in my stomach.

Ames laced his fingers together. "Is that all, Lilly?"

I ground my teeth. I knew when I was being dismissed.

"Yes, sir," I muttered, pushing myself to my feet and giving Ames a half-hearted salute.

I may have left Ames's office, but the knot in my gut stayed. Now, I had no choice. Ames made it clear that he was too busy to accommodate my suspicions. Yaozu was my problem now.

Which meant that I had two options: catch her before she could do any damage or pray to Greysoft that I was wrong.

- 38 -
C.E. 2253 September 7
2200 hours

Hong Kong Island loomed like a lonely mountain in the distance, jutting out from the dark blue sea against an even darker, starless sky. Tonight, the entire island was aflame, lit with a myriad of paper lanterns, LED torches, and bonfires flickering in every color of the rainbow. White-capped waves crested around the landmass in a gentle, silent dance. I watched those waves with a knot in my belly, allowing their rise and fall to lull me into a false sense of calm. The Rebirth of the Moon celebration was in full swing, and we were there to ruin it.

The hovervan was crowded and stuffy. Mezei and Brit from the Black Cats had joined my squad for this mission, and along with Mara and The Ox, the Tanks' collective bulk pressed the rest of us into the corners of our seats. JR had taken his place by the window, his leg jittering almost as much as Ru's, who sat across from him. Chet muttered some complaint about Jun's tech digging into his ribs, but I also noticed her human fingers intertwined with his. Yaozu, on Jun's other side, echoed Chet's complaint in a light-hearted fashion, while giving Jun a friendly punch on her human shoulder.

I watched the Auraseer through half-lidded eyes. Despite my concerns, Yaozu had acted like a veritable angel in the months since our confrontation, with more "yessirs" and "no sirs" than even Niu himself. It made me suspicious, and I noticed that Chet hardly let the woman out of his sight, but what could I do? Report her for being *too* compliant?

"Something you need, Boss?" Yaozu asked, when she noticed my stare. She flashed me a friendly smile, her expression so unlike the one from my first interaction with her.

"Just thinking," I said, trying to give her an equally fake smile. Then, I looked around to my squad.

"Okay team," I began, trying to keep the tremor from my voice, "we'll be under a comm blackout once we arrive in the city. We can talk to each other, but long-range signals are too easy to track. We have our orders— find Naira and get her out of Hong Kong." I paused, dreading the next words. They would be a surprise to my squad, though I'd known the full plan for weeks now. "We've tracked her to Lightbar Spire."

"The most secure place in Hong Kong?" JR asked, raising a worried eyebrow. "*That's* where we have to go?"

I nodded.

"Well fuck me," Chet said with a whistle. "And the officers are trusting *us* to get in there?"

I nodded again. "We've also been given additional orders." A breath. "Kill Rose."

Nine mouths gaped at me.

"The officers are trusting us *with an assassination*?" JR asked, panic burning like a hot iron on my skin. "And not just *any* assassination, for that matter. They want us to kill the third most powerful person in the world?"

Ru squirmed, hands twitching in and out of fists. Jun and Yaozu shared a worried look, but Chet wore a slight grin. The Tanks just looked determined. Well, at least some of us were ready for this.

"That is correct. The officers are implementing an all-out assault on Hong Kong. Many groups. Many missions. Most of them to divide up Lightbar's forces and distract them…from us."

I swallowed hard and sat up straighter, despite the tight confines.

"Once we're in The Spire, we will split into two groups," I continued with a second breath. "Rostbane, Yaozu, Niu: you're with me to look for Naira. Mara will take Jun, Ru, Ferryman, and Mezei to find Rose. Brit, stay with Mendez to ensure we have a ride out."

My two on-loan Tanks nodded solemnly, but my regular squad still seemed ill-at-ease.

"How do we even know Rose will be *in* The Spire?" Chet asked. "Ain't there a festival going on?"

"Rose hate this festival," Jun said, scrunching up her face in disgust. "Says it's too…" She snapped her human fingers. "What is word?" She tapped Chet's leg.

"Working-class?" he gave a dry chuckle.

"For peasants," Jun agreed.

"So, he'll be hiding in his tower, pretending it doesn't exist?" Mara asked, her eyes sparkling with understanding.

Jun gave her a hesitant thumbs-up. "Exactly."

"Works for me," Mezei said, crossing his massive arms to the annoyance of JR, who sat next to him.

"Once we have Naira," I said, "Rostbane, you'll take her from The Spire with Yaozu and Niu."

Mara furrowed her brow, fixing me with a hard stare. "What about you?"

I twisted the hem of my T-shirt. "The officers have asked one more thing of me."

She frowned.

"I'm to…disable the rods…if I can."

The Ox shifted in his seat, studying me, as if his deep brown eyes could glean my thoughts. "What does that mean?"

"Can—it's a word that expresses a possibility—" JR began, but I held up a hand, cutting him off.

"The only other way to access the rods is from a control center inside The Spire. If we want to disable them, this is going to be our only chance."

He shook his massive head. "What do you mean by 'if you can?' Is there possibility of failure?"

I sighed, already exhausted. "There's a possibility of failure, yes. I can lock up their systems, scramble the code, impose layers of digital security, but as long as there are hackers in this world even half as good as me, someone could still break in someday. And unfortunately, they're stored in an exospheric orbital hangar. Even Rose himself doesn't have the kind of technology needed to visit a satellite."

"So, no way to physically destroy them," Mara said.

"Correct."

"Can't we just blow them up in their hangar?" The Ox asked.

I shook my head. "That's the thing about these rods. In storage, they are totally inert. Harmless. Just a massive tube of tungsten. Their destructive power comes from the sheer force of their impact."

Chet whistled. "They use gravity for energy." He raised his eyebrows in admiration. "That's slick."

"Something like that," I said blandly. While the rods were intellectually fascinating in theory, in reality, they terrified me.

"So, what happens if you can't disable them?" The Ox asked.

I didn't want to answer. Didn't want to face my squad and the concerns that would follow. They all watched me expectantly.

"I must launch them all."

All the previous heavy news must have numbed my squad, because this time, hardly anyone reacted, save for the occasional eye twitch.

"What are we launching them at?" Chet asked, the characteristic dark twinkle in his eye.

"Technically, that information is classifi—"

JR booed loudly, interrupting me and inspiring everyone else to do the same. I listened to their jeers with the sternest expression I could muster.

When they'd quieted I said, "Seriously. I'm not supposed to—"

JR hissed. "C'mon Rob. Some of us may die today, don't you think we should know what we're dying for?"

He had a point. "Dammit, JR," I snarled. He hadn't even needed his Aurawave to guilt-trip me, the imminent danger was enough. "We're launching them at Hong Kong Island."

A collective gasp sucked all the air from the hovervan. I tried to swallow, but my throat had gone dry.

"*What?*" Mezei replied, his brow furrowing in confusion, "My English may not be that good. Did you say, 'suicide mission'?" A rumble of agreement ran through the van.

"No," I kept my voice stern. "I won't launch until everything else is taken care of. Mendez will be on standby to get us out."

Chet shook his head. "She is a good pilot, but I'm not sure *that* good of a pilot."

"Don't worry about it," The Ox said with his characteristic goofy grin, "even if Mendez fails, us Tanks will probably survive."

"Hey!" Mendez shouted from the driver's seat, "I've gotten people out of tighter scraps than this! Don't you doubt me now."

"Still…" Yaozu began, initial worried expression transforming to full-on trepidation, "we may not survive this, yes?"

I took a breath to respond, but before I could, Mara said, "More importantly…Robert, you're really going send the rods at another city? Why not just drop them in the ocean?"

Her frown had deepened, dark eyes flashing in accusation.

"Makes perfect sense," Chet said, his chuckle wicked. "Hit the CORPs where it'll hurt—"

Mara glowered at him. "Do we *want* to hurt the CORPs that badly?" she interrupted, "*Millions* of innocents will die, Robert. Do you not remember Xi'an?"

I raised both arms in a gesture of submission. "Wasn't my choice," I muttered, suddenly feeling tiny, weak, and terrified. "Mazet's orders."

"So, we *are* just as evil as the enemy," she spat.

"Boss," Yaozu said, leaning forward suddenly and putting her hand on my knee. Her face contorted as she pressed it near mine and whispered urgently, "You *can't* do this. There are families in Hong Kong. Lots and lots of families." Her hand trembled. "My…" she breathed, then shook her head. "You can't…"

Chet frowned. Our eyes met. He gave me a subtle nod, as if to say, *"Toldja!"*

I didn't let my gaze linger, forcing my expression to become neutral. I knew none of the squad was happy about this plan, but Yaozu's reaction did seem overly dramatic. As if…she had some vested interest in keeping Hong Kong whole.

"Well, hopefully it won't come to that," JR said, cutting through the tension with false bravado. "I know Rob. He's a squirrelly fucker for sure, but great with machines. He'll find a way to disable them."

I gave him a light laugh, knowing he was trying to be brave for me, though my stomach twisted itself into knots. "Thanks, JR," I said. "I will certainly try."

And I wished it, too. Wished I *could* disable the bombs. Wished I was as brave as JR pretended, as strong as Mara, or as…*certain* as Chet. But, I was none of those things. Just a lone sergeant, trying to do right by his superiors—and do it without getting my team killed.

Besides…I'd been given my orders, and there was no way to back down now.

* * * * *

Sounds of a celebrating city drifted on a light breeze through the open windows of our vehicle—drumbeats, pan flutes and the distant peal of laughter. I felt a deep, heavy nostalgia for a memory I would never experience. I wanted to take my son to such a festival. Wanted to see him running from stall to stall with a huge childish grin on his face, tasting the sweets, marveling at the costumes, watching the fireworks.

Instead, I sat with my squad at the hoverdock of a large plaza, going over logistics. Lightbar Spire stood at the other end of that plaza. The tall building on top of this mountainous island reached upward like a giant obsidian needle, carving a glistening scar of blackness into the surrounding starry sky. Traffic had died down as we climbed, most of the revelry confined to the lower levels of the island—the "working-class levels," as Chet had called them.

By the time we arrived at Lightbar Plaza, we were the only car on the road, save for a lone, lost tourist who made an illegal U-turn over a curb right in front of us. They sped away as if we'd give chase, but Mendez just flicked off our lights and slipped the hovervan into the dark, covered dock.

I was beginning to regret our part in this mission, though at the time I saw it as a way to redeem myself—not to the officers, they didn't blame me for my previous failure—but to myself, and perhaps also to my squad.

But what if I failed here, too?

You probably won't be alive to regret it, my inner voice said to me. Immediately, my inner logic rebutted, telling me this wasn't the time for second thoughts. We had the mission, now all we had to do was complete it.

Easier said than done, I know.

"Boss?" Mendez asked me, turning in her seat to look over the squad. "Any final words?" She nudged my shoulder with her elbow. "Maybe… *encouragement?*" she whispered.

With a calming breath, I tapped into my frustration and my anger at the CORPs. At my lost youth. And at any chance I had of living a normal life. Who could live peacefully, after knowing they held millions of lives in their hand and then decided to close their fist?

"Street Dogs, Black Cats," I said, deepening my voice, "tonight ends more than a year of running, of watching helplessly as Norman Rose and Lightbar bled this country dry. We've seen too many innocent lives crushed under their greed. But tonight… Tonight, we fight back. We'll show them that every life lost, every friend we've buried has meaning, and we'll strike so hard they'll never forget our names. Tonight, you're not just soldiers. You are the spark that sets the whole damn system on fire. Tonight, we'll make history—together."

I kept one eye on Yaozu as I spoke, noticing her eyes flick toward her lap, hands clasped tightly. My squad sat in silence for a moment, each member contemplating their part in this operation.

JR, handheld tilted toward me, recording on, was the first to speak. "Hear, hear!" he said, a rush of pride swelling through the cab.

"Hear, hear!" the others roared, though I caught Mara's disapproving frown, even as she egged on the others. She was with me, no matter what she felt about the plan. My heart thumped with gratitude.

Yaozu, on the other hand, mouthed the words, but her eyes were dead. Cold and emotionless. Almost….resigned. Was she—? I shook the thought away. Everyone had reacted differently to my news, to the heightened danger of our mission.

I remembered Ames saying, *"If you analyzed every abnormal reaction that happened during war…"*

So, I didn't analyze. I took a deep breath, and I opened the door.

"We are going to be exposed as fuck," Mara muttered, low in my ear.

I uncurled myself from my seat and surveyed the wide plaza stretching out before us. Decorative hedges clustered against the wall of a small maintenance building, and a fountain bubbled in its center. Tall lights glowed along the fountain's edges, illuminating the grounds and providing little in the way of shadows.

"Yeah," I muttered back. "I don't like this."

Fortunately, the plaza was empty this time of night, save for a lone security detail pacing its perimeter. There were only two of them, and currently they were on the opposite end, in front of Lightbar HQ's massive obsidian doors.

Huddled in the shadows of the hoverdock's garage, I briefed my team.

"We need to take out the lights and the guards first," I said. "Ru, the breaker is on the backside of that building. Go kill the lights." I pointed to a power box about nine meters away, its hum steady.

"Copy, Boss," Ru said, and slipped out of the dock without another word, keeping his slim form pressed into the meager shadows.

"He need cover?" Yaozu asked, holding up her pistol.

I shook my head. "He'll be stealthier alone."

Yaozu lowered her pistol with a frustrated huff.

"The rest of us will take cover behind those bushes," I continued. "When the lights go down, Mara will neutralize the guards. Then, we make a break for the building."

"Copy," came a smattering of voices.

"Mendez, we'll see you up top in two hours." I hoped that was enough time. "Don't wait for us."

"Boss, you should really have more faith in yourself," the woman responded, gripping my arm. Her smile was feral and bright. "You'll be there."

"Thanks," I muttered into her head of wild hair. I gave her shoulder a quick squeeze. Then to everyone I said, "Let's move out."

The drumbeat came first, a steady, hollow thrum that echoed from somewhere beyond the plaza. I pulled my rifle, providing cover as Mara and the others disappeared behind the bushes. No movement across the plaza. Good.

Still, the drumbeat pounded into my chest, matching the quickening rhythm of my heart. My visor's HUD flickered as Ru's EMP pulsed but only half the plaza went dim. The neon lights along the fountain's edge remained stubbornly bright.

"Boss," came Ru's raspy voice through the comm, "not same circuit. The lights…"

"You check the map?" I asked him.

"Shì de," Ru confirmed, voice rising. "Don't see it."

I pulled up the schematics Query had given us and quickly searched for the other breaker box. Ru was right—it wasn't listed. I scanned the plaza with my handheld, looking for energy signatures. The results were as I expected—the remaining lights, the two guards, nearby power lines and… *wait a minute!*

The energy sigs of the two guards had split.

"Shit," I muttered, "we've got company."

"Tā mā de!" Ru swore. "They see—"

The guards emerged from the shadows of the Spire's far side. Not two, but ten. One knelt, an RPG balanced on their shoulder. The drumbeat quickened.

"Take cover!" someone shouted.

The RPG spat fire.

Chaos erupted.

A rocket streaked toward us, trailing smoke. Mara yanked JR into a doorway. Mezei hurled Jun behind a low wall. The Ox threw himself in front of Yaozu and Chet. The warhead hit the hoverdock with a deafening roar.

The shock wave hurled me backward. Concrete cracked under me as I slammed into a low wall, rifle tumbling from my fingers. My forehead hit the ground, visor blossoming into a spiderweb of cracks, Heat licked at my exposed skin. Dust and debris rained from the sky.

Another rocket landed farther away. Another explosion.

The plaza twisted into blurred shadows and shards of orange flame.

I blinked. All sound dulled to a muffled ringing. My breath came in sharp, jagged pulls. I moved my fingers—they responded. My knees wobbled but held as I staggered to my feet and ripped off my cracked helmet. The night air burned my throat.

The hoverdock was gone, replaced by a smoldering crater. The outbuilding had collapsed into rubble. Figures moved through the smoke. The drumbeat had stopped.

"Mara?" I tried the comm. Silence. "JR? Ox?" Nothing.

My chest tightened in panic.

The rubble pile moved. With a roar, Mara flung rebar and concrete chunks into the air. She was red-faced and panting, sweat streaking through the concrete dust on her cheeks. When her fiery eyes met mine, she smiled.

"Thank Greysoft," she said. Tossing several more slabs of concrete out of the way, she bent down and pulled out JR.

"You guys okay?" I asked.

JR nodded. "Thanks to Mara and that doorway." His visor had shattered, cutting into his forehead. He wiped the blood from his eyes and pulled the ruined helmet from his head. "Anyone else make it?"

In fear, I turned toward the dock. Or at least, where the dock used to be. The hovervan was nowhere in sight.

"No…" I breathed, refusing to recognize failure.

Another dark shape hurtled toward me from above. Another bomb? My muscles seized. Before I could move out of the way, it collided with me, slamming me back into the concrete. I struggled to breathe. The weight shifted, and a familiar gravelly chuckle cracked through my fog.

"Charger's Beard! I can't believe that worked!" Chet crawled off me, wiping blood from his lip where our heads had collided.

"What the hell'd you do?" I snapped, using anger to cover my confusion.

"Never lifted myself before," he said breathlessly. "Heard it was possible, but only idiots tried it." He extended a trembling hand to help me up. "You okay, boss?"

I groaned in confirmation.

The rubble shifted again. Mezei crawled free and shook dust from his bright red hair.

"Bazdmeg!" he roared, kicking a piece of rubble down the hill. When we all stopped to stare, he ducked his head. "Sorry. Where's Jun?"

A spidery shape unfolded from a streetlight behind us. Jun settled to the ground, using one mechanical arm as a crutch while another dragged uselessly at her side. Her lower leg glistened with blood, the white tip of a bone protruding through her shin.

"Jun—?" I asked.

"Still breathing," she hissed.

The ground trembled. A shriek of metal turned my head in time to see Mendez's hovervan, trailing smoke and sparks, lurch sideways from behind the Spire. The vehicle groaned, barely staying airborne as it rocketed toward us and the remaining cluster of soldiers. A bright burst of light erupted from the side hatch. Mendez ejected, her parachute flaring open as the wreck detonated. Brit leapt forth when the van's nose dipped, metal shrieking against concrete. The hovervan tilted and slammed into the enemy knot with bone-jarring force. Figures scattered.

"That'll keep 'em busy," Mendez, said breathlessly, sliding to take cover behind the ruined outbuilding. "But not for long."

She cradled her right arm against her chest.

"Yeah, that's probably broken," she continued. "I'm fine," she added at my worried look.

A low groan came through the haze. I pivoted, rifle raised. Two figures emerged from the gloom, limping through the swirling debris.

"Ox?" I called, voice hoarse.

"It's us," came the rumbling reply.

The Ox staggered into view, suit blackened and torn, handheld cracked. A dark bruise crept along his neck and into the collar of his jacket. Yaozu trailed behind him, her helmet missing, dark hair matted with sweat. Soot streaked her pale face.

"What happened?" I asked, lowering the rifle.

"Took the rocket," The Ox said, grimacing.

"A whole rocket?" JR asked, helping Jun get comfortable.

A syringe shot from one of her mechanical hands, and she jabbed it into her thigh with a sharp intake of breath. The Ox waited until she was finished before nodding.

"Dayum, yer a beast," Chet chuckled.

He gave the Kinetic a lopsided smile, despite hunching in pain. "Ru?" he asked.

I checked the monitor on my handheld, somehow miraculously intact. The heartbeats of all my squad pulsed there, including Ru's.

"Looks like he's alive," I said with a worried frown. I glanced at the rubble of the outbuilding.

"I see him," Yaozu said, "under there." She pointed to the far side, where Ru had been working moments before the explosion.

"Robert," Mara said in my ear, her voice edged with urgency. "Some of the enemy are rallying."

I looked where she pointed. Flames still licked at the hedges, and smoke curled from the ruined hovervan. Several dark shapes moved haltingly among the wreckage.

"Yaozu, show Chet," I said, pointing to the rising mechs. "Get Ru. If he's still alive, maybe he can help us with *that*."

"Aye, Boss," Chet said, cracking his knuckles.

Yaozu hesitated a second longer, her eyes flitting toward the pile and then toward me. There was a shadow in her expression, but she gave a sharp nod and followed him.

"Everyone else," I continued, "keep those guys busy. Tanks, don't go out unless they begin advancing."

"Got it," Mara said, pulling her rifle.

The others nodded, then did the same. Soon, the hiss of laser fire and pop of mag bullets filled the air.

"Jun?" I asked, kneeling beside her. "How are you?"

She cast me a deadpan glance, features lined with pain. "I'll live."

Using her three mech arms with delicate precision, she enveloped her leg and twisted, all in one fluid motion. The wet crunch of the setting bone and Jun's strangled grunt churned my stomach. White receded back into red.

Reaching behind her, Jun extracted a long strip of plastiband from her medpack, and wrapped it around her leg, using the broken hydraulic pump from her dead arm to pull it tight. She panted, sweat pouring down her face.

After several shaky breaths, a determination settled over her features. She shouldered her rifle. "I'm ready," she said, twisting into position and resting the barrel of her rifle on the rubble.

"Are you sure?" I asked her.

A piece of debris sailed over my head, landing with a crash on the other side of our barrier. Chet's Aurawave at work.

Jun nodded. "Not worse pain than getting these," she said, waving one of her mods.

I cracked her a grateful smile, giving her human shoulder a squeeze. "Then get to it," I said and the mech smiled back.

"Boss," came Chet's gravelly voice through the comm. "We see Ru. He's alive."

"Good," I said, relief flooding me. "Get 'im out of there. We got mechs to fry." I glanced at Jun. "Uh…sorry."

She quirked me another smile. "No problem. I not dumb." She tapped her mechanical backpack. "Protected. Faraday."

Of course she was. I let out a soft laugh and shook my head. "Smart thinking."

The comm crackled with static, followed by Chet's voice, strained and frantic. "Rob, she's got her pistol—what the hell?"

The words shot through me like ice. "Chet! What's going on?"

"Yaozu!" he shouted, his breath ragged. A sharp pop cut through the air from this side of the debris. "Fucking hell! She just shot Ru. She—"

Static engulfed the line. Shuffling. Another pop. A pained cry.

"Chet?" I barked, sprinting toward them. "Talk to me!"

The Ox followed close on my heels.

We rounded the corner just in time to see Chet scrambling up the rubble, pushing Yaozu, one arm twisted behind her back. Blood streaked his face; his other hand clutched his side. Yaozu fought him every step, teeth bared, eyes wild.

"She shot him!" Chet shouted, voice cracking as he threw her in front of me. "She shot Ru. In the head. Pulled her pistol and—just…did it. Point blank."

"You are lying!" The Ox surged forward, fists clenched. "Yaozu wouldn't do—she's ours!"

Chet moved his hand. Beneath, his black suit was wet with dark blood, his hand already stained with it. The bullet hole didn't look deep, but I understood its intention.

"Does this look like *ours* to you?" he snarled, challenging Niu with crazed, red-rimmed eyes. "Tell them!" he kicked Yaozu. "Tell them what you did, you traitorous bitch!"

The Ox lunged for Chet.

I threw out an arm to stop him, but he just thrust it away like driftwood.

"Niu, stop!" I shouted.

The Ox froze at my words.

My gaze locked on Yaozu. Her chest heaved, breath ragged. Her hands, scraped and dusty, were empty now—but her holster hung loose, the pistol missing. Deja vu brought be back to another similar scene, just a few months before.

"Yaozu," I said, my voice low, dark, crouching down beside her. "Did you shoot Ru?"

Her lips pressed together, eyes flicking from me to Chet to the Ox and back again. The muscle in her jaw jumped.

"Like you shot Cheng?" Chet added, tone menacing.

Tears welled in her eyes, but it wasn't regret I saw there—just fear. Her mouth opened, closed again. "Wǒ bié wú xuǎnzé," she whispered.

The words landed like a punch.

The Ox froze beside me. "No," he muttered, shaking his massive head. "Yu Jie, what do you mean, you had no choice?"

Chet swore and turned away, running a blood-streaked hand through his hair. "I told you," he said, voice trembling. "I told you, boss. I saw her."

"Why?" I asked, heart hammering.

Her chin trembled. "Lilly, your plan cannot succeed. Hong Kong Island…my family is here. I had no choice." She repeated that last phrase, eyes pleading not at me, but at Niu. "I had no choice."

The Ox staggered back as if she'd struck him. "Yu Jie, you *always* have a choice." Then, without another word, he turned away, his shoulders hunched. He waved a careless hand as if to say, *"I don't care what you do with her now."*

"Niu!" Yaozu wailed and slumped, head in hands.

My whole body shook, and my mind went blank. One of my soldiers was dead—and another had pulled the trigger.

"Boss!" Chet snapped, face close to mine.

I blinked and took a staggering step backward. "Huh? What?"

He shook me, his chest heaving. "Hey, stay with me. We can't just let this go."

The plaza around us crackled with gunfire, smoke curling in the warm night air. Yaozu knelt near me, eyes downcast, hands limp by her sides.

"She killed Ru," Chet said again, voice raw. "She's a traitor. We need to take care of her."

I stared at Yaozu. Her face was pale, smeared with dust and blood. The corner of her mouth twitched when she noticed me looking, as though she wanted to speak but thought better of it.

"We'll bring her to justice," I said, swallowing the lump of dread in my throat. "Let the officers deal with it."

"Officers?" Chet hissed. "There's no time for that. I say we kill her now."

"We're not executioners," I snarled back, aware of the hypocrisy of my words. I looked at Yaozu, eyes focused on the cracked stones of the plaza, repeating something softly under her breath.

"Yaozu. If you confess. I'll let you walk away. Right now."

She jumped when I said her name, but didn't look up.

"What?" Chet whirled on me.

Yaozu's lips parted, eyes shimmering with tears. "Not me," she whispered. "My family."

"Fine I'll let you go. Get them somewhere safe." My hands curled into fists. "But first, I need you to look me in the eye and *say it*."

Yaozu squeezed her eyes shut. Her chest heaved with a single sob. "Doesn't matter anymore. *She's* not here," she muttered.

Slowly, she tilted her chin toward me, features contorting into an expression of fear mixed with anger.

"You were right. It was me. I shot Ru. And Cheng. " Her breath hitched, eyes going hollow. "I told them—"

The wet crack of bone snapped through the air. Yaozu's head twisted unnaturally to the side, and she crumpled like a discarded puppet. Chet stood over her body, hands raised, breathing hard.

I stared at him, stunned.

"Niu already said it." His eyes glistened. "She always had a choice. She should have chosen to die."

A gunshot cracked across the plaza.

Chet staggered, red blooming across his chest. He collapsed beside Yaozu, mouth opening and closing in shock.

"Sniper!" I yelled over the comm.

2300 hours

Someone slammed into me, knocking me into the ground.

Mara.

She froze when she noticed Yaozu's corpse, Chet's bloody jacket.

"What the hell happened here?" she ground through her teeth, scrambling off me.

I rushed to Chet, pressing my hands to the wound. His blood poured through my fingers. "Yaozu," I gasped, "shot Ru. Betrayed…" but I couldn't continue, the weight of the truth threatened to crush me. "Get Jun," I said instead. "We need her medpack."

"Robert," Mara urged, "we need to do something about the soldiers…"

But I couldn't think with Chet gasping beneath my hands.

"Mara…" My voice squeaked, tears slipping down my cheeks. "I… need…"

Understanding flashed in her dark eyes. "Right. I'm second-in-command. I'll take care of it." She cast Chet a worried look. "Hang in there, you scrappy bastard," she muttered.

The she stood, booming her voice across the line, scooping Jun up as she spoke. "Ferryman down! He needs medical. Mezei, Niu, neutralize those snipers. Mendez, take Brit and find us transpo. JR, for the love of Greysoft, please *hit* something!"

My heart hitched as I watched her. Pride swelled.

Chet's breathing slowed, his eyes fluttered closed.

"Stay with me, you impulsive son-of-a-mech," I muttered, turning my attention away from Mara. "You hear that? Stay with me."

He coughed, blood trickling from his lips. "Was worth it," he whispered. "I was right."

His eyes slipped closed.

"Hey!" I shouted at him, shaking his cheek and remembering my combat injury training. Gotta keep his mind active. "Chet! What food do you miss most from back home?"

"What?" he asked with a wheeze. Then, after a moment, he added, "steak. A juicy, rare steak, rubbed with pepper. Only had it once."

"Where did you eat it?"

"Senior Effrain's…" he croaked.

Mara set Jun down next to Chet, trying not to jostle her injured leg.

"She wants to help," Mara explained. "*Insisted,* even."

Jun nodded with a frown, studying Chet's wound. I tried to keep him talking, but he coughed again, painting a red spray across the front of her uniform.

"Mag bullet," she said, her face a hard mask.

"I know," Chet gurgled, scrunching his eyes shut. The bullet slowly inched from his wound.

"Stop," Jun scolded. "You bleed more." She thrust his jacket open, cutting off his shirt.

"No. No…tech," he croaked.

I realized he was trying to push the bullet out using his Skill. "Chet," I tried to cajole, "stop." But he ignored me.

The bullet popped from his chest and rattled to the ground.

"Your funeral," Jun muttered, but she bandaged the wound anyway, the three-way plastiband valve whistling with his exhales.

He flashed a tired grin, teeth stained red. Then his eyes rolled back in his head, and he passed out.

"Will he survive…?" I asked Jun. The adrenaline leeched from my body, leaving me cold.

She shrugged, face drawn, then gave me a plaintive look. "Will any of us survive?"

The growl of engines filled the air. A scorched hovertruck rattled across the plaza, slamming through debris and screeching to a halt. The side door clanged open, revealing Mendez behind the controls.

"Get 'em in!" she barked.

Mara and I hauled Chet into the truck.

"Boss," JR nudged me from behind, "we may be meched here."

Stealing a glance above the berm, I looked toward the plaza. Five soldiers lay dead on the ground, but the remaining half had managed to barricade themselves in a ring of riot shields, pressed up against another short wall.

"The Tanks got the sniper, but we can't get any shots on the others," JR continued. "Though, the way they're clustered up, they're not coming after us either.

I gave a heavy sigh.

"Boss?" Mendez said from the driver's seat of the stolen hovertruck.

I looked up at the Zephyr.

She clicked her tongue, "During the Suria police action I was in several standoffs such as this."

"What did you do?"

"Charged them." She flashed a grin. "We got Tanks, right?"

I nodded.

"Use them."

Mara, standing next to me nodded in agreement. "We're ready."

Swallowing hard, I called over Mezei, Niu, and Brit.

"I want you four to charge the line," I began, cobbling together a plan. "Focus on the shields. Then, the rest of us can pick them off. Got it?"

"Yes, Sir," the group said as one, their faces set in resolute determination.

A small canister bounced beside me, trailing green smoke.

"¡La hostia puta!" Mendez swore when she noticed it. "¡No, aquí no!"

She leapt from the truck and kicked the cannister away. It skittered along the ground, the noxious yellow smoke spiraling out of it.

My eyes burned. Tear gas.

Most of us had lost our helmets—or, in the Tanks' case, never had one —except Jun and Mendez. The latter snapped her visor shut, picked the cannister off the ground with her good arm, and tossed it back at the mech. The former, settled against the barrier, rifle at the ready.

"Tanks, go!" I coughed, trying to scrub my itching eyes, but only succeeded in smearing Chet's blood across my forehead.

JR hacked beside me, though I noticed he'd managed to don a pair of bug-eyed goggles.

The four bolted into action, vaulting over the barrier and launching themselves toward the soldiers. Mezei and Niu went left, while Mara and Brit went right—as if they'd already discussed this.

Mezei sprang several feet into the air, heels busting a large dent into one shield and crushing the mech beneath it with his momentum. The Ox also took down his target by simply ripping the shield away and grabbing their helmet with both hands. Before they had a chance to react, the Tank slammed his head into the soldier's helmet, shattering into its owner's face.

Mara and Brit took a different approach, sliding into the bottoms of two shields, pulling them flat over their bodies. A laser hiss from JR beside me, and a perfect hole formed in the soldier's faceplate. They fell sideways, staggering their neighbor.

"Rob!" JR practically screamed in my ear through raspy coughs. "Did you see that shit?"

His white smile glowed from a soot-streaked face.

"I did," I said, shooting my own mech just below their chin—where their helmet and body armor failed to meet. "Nice shooting."

He beamed at me a moment more, but managed to miss the last soldier before Niu broke their neck. He shrugged at that.

"Can win 'em all," he chuckled, jabbing me with his elbow.

I grunted and doubled over, wondering if the explosion earlier had broken any ribs. Nonetheless, I patted JR's forearm, watching the sweaty Tanks rejoin us, leaving a gleaming pile of black and chrome in the square, reflecting the streetlights like stars in a broken night sky.

"You all okay?" I asked the panting crew as they settled behind the barrier.

The Ox had laser burns on the bare skin of his forearms, mere pinkish stripes that didn't even break skin. A black eye was developing on Mezei, and I wondered if he'd been shot in the face (not that it had slowed him much). The four of them shrugged, giving me ragged smiles.

"Better'n that guy," Niu said darkly, gesturing toward Ferryman in the van. Though the Tank seemed to accept the actions of the evening, the smile lines that usually adorned his earnest face had faded.

"What do we do now, Boss?" Mezei asked, coughing from the residual gas that lingered in the air.

"Three soldiers are down," I said, my throat tight and my shoulders heavy. "Jun's hurt pretty bad. Mendez, too."

I looked over the rest of my team, the exhaustion in their faces, the twinges from their minor injuries—not enough to take them down, but enough to feel disheartening.

"With Brit assigned to Mendez, that only leaves me with JR and three Tanks," I swallowed hard. "But there's still the mission."

The Ox put a heavy hand on my arm. "Yu Jie," his voice hitched, slurring at the end. He wrinkled his nose in an expression of distaste. "Yaozu," he tried again, "said, 'She's not here.' Said, she told…" He flashed me a pleading look, gesturing toward the Spire behind us.

"She told Lightbar about our plan," Jun said flatly.

I turned to her.

"I knew," she said with an angry sigh. "I…suspected. There were signs. But I… didn't believe it could be her. Always…consp—" she faltered at the word. "Conspires…?"

"Conspiracy theories," The Ox helped, his jaw twitching with anger. "She always had conspiracy theories. We didn't—" he coughed.

"We never listened," Jun said. The utter shame on her face broke my heart. "And Ru paid the price."

"Oh, Jun…" Mara breathed.

Everyone else just sat in stunned silence.

"She…" Jun continued, "was like a sister. Protected me after my parents died…I stood up for her. Thought I—owed her."

Then the mech did something I hadn't thought her capable of, she took my hand tenderly in hers. She kissed my fingers and pressed her forehead against them.

"I am guilty, too. I should go…like Yaozu."

I watched her, the defeat in her posture. On Niu's face. They waited on me to decide their fate. Fearful, expectant.

"Fuck that," I said.

Jun stiffened, but I held her hand tighter, anchoring her.

"Yaozu betrayed us. You didn't."

Her lips parted, protest trembling on her tongue, but I shook my head.

"You doubted. You hesitated. But you didn't turn on us." My voice dropped lower, cutting through the deadened air. "And when it mattered, when it was life or death, you chose life. Yaozu didn't."

She swallowed, her fingers icy.

"Chet is still breathing, because of you. If you want to pay a price," I went on, "then help us save him." I exhaled. "I'll put a medal on your chest before I ever put a bullet in it. Same goes for Niu. You two have proven your loyalty. I trust you."

I looked at the squad—bruised, bloodied, beaten down.

"And if anyone else has a problem with that, they'd do best to keep their mouths shut."

No one spoke up. A few shook their heads. Mendez smiled.

"Boss," she said, "I can still drive." She tilted her head to the hovertruck, with Chet wheezing inside.

I shook my head, the weight dropping deeper into my core, making my limbs heavy. As much as I didn't want to press on, I had to. I knew that. "Naira may well be gone from this island, but I still have my orders. You all should get out of here. I'll take care of the rest."

"Fuck *that!*" Mendez snapped. "The officers have no *right* to ask you to do this. They have no *right* to put your life at risk. Discard you like a puppet. A fucking *cog!*" She spat on the ground, her expression softening. "Come with us. Worry about the rods another day."

"I can't," I continued hoarsely, though all I wanted to do was leave this accursed island. "This is our only chance. We fail this, and hell will rain from the sky. I still have the chance to stop it…and I have to at least try."

"Dios mio!" Mendez moaned, slapping her forehead with her good hand. "You kids are always so determined. So stubborn. So…" she spat again, "estúpido!"

I watched the Zephyr. Sure, she had a good decade on me. Had been in more fights than me. But, she'd also been young once, like me. "Don't tell me you wouldn't have ever done the same. Been," I gave her a mischievous grin, "estúpido like me?"

Mendez studied me, chewing on her lip.

"Pues si," she finally said with a nod. "Go," she waved her hand at me, "but take my girl with you. Someone's gotta protect your stupid face!"

Mara put her hand on my shoulder. "I've got your back," she said, though her voice still sounded hollow, far away.

"Me as well," The Ox said, standing to his full height. "For Cheng. And Ru," he paused a moment, looking at the corpse only a few feet away, "and for Yaozu. "

I gave him a grateful nod. "The rest of you," I continued, "get out of here. You've done enough. We'll find our own way off this island."

I stood, rubbing dried blood and dirt from my hands.

"Nuh-uh, Rob," JR said with a vehemence. "I'm not going anywhere, unless that place is with you."

"JR, this is really not up for debate," I began, placing my hand on his arm.

"Shut the fuck up, Rob," he snapped, snatching his arm away. "You've seen me through more shit than I can remember. Now, it's my turn."

I shook my head but didn't argue. JR wouldn't listen anyway, but that's what I liked about him. And, I had to admit, his brash presence gave me some comfort.

"Thank you, Mendez," I muttered, pulling her in for a gentle hug.

"It's *estúpida* for me, by the way," she whispered as she kissed my cheek. She grabbed my chin in a tight grip. Her breath rushed over me, "Don't be a hero, niño. I don't want to hear about your death."

"I don't plan to," I replied with a weak smile.

Mara hugged Mendez, exchanging quiet words, their eyes shining.

I helped The Ox maneuver Jun into the van. She turned to look at me. "Boss," she touched my cheek, "You—not so bad after all."

I choked back a sob, already bone-weary. It was the last thing I had expected to hear, but it was the thing I most needed. My squad was breaking apart, and the finality of this moment lingered in my gut.

I stepped back as the truck's engine rumbled to life, the glow of its lights carving long shadows against the wreckage. Jun's gaze lingered on me through the window, her face unreadable. Then they were gone, swallowed by the night.

I exhaled, the weight of it pressing down on my ribs.

The island felt different now. An opportunity. A promise. But also, a prison. The night pressed in, thick with the scent of blood and smoke.

I turned to my squad—what was left of it.

"Let's move."

No one argued as we fell into step, heading toward the Spire.

I didn't tell them I had no way out.

I didn't tell them what waited in the tower.

And worst of all—I didn't tell them the truth about the bombs.

There was no disabling them. No way to turn back.

We were walking toward the end, and they didn't even know it.

- 39 -
C.E. 2253 September 8
0100 hours

The pile of twisted mech bodies lurched. The low hiss of hydraulics cut through the night air. A battered shield pushed up, hesitating, then dropped back down. I realized too late that someone still breathed beneath the carnage.

We were already sprinting for the Spire's entrance when the scream rang out.

I spun, pulse hammering.

JR—never the fastest runner—was down. A hand, slick with oil and blood, locked around his ankle, dragging him across the ground. He twisted, kicking wildly, but the grip was ironclad, made of literal metal.

Then the wreckage heaved. Metal groaned. And something rose from the carnage.

A man. If you could still call him that.

Half his face was human, but the other half gleamed in the dark, an intricate mesh of steel and circuitry, his ocular implant pulsing an eerie blue. My breath locked in my throat.

"Hex Tristan," I breathed.

And he had JR.

"You move, he dies," the Hex said in a booming voice.

Mara and The Ox backpedaled, taking their positions on either side of me.

The Hex yanked JR up by his collar, mech arm locking around his throat. His human arm slid a knife from a forearm sheath, pressing its edge against JR's collarbone. The Sway made a strangled grunt and froze, panic tightening his features. The Aurawave that crashed over me was pure, unfiltered fear.

The Tanks bristled beside me, but I placed a hand on each of their arms, stilling them. Mara's face twisted with rage and The Ox scowled daggers.

"Tristan!" I shouted back. "What the hell do you want?"

"You," he purred. "Did you really think you'd get away so easily from that shit you pulled in Chengdu? Taking my eye. Humiliating me." He tightened his grip on JR's throat. "I've been tracking you. Waiting for this moment."

The last words slithered under my skin like ice, making my insides tremble. Maybe it hadn't been Yaozu who'd given away our position, after all.…

I swallowed down the tight knot in my throat, forcing my voice to stay steady. I needed to stay in control. JR's life depended on it.

"Oh, is that what this is about? Revenge?" I sneered, masking the unease curling in my gut. "And here I thought you actually cared about the cause."

Tristan's lip curled. "This is more than revenge." He pressed the knife against JR's cheek, just below his eye. A thin drop of blood welled up. "It's about retribution. An eye for an eye."

JR sucked in a sharp breath.

My stomach twisted.

"Let him go," I snarled, forcing the tremor from my voice. "Your grudge is with me."

"A trade then," he replied. "You for him."

I contemplated this proposal, my mind working furiously.

JR pleaded at me through clenched teeth. "Rob…no…"

"Abandon your mission," Tristan continued, his voice cold. "I've watched you stumble through this war, pretending you're a leader, when you're really just a scared little boy. You could end it now. Save your remaining people. Stop playing sergeant."

My jaw clenched. He was trying to get under my skin, and it was working.

But I couldn't let him see that.

I exhaled a slow, trembling breath. "And yet, here I am. Still standing, while you skulk about beneath a pile of your own dead men. Men *we* killed." I flicked my eyes over the pile of bodies who were once Tristan's soldiers. "Remind me—who's the failure again?"

Tristan's smile faltered, just for a second. Then, his knife pressed into JR's cheek, digging deeper. Blood well, a single droplet rolling down the blade.

I tensed, flinching. *Don't push too hard.*

"Enough stalling," Tristan snarled. "You have two seconds to make your choice."

My eyes darted between the two Tanks. The Ox gave a small, sharp nod. Mara squeezed my arm.

Fine. I'd listen.

For now.

"All right," I said, taking a hesitant step forward. "You can have me."

When I was within arm's reach, the Hex uncurled his mech arm in a smooth, almost serpentine motion. JR shoved me away with a yell, but he wasn't fast enough. A metal hand gripped my wrist like a vise. Something sharp bit into my forearm.

I stiffened. A slow, burning warmth curled beneath my skin. A sense of *wrongness* accompanied it, slithery and cold.

Tristan leaned in, voice barely above a whisper. "Finally, you can see what it's like…"

"Now!" I shouted and jerked against Tristan's hold.

At my command, The Ox sprang into action, dropping to one knee. Mara stepped in the cradle of his grip, and he shot up, launching Mara through the air. Tristan barely had time to react before she crashed into him, knife flashing.

The three of us collapsed into a pile, his iron grip wrenching my arm at an awkward angle. My shoulder popped. Pain shot through me. The Hex snarled as Mara's blade tore into his side, his metal arm going slack. I scrambled to my knees, using my good arm to right myself, even as stars sparkled in my vision.

JR grabbed at me, pulling me to my feet. Blood dribbled from a cut on his face, from cheekbone to chin.

Tristan roared, shoving at Mara. His mech arm shot out, slamming into her ribs, sending her tumbling across the broken stones of the plaza.

Then he turned to me.

"You think you're clever," Tristan spat, gripping the wound at his side, blood already staining his fingers. He tried to get to his feet. "But it doesn't matter. You're already—"

I didn't let him finish. I slammed my boot into his jaw, cutting his monologue short.

His head snapped to the side, and The Ox was on him before he could recover, tackling him with bone-rattling force. The impact sent a shock wave through the plaza. Tristan let out a choked grunt, trying to repel The Ox—but Mara was back on her feet, driving her knee into his ribs.

He didn't get back up.

I stood there dazed, breathing hard, my shoulder throbbing. The wrongness pulsed beneath my skin. Almost…alive.

I swallowed against the rising dread, but there was no time to be afraid.

JR still held me by my good arm and Mara watched me, wiping her hands on her pants. Even The Ox, stepping back from Tristan's unmoving body, waited expectantly.

Waiting for me to lead.

I winced at my dislocated shoulder. "We need to keep moving," I said, voice hoarse.

"We *need* to fix that shoulder," Mara said, the ferocity in her expression transforming to concern.

The Ox flicked his eyes toward Tristan, who still hadn't moved. "Maybe we get inside first?"

I nodded, breath still coming in frantic gasps.

The Spire's lock was easy to crack. Too easy. I pried off the panel, fingers flying over the wires, rerouting power. Pain, white-hot like fire licked up my arm. I jerked back. The small hole in my sleeve seemed innocuous; it barely bled. But, whatever Tristan had injected me with packed a punch.

Whatever.

I had to keep moving. I finished the reroute, pushed everyone inside, and reversed the lock. I stood for a breath, eyes roaming over the Spire's pristine lobby, disoriented, nauseous, mind buzzing. My arm twitched.

It twitched again, faster.

I couldn't control it as the muscles shook as if a strong current ran through them. I shoved up my sleeve. A silver patch had formed on my skin, glistening like the scales of a fish. I touched it. It burned my fingers.

With a gasp, I swallowed bitter bile and fought against the urge to retch. I touched it again. A thousand tiny pulses. Each one different. Each one… active. Sentient.

"Shit," I muttered as everyone leaned close to examine.

"What," Mara asked, brushing her fingers over my arm, "is *that?*"

"Nanobots," I mumbled, the shock overwhelming me.

Static overtook my vision, the lobby dissolving to a pinprick until it blinked out in darkness. I sank to the floor, barely even registering the pain in my dislocated shoulder.

* * * * *

"We are here," they whispered to me. *"We are you."*

I felt the nanobots, a hundred-thousand microscopic robots, burrowing into my flesh, my nerves, my bones. My blood. Was I hot? Or cold? Or did I feel anything at all? Anything, that is, besides the machines.

"Soon, you will be us," they whispered in my mind, bits and bytes of information, encoded in ones and zeros.

Someone shouted my name; it felt far away. I think it was Mara. But I couldn't remember Mara. Her very name slipped from my thoughts like an eel, slipped away with the machines. High frequency vibrations rattled my teeth, jerked my body like a puppet.

My head pounded, my limbs a heavy, dead weight. My heart made a stutter-stop beat. I gasped for air. Took a labored breath. Focused on the beating of my heart.

I had to fight them. Had to *stop* them. *They're just machines,* I thought to myself, though even that thought slipped away as if coated in oil. Each time I locked onto a nanite, it skittered away, evading me like a cockroach in the light. Wrong. All wrong. A voice in my head screamed at me to fight.

Reaching out with my sixth sense, the one I used to manipulate a lock or the ignition of a speedcycle, I focused on the nexus of activity in my forearm. Single nanites broke away from the cluster, scouting parties through my bloodstream. I screamed at them to stop.

But they didn't stop. They had a purpose, which they pursued with the dogged determination only machines could muster. Usually, when I manipulated tech, all I had to do was encourage the true purpose. But now, I had to dissuade them.

Stop. Go back. Go away. I pushed my thoughts toward the invaders.

Even still, the first nanobot made it into my chest cavity. My lungs seized. My breathing faltered. I struggled to draw in air, trapped in my own body.

No, I told myself; my thoughts dragged. *I* was in control, not these artificial monstrosities.

Stop now!

My chest suddenly expanded as all the air rushed in at once. I choked on my breath, my will pushing the bots backward. Pushing them *away.*

Go! I felt the snarl in my thoughts.

The bots receded, but didn't stop. They chose a new route; toward the stutter-stop motion of my heart. My toes curled in my boots, my hands into fists.

My body is my own, I mentally shouted. *I intend to keep it that way.*

The bots receded further, back through my arteries, through my veins. With fiery, needling pain that flowed down my arm, settling where they'd entered. Pulsing. Angry, yet also confused, and weakened—but not gone.

My vision returned, and I blinked stinging eyes. Lightbar's lobby opened before me, too bright. Shapes milled about, just shadows, whispering, breathing. I didn't recognize them, didn't understand the looks on their faces or their hands on me. I tried to remember…where was I?

A sharp snap, like a rubber band breaking loose speared through my forehead.

They were there. In my brain. Prodding at my thoughts. Exploring. Seeking.

"Get out!" I bellowed, my voice tearing from me. I gripped my face with both hands.

Get out of my head!

Focusing on my memories, I struggled to dredge up meaning through the chaos. A great wall, stretching into darkness. Cinnamon-scented cigarettes. Strong baiju, burning my tongue. Boisterous laughter from half a dozen throats. The word 'bro.' The touch of soft skin against mine. A smile in deep brown eyes. Hot lips against my own.

The War Room in Tianjin…

"No," I slurred. I knew what the nanites sought. But they wouldn't find it.

I clung to happy memories. To memories of my own fear and inadequacy. To memories of shame.

The probing faltered. I pushed deeper into my emotions.

My *uselessness*. My frivolity. My lofty dreams.

Get out. Go home.

I clamped my teeth shut, shearing through a piece of my tongue. The pain grounded me, numbed me. I shoved at the bots with another breath.

The world went dark.

Then—light, voices, pain.

The fog receded with the speed of a maglev train. My mind burned. Clear. Bright. I pulled cool air into my lungs. I heard people saying my name.

Mara. JR. The Ox.

Someone else. Someone I recognized.

I opened my eyes.

"Nic Saint Claire?" I croaked, exhausted, confused.

Okay, this Saint Claire guy was literally *everywhere*.

He wore a black uniform with the HumanSource logo on its breast. Three dark-helmeted guards stood behind him, similarly dressed. They carried vintage automatic rifles; the name *AK-2147* adorned a plaque on the side. Information flooded my thoughts. I latched onto it. Onto something real.

"The AK-2147," I muttered automatically, "a reboot of the millennium's most popular rifle."

"What?" JR asked.

Shaking my head, I looked around. They'd moved me from the stark, bright lobby and into a dim stairwell, though I had no memory of that. Someone had fixed my shoulder and bound it in a crude sling. It ached with a fury, but after what I'd just experienced, I practically reveled in something as mundane as physical pain.

I glanced at my forearm. The silvery spiral patch was still there, but it didn't seem to have grown. It itched. And burned. But I ignored it.

"How long was I out?"

"Ten minutes, maybe?" Mara said.

Minutes? It had felt like hours. Like an entire lifetime.

"What happened?" she asked, stroking three fingers down my jaw, a grimace of worry on her blood-splattered face.

I gasped at the sudden heat, fanning my already sweat-soaked T-shirt. My MOPP suit had been unzipped to the waist. "Nanobots," I grunted. "That dirty mech stuck me with some kind of tech serum."

"Nanobots?" JR repeated. "That's it? We thought you were dead and were gonna have to restart your heart!"

I brushed a finger over the bots again, a shudder going through me. "That's not 'it' JR," I said acidly. "They're the whole shebang. I've never seen them like this before, but I understand they can convert flesh to metal in a matter of seconds."

JR swallowed, as if he'd eaten something off, his face going pale.

"I've got them contained—I think."

"For now," Nic said with a frown. "I've seen a few people get infected. It's not pretty."

"Can they be removed?" The Ox asked, shaking Nic's arm.

Nic shook his head. "I don't know. I didn't even think they could be contained."

JR's face fell.

"Well, if anyone can figure it out, it would be Robert," Mara said, giving me a weak smile.

I wasn't convinced. The others had more faith in me than I did. "We'll deal with it later," I said. "First, we finish what we came here to do."

Nic gave a small approving nod. "Good. You're going to need that kind of focus."

"Why are you here, Saint Claire?"

"Helping you," the man said with a grin. "I rearranged the security detail of the Spire's ground floor."

Mara crossed her arms. "You're everywhere, aren't you?"

Nic smiled like that wasn't a bad thing. "I like to keep an eye on interesting people."

I kept my expression blank, but something about him still made me uneasy. He was always where we needed him—just before we needed him.

"But Naira's not here," I said. "We already know."

Nic gave a sad nod. "We were not aware she was being…removed."

I slumped against the wall. "Yaozu."

He raised an eyebrow.

"She was the mole. We found out. Tonight."

"Ah. I had my suspicions," he said lightly. "Though I hoped I was wrong."

Mara scoffed. "Really? Because we could've used that information before she nearly got us killed."

Nic tilted his head and threw up his hands in defeat. "People in power don't like hearing they've made a mistake," he said, "Sergeant Lilly, should know that by now."

I didn't have a response for that, so I just scowled.

Mara, however, wasn't done. "People say you're a double-agent. A deserter. Maybe even a traitor yourself."

Nic smirked. "People say a lot of things. But right now, I'm helping you. And you're running out of time."

I exhaled through my nose. "Fine. Can you get us to Rose?"

He tapped his forearm computer. "I've just piped the route to your handheld. Fifty-second floor. Service elevator at the end of the hall should get you close. My men will clear the building."

I studied him for a long moment. His presence, his resources, his uncanny ability to be exactly where the battle tipped. A storm raged behind his bright blue eyes; a storm that was bigger than us, bigger even than Nic himself.

"Won't taking down Lightbar make things harder for you?" JR asked.

Nic only shrugged. "Depends on who's left standing."

That was the closest thing to honesty I'd heard from him all night.

Mara's jaw tightened, and she narrowed her eyes.

Before she could snap back, I pushed off the wall, nodding to my team. "Let's move."

Nic gave a short, knowing nod. "Good luck, Lilly."

I didn't answer. Luck wouldn't save us.

0200 hours

"That was hardly *close*," JR wheezed as we ascended our sixth set of stairs.

I grunted an agreement. Nic's service elevator hadn't been as convenient as expected.

"Only two more to go," Mara said cheerily, hardly winded, tapping on a metal plaque that read *FLOOR 50*.

I huffed, planting a foot on the next step without thinking. My toe caught, and I stumbled, reaching out to catch myself. I landed on my injured shoulder and let out a strangled yell.

"Boss," The Ox cooed, lifting me to a seat, "you all right?"

Wiping tears from the corner of my eye and trying to unscrew my face from its pained grimace, I nodded.

The big man's eyes sparkled as if I'd just said the funniest joke.

"I think you're lying," he said, swinging Jun's medpack from his shoulder. "Go on," he called to Mara and JR. "We'll catch up."

Rummaging around in the pack, he pulled out two small bottles and a syringe. He tutted like a grandmother, while simultaneously preparing a cocktail of painkiller and stimulant, tongue wedged in the corner of his mouth.

Now it was my turn to smile. I watched him in wonder.

"What?" he asked when he noticed my stare, the cap of the syringe between his teeth.

I glanced down to the meat hooks he called his hands daintily holding a glass bottle and chuckled.

The Ox furrowed his brow, though he never stopped his preparations.

"It's just that…" I said, almost giddy, "you could crush my skull before I said 'no!', yet you're so gentle and—Ow!"

He stuck the needle into my forearm.

I shook my head as the sting of stimulant raced through my blood. "—and kind," I finished.

The Ox smiled wryly.

"Mara, too," I continued. "I always thought Tanks just wanted to break shit?"

He grinned. "I like being an en-enigma," he said slowly, sounding out the word. "Just learned that one."

I snorted as the sickening ache began to recede. My pulse quickened.

"But breaking shit is fun too." He gave me a wink, hauled me up, and we continued up the stairs—me breathlessly, him as if it were just another day on the job.

With the pain gone, I was able to feel the nanobots again—more of an annoyance than a hindrance, but it still had me worried. Would I really be able to reject these machines? And if not, what would I have to sacrifice? My arm? My life? I shuddered but resolved to do what was needed to avoid becoming a mindless automaton.

By the time we reached the landing of the fifty-second floor, I was thoroughly over stairs. JR sat panting, back against the wall. His cuts had been sealed with sani-strips, and he'd unzipped the front of his MOPP suit, the T-shirt beneath sweaty and grimy. Clasping his forearm, I helped him to his feet, then pulled him in for a hug.

He squeaked in surprise.

"You okay?" I whispered into his hair. He smelled of sweat and blood, and still the barest fruity hint of that silly conditioner he hoarded.

"I'll make it," he grunted and pushed me away, almost embarrassed, though the hint of a smile twitched on his lip.

I could almost hear his sarcastic thought: "aw, Rob, you *do* care!"

"What do we do from here?" Mara asked.

She gestured toward the door, topped by a bright green *EXIT* sign, a *FLOOR 52* plaque next to it.

"Go through that door and hope there are no guards?" I teased.

JR flashed me a look. "Shouldn't that be *my* line?" he grumbled.

"It's okay, you didn't have the breath for it." *Wow,* that stim was making me into a true comedian.

The Sway groaned, his Aurawave of—something—passing over me. He pointed to the maglock flashing beside the door. "Well, this is your show, *wunderkind.*"

I touched it. Power resonated from within. It was of a different quality than maglocks I'd seen in the past—stronger, sharper somehow, and deeper—though when I snapped off the plastic plate, it revealed the same internals. With practiced motions, I rearranged the wires one-handed until the door latch clicked. The unique power signature faded from my mind. I pushed the door open.

The room that expanded outward was no mere corporate office. Taking up what looked like an entire floor, it was packed with server bays and workstations only feet apart. Holo projectors blinked overhead, some displaying views of the city, while others depicted quiet fields or tree-covered mountains. Lights blinked in a myriad of colors and the machinery hummed alongside the whispered breeze of cooling fans.

My head exploded with the voices of the machines—louder than the usual rumble of tech I was accustomed to, and louder even than a room full of mechs. These were powerful computers, with yottabytes of computing power, thrumming on high-tech dytraxihydrade power cores. The presence of these voices caused the nanites to stir, sending their subversive whispers into my consciousness.

"We are here," they breathed.

I pressed my hands to my forehead, an unwanted yowl escaping my lips as pain blossomed behind my eyes.

Leave me alone, I pushed back at the bots—at the tech.

"Robert, what's going on?" Mara asked, placing her hands on my bare arm.

I flinched away, her touch burning.

"Rob? What is this place?" JR said, in my other ear.

Simultaneously, the nanobots whispered or screamed, directing me to one computer or another.

"Robert?"

"Boss?"

"Rob?"

"Shut up!" I groaned, squeezing my eyes shut. "All of you, *shut up!*"

A sharp sting on my face, followed by a numbness. I opened my eyes. Blinked back tears. The Ox watched me, his dark brown eyes alight, a scowl on his face. His hand raised once more.

"Did you just slap me?" I asked in shock.

"Job needs to get done," he snapped at me in Chinese. "Zǔmǔ always told me weakness was laziness. Don't be weak, Boss."

An image of Niu's deceased grandmother materialized in my head, brandishing a spoon at the children while she made dumplings for the family. I snorted. Then I laughed. I couldn't help it. A coppery film coated my tongue from where my teeth had cut my lip, but I didn't care. I spat blood. And then I kept laughing.

The Ox's scowl faded, replaced by a mischievous smile. I felt silly, but the futility of this whole evening finally struck me. From the moment we'd set foot on this island, we'd gone through one blunder after another. Yet here we were, so close to our goal, I could almost taste it. Or at least, I could if my mouth hadn't been filled with blood.

Mara and JR looked on in confusion.

Taking several more gasps, I composed myself, head much clearer. The nanobots had quieted, and the equipment hum reduced to a dull ache within my bones. I looked around the room.

"Now that you're done cracking up," JR said blandly, "you wanna tell us where we are? Rose isn't here."

I had suspected that would be the case, and the earlier appearance of Saint Claire had confirmed my suspicions.

"Rods first," I said, my mind honing to a pinprick of focus even as my gut twisted, "then Rose." The last lie I'd ever tell them.

I found the KEWP control console from its whispers alone, a deep reverberation in my eardrums.

Approaching the computer, I performed a quick scan of its programming. Locked out, of course—bio-activation only. I pulled a small pouch from my MOPP suit. It contained two items to force activation—one slim and pink, the other perfectly round and smooth. I chuckled despite myself.

Rolling them in my hand for a moment, I pressed Query's right index finger and left eye against the sensors and prayed. The cyborg claimed to have buried their credentials so deep within the code no one would ever find them. I hoped they were right.

WELCOME TO THE KINETIC ENERGY WEAPONS PROGRAM, PROFESSOR QUERY.

Professor? That was a new title.

Quickly, I scanned through the protocols until I found the link to the missile satellite. Navigating the few remaining security levels with the passquotes and code combos Query provided, I set up the launch. A confirmation notification appeared on the screen.

LAUNCHING KEWP POWER RODS
DESTINATION:
HONG KONG ISLAND
22° 15' 31.5324" N
114° 11' 27.8556" E
SCHEDULED TIME:
0300 HOURS

That gave us forty-five minutes to get out of there. I hoped it would be enough.

ACTIVATE? ***YES | NO***

I stood there for a moment, staring at the screen. The words burned into my vision even after I looked away.

My hands felt numb. This was it. The part of the mission I hadn't told them about. The part I feared they wouldn't forgive me for.

"Street Dogs, bring it in," I called.

My squad, those few stalwart members who would see me through anything, gathered close. They must have noticed the worried crease of my brow, because one by one, their faces fell.

"Robert? What's the matter?" Mara asked. She reached out to touch me, but something stayed her hand, and she pulled back. Her face pinched. Fear.

"Rose was never part of the mission," I said somberly.

"What?" JR snapped. "What do you mean?"

I took a breath. "Neither was disabling the rods."

Mara glared. "What the hell are you talking about?"

I exhaled, steadying myself against the control panel. The truth sat like a stone in my throat. The word *ACTIVATE* blinked on the screen. I'd known this moment would come but saying it out loud felt like cutting apart the thin thread that held us together.

"There's no surefire way to disable the rods," I said. "Not permanently. They're rigged with redundancies. If we try to shut them down, the system overrides. And since we can't destroy them…the only way to end this for good is to launch them all."

Silence.

Mara's glare sharpened. "That's not funny."

"I'm not joking."

JR took a step forward, face pale. "You're saying you want to drop these things—these bombs on Hong Kong Island? On *people*?"

"No. I want to drop them on Lightbar." My voice was steady, but my gut churned. "Hong Kong *is* Lightbar. It's their headquarters, their factory, their financial heart. Every credit they earn flows through Lightbar Spire. Every project, every new division, every war crime they commit—it all comes from here. If we take it out, we take everything out. Lightbar won't be able to rebuild. Ever."

Mara scoffed, shaking her head. "That's insane."

"It's the only way."

JR's voice wavered. "No, it's not. It can't be."

I slammed a fist against the console. "You think I don't hate this?" My voice cracked, but I didn't care. "I've gone over every possibility. Every route, every workaround. There's *nothing*. This whole mission—our whole goddamn war—was never about assassination. Lightbar will just replace Rose. They'll rebuild, no matter how many heads we cut off. The only way to stop them is to make sure these rods never get used again."

Mara took a step back, like I was a stranger. "So, you're just making the call? Deciding for all of us?"

"No. But Mazet did. Qian. All the officers agree."

"And you're going to listen to them, like a good little soldier?" Mara snarled.

I hung my head, watching the minutes tick by on the console. Watching the one word that would seal the fates of millions. Feeling like the biggest piece of garbage on the planet.

"Yes."

A beat. Then she lunged at me.

I barely got my arm up before she shoved me hard into the console, teeth bared in fury. "You self-righteous son of a bitch! You lied to us—again!"

I let her shove me. Let her rage. I deserved it. If she bashed my face in, I wouldn't have even blamed her.

JR grabbed her arm before she could hit me. "Mara—"

"No! Don't you dare defend him!" She wrenched away. "All this time, all the sacrifices we've made, all the *people* we've lost, and he just—he just chooses to wipe an entire city off the map?"

I swallowed. "It's not my choice."

She laughed—harsh and humorless. "Oh, screw you, Robert. You *always* have a choice."

JR hesitated. "Boss…"

"I tried to find another way," I said. "But the truth is, we don't have one. If we don't use them first, Lightbar will. It'll be hell."

Mara exhaled sharply, shaking her head. "That's what they told you, huh?" Her voice was quieter now, but no less furious. "And you just nodded along? You're better than this."

I wasn't. Not anymore.

A heavy silence settled between us. The minutes ticked by.

The Ox, who had been quiet until now, folded his arms. "Boss," he rumbled, "if we do this, there's no turning back."

"I know."

Another silence. This one heavier.

Mara clenched her jaw, breathing hard. I saw it—the war in her head, the sheer weight of it. She whirled at Niu. "And you're okay with this?"

"No," he replied. "But I don't have to be. Lightbar's too big. If we leave even a piece of it standing, they'll find a way back. They *always* do."

She looked at JR next, eyes pleading, like he would have an answer, or at least the strength to put a stop to this. But he just stared at the screen, at the cold, unfeeling message. He bit his lip. There was horror in his expression, but also loyalty. His eyes met mine. He needed a clean way out.

There wasn't one.

He swallowed, lips parting as if he wanted to argue, but said instead, "If we go through with this and live, we'll never be the same. We'll never feel like heroes."

I nodded. "I know."

Mara closed her eyes. She was shaking—not in fear, but in rage. And grief. I wanted to say something. To tell her I was sorry. That I understood. That I didn't blame her if she hated me after this.

She reached for me.

Her fingers curled into the front of my suit, yanking me forward. "I could stop you," she growled. "I could stop you all—yes, even you, Ox— and kill Rose myself."

"I know that too," I said quietly. "And I wouldn't blame you."

Her stormy eyes challenged me for one heartbreaking moment.

Then, she leaned in, pressing her forehead against mine. Not a kiss. Not forgiveness. Just something raw and wordless. I closed my eyes and let myself lean into it.

"You don't deserve this," she whispered. I wasn't sure if she meant Hong Kong or her mercy.

Then, she let me go. And stepped aside.

"How long will we have?" JR's small voice broke the tension.

"Thirty minutes."

"Then we'd better make it count," The Ox rumbled.

I turned back to the console. The screen was waiting. One press. One final order.

I sucked in a breath and gave the last command.

0300 hours

"MISSILE THREAT DETECTED. PLEASE EVACUATE THE SPIRE. THIRTY-MINUTES TO IMPACT."

Overhead sirens came to life, blaring through my eardrums.

"We need to get out of here," I told my team. "Thoughts?"

"Uh, is this not a suicide mission?" The Ox asked genuinely.

"I never intended it to be." I placed my hand on his shoulder. "I know I've asked you guys to do a lot. Too much. But I never wanted your deaths on my hands, too. And *dammit,* if I can only do one thing right in this whole fucking war, it's going to be saving my friends. So, how do we get out of here in thirty minutes?"

A smile spread across Niu's face and JR's mouth began to run.

"Well, we can't go back downstairs. It's too far, and who knows what will be waiting for us in the plaza? But Mendez isn't coming so…"

"Up?" Mara suggested. "These fancy 'scrapers usually have a rooftop launchpad. Maybe we'll get lucky there'll be a plane available?"

"Or we may be able to reach Mendez!" JR added, eyes alight. He was already pointing toward an elevator on the far side of the control room.

I looked between them, a grateful smile on my lips. "Good thinking. Let's go."

"And if there isn't, we'll likely die before we regret our decision," The Ox added, picking up the rear.

JR chuckled. "Damn Ox, that's real morbid, especially coming from you. Welcome to the cynical side."

He just slapped JR on the back, hard enough to make him cough and stumble. "Well, if I survive, I'll make sure you are remembered. How's that?"

"Much better," JR replied with a roll of his eyes. He pushed the elevator open button, slipping inside. "Well, that sucks," he continued, contemplating the menu.

"What?" I asked, glancing at the row of buttons.

"The sixty-fourth floor has a *P* next to it. Penthouse. You need a key to get up there."

Crap. If we couldn't get to the top floor, then we couldn't get to the roof. Shouldering him aside, I ran my fingers along the panel. However, when I touched the lock for *P,* a spark jumped toward me. I pulled my hand away, sucking on a finger.

"Anti-tamper device," I said, rummaging around in my pockets. "Not sure I have the right tool for that."

"Well, let's get close," Mara said, punching the button for the sixty-third floor. "There have to be emergency stairs."

I sagged against the handrail and gave an exhausted nod. The strain of fighting, the pain, and the drain of adrenaline dragged on me. My brain felt sluggish as I sought out solutions, all while my heart hammered in time with the ululating shriek of the alarm.

The elevator dinged on floor sixty-three.

"Guess we'll find out right now," JR muttered.

In the lobby, an emergency exit sign glowed above a side door. Past that, a dusty staircase spiraled upward into the black depths of the Spire. We only had to ascend one floor this time, before the stairs dead-ended at a locked door that read *P.*

"Electrical?" The Ox asked.

"Mechanical," I confirmed when I spotted neither maglock nor ID-reader beside it.

"No problem," he snorted. With a single kick, he crumpled the door like tissue paper. The time for stealth was over. He shot me a questioning glance.

"Let's do this," I said grimly.

The Ox slid through a rift between two pieces of cloth—curtains, maybe?—and the rest of us followed. We emerged into a dim sitting room that reeked of heavy, floral perfume. I wrinkled my nose. Plush red carpet stretched from wall-to-wall, tacked down by gilded baseboards. A chandelier glittered from the ceiling, and a fancy tea set sat on a table next to several overstuffed couches, all upholstered in garishly contrasting jewel tones.

"No. Fuckin'. Way." JR muttered, as he pushed the fabric aside to help Mara through.

I turned to look.

A large tapestry hung over the door we'd just exited, from ceiling to floor—a portrait, now damaged where The Ox burst through. However, despite the rent down the center, we could still make out one half of the face: orange skin glowing of its own volition, messy hair, and snake-like eyes in red-rimmed sockets. He held a red rose in one hand, draped over his shoulder. A foolish pose for a foolish man.

"So, I think I know who this penthouse belongs to," JR said sarcastically.

"Of course, Rose would cover the emergency exit with a portrait of himself," Mara snorted.

"Hold!" someone shouted from inside the room.

I whirled, gaze falling upon the barrels of two mag pistols aimed straight at us. These were no HumanSource guards. Judging from the red flower embroidered on their jackets, I gathered they were Rose's personal security detail. Great.

"Wait!" I said, holding my hands up, while trying to form a coherent plan.

They didn't wait.

The Ox lunged at me, two guns firing simultaneously.

He slammed me against the wall, just as the bullets sprayed against his back. Though the big man gave a strangled grunt, he barely stumbled, sheltering me with his larger form. At the same time, Mara grabbed JR's arm and flung him into the open doorway, blocking the entrance with her body. Two more bullets hit her in the chest, sending her to her knees. She coughed and swore, expression twisting with fury and pain.

Mashed up against mine, The Ox's face contorted into something like irritated determination. His cheeks flushed red, and he pushed off the wall, launching himself toward the right-most guard. The man didn't even have time to scream, before Niu's uppercut took him in the chin. He dropped like a sack of rocks. Mara, equally as quick to recover, followed. She leapt low, toward the other's legs, taking him down. Rolling over like some kind of bullet-proof alligator, she snapped his neck between her thighs. His final two bullets chewed holes in the far wall.

It was over in a matter of seconds.

Panting, I pulled myself up straight, tugging down Rose's ruined tapestry in the process. It flopped onto my head, the dust making me choke, and I flailed for freedom. When I'd finally discarded the heavy, musty fabric, I surveyed the room. JR peeked his head from the doorway.

"They dead?" he asked.

Mara and The Ox, crouched over the bodies like wolves, nodded. They stood and stretched, both wincing, and wiped their hands on their suits.

Niu's face once again transformed into that easy-going smile. "You're lucky you brought us with you, boss."

"Very lucky," I agreed.

"I fucking *hate* getting shot," Mara moaned, massaging her collar bone as she retrieved the pistols from the dead guards.

She passed them out while JR did a quick search of the bodies for anything else useful. Not finding much, he stood.

"Ready?" he asked.

"MISSILE THREAT DETECTED. PLEASE EVACUATE THE SPIRE. TWENTY MINUTES TO IMPACT."

A frantic shuffle erupted in the next room.

The Ox, still in the lead, got there first. His deep bass laugh echoed back. "Boss. Guys. You must see this."

"This" was a half-dressed Rose in lounge attire, wheeling about in a frenzy, his chubby hands waving in the air.

"Mercy," he said to The Ox, who aimed a pistol at the man's head. Rose repeated the request in bad Chinese.

"Mercy, my ass," JR mumbled in a low voice. "Should I shoot him?" He pulled out his laser pistol.

"No," I said firmly, then muttered, "rats always know how to abandon a sinking ship." I stepped toward Rose. "If you get us out of here, we will let you live."

"Yes!" the CEO stammered, spittle greasing his lips. "I have a helio. Just on the roof. The pilot is already there. Come! Come!"

He turned and wheeled toward his personal elevator.

The four of us exchanged quick glances. No one *wanted* to follow this scumbag, but none of us were keen on dying, either. We nodded in unison.

"Niu, Dark, escort Rose," I said. "If he so much as *breathes* out of line, break his neck."

Rose paled when the two Tanks each grabbed an arm.

"JR, keep that gun on him."

"Really great of you," Rose continued with platitudes, though his hands shook. "You will be…will be well rewarded for your…for your service…"

"Shut up!" JR snarled, shoving the pistol into his back. "Just walk. Or roll…I guess." He muttered that last part and, despite the danger, I smirked.

As JR passed a brown brocade chair, in a seamless—and I should probably say sexy, though I'd never tell *him* that—one-armed move, JR flipped a burgundy velvet tailcoat over his shoulder without even dropping his aim on Rose.

I gave him an incredulous frown.

"Souvenir," JR said with a wink.

I shook my head, hiding my smile. No matter how much JR had grown into his new role as a soldier, he'd *always* be a bit of a glitterpony. I placed a hand on his shoulder and followed him to the exit.

Awkwardly, Rose entered the elevator key code with his bound arms.

He stammered again, "I'm a man of my word, gentlemen…and woman…you could let me go, you know."

"Not a chance," JR grumbled.

"MISSILE THREAT DETECTED. PLEASE EVACUATE THE SPIRE. FIFTEEN MINUTES TO IMPACT."

I fiddled with my weapon nervously as the elevator ascended at a snail's pace toward the roof. Queasy anticipation roiled in my belly, and I tingled. The nanobots swirled restlessly over my forearm, the silver patch undulating like a snake.

The doors crept open. A sizzle of current tickled the roof of my mouth, then Mara yelped. She and Niu pulled their hands away as if they'd been burned. No…not burned, shocked. And, from the heavy metallic tang in my mouth, I could tell it had been one hell of a current.

The doors finally clicked open. Rose bolted on his one wheel faster than any of us could recover. JR fired his laser pistol, but the beam went wide, tracing across a bright red helio idling on the tarmac.

"Dammit!" He shouted. A spike of frustration shot through my gut. JR's frustration. Swallowing it down, I focused on the task.

"Get to the helio!" I shouted, though the elevator doors had already begun to close.

The Ox jammed his shoulder between them, forcing them open, and the rest of us piled out at once.

A dark-haired man with a bushy mustache and flight goggles perched atop his head stood up at our appearance and pulled his gun. Our eyes met. He raised a confused eyebrow. I trained my pistol on him.

JR fired again, his second shot burning through the gyro-drive core of the CEO's scooter, sending the man skidding to a halt. Rose whirled.

"One more move and I'll blow your head off," JR said, trying to steady his grip. His hands shook so badly I doubted he could hit anything.

Rose lifted his hands, his tone shifting from shock to pleading. "I'm sure we can talk about this, right? Mister VonBuren—"

The pilot flicked his gaze to the CEO but didn't lower his gun.

"These dirty savant rebels are trying to use me as a hostage to escape the island! Shoot them!" Rose barked.

JR's fingers twitched on the trigger. I reached out, just barely brushing his little finger—enough to ground him. Something about this felt wrong.

"You're—you're outnumbered," JR said, voice unsteady. "Shoot me, and they'll kill you both." He indicated the others with a flick of his pistol.

His Aurawave curled toward the pilot, tendrils reaching, searching— then faltered. They fizzled. Dispersed. JR's whole body was taut, his face slick with sweat, his hands bloodless. Fear, not compulsion, poured from him in waves.

He was terrified.

"Shoot them, you idiot!" Rose snapped. "Kill the bastard savants!"

The pilot hesitated. His grip tightened, but his jaw worked, uncertainty clear in his eyes. He had to know the truth—we'd win this fight. He and Rose wouldn't make it out alive.

But even if we survived, none of us knew how to fly a helio.

"MISSILE THREAT DETECTED. PLEASE EVACUATE THE SPIRE. TEN MINUTES TO IMPACT."

"Look," I said, voice low, steady. "We just... we just want to go home." It sounded pathetic, but it was the truth.

"Home?!" Rose shrieked. "You don't deserve a home after what you've done. VonBuren, you genetic trash goblin, shoot those fucking savants!"

The pilot's finger twitched toward the trigger.

A shot rang out.

A hollow crack in the heavy wind.

JR flinched, his own gun bucking in his grip.

Rose staggered, half his face gone. He crumpled onto the ramp.

JR gasped, staring at his shaking hands as if they belonged to someone else. But his gun still had a full charge.

The pilot lowered his smoking pistol—an old combustion-type—his expression blank.

I exhaled and pried the gun from JR's trembling fingers.

We stood in stunned silence, open-mouthed like dead fish.

"I never liked that wanker anyway," VonBuren said in a thick Irish brogue. He looked us over for one more tense second. "You mates wanna get out o' here?"

On cue, a loudspeaker blared on the roof.

"MISSILE THREAT DETECTED. PLEASE EVACUATE THE SPIRE. FIVE MINUTES TO IMPACT."

We looked at each other. Color had returned to JR's face. The Ox smiled and Mara slipped her hand in mine.

"Weh-hell," JR said tremulously, "I suppose I'm not one to look a gift assassination in the face." He tilted his head toward the helio. "Shall we?"

The others nodded.

"Let's go," I replied.

We tripped over each other in our eagerness to get to the helio.

* * * * *

"Name's Quentin VonBuren," the pilot said as he lifted the helio off the pad. His voice was steady, but his hands clenched the controls too tightly.

No one responded. The weight of what we'd done—what I'd done— pressed down like a lead blanket.

As we jetted away from the island, the city sprawled beneath us, fading into the distance. Despite the late hour, its standard lights still blinked, hovercars zipped along the spiral highway, and waves lapped gently at the sea docks. Boats bobbed in the water, some moored to the island, others slipping quietly into the ocean. It was heartbreakingly normal.

For a few more moments, at least.

"There!" JR gasped, pointing.

Red streaks split the starless sky. They were fast. Too fast.

My throat closed. My heartbeat slowed. Every fiber of my body screamed to look away, but I couldn't.

This is what you've done, Robert. Watch what you have done. The voice in my head did not sound like my own.

The bombs struck faster than expected. The sky burned brighter than daylight, a violent haze of oranges and yellows. A fireball erupted, impossibly large, swallowing the city whole. Black smoke billowed, tinged with angry orange cracks, expanding outward like a living thing.

The shock wave hit us next. The helio rocked, but VonBuren held it steady. The heat pressed against my skin, seeping into my bones. My stomach twisted. My breath turned ragged.

JR made a strangled sound. His breath was hot against my ear as he leaned in close, his cheek wet. A single tear fell onto my shoulder.

Mara's grip crushed my hand. Her gaze stayed downcast, pools of shadow against her tan skin. A loose lock of hair slipped from her ponytail, veiling her face.

The blood drained from my head. My vision blurred. I thought I might vomit. But this time, it wasn't the nanites.

This was *me*.

I wanted to disappear—crawl under a seat, leap from the helio, anything to escape this feeling, but I couldn't. My eyes were glued to the devastation below.

This is what you've done.

Debris rained down on the ruined city. The fire swallowed the streets in waves.

No matter how much I tried to justify it, no matter how many times I told myself there was no other way, I felt nothing but contempt for myself. I did this. I set the bombs off. I brought them here.

I glanced at the pilot's reflection in the windshield. His goggles were still pushed up, leaving his eyes exposed—wide, gleaming, caught somewhere between horror and disbelief. The yellow glow of the fire reflected in them like dying stars.

His mustache turned down, his mouth half-opened in a silent cry.

Did he have family in Hong Kong? Had he warned them? What had he lost because of me?

"I'm so sorry," I whispered. I wasn't sure to whom.

VonBuren finally spoke. His voice was quiet, resigned.

"I suppose ye lot are responsible for all of this."

I didn't answer.

He exhaled, long and slow. "I figured as much."

"Why did you help us, then?" the Ox asked, his face carved from stone.

VonBuren kept his eyes on the horizon. "My life has been defined by one terrorist action or another. This is no different."

"That didn't answer—" JR began.

"I'm a Zephyr," the pilot said, his voice steady.

I gaped. A savant working for that piece of garbage, Rose? How did *that* happen?

Before I could ask, the pilot continued in a strong voice, as if making a declaration that had resided too long in secrecy.

"I am the son of Trentino VonBuren, also a Zephyr, and the grandson of Cardie VonBuren, Prime Minister of Greater Ireland."

He exhaled again, the weight of something unseen settling into his shoulders.

"And I have been on the wrong side for too long. This is my penance."

- 40 -
C.E. 2253 October 25

After the bombing, I sat through briefing upon briefing with the Citizen's Army, drowning in words I only half-understood. I spiraled, sinking deeper with each passing moment, suffocated by what I had done—and what was being done to me. Hong Kong Island had been leveled, nanobots ran rampant through my bloodstream, and I hadn't even had a moment to understand what it all meant.

On top of that, my squad broke apart. Ru and Yaozu were gone and Chet discharged for wounds that went deeper than his flesh. He shipped back to America as soon as they could transport him. The rest healed and went off to new assignments, save for Mara and JR, who refused to leave my side. And me...

Well, no one knew what to do with me, including myself. I was lost. Adrift.

I took what remained of my squad to Huairou Base by the Great Wall hoping to find some peace. How do you recover from the murder of ten million people?

To make things worse and despite my best efforts, the nanobots slowly broke free of my control, meching more and more of my arm. It still worked but no longer felt like mine. It was stiff. Numb. More machine than flesh.

The tiny bots were relentless and alien, driven with their purpose, and too advanced to influence. I'd already exhausted my resources trying to find a solution. And I had little progress to show for it. Thus, I gave up, spending most of my days languishing in my bunk, pretending the world at large didn't exist.

It was on one of these particularly bad days, as I turned Saint Claire's strange coin between my fingers, that I finally admitted defeat. The coin was still hard to look at, so I didn't, instead running my fingers over the engraving of a fist, memorizing its shape. He had told us the resistance was bigger than we knew; that there'd come a time when it would need people like me. But not *me,* I realized. If I wasn't even fit for civilian life, I *definitely* wasn't fit for the resistance.

A knock rang upon my door.

I stared at it blankly, before dragging myself up.

Captain Ames stood there, two beers in hand.

I smoothed my rumpled civvies, brushing crumbs from my pants. "Captain," I said, embarrassed, "if I knew you'd be coming by, I' d—uh—have changed."

He smiled thinly, handing me a beer. "Thought you might need this. You seem troubled."

Troubled. Right. But how could I not be when the media was tearing itself apart over Hong Kong. Mech talk shows like Monsieur Baudelaire's spouted theories on who—or what—leveled the city. Religious zealots called it divine wrath. Mechs blamed savants. Savants praised an unseen hero.

And on every savant network, my face played on a loop. JR's footage —my speech before we stormed Hong Kong Island—was everywhere. They called it the rallying cry of the revolution. They dissected every word. Painted me as a visionary.

But, I knew what the press didn't see. The shaking in my hands. The hesitation before I spoke. No one could understand the weight that had sat in my gut, in knowing what was coming, but being unable to say it.

As much as I hated it, I knew people only saw what they wanted to see. Heard what they needed to hear.

Ames flicked off the cap of the bottle with his wedding band.

I startled, torn from my thoughts. "Sir, I didn't know you were married."

"There's a lot of things you don't know about me," he said, a twinkle in his eye. "Take a walk with me. It's a beautiful night."

I shrugged and saluted half-heartedly. We walked in silence, my feet choosing the path, Ames making no effort to correct me. We exited through the side door, into the lush landscape, just beginning to brown. The cool fall air caressed my face, but it did nothing to quell the fire of despair smoldering in my breast.

Twenty paces or so from the building, Ames spoke. "Any progress with that?" he asked, nodding to my arm, which I held close to my chest.

I shook my head. "No matter how hard I fight the bots, I can't convince them to leave. Being meched is a savant's worst nightmare. I only have one solution right now."

"And that is…?"

I sighed, hunching into myself. "Say my goodbyes."

Ames stopped. Looked at me. As much as he tried to maintain a neutral expression, I caught a hint of melancholy there. Loneliness.

"That doesn't sound like the Robert I know."

Hearing my name from him—not my surname or rank—made something in me crack.

I shrugged. "I don't think I'm that Robert anymore, Sir."

We climbed up the trail to the Great Wall—the same one my squad had walked only a few short months before. This time, however, I took it with a much heavier heart.

"Call me Jeremy," Ames said. "I'm not here to speak to you as your captain."

Jeremy. So, this is where it was going…My stomach twisted.

"Yes, Sir—uh—yeah, okay…Jeremy."

He chuckled dryly and touched my meched arm. "Have you thought about methods outside of rejection?"

I looked at him. "As far as—?"

"That robot—AI or whatever they consider themself—Query," Ames continued, "what about their program?"

"Won't work," I said, though even as I spoke, the gears in my head began to turn. "We don't have the infrastructure to build me a body."

"I'm sure you could come up with something."

"Everyone always says that," I sighed in frustration, my voice taking on a high-pitched, mocking tone. "I had *one* good idea and now it's all—Oh, *Robert* can figure it out. *Robert* is a top-notch Mechanic. If anyone can find a solution, it's *Robert.*" I spat on the ground, then took a swig of my beer.

Ames let me rant, listening with attention, his expression sympathetic.

I leaned on the wall, my meched arm hanging from my shoulder like a dead weight. "But what does it matter anyway?" I asked. "I killed millions. Why is my life more important? Why should I survive when they didn't?"

"You carry a burden, that is true," he said pulling another pair of beers from his satchel. "And it's one not many understand. But that doesn't mean you just give up."

I laughed humorlessly. "Am I that obvious?"

"Yes," he said, setting the bottles on the wall. "I don't need to be an Auraseer to see the weight on your soul. Have you talked to anyone about it?"

I shook my head.

"Do you want to?"

I sighed. "Frankly, Sir—Jeremy…I wish I'd never been a part of this whole war. If I had to go back in time…"

"You would have done it differently?" Ames said. "Really?"

The breeze teased through my unkempt hair. I traced a line of condensation on the bottle, then shrugged.

"Probably not. But a guy can dream, can't he?"

"We needed a show of force, you know that as well as I. We needed the world to stand up and take notice."

"Well, the world noticed alright." My laugh was bitter. I took another long drink.

"The Firebrand is in a position to become a legend."

"There's that word again." I ground my teeth. "I hate it. What's it even mean?"

Ames stared into the distance. The electric lights of the city reflected in his gray eyes, like silver stars in an abyss.

"In the coming years, mechs will rewrite history saying the Firebrand didn't just destroy Hong Kong Island, but also Lanzhou and Xi'an, with kinetic energy no human should ever possess. Conversely, savant lore will paint them as the catalyst that ended Lightbar's oppression."

"And that's me?"

He nodded.

"I don't want to be remembered like that."

"You won't." His voice was steady. "The Firebrand will be. People need a symbol. A hero."

"Or a villain," I laughed derisively. "I get it."

Another solemn nod from Ames. His eyes grew far away, and I knew he was looking into the future. "They'll call this the Savant Uprising, even though it involved more than just savants. The conflict will get bigger before it's over. Not just here in China. But in Europe. The UCCA."

"So, all we did means nothing?"

"On the contrary. It means everything."

I looked at him, furrowing my brow.

"For one person to do all that—whether it's good or bad—that's powerful stuff. People will rally behind it."

"But it's a lie!" I snapped. "I didn't do all that. Lots of us did."

Ames shrugged. "People don't want the truth."

"Well, people are stupid," I grumbled, staring out over the twinkling lights of Huairou base. The yellow and red gems spread among a tree-darkened plain, making the landscape feel magical, otherworldly.

"Robert," Ames said, tone serious, "we didn't put you in a good position and I am truly sorry for that. But again, there was no other option."

There was that phrase again: no other option. I snorted.

"Do me a favor," I said, though now my voice felt far away, like it was coming from someone else.

"Anything."

"Make sure I'm remembered as more than a villain. As more than the Firebrand. I don't want my name, my truths, to die with me."

Ames nodded. "The Citizen's Army will not forget your sacrifice."

Sacrifice. Ouch.

But I supposed that was better than nothing. Maybe a handful of soldiers would remember my name—just a whisper in war stories, a footnote in someone else's legend.

Still, the weight in my chest didn't lift. I wasn't going back. Not to the fight, not to the cause.

One way or another, this war had already taken me.

* * * * *

I stood in the darkness for a long time after Ames left, thinking about everything and nothing. I wished my squad was here with me—Mara or JR, or even Chet. One of them would have something witty or asinine to say that would distract me from the inevitable. The memories.

I pulled out the resistance coin again and tried to study it in the dim light.

I felt fear in that symbol, despair. But also hope. My vision blurred. Stomach churned. I thrust it into my pocket.

The familiar numbness of feeling sorry for myself returned. A shuffle behind me tugged me from my self-destructive thoughts. A tall, muscular man approached, clearing his throat politely. He waved.

"Ah, Firebrand, it's you," he said in his lilting brogue.

"VonBuren, you know my name is Robert." I scowled. I really did hate that name.

"Quentin, please," he said, smirking. I huffed.

Quentin VonBuren was an enigma. The pilot who'd flown us from The Spire. The one who killed Rose. In one blink—in one breath—he renounced a lifetime of employment with Lightbar and thrown in with us. We didn't get a chance to talk in the days following the bombing. He'd turned right around to search for his family in Hong Kong.

Secretly, I was grateful. I didn't know how I'd look the man in the eyes and see anything aside from my own guilt reflected back.

"I'll leave," I said, pushing away from the wall.

"Stay," the man replied, coming up next to me. "What's the story?"

Every fiber of my muscles screamed at me to flee, but that would only amplify my guilt. I forced myself to be calm. I swallowed.

"Thought it'd be a nice night for a walk," I said sarcastically.

He nodded. "'S quiet out here. Nice place to think."

I grunted my agreement, though I had hoped to do the opposite.

Opening a canteen, Quentin poured a clear liquid into the small lid. Downing it in one shot, he gave a dramatic sigh.

"Baiju," he said as I watched him refill the cup. He wiggled his eyebrows in the silvery moonlight. "Care for some?"

I gave a groan but held out my hand anyway. He passed me the cup.

"Why'd you bring your family here?" I asked suddenly. "Why not a CORP hospital?"

He spat. "I'm done with the CORPs. Even though only a few know what I did, I won't go back. Huairou has some of the best medical care. My family needed it."

"How are they?"

Quentin was silent for a moment. "Zhìwàng is recovering. He's a strong wean, like his da."

I released a small sigh. Quentin's son was just a few years older than Sam, and yet he had been a presence in his father's life—someone Quentin had held, spoken to, and watched grow. My own remained a stranger, a memory of a life I'd never had.

"Chenguang, my morning glory," Quentin continued, "Did not survive. She's been gone a week."

I felt as if I'd been punched in the stomach. My breath caught in my throat. *You did that.*

"I'm sorry," I croaked, unsure of what else to say.

"I don't blame you. You are as much a casualty of this war as they."

I froze. "What do you mean?"

"Have you looked at yourself, Robert? You look like shite." He studied my face in the moonlight.

I laughed, caught off guard. "I suppose a rampant nanovirus will do that to ya."

He shook his head. "Not talking about that, though it does look serious. Something's on your mind, boyo. What's the story?"

The way he said it—casual, almost familiar—told me everything. Ten seconds with Quentin, and he'd already drawn the same conclusion as Ames.

"I'm not who they say I am," I blurted.

"You're not the man who pushed the button in Hong Kong?"

I snorted, "Okay. I am that man…*was* that man. One time. But never again."

Quentin nodded slowly as if waiting for more.

"It was a mistake!" I said with vehemence. "It was a stupid choice on my part and that of the officers. I will always—*always*—regret my part in the destruction. I know there was more to Hong Kong than a parasitic corporate HQ. I know it was filled with *people*."

I was whining now but couldn't help myself. My despair had sunk deep.

"And yet, I killed them all with the tap of some buttons. Mechs *and* savants. True Humans. Families. Hard-working laborers. Brilliant scientists. People whose only transgression was to be in the wrong place. I know some will say those people were complicit. Or that I killed some to save the rest."

I turned to look at the Zephyr, tears streaming down my cheeks.

"But all I can think of is how I silenced their voices."

I buried my head in my hands, resting my elbows on the wall.

"Despite everyone before me who made the decisions, every officer whose orders I followed, *I* was the one to break the heart of China," I mumbled through tears.

Quentin said nothing, just patted my shoulder and held the little cup of baiju toward me.

I squinted at him, the effects of the alcohol blurring my vision.

He shook his head sadly and muttered soothing words under his breath as if I was just another son with a scraped knee.

"How can you be so understanding?" I snapped at him. I wasn't sure if it was the liquor or bile that burned my throat, but suddenly I *ached*. Ached to feel…ached to hurt.

"You should hate me!" I continued. "You, of all people, saw exactly what I did."

"Jesus, Mary and Joseph!" Quentin cursed, pulling back his hand. "Are you questioning my judgment?"

"Yeah," I rumbled, voice hoarse. "I'm questioning your judgment. *And* your sanity. If you had known I was the one about to shatter your family, would you have rescued us?"

Looking away with the bitter taste of baiju on my tongue, I moaned, "You should have left us to die."

Quentin slapped me, his beefy hand hitting more like a cudgel than skin and bone. I reeled backward, stars flashing in my vision.

"Is that better?" the man snapped, shoving me hard. "Do you feel sufficiently punished?"

I blinked in confusion. Blood dripped from my nose.

"Do you need a belt to the gob from each person who lost someone in Hong Kong, or d'ya want more from me?" He went to hit me again, but I caught his arm this time, shrinking under the blow. Slowly, I lowered myself to a hard seat on the weed covered stones. The tears came again in a violent, ugly wave.

"What's done is done, lad." He dropped into a crouch beside me. "No sense in punishin' yourself for it."

When I'd finally cried myself out, I slumped against the parapet, exhausted and drunk. Wiping tears and snot from my face I sighed. "What's *your* story, anyway?"

He passed his canteen to me. "It's complicated."

I took a drink, tiny cup forgotten.

"I'm not going anywhere." The baiju had me floating and feeling as if I could sit there all night.

Quentin began. "Like most Irish savants, we'd thrown our lot in with the CORPs after The Third. The English called us turncoats, but our ancestors had wanted more. Hundreds of years of oppression will do that to a people. My grand da was the Prime Minister of Greater Ireland from '20 till his death in '44. He died at the hands of English rebels during the Small English Revolt. My whole family perished from their scatterbombs—my da, my mam, my sister. With my family gone at fifteen, I was so angry. Angry at the English for killing us. At Europe and The UCCA for not doing anything. So's I ran away to Hong Kong for work."

He took another shot of baiju.

"Initially, I believed what the corporations wanted us to hear. I ate up their drivel of freedom and a country of our own. In short order, I found out they lied. We traded one oppression for another. The Crown was gone, Londyn City set adrift in the overfull ocean, but we were still trapped in the same kind of shite."

"A savant with the CORPs?" I asked. "How'd that work?"

"Carefully," Quentin rumbled with what I thought was a chuckle, but it held no humor, "The CORPs employees looked the other way as long as we lied about it. As a Zephyr, I couldn't ever fly to the best of my ability. I had to pretend I was True."

"Were there no Aurasniffers? No way to detect savants working for the CORPs?"

Quentin shrugged, "As long as we did our jobs and were mindful of who we did—and didn't—piss off, they left us alone. We quietly worked in anonymity."

"Did you hate us?" I asked before thinking. "I mean the other savants? The resistance fighters?"

He shook his head. "I didn't. But I didn't do anything to stop it, either, which was almost as bad. There were many like me. Do you know much about Hitler?"

"The German dictator in the nineteen-forties who killed millions of people?"

He nodded. "But it wasn't just anyone. He targeted citizens from specific subgroups—Jews and Romani, those with disabilities—anyone who didn't fit into his ideal society."

"How'd he kill them? With a bomb or synthetic virus ?"

"One by one," Quentin said, his expression grim. "Early twentieth century technology was rudimentary, compared to ours. They didn't have super-fast communication or mega-bombs. Hell, they barely had planes. Instead, he rounded his citizens up. Used soldiers and trains to take them to prison camps. Killed them in batches with guns and chemicals. It took him half a decade to kill six million people."

"Camps and guns?"

Six years to kill a third as many people as one rod could in seconds. I thought back to Zhelan's declaration, *"We shall not suffer a tyrant's rule."*

"How did people allow that?" I asked in awe and horror.

"He shouted his way to the top, spewing hatred and vitriol. He preyed on the fearful. On weakness. It was insidious. His government wasn't the most popular, but it was the loudest. And in turn, his followers were loud too. Those that didn't agree stayed silent, holding onto a different kind of fear. A crippling fear. All they wanted was to keep their heads down, do their jobs. In refusing to acknowledge this fear, they passively helped their country fall down around their ears."

"They did nothing to resist?"

"Not at first. Does that sound familiar?"

I nodded.

"We are a product of our time, you and me. We both have done things we're not proud of—things what will haunt us. But that doesn't mean we're awful people, yeah? Doesn't mean we can't grow."

I blinked, staring into the man's dark eyes. To my surprise, they held no hatred or bitterness, but instead a sad solemnity.

"Thank you," I said. "Though, I'm not sure what to do now."

Quentin clasped my hand, firm and certain. "Well, whatever you decide, boyo, it'll be the right thing for you."

I quirked an eyebrow at him. "What about you?"

"Me?" He set his jaw in a determined smile. "I will use this second chance you've given me. I won't sit on my arse and marinate anymore. Instead, I will spread the word of the Firebrand. Of hope."

I let out a slow breath, exhaustion pressing down on me like a weight I could no longer bear. The Firebrand. The symbol they wanted, the legend they were crafting—one I had no say in.

I wasn't hope or salvation.

I was just a soldier who had followed orders, done what had to be done, and now had to live—or die—with it.

But maybe Quentin was right. Maybe I didn't have to be proud of what I'd done to believe something better could come from it. Maybe, in the end, it didn't matter if I wanted to be remembered or how it was portrayed.

Maybe what mattered was that someone—someone like Quentin—was willing to take the torch.

He stood, his resolve set. "People need something to believe in. You lit the spark, Robert Lilly. Now it's time to see if they'll rise from the ashes."
I watched him go, that sense of peace I'd sought, finally settling. My war was ending, but for others, it had only just begun.

- 41 -

C.E. 2253 November 10

"We should have turned the fucking car around!" JR railed. "Fuck this *fucking* war!"

He rose from his chair, a scowl bisecting his face.

"Are you *sure* there isn't any other way?"

He grabbed my left arm, meched now from collarbone to fingertips.

Warmth from his touch radiated through me, but I could no longer feel his skin.

"No," I sighed, resigned. "Query and I have been banging our heads together, but we have no resources, no infrastructure. The bots have replicated beyond my awareness. I can't keep track of them anymore."

JR huffed, his voice heavy. "But your proposal—your *solution*—is gonna kill you!"

"So will the bots, eventually."

"But, Rob, there *has* to be something else. Maybe another scientist?"

He gripped my hand. Desperation hit me in a wave, laced with hope.

I shook it off. "Don't you understand? There *aren't* any other scientists. There's not enough *time*." I rubbed my forehead with my good hand. "JR, they're in my *mind*."

His eyes, glistening with tears, pleaded with me. "But Rob…putting your consciousness into a machine? That's crazy!"

"I already feel like I'm crazy!" I snapped back. "If I don't do something soon, I will lose what little sanity I have left."

I paced, itching all over.

But it wasn't just an itch—it was a deeper, crawling sensation just beneath my skin, thousands of insects burrowing through muscle and marrow. My blood felt thick, sluggish, and buzzing. Syrup laced with static. Every breath carried a faint metallic tang, the taste of copper and ozone clinging to my tongue. The air smelled wrong—too sharp, too clean. My throat burned. And my thoughts—

My thoughts stuttered, flickering like a dying signal. It had become hard to tell which ones were mine and which ones were…other.

"It will work," I pressed. It *had* to work. "Query's done this before. Granted, they had better tech then, but…It'll work." I said the last words with a finality I hoped JR would interpret as confidence.

"Okay, but where you gonna get this robot? You said it yourself. We don't have the resources."

He still hadn't let go of my hand. I felt his irregular pulse, first quick, then slowing.

I bit my lip and wiggled my metallic fingers with difficulty. "Right here."

He cocked his head at me. "Wha—huh?"

"I'm going to extract the nanobots, then rebuild them into an artifact."

"Rob," JR snapped, "that's ridiculous! If you can extract the nanobots, why not just do that in the first place?" He kicked the rolling chair across the floor. It clattered into a wall.

"Because that would kill me," I said. "I know it doesn't make sense to you, but the bots have already consumed my flesh. If they just go, they take me with them."

JR roared, burying both hands into his mess of curly hair until he gagged. He stomped across the room and kicked the chair again, causing it to tip over. Anger and agitation filled the room with an almost palpable heat. I wiped sweat from my brow.

"Hey," I said gently, placing a hand on his shoulder. "It's all right."

He whirled on me. "All right? It's *not* all right. You're gonna become a machine. A common tool!"

I tried to give him a wry smile, "So, not much different than now, huh?"

He froze, taken aback. When he got my joke, he wrinkled his nose and refused to play into it.

"Much different," he said. "Right now, you control machines. They don't control you." He swiped angry tears from his cheeks.

"JR," I said, grabbing his sleeve to stop his erratic pacing. I stared into his wild eyes. "You know this is not a choice I take lightly. But it's the only option."

There's that 'only option' phrase again. Shit, I'm sure JR was getting as sick of hearing it as I was.

He gripped my forearms tightly, "It can't be, Rob. You know that. You know you can't leave…"

His voice caught, and rose an octave, even as he dropped to a whisper.

"You can't leave *me*. You are the only good thing that's *ever* happened to me. Without you, I would have died at least ten times. I don't know how I'll survive."

My heart sank. For all his bluster and teasing, JR was the truest friend I had. Normally, I kept myself closed to the Sway's Aurawave but this time, I opened up, allowing all his feelings to flow through me. Despair. Denial. Loss. Helplessness.

His honey eyes locked with mine.

"PFC Judas Rostbane," I said finally, talking around the lump in my throat.

JR frowned, but this time, he didn't bother to correct me.

"You underestimate yourself. For Greysoft's sake, your dad was a syndicate boss! You've got grit and steel in your blood. But, even better, you're also kind and genuine. Honest, even. You may still be a pretty crappy shot…"

JR chuckled, despite himself.

"But you're a survivor. You *will* do amazing things." I pulled him in for an awkward, one-armed hug. He gripped me tightly with his skinny arms. "I'm sorry we never got those shrimp wontons."

He grunted. "I'll just have to find the best ones and eat them without you."

Removing the dog tags from around my neck, where I had also hung the resistance coin, I placed them over his head.

"Don't forget me, okay?"

Pressing his forehead against mine, JR sniffed, letting the tears run down his cheeks. He moaned. "Charger's Balls, how could I ever forget you, you insufferable cock?"

C.E. 2253 November 11

I walked like a robot back to my bunk. During the Battle of Sky Plaza, I had already accepted the fact that I may not survive the war. At the time I thought I would flame out—die so suddenly that I didn't have time for goodbyes or regret.

This way was both a blessing and a curse. And *Charger's Balls,* it was harder than I expected.

Opening the door of my bunk, I slipped inside. Mara was already there, sitting on the edge of my bed. Her face was pale and her sunken eyes bright red. Clearly she'd been crying, though I knew better than to bring up that fact. Sitting next to her, I said nothing.

"So, it's time?" she asked.

"Yes. Tomorrow…" I choked.

"You fucking son-of-a-mech asshole!" she snapped, punching me in my robotic arm. Her fist connected with a hollow *clang,* and she pulled it back in surprise. "Ow!" She shook the tension from her fingers.

I felt nothing. I couldn't help but chuckle, "Well I guess the bots did one good thing for me. That punch would have broken my arm."

She scowled, having none of it. "If you hadn't gotten meched in the first place, I'd have no reason to punch you."

I sighed. Mara was right. Turning to her, I used my human hand to push strands of dark hair from her cheeks. Cupping her face, I stared at her. "I'm so sorry."

She pulled away, allowing the hair to fall back down over her face, "It's not your fault. It was that shithead, Hex Tristan. When I find him, I'm going to rip out every wire, every fuckin' nerve, until he dies screaming the name of the man he condemned."

I shook my head. "Please…can we…not…" I touched her shoulder again as she looked back up. "Mara," I said slowly, hand shaking, all my muscles tense, "I love you."

Her mouth opened halfway and closed. "I know," she said, "but what about your wife?"

"Fiancée," I corrected her. "And I don't know. I love her, too, I suppose. But I'm a selfish, horny, destructive, arrogant fool."

"That you are," she smiled wryly.

"Am I a bad person?"

She shrugged. "We're all bad people I guess. We do what we can to survive. And…make our days bearable."

"I never thought I'd find love here," I said.

Mara snorted. "You and me both."

Pulling the data ring and my rank badges out of my pocket, I pressed them into her hand. "Please make sure Sam gets these." She nodded, slipping on the ring. "And also…"

I choked.

"And also, give him whatever is left of me."

She looked as if she'd swallowed something sharp but nodded again. "Are you sure this is the right thing to do?"

I nodded, not trusting my voice.

Then Mara kissed me, a hesitant kiss, full of uncertainty. I returned, pressing my lips hard into hers, taking in all the warmth and vitality I could from that kiss. Slipping her tank top from her shoulders, I moved my lips to the hollow of her neck, her collarbone, her breasts.

She took me with urgency, as the minutes ticked away. I'd never felt so fulfilled or so empty at the same time. I couldn't get enough of her skin, her scent, her kisses. When we were spent, laying there breathless, she spoke.

"Call JR. He deserves to be here as much as I."

I cocked my head at her.

"It's been you two from the beginning," she continued, "then me. It's appropriate we're here for the end too, hmm?"

I nodded and did what she said. Loving her for her encouragement and for sharing me with my best friend.

In the meantime, she dressed and pulled out a bottle of alcohol from a bag—not bathtub spirits or the homemade baiju that tasted like feet—but dark, brown whisky.

"From Quentin," she smiled, pulling several cups from the bag. "He said he'd been saving it for just an occasion."

My gut twisted and my face warmed, overwhelmed by the care taken by my friends.

JR arrived shortly thereafter with a case of beer, not nearly the quality of the whisky, but good, nonetheless.

The rest of the night, there was no more talk of finality. We told stories about the squad, speculated where Ox and Mendez ended up, laughed at

JR's drunken antics, and killed off the beer and the entire bottle of whisky. A haze of booze settled over us, a thick shroud that drowned out the rest of the world. When the first rays of sunlight hit the barracks wall, we'd finally exhausted our supply.

Collapsing in a tangle of arms, legs, and blankets, we held onto the warmth of each other, as if we could stop time with the weight of our bodies alone. No one spoke of what came next, of the choices already made or the dawn creeping in through the window. For one last moment, we were just us. Before sleep finally claimed me, I clung to the sound of their breathing, the steady, fragile proof that for now, for this fleeting moment, I was still here.

When I awoke, the room was thick with the scent of sweat, spilled whiskey, and something quieter—something like goodbye. JR snored softly beside me, an arm draped over his face, while Mara stirred, blinking at the morning light. My head throbbed, my mouth tasted of ash, and for a second, just one second, I let myself believe that nothing had changed.

But today, everything would change.

Epilogue

C.E. 2253 November 11

Dear Sam,

You need to know the truth.

I came to China, broke and apathetic. I fought beside people I didn't know, and didn't care about. Somewhere down the road, something changed. I began to believe. When people work together, we can do great things.

The people of China invested in this war—those mechs, savants and Trues who put their differences aside to push toward a common good, showed a level of compassion I've never seen in the UCCA. When Nic Saint Claire talked about a future for everyone, I didn't believe him. However, throughout my time and especially in the last two months, I have seen this in action. As much as humans find a way to fight, they also find a way to persevere.

People can be loyal. I am still not sure when I earned such loyalty from Mara, JR, Chet, and the others, but there it was. I thought I was just doing my job, making the best choices with the orders given. Along the way, I tried to look out for my people, though they both challenged and bolstered me.

I never considered myself a charismatic person—especially not compared to JR or even Captain Ames. But I found it takes more than charisma to command loyalty. It takes faith, trust. In both yourself and your people. By the end, I trusted these men and women with my life and will always be grateful for their returned trust. I hope I did them right in the end.

Loyalty can become friendship. This war was the last place I thought I'd find it. JR challenged me most of all, but even still, he was willing to ignore my flaws. Somehow, we worked our way in to a "bro-manship" I never thought possible. His friendship saw me through my darkest days. Never underestimate your friends. You will need them during your own dark days.

Love blindsides you like a maglev truck. When I left for China, I was a brash young man who followed my lust. I loved your mother, to the extent any young man with no life experience could love someone. But even that scared me, so I ran. Not my finest moment, for sure.

The thing about love is, it is not a finite resource to be doled out sparingly. It comes from within and makes no demands. You can love many —at the same time. Remember this, Sam. You can love your friends. Your family. Your partners. Never sacrifice one love for another, or you'll never be fulfilled.

Machines—my greatest gift, my Skill—will be my downfall. Try as I might, I cannot eject the nanobots. If I do nothing, they will turn me into an automaton. However, with help from a cyborg named Query, I came up with a plan. If I can infuse the nanites with my conscience—my soul if you will—maybe I can take control of them. It's risky. It could kill me. Or erase me. But if it works, it would be a breakthrough.

Many of the savants don't understand this choice. For one of us to willingly become a machine, or part machine, is nearly unheard of. Yet, we are not all that different, savants and mechs, contrary to what both sides would have you think. Again, we are all people and if we can work together, we will be stronger.

It is my hope we are reunited when I am in my new form. Perhaps there will be enough left of me to recognize you. I've entrusted Mara to find you with this letter. I hope you will give me a chance and read it.

Lastly, I wanted to say I'm sorry. I don't expect you to understand why I did what I did, but I hope you will forgive me. You did not deserve to be fatherless. I regret that more than anything else I've done. Please know, though we've never met, I've always loved you and will continue to love you until the last breath leaves my body.

Sam, be amazing. Fight for what you care about. Fight for *who* you care about. And don't give up on yourself. Not ever.

Your loving father,
Robert Lilly
Staff Sergeant of the Street Dogs
Citizen's Army, China
P.S. If I'd had any say in the matter, I'd have given you the middle name Jeremy, for my captain. He's seen a future for you. You will be magnificent.

Read on for a sneak peek of Book 2 of *The Savant Uprising*.

Anamnesis

A street kid, a deadly assassin, and a war for the future—Sam doesn't want
to join the revolution, but he has no choice, it's in his blood.

C.E. 2267 February 19

Anamnesis [an-am-NEE-sis] (n): the recollection of the Ideas, which the soul had known in a previous existence, especially by means of reasoning. - Plato's dialogs: Meno & Phaedo

* * * * *

Sam startled awake, heart clamoring in his chest and throat tight.

Bad dream? he wondered, but he couldn't remember it. He just knew that every nerve thrummed in anticipation.

A tension hung over him, and he glanced around the darkened warehouse. The cadence of soft snores drifted toward him through the chill spring air—the bodies of the homeless teens pressed against each him for warmth.

"Hey Grant," he said, shoving an elbow into his best friend's ribs.

Grant's eyes fluttered open, and he yawned, raising a sleepy eyebrow.

"The hell, Sam?" he mumbled, pushing up to an elbow. Sitting up, Grant shivered, spreading out the hoodie he'd been using as a pillow.

"Something's wrong," Sam said, keeping voice to a whisper, so he didn't wake the others.

"What's Wrong?" Grant looked around. He pulled on the sweatshirt. "Something besides the fact that it's fucking cold in here?"

"Yeah. Dunno what, but I have a bad feeling." He touched his chest, feeling his frantic heartbeat. A prickle ran across his skin that had nothing to do with the cold.

"You've had bad feelings before, you know," Grant chided, words still slurred by sleep. "And they've always been false alarms…"

Sam sighed. "I know, but this time it's—" *It's what?* He thought. His head throbbed with each beat of his heart. "It's different, there's—something," he practically whined, begging Grant to believe him. Ragged breath tore past his teeth. His eyes unfocused, the world narrowing to a pinpoint.

"Hey," Grant said, his tone now gentle. He put one hand atop Sam's and gripped his chin with the other, forcing Sam to meet his eyes. "It's okay. If you say there's something wrong, we'll take a look."

Sam nodded, swallowing through a tight throat. Bright moonlight filtered through a high window, turning Grant's skin a silvery gray that matched his friend's sparkling eyes. His friend looked like one of the mysterious fae from old fairy tales. Sam tore his eyes away and released another shuddering breath. The dizziness receded. His heart slowed, if only a fraction. Cold seeped through his crossed legs from the concrete floor. At least that still felt solid.

"Do you think I'm crazy?" he muttered as they picked their way through sleeping bodies. Life on the streets of The Sink were already hard enough, but it would be worse if his best friend thought he was crazy on top of it.

"Of course not," Grant said, "You're just not—"

"Like you guys," Sam filled in, his saliva going sour. Grant was a savant, a reclaimed term from a hundred-plus years ago, used for the descendants of the first genetically modified humans. Savants had an extra sense, their Skill, which gave them an edge over normal humans. This had earned them disfavor in the eyes of the Triumvirate, America's corporate government, run by cybernetically modified individuals called mechs. Despite the danger, Sam envied savants. He thought having a Skill and being hunted would still beat being ignored as a weak, normal nobody.

"That's not what I meant," Grant said with a snort. He understood Sam's frustration and usually tried to be sensitive to it. "I was gonna say, 'You're not known for your accuracy'."

"Ass," Sam muttered, giving his friend a good natured shove.

They stuck to the edge of the warehouse, the large room yawing cavernously before them. Sam strained his eyes so hard they hurt but could still barely make out the faded letters on a partially-collapsed interior wall, M-A-C-H.

Sam caught his toe on a piece of concrete and tripped, falling toward a pile of rubble. Before hitting the ground, an invisible force stopped him. Grant's hand worked like a conductor, pushing against the air. Without touching Sam, his friend helped him regain his feet.

"Careful," Grant breathed, swiping his hands away from each other. Bits of concrete, dirt, and gravel skittered from the path as if blown by a strong gust of wind, but not even a breeze ruffled Sam's hair.

"Thanks."

"What?" Grant asked, catching Sam's half-lidded scowl.

"Do you have to be so fucking perfect?" he sighed. It was easy to pretend Grant was just a normal kid like him—albeit a charming, strong, and street-smart kid—until he did something like that.

"Oh, my Skill. Sorry, I know you don't like when I use it, but I wasn't just gonna let you fall."

And, dammit, he was humble too.

Sighing again, Sam gripped Grant's hand, intertwining their fingers. "Don't be sorry," he said. They'd made a half circle and already the feeling of unease had begun to fade. As long as Grant was there, everything would be okay. "It's your Skill. You shoul—"

Something caught Sam's eye: a small red dot on the far wall by the entrance.

At first, Sam didn't realize what was seeing—a fuzzy line growing from the dot, reflected in the dusty darkness. Moonlight glinted off a shiny faceplate.

"Get down!" he hissed, dropping to the floor and pulling Grant with him. A tiny tranq dart flew above their heads to lodge into the half-wall.

Gasping for breath, the two lay on the floor, Sam's heart hammering once more. An electric anticipation filled the air and for a brief moment, Sam hoped it had all been in his imagination. Two more darts zipped across the darkness, but Grant brushed them away with a flick of his hand. So much for imagination.

"Raid!" he shouted, before Sam dragged him again behind a pile of rubble.

The warehouse exploded with noise. Teenagers scrambled to their feet with muffled shouts, tranq darts whizzing over their heads. Enforcers burst through the door, covered in head-to-toe riot gear.

"How many?" Grant gasped under his breath. "And who are they?"

Sam stole a glance from behind the pile. He could only see fast-moving dark blurs interspersed with glowing digi-ink. "I can't tell. What's T-SEC?" he asked, noting the company name painted on one of the enforcer's suits.

"Triumvirate Security, the government's police force. Shit. This is bad."

Sam pressed himself further into the shadows of the broken wall. The commotion had risen to a din, and already the situation felt hopeless.

Many kids were already down. Some lay still and others struggled beneath taser nets made of red light. The rest had scattered. He noticed a couple already working their hands to ready their Skills. Though Sam wondered how effective that would be against the fully-armored T-SEC enforcers that stalked the perimeter.

"Should they be here?" Sam whispered to Grant. "I thought this was the cartel's city?"

"You wanna tell them that?" Grant ground out through clenched teeth, his whole body shaking. "Greysoft knows, the CORPs do whatever they want."

His friend's face was pale, lips a bloodless line and Sam realized how afraid Grant was—and he wasn't supposed to be afraid of anything. Palms clammy, he gripped Grant's sleeve.

"What do we do?" he whispered. No escape plan had materialized in his frantic brain.

Enforcers, positioned on three sides of the warehouse, stood with weapons raised. One man adjusted something on his visor, and somehow Sam knew he was adjusting his sight. Another man motioned toward the fourth, unoccupied wall. They were about to be surrounded.

A tingle ran across Sam's skin, indicating the building pressure of an electromagnetic pulse. One of the teenage savants stood up from the rubble. The EMP fizzled through the warehouse killing the lights on the guards' uniforms. The sudden quiet as tranq guns went still, formed like cotton in Sam's ears. His head spun. He'd forgotten how noisy tech could be.

"This won't last," he whispered in Grant's ear. "C'mon!"

The feel the gentle whir of the enforcers' backup powerbanks coursed across Sam's skin.

He tugged on Grant's arm.

But they'd wasted precious second, and everything blinked back to life. He staggered beneath the flurry of noise. Grant caught him, this time with a shaking hand. Sam blinked fuzzy eyes at the young woman who'd caused the EMP, a Spark named Corine. She made to clap her hands together for another, but the grating buzz of a laser weapon cut her actions short. She screamed as a net engulfed her, dragging her to the floor.

Someone grabbed him, another young woman with dark skin and kinky brown hair. It was Ryann, the newest girl in their group.

"This way!" she hissed at Sam. "There are no Auras at the south wall!" She pointed to a darkened alcove where Sam could barely make out the rusty rungs of a ladder.

"Where's it go?" Grant asked.

"The roof, I think—"

Another hiss. A net headed their way. Sam tried to grab both Grant and Ryann, but one hand came away empty. Ryann tumbled under a taser net, immobilized before she even had a chance to scream. Sam shoved Grant behind a pillar.

"That was close," Grant said with a frown toward Ryann.

"We should help her," Sam said, though Ryann had already gone motionless from electric current.

Grant shook his head in desperation. "No. We'll just get caught too."

With an aching heart, Sam nodded. Grant was right. Even though Sam was good at working with technology, it would take far too long to disable the net, leaving them both vulnerable.

"That ladder Ryann pointed to. We'll run there on three," Grant said in a trembling whisper. "Don't look back."

Sam nodded again, his fragile grasp on calm slipping away with the dying of Ryann's screams.

"Promise me," Grant said, holding Sam's face in his hands. "Don't look back. We can't afford to stop."

Sam swallowed hard but managed to croak out, "I promise."

Grant began to count.

"One."

The warehouse swarmed with T-SEC Enforcers. One launched a cannon with fine powder into the the air. It settled on the two, and Sam gagged at the sour smell, the chemical fumes burning his eyes.

"Two."

What the hell was it? It didn't stick around like the tear gas they'd breathed during the protest last summer. Already, the burning had receded, though the scent of something off lingered in his nostrils.

"Three!"

The word sent a bolt of lightning through him and Sam took off, with an uncharacteristic burst of speed. Pumping his legs hard, he leapt over the fallen bodies of several kids, but managed to keep his footing.

"Hey!" a guard shouted. "Get that one!"

Sam looked back.

Grant wasn't running. Instead, he gestured toward an old steel drum and lifted it from the ground. With his hands in the air, he flung the drum toward the guard, shattering their glass faceplate and snapping their head to the side. The guard fell, blood seeping through the cracks of their helmet.

Sam stumbled, another piece of rubble catching his toe. This time, Grant wasn't there to save him. He sprawled across the floor, banging his elbow on the uneven floor. A bar of black flashed in his vision, followed by sparkling stars of pain. He writhed, arm numb, and tried to call to Grant. But hand grabbed him under the arm, hauling him to his feet. Sam whirled to fight, and the figure shoved a gloved hand over his mouth.

He struggled against his captor, but the person caught his punch and held him tight. Slowly, he was dragged farther and farther away from Grant, who still fought—trying to confuse the enforcers in a swirl of debris. The figure pressed him against the rusty ladder, their face close to his.

"You can't save him," came the harsh male voice. "Climb and you may survive."

In the shadows, Sam couldn't make out the face of the man, who smelled of leather, sweat, and some unknown spice, but immediately knew he had to listen.

He gave a hesitant nod, but the man had already slipped away, becoming part of the darkness in his night-black clothing. He placed a foot on the ladder, limb carrying him upward of their own volition. Something in the back of his mind screamed at him to stop, but he couldn't. The ladder disappeared into the ceiling.

As he went higher, the compulsion to climb bled away, leaving Sam cold and empty. And thinking of Grant. He froze, ears straining.

He could go back to look for Grant, but he recalled his friend's own words.

"They'd just catch us too."

If Grant was *not* on his way up to Sam, he might be stuck down there like Corine. Like Ryann. Besides, that mystery man might still be down there, and Sam wasn't sure he wanted to encounter him again.

He felt a cool draft across his cheek, and turned to see the grate of a ventilation shaft on one side of the ladder. Maybe he could wait in there for Grant? Slamming his fist into the grate, he was able to cave it inward. His hand ached, and the jagged metal edges of the shaft tore at his already worn clothing, but he managed to wiggle through, choking on a face-full of dust.

He could hear the sounds from down below much better now, so he slid along until he reached an open vent with a view of the floor. What he saw turned his blood turned to ice.

Grant, chest punctured by not one, but two sets of taser pins struggled against the paralytic current, roaring like an animal. Debris, broken crates, and steel barrels flew around him in a whirling tornado, but that only slowed the enforcers. Using batons and riot shields, they fought through the maelstrom, until one planted the butt of a magrifle into Grant's temple—once, twice, three times. Grant crumpled.

"No!" Sam breathed a strangled cry.

Bile rose in his throat. Taking one slow breath through his nose, he tried to stop trembling. *I have to do something! Grant's all I have.*

But he didn't do anything. One clumsy, normal street kid was no match for a contingent of armed T-SEC guards.

At least, if he remained free, he had a chance of finding his friend. So, he watched and tried to remember everything.

The soldiers dragged all the kids into the center of the room, including Grant, fitting hoods over those who were still awake. Sam choked down a sob.

A door on the outside of the building opened, the sound causing all the guards to snap to attention. From the hurried salutes, Sam guessed the new guy was the leader. Illuminated by a golden shaft of street lights from the open door, the new man wore no helmet. By the looks of it, he didn't need one. A shiny plate, crawling with glowing circuitry, and a bright blue monocular covered half his head, ending on one side of a short black mohawk. The other half of his face remained human.

The unnatural mosaic of metal and flesh continued down the man's torso where he wore some combination of plated battle armor and cybernetic modifications. One arm seemed human enough, but the other was a shiny, gunmetal gray. His hand had taken the form of a laser pistol. Once he verified the scene was secure, the man slipped the pistol slipped back into the arm casing and removed a blackened metal hand.

This guy was a classic mech, if Sam had ever seen one. If savants were considered mutated freaks born from reckless science, then mechs should be seen as the bastard children of capitalist excess. Yet, Triumvirate propaganda touted the opposite.

Tech rules supreme.

Better living through modification.

Machines elevate. DNA subjugates.

Mechs were the Triumvirate's people, first class citizens. They made up over half the population of the United Corporate Cities of America. While at first, only those without savant DNA chose the mech path, but a hundred years later, even some savants had begun buying into the lies. True Humans like Sam, those without either modification or savant DNA, were becoming an endangered species.

"How many, Agent Six?" The leader twisted his lips into a grimace.

One of the enforcers lifted his visor to scan the group, and Sam noticed light shining from unnaturally blue eyes. "Twenty-three, Vox Tristan," he said in a raspy voice. "No…twenty-four."

"Twenty-four?" the general repeated, "Our heat scans showed at least twenty-nine. Where did the rest go?"

Sam's heart jumped in his throat. He clamped his lips shut, afraid the guards down below could hear even his breathing.

"Run off, Sir. This warehouse had more exits than we anticipated."

"That is not acceptable, Six," The Vox said, his voice tense. "We need them *all.* What we're doing here is not remotely legal…we must have no witnesses."

"Of course, Sir," Six said with a sneer, "I planned for this. Tagged them with a traceable chemical that has as slow breakdown rate. We'll find them."

"You'd better," The Vox's cold voice made Sam's skin crawl, "or it'll be your hide the doctor experiments on."

The Agent chuckled, an equally unpleasant sound. "Oh, no, Sir," he said slowly. "I don't fit in the doctor's age or DNA demographics." He gestured over the captive teens. "But I appreciate the threat. I will personally oversee the hunt."

"Do that," The Vox said, crossing his arms. "Get the rest loaded up and into holding. The transport leaves in a week."

Sam bit his tongue to keep the anguished cries from escaping his throat until he tasted copper. Silent tears streamed down his cheeks. Grant's now motionless body flopped like a ragdoll over a guard's shoulder.

"I'll find you, I promise," Sam mouthed without sound, though he immediately realized the futility of that statement.

He had no idea where to start looking and it would take a lot of cred to buy that kind of information, especially on a deadline. And cred wasn't something a broke street kid just had lying around.

You're gonna need some help, he told himself, fighting through tears as the last of the kids was hauled away. But there was only one problem...

Sam didn't trust anyone but Grant, and now Grant was gone.

Appendix 1
Chinese Phrases Used in the Story

The Chinese phrases, characters, and pinyin used in this book have been carefully reviewed by a native Mandarin speaker to ensure accuracy. However, as I am not a native speaker, there may still be occasional errors or inconsistencies. This book uses Simplified Chinese characters and Mandarin terminology exclusively. Any mistakes that remain are entirely my own.

Key:
Pinyin (拼音): The Romanized pronunciation of Chinese words.
Simplified Chinese (简体中文): The modern standard form of Chinese characters used in mainland China.
English Translation: The meaning of the phrase or term in English.
Chapter: The section of the book where the phrase appears.

Pinyin	Characters	English	Ch. #
Wǒmen xūyào bāngzhù.	我们需要帮助	We need help.	1
Yéyé, Tā shòushāngle.	爷爷,他受伤了。	My Grandfather, he is injured.	1
Nǐ de míngzì?	你的名字？	Your name?	1
Nǐ de fángjiān shì sānshíwǔ hào.	你的房间是三十五号。	Your room. Number thirty-five.	1
Jiùmìng	救命	Help	2
Wǒ de háizimen… Wǒ de jiātíng	我的孩子们… 我的家庭	My children… my family	2
Tiānkōng guǎngchǎng	天空广场	Sky Plaza	4
Nǐ fǎnduì Lightbar ma?	你反对 Lightbar 吗？	You oppose Lightbar?	6
Tàitài Zhelan	哲兰夫人	Mrs. Zhelan	6
gǒu cāo de	狗操的	Offensive slang (Literally "dog-fucking"?)	17
Zhōngxīn jūmín	中心居民	Center dwellers	23

wùdǎo xiǎoduì	误导小队	Misdirection squads	24
Tā sìhū méiyǒu nàme zìxìn.	他似乎没有那么自信。	He doesn't seem that confident.	25
Nǐ yīdìng bùyào huáiyí tā.	你一定不要怀疑他。	You must not doubt him.	25
Nín de zǔxiān tīng dào nín zhèyàng shuō huì gǎnjué rúhé?	您的祖先听到您这样说会感觉如何？	How would your ancestors feel if they heard you say that?	25
Tāmen huì juéde xiūchǐ	他们会觉得羞耻	They will feel shame.	25
Měiguó rén shì yīgè shībài zhě.	美国人是一个失败者。	The American is a failure.	25
Jūnshì	军士	Sergeant	25
Zǔxiān	祖先	Ancestors	25
Jiàn nǚrén	贱女人	Bitch	25
Tīng wǒ shuō.	听我说。	Hear me out.	26
Wǒmen néng zuò dào.	我们能做到。	We can do this.	26
Liánmǐn	怜悯	Mercy	28
Chāo jí bái	超级白	"Super-white"*	29
Nǐ méiyǒu líkāi wǒ.	你没有离开我。	You didn't leave me.	29
Nǐ shuō shénme?	你说什么？	What did you say?	29
Méiyǒu!	没有！	No!	29
Duìbùqǐ	对不起	I'm sorry.	29
Mèi mèi	妹妹	Little Sister (a term of endearment for a young woman)	29
Míngxiǎn	明显	Obviously	30
Zǒng shì	总是	Always	30

Zhǔnbèi	准备	Ready	30
Yī' èr sān	一二三	One, two, three	30
gōngjī yīyàng de rénzào zhìzhàng	公鸡一样的人造智障	rooster-like artificial moron	31
Wǒ jiǎnzhí bù néng xiāngxìn tā de ěxīn de shǒu zhěnggè fùgài zài tāmen shàngmiàn	我简直不敢相信他到处都是恶心的手。	I can't believe his disgusting hands are all over them.	31
Xīwàng nǐ jiānqiáng yīdiǎn er.	希望你坚强一点儿。	I hope you will be strong.	31
Rose jiào 'Xiānshēng	叫)先生 Rose	Mr. – but with the preface "so-called" to make it insulting.	31
Shì de	是的	Yes	38
Wǒ bié wú xuǎnzé!	我别无选择！	I had no choice!	38
Xièxiè	谢谢	Thank You	1, 28
Tā mā de	他妈的	Expletive**	26, 28, 31, 38
Zǔmǔ	祖母	Grandma	31, 39

* This is also used as a slur against someone with white skin.

** Tā mā de is roughly equivalent to "your mother's…" in English. It is commonly used as an exclamation of frustration or anger, similar to "damn." It's considered quite rude and usually avoided in polite or formal settings but is popular among young speakers.

Appendix 2

The Soldiers

In addition to the dedication page, this story pays tribute to my own military family members dating back to the American Civil War. I have listed them below, so they may never be forgotten.[2]

<u>The Skinners</u>

All Skinners listed are descendants of John Skinner, who came from England in 1635 and became one of the one of the founding fathers of Hartford, CT.

Private William H. Skinner: (b. 1858, d. 1935). Served in the US Army during the Civil War. He was also associated with the Winchester Arms Company.

Colonel George A. Skinner: (b. 1870, d. 1949). A US Army medical officer and surgeon during WWI. Helped set up hospitals in France to serve the wounded. George was the first surgeon to successfully transplant an animal bone into the arm of a soldier to save it from being amputated, though this story was not publicly documented. After retiring from the military, he taught at the Mayo Clinic and the Washington University Medical School in St. Louis.

Colonel Leslie A. Skinner: (b. 1900, d. 1978). Leslie was an American rocket engineer with the US Army and held a Master of Science degree from MIT. He originally produced sketches of a tube-launched anti-tank rocket but had no suitable warhead to use until the development of the M8 rocket, which he tested at Aberdeen. In addition to being the inventor of the

[2] A big thank you to my mom Marian, my Aunt Peggy, my Uncle Walter, my great-uncle Breck, and all the genealogists before them who compiled and passed along this information.

Bazooka, Leslie was also a sculptor and poet in his later life.

Lieutenant Col. George Breckenridge Skinner: (b. 1927, d. 2017). Uncle Breck, as he was known to me, served in the US Army Corps of Engineers during the Korean and Vietnam Wars. During his service he earned a Bronze Star Medal, a Legion of Merit, Vietnam and Korean Service Medals, and a Korean Presidential Citation. He took me wine tasting in Sonoma Valley and loved sharing jokes and silly stories.

The Jagiellos

Master Sgt. Anthony Jagiello: (b. 1899, d. 1988). A US Marine Corps retiree of thirty-four years, Anthony was born in Krozno, Poland and emigrated to the United States in 1905 at age nineteen, with barely any English language skills. He enlisted in the Marines because he always wanted to "wear a uniform like the Polish officers." He served under General Pendleton during WWI in Nicaragua and then enlisted for a second term because he "didn't know what to do with his life after the war."

Major Walter Albert Jagiello: (b. 1921, d. 1995). My grandfather Walter attended the US Naval Academy at Annapolis (class of 1944) and graduated from West Point Academy in 1945. Serving during the Korean War (1953 and during armistice in 1956), he earned two Silver Stars and a Purple Hearts. I remember him throwing "mouse" toys for his kitties, and I loved laughing at his goofy jokes. The smell of cigars always reminds me of him.

Colonel Helen D. Jagiello: (b. 1929). Helen served in the US Army Nursing Corps during both Korean and Vietnam Wars.

Staff Sergeant Joseph A. Jagiello: (b. 1924, d. 1950). Joseph served in the United States Marine Corps during the Korean War. He was Killed in Action in North Korea, just before a cold front from Siberia descended over his platoon at the Chosin Reservoir, and the temperature plunged to as low as −36

°F. He was buried in a mass grave in North Korea, and it took the family years to recover his body. He was twenty-six years old.

Staff Sergeant Walter Anthony Jagiello: (b. 1958). My uncle Walter served in the US Air Force, District of Columbia Air National Guard, 113th Tactical Fighter Wing as a weapons munitions technician. Currently, he drives a bus for special needs children for his local school district. He once took me beach camping with his family and to see wild horses on Assateague Island.

Other Relatives

Private John C. Holme: (b. 1836, d. 1885). Holme served in the Union Army, Company F during the American Civil War. He served through the July 1861 First Bull Run Campaign and was honorably mustered out on August 2, 1861[3]. He is my great (times 3) grandfather.

Private Chester H. Clark: (1915-1999). My grandfather Clark worked for the US Army from 1940-1947. He never went on deployment because he broke his back during basic military training and instead took an office job in the US. Had he gone to Buganville, an island in South Pacific, with the rest of his unit during WWII, he may not have made it home. Instead, he was able to have a family, that ultimately led to me. He was very grateful for his good fortune.

Petty Officer Second-Class Robert A. Frazer Jr.: (b. 1947, d. 2014). My uncle Bob served in the US Navy from 1964-1969 as a Fire Control Technician for Missile Guidance Systems, spending seven months on a ship in Vietnam and earning Outstanding Evaluations. He was a very loving family man who unfortunately died from a self-inflicted gunshot wound, never able to ask for the help he needed.

[3] "John C. Holme." Find a Grave. https://www.findagrave.com/memorial/34307037/john-c-holme.

Petty Officer First Class James Swayze: (b. 1985). My partner and "#1 Superfan," James served in the US Navy as a nuclear-trained Electrician's Mate on the USS Nebraska submarine from 2005-2009, spending up to three months at a time underwater for a total of two-and-a-half years. After spending almost ten years faithfully serving his country, he left the Navy to be a better father and spend time with his two children, Ben and Sidon.

Acknowledgements

As this is my first novel, it's tempting to thank everyone who ever helped me in my writing journey, but then I suppose I wouldn't have anyone to thank in future novels. Self-publishing is a complicated, self-doubting journey, but with the help and encouragement of some awesome people, NANOWRIMO writing groups, critique groups, and beta-readers, I am finally able to realize the crazy dream I had in 2012, when I started writing content for my *Savant Uprising* series.

For this first book in this series, I have some huge thanks to give. First of all, I promised my partner, James, that he would get a sweet, heartfelt dedication in this book for all his help and encouragement throughout this process. But well, he gets this instead. I have come to learn that it is not easy to be a writer's partner. We are persistent in chatting about our ideas, fatally despondent when inspiration dries up, distracted, geeky about words, and sometimes tone deaf to someone else's needs to turn off their brain. However, James not only tolerated all this, but also supported me both financially and emotionally while I went on this author journey. He worked with me to bring my ideas to life and steered me back on course when I tried to write (yet another) side quest.

He put up with the late-nights/early mornings of typing, missed hang-out time during NANOWRIMO, and endured hours on end of "just *one* more question about my novel," and he continues to encourage me to keep pushing forward, even when the brain weasels of impostor syndrome rear their little heads. And it can't be left out how many meals he provided when I was stuck at my desk writing. Move over breakfast-in-bed, because breakfast-at-desk feels so much more decadent!

I'd also like to thank Jon Gray Lang, author of *The Saga of a Space Freighter Series*, who helped me navigate the terrifying world of self-publishing, gave me lots of momentum for writing, teamed up with me to publish this book, and provided some of the weirdest inspiration I never knew I needed

(I still haven't used the line "I feel like the freak at a stump-fuck show" but someday I totally will).

And where would I be without my editors? A huge thank you goes out to Gabino Iglesias, editor and author of *The Devil Takes You Home*, who gave me the first sign of hope that this book wasn't a total pile of garbage, and to Angelle Horste of Finally Write Book Coaching & Editing, who helped me find the "heart" of my stories. Lastly, thank you to Karen, my mother-in-law and an awesome proofreader who, at times, saved me from myself and spotted the errors that no one else did.

However, the biggest thanks of all goes to the tribe of people who took part in my 2024 Kickstarter, causing me to meet my funding goal and be able to publish this book! When you're working as an unpaid and unpublished author, funding your first book is terrifying but Kickstarter made it possible. Thus, I will be eternally grateful to everyone who helped me develop the campaign, pledged to a reward tier, or shared the campaign. This includes Nova Kodex (cover design/promo art), Chris (video music), Eric (physical rewards), and James (voice-over), as well as all my backers:

StoicMan	Rob Clark	Alicia	Samantha Seaman
Ed Clancy	Liz Winterslice	Heiko Koenig	Steven Mason
Joe Bayes	D Sampsel	Cecile Penland	Chris Perrotta
Farm Dog	Jeff Womack	Suzanne Perkowski	Historical Martial Arts Nerd
Simon K	Sara Feinberg	MusingsofMuse	Meredith Carstens
heiditodd	Joshi Solomon-Freville	Carrie Vaughn	dw_dreamer
Kim Baright	Lianne S. Hill	Melissa Morman	Karl Kieninger
Tek	CGKat	Mary Hoppe	Ashley Beitz
Deborah Frazier	Jason Lantrip	Amanda Perrillioux	Tom McGrath
Pyndan	amara	Dawn DeHoag	Jswayze85
Sharon Ahrens	Lukas DeVries	Lillian Cordaro	bill
		Jennifer M	

Randall Jackson	Brandon Sivret	Thompson	Grace
John Swayze	Jon Lang	Andrew	Alice Robinson
Lexi Baisa	Lisa C Adams	Wil Corvey	Bree Pye
Jonathan Sabar	Meshia	Eric Hodges	Donna Curry
Lori Olcott	Matt Beins	Tori	Jacquelyn
Hawk Zindell	Zachary	Perry Rogers	Chris Bristow
Carolyn	Caroline	Terry Dawson	Grace Nicholson
William Bowman	Shyanne	Karen House	Andrew Ryan
Lena Johnson	Maxie Froelicher	Andrea Tremblay	Jack Sherven
Christopher Holtorf	Campbell Scott	Kyle Cisco	Dan Roop
Andrew Gilbert	Ashmash	Thomas the Seeker	Ringmaster
Tori Gilbertson	Toni Tadolini	Theresa Duck	Olivia Newby Doll
Alyssa Faller	Michelle Lang, MC	Lori Schiess	Marian Clark
John Fearnside			The ladies of the Beledi Dance Caravan
	Geoff Charlwood	Madge	

About the Author

Photo by Cassidy Wayant Photography

Lyndsie Clark is a sci-fi author, linguist, and self-proclaimed geek with a love for gritty dystopian stories, her tiny feline overlords, and a well-crafted pint of beer. Raised by hippie parents in Boulder, Colorado, she spent her childhood lost in stories and never quite found her way out. Armed with a Master's in Linguistics, a certificate in copyediting, a knack for world-building, and a questionable grasp of Spanish, she brought *The Savant Uprising* series to life after more than a decade of marinating in her head. When she's not writing, you can find her sword fighting, cosplaying, or tracking down the best food trucks in Denver.